BURY
ELMINSTER
DEEP

SAGE OF SHADOWDALE

Elminster: The Making of a Mage
Elminster in Myth Drannor
The Temptation of Elminster
Elminster in Hell
Elminster's Daughter
The Annotated Eliminster
Elminster Ascending
Elminster Must Die
Bury Elminster Deep
Elminster Enraged
(August 2012)

SHANDRIL'S SAGA

Book I
Spellfire

Book II
Crown of Fire

Book III
Hand of Fire

THE KNIGHTS OF MYTH DRANNOR

Book I
Swords of Eveningstar

Book II
Swords of Dragonfire

Book III
The Sword Never Sleeps

ALSO BY ED GREENWOOD

The City of Splendors: A Waterdeep Novel
(with Elaine Cunningham)
The Best of the Realms, Book II
The Stories of Ed Greenwood
Edited by Susan J. Morris

FORGOTTEN REALMS

ED GREENWOOD
SAGE OF SHADOWDALE

BURY ELMINSTER DEEP

Wizards
OF THE COAST
®

Sage of Shadowdale

BURY ELMINSTER DEEP

©2012 Wizards of the Coast LLC.

Published by Wizards of the Coast LLC. Hasbro SA, represented by Hasbro Europe, Stockley Park, UB11 1AZ. UK.

Cover art by Kekai Kotaki
Map by Robert Lazzaretti

Original Hardcover Edition First Printing: August 2011
First Mass Market Paperback Printing: June 2012

9 8 7 6 5 4 3 2 1

ISBN: 978-0-7869-6024-8
ISBN: 978-0-7869-5931-0 (e-book)
620-39846000-001-EN

The Library of Congress has catalogued the hardcover edition as follows

Greenwood, Ed.
  Bury Elminster deep / Ed Greenwood.
    p. cm. -- (Sage of Shadowdale ; 3)
  ISBN 978-0-7869-5815-3
  1. Forgotten realms (Imaginary place)--Fiction. 2. Elminster
(Fictitious character)--Fiction. 3. Wizards--Fiction. I. Title.
  PR9199.3.G759B87 2011
  813'.54--dc22

                                          2011015517

For customer service, contact:

U.S., Canada, Asia Pacific, & Latin America: Wizards of the Coast LLC, P.O. Box 707, Renton, WA 98057-0707, +1-800-324-6496, www.wizards.com/customerservice

U.K., Eire, & South Africa: Wizards of the Coast LLC, c/o Hasbro UK Ltd., P.O. Box 43, Newport, NP19 4YD, UK, Tel: +08457 12 55 99, Email: wizards@hasbro.co.uk

Europe: Wizards of the Coast p/a Hasbro Belgium NV/SA, Industrialaan 1, 1702 Groot-Bijgaarden, Belgium, Tel: +32.70.233.277, Email: wizards@hasbro.be

Visit our websites at www.wizards.com
www.DungeonsandDragons.com

Res tam malae sunt quam putas,
et inimici re vera te persequuntur

For Abby Glicksohn-Coté, because in my world
even long-ago promises get kept.

Northwest Suzail

1. The Royal Palace of Suzail
2. The Royal Court of Cormyr
3. Horngate
4. The Promenade
5. Home and Shop of Immaero Sraunter, Alchemist
6. Mansion of Larak Dardulkyn, Wizard for Hire
7. Rented Lodgings of Amarune Whitewave, Dancer
8. The Dragonriders' Club
9. The Bold Archer
10. Delcastle Manor
11. Stormserpent Towers
12. Trueturrets
13. Huntcrown House
14. Goldengates
15. Emmarask Towers
16. High House of Crownsilver
17. Rathspires
18. Staghaven House
19. House with Access to
    Palace Cellars and Royal Stables
20. Royal Stables
21. Haunted Wing
22. Royal Gardens
23. Graethrunposts

Welcome to Faerûn, a land of magic and intrigue, brutal violence and divine compassion, where gods have ascended and died, and mighty heroes have risen to fight terrifying monsters. Here, millennia of warfare and conquest have shaped dozens of unique cultures, raised and leveled shining kingdoms and tyrannical empires alike, and left long forgotten, horror-infested ruins in their wake.

A LAND OF MAGIC

When the goddess of magic was murdered, a magical plague of blue fire—the Spellplague—swept across the face of Faerûn, killing some, mutilating many, and imbuing a rare few with amazing supernatural abilities. The Spellplague forever changed the nature of magic itself, and seeded the land with hidden wonders and bloodcurdling monstrosities.

A LAND OF DARKNESS

The threats Faerûn faces are legion. Armies of undead mass in Thay under the brilliant but mad lich king Szass Tam. Treacherous dark elves plot in the Underdark in the service of their cruel and fickle goddess, Lolth. The Abolethic Sovereignty, a terrifying hive of inhuman slave masters, floats above the Sea of Fallen Stars, spreading chaos and destruction. And the Empire of Netheril, armed with magic of unimaginable power, prowls Faerûn in flying fortresses, sowing discord to their own incalculable ends.

A LAND OF HEROES

But Faerûn is not without hope. Heroes have emerged to fight the growing tide of darkness. Battle-scarred rangers bring their notched blades to bear against marauding hordes of orcs. Lowly street rats match wits with demons for the fate of cities. Inscrutable tiefling warlocks unite with fierce elf warriors to rain fire and steel upon monstrous enemies. And valiant servants of merciful gods forever struggle against the darkness.

A LAND OF
UNTOLD ADVENTURE

PROLOGUE

Sometimes, Lord Arclath Delcastle thought he was going mad.

Right now, for instance.

He'd risen out of a very pleasant dream of lazing abed with his beloved Amarune, which had turned suddenly into a nightmare of thunderous voices in his head, a scrambling of frightened clawing and clutching, and a rising dread. Hurled into fearful wakefulness, he grabbed for his sword.

Only to find the rafters of a simple King's Forest royal cabin above him, his Amarune hastening out into the night—and Storm Silverhand throwing herself on top of him, seeking to hold him down.

And managing that very effectively.

Grunt and heave though he might, he couldn't reach the waiting, *just*-beyond-his-fingertips pommel of his sword . . .

Storm's long, silver hair was *alive*, its tresses like the monstrous vines of half-remembered nursery tales, lengthening and winding to bind him fast. Those gods-cursed strands shone like armor in the dancing glow of the brazier. Moreover, her warm and sweet lips were glued firmly to his, keeping his cries and curses to muffled mumblings.

No matter how he bucked and strained, her long limbs kept him down. She was stronger than he was—stronger than a smith he'd once wrestled! Not to mention sleek and shapely and pressed against him ...

Arousing him, all gods blast it, despite his anger and worry.

Arclath shook his head, managing to free his mouth from hers at last. "Dragon take all!" he gasped. "Will you not let me *go*?"

"No," Storm replied firmly, her voice low and regretful. "Not while you're this upset. You'll go rushing off into the night and get lost or hurt. And if you do find Rune, you'll interrupt something needful. Something very important. Something *wonderful*."

Was that ... *awe* in her voice?

Arclath swallowed, trying to think through his panting rage, to fight down his anger and frustration.

"Let ...," he gasped, "let me up. I'm ... I can't spend much longer tussling with you in this bed. 'Tisn't seemly, as ... older nobles say."

"Aye," Storm said in a dry voice, running one finger along his thigh—past the part of him that was stirring uncomfortably. "I've noticed."

She raised herself on one elbow. "If I let you go, have I your word you'll not depart this cabin, Lord Delcastle?"

Arclath crooked an eyebrow. "You really think you can hold me?"

Storm descended in a lunge that brought one of her hands around his throat. Her grip was like iron.

"Yes," she replied calmly. "Yes, I do."

She was giving him just enough space to breathe. Arclath used it to swallow, sigh, and tell her, "You have my word. Just as long as you tell me *where* Rune went, and *what's* going *on*!"

Storm grinned. "The eternal demands of the young. I can answer your first. She's gone somewhere near in the forest, taking Elminster to an ... unexpected meeting. As for your second question, your guess, Lord Delcastle, is as good as mine. They should return soon, though, and you can be sure I'll demand answers from them just as strenuously as you."

Arclath nodded. "Your terms are accepted. Upon my word as a Delcastle."

"*That's* well spoken, lord," she replied, in precisely the indulgent tones he'd heard matriarchs of Cormyr's haughtiest noble Houses use.

Ah, but she *was* one, now, wasn't she? Marchioness Immerdusk, and a few more titles since . . .

Huh. A matriarch less like his mother he couldn't imagine.

His words were obviously what she'd been waiting for, so she released him.

"Someone," Arclath said slowly, as he sat up and rubbed his throat, "was speaking in our minds when I awoke. Someone of great power."

"Yes," Storm replied calmly, handing him his sword and settling herself in a comfortable sitting position beside him. Her long, silver tresses curled almost demurely around her. Watching Gods, but she was beautiful.

Arclath forced himself to think of Rune, alone in the night.

No, not alone. She had Elminster with her, riding her mind.

He grimaced, his irritation flaring. Storm hadn't handed him the answer he was seeking. He gave her a glare.

And found her half smiling at him, a knowing twinkle in her eyes. She looked like someone bursting with a happy inner secret.

"Well," he snapped, "who was it?"

"*Such* manners, Lord Delcastle," she reproved him. Then she laughed like a little girl and said, "It certainly seems to be a goddess many have long thought dead. Mystra, the Greatest of All. The One. Our Lady of Magic."

Arclath stared at her, his mouth falling open.

Was she mad? Or mistaken?

And if not, what doom would *this* bring down on Cormyr, and all the world besides?

Chapter
ONE

Kneeling to a Goddess

I've had my share of bright moments, mind ye!
Bedding a princess on dragonback, by moonlight,
Dancing with elves in the blue mists of a great spell
And once, kneeling before a goddess.

Old Lokhlabur in Act I, Scene IV of the play
A Throne O'erthrown by Mandarjack the Minstrel
first performed in the Year of the Hidden Harp

As he directed Amarune's borrowed body to pad cautiously
through a pale white labyrinth of moonlit trees, Elminster
felt himself trembling.

This almost had to be a trap, after all this time—yet, nay,
nay, it was *her*, his Mystra! It *was*!

He could feel her! He knew that feeling, could never
forget the touch of her mind on his . . . this *was* Mystra, the
vivid blue mists of power swirling around the edges of his
mind . . .

A sharp stick underfoot hurt his—Rune's—bare feet, and
El sank to all fours to crawl like a beast. He tingled with eager
haste and had to remind himself to look for what peril that
might be aprowl in the King's Forest.

Halting on a tree-cloaked ridge in the rolling, deepening
woods north of the cabin, one hand raised like a questing cat's
paw, he listened hard.

He heard distant stirrings of brush to the northeast, probably well across the Way of the Dragon, then silence. Broken by
a brief, faint hooting even farther westward.

Still and silent, Amarune's dancer's body poised like a
statue, El waited.

Long enough for even a lazy hunter to become impatient he held still, but nothing else moved that he could hear. And the sleekly muscled body he was occupying had far better hearing than what he'd grown used to in recent centuries.

Some of his excitement washed into her sleeping mind, at rest in one dim corner of the brain he steered. Amarune rose slowly toward wakefulness, her dreams growing restless, as she tasted his eagerness.

Ye're as giddy as a lass fleeing her first kiss, El reproached himself, as he crawled on down a ferny slope of wet dead leaves toward a dark bank of old, leaning trees. Steady, Sage of Shadowdale. Where's that world-weary yawning that ye do so well?

Part of him smirked, but through the lacy curtain of his mirth, El fought to quell ever-wilder excitement as he reached the bottom of the slope.

Only to lose his breath under a thrilling onslaught of fresh nerves as he felt the nearness of Mystra. Right ahead of him.

A weighty taste in the air came from the silent gloom behind a rising old tree that smelled of bear.

He didn't even have time for a hint of fear before he saw a dark wall of fur that must be that beast shambling away along the line of trees, afire with Mystra's power just as his own mind was.

Blue fire deepened in his brain, bringing certainty. The goddess of all magic was riding the bear's mind just as he was riding Amarune's.

Before El knew it, the moonlit trees were behind him, and he was crawling into bear-smelling darkness, over muddy, loose stones in a musky earthen den tapestried in descending roots and floored with gnawed old bones green with mold. As he crawled on, the ground dropped down into a stony cavern tall enough to stand in, aglow with Mystra's fire.

Where two great, keen eyes he'd not seen for long centuries suddenly opened in the air in front of him.

Stealing away his breath again.

Elminster gazed into them, dumbstruck. Floating orbs of silver-blue fire regarded him with love and an excitement to match his own. Eyes he'd feared he'd never see again.

Amarune's body lacked the feel for the Art that his aching old frame had possessed, but strain though he might, he could sense nothing false about what loomed before him. This *was* Mystra, though the heat in his mind remained a whispering echo of her full power.

Yet Our Lady of Mystery could easily hold back, cloaking her divine might to seem less than she was, and often—usually—did so. The eyes of deepening silver-blue fire were linked by softly coursing threads of the same radiance, lines like lightnings too gentle to crackle or spit, to . . . things strewn among rocks on the cavern floor.

A gauntlet with gems inset in the knuckles, a wand, a ring, other small items still hidden among the stones.

"Some blood of my mortal self spilled on these trifles of Art in the time before I became Mystra," came the warm whisper of the goddess, both in his head and filling the cavern as if she were awakening in purring languor right beside his ear. "When you came nigh, El, the nearness of your mind alerted me. I am . . . preoccupied much, now."

"Ye collected these things when ye were Midnight?" El blurted, trembling in a sudden chaos of wanting to know so much, yet not knowing what he dared ask. Her love—or at least fondness—was in his head and all around him, But something was subtly different in it, a distance that had not been there once, or rather one that had grown since Midnight had ascended to replace the Mystra his far younger self had first touched and tasted. Gone was the Mystra whose mind would long ago have merged with his to let them converse wordlessly, thoughts flashing.

Something was rising in him, something urgent. Before he quite knew what it was, he felt a flash of confusion and wonder, alarm strangled by awe. Amarune Aumar had awakened.

"I did," the Lady of Magic replied as if nothing had happened, though fond regard washed out of her bright silver-blue fire into Amarune, causing a mental turmoil of astonished pleasure tinged with bewilderment. "The bear keeps them safe here, and I see through his eyes and guide him. It is good you came to me, El; I have many unfinished tasks for you."

"L-lady?" Rune dared to blurt, then. "Who *are* you?"

"I," the fire behind the eyes replied, as tenderly as any gently drawn sword, "am Mystra. I am *magic*."

That last word became a thunderclap that raced away into unseen distances, only to return a rolling echo of deep, teeth-chattering force that made small stones fall and patter in the bear's den, and the living roots groan and murmur all around them.

I am the fire in all things. That whisper came soft and calm, uttered only in the depths of their shared mind.

Then Mystra seemed to shake herself and added, "More than ever, El, I need your service. You I can truly trust, where so many others have turned from me or fallen. I can coerce, of course, but I will no longer make that mistake of lesser gods. The work of slaves is nigh worthless. For deeds to have true and lasting meaning, they must done willingly. Elminster Aumar, El mine, *are* you still mine? Are you with me?"

"As ever," Elminster burst out, finding himself on the choking edge of tears in an instant. "Goddess, command me!"

Blue fire flooded through him, leaving him gasping, overwhelmed by Mystra's pleased satisfaction.

"You must be my roving hands, skulking alone," she said, eyes flashing with resolve, showing power enough to make Amarune's mind cower. "I charge you to preserve magic wherever and whenever you can, keeping to the shadows as much as possible. Bold confrontations and invoking my name are clumsy marks of pride I would fain put behind me forever. So, El, be my—forgive me, Amarune—my Silent Shadow."

Amarune fought to make her lips gasp; El was too distracted to relinquish control over them. He felt amusement washing his mind on tides of blue fire as Rune managed her gasp, then gave him a rueful mental shove as she yielded her mouth back to him. It was some moments later before he managed to reply, "Lady, I will."

"Employ disguises. Be the thief you once so ably were in Hastarl. Steal and copy magic, and then hide the copies so that, whatever befalls the originals, my Art will survive for those yet unborn."

"Lady," Elminster repeated, "I will."

"Recruit new Chosen, and gather them here for me to confer with. I need many, and they must be different from my daughters and from each other, for that kinship was another misstep. Yet, we both know how rarely the needed loyalty and strength are found together—and above all, I *must* have those I can trust."

El nodded, remembering Khelben and Sammaster, Laeral, and too many elven ladies who were all so willing, yet had faded so swiftly under the ravages of too much Art. Betrayals, defiances, independence, and weaknesses. Gone, now, all of them. Gone . . .

His Alassra, fled and mad somewhere, brain-burned by the roaring Blue Fire that was not Mystra, the plague of wild fury that had snuffed out the lives of thousands in a blazing instant, and many more in the days and seasons that had followed . . .

"Lady," he said huskily, "I will."

"Continue what you have done so well for so long: preserve and strengthen the Art—not magic bestowed by others, but magics worked by the caster's own craft and knowledge."

"Lady, I've done that for so long," El told her truthfully, "that I do not know if I could now refrain from doing so. It is what I *do*."

"It is. Yet the fall of Azoun heralded your newest task. It is time to do what Storm and Dove have both suggested. By any means you deem best—becoming their head or turning their leaders to my service—recruit Cormyr's wizards of war. They must become the ready allies, helping hands, and spies for all my Chosen."

All my Chosen?

Ah, Storm and Alassra, of course. If there were more, and Mystra desired him to know of them, she would reveal them . . .

She was right, of course. If he was to manage any of these tasks, he sorely needed new allies—with his own body lost to him, Alassra crazed, Storm's magic all but gone, and the work already far more than he and Storm could handle.

"Soon enough, you'll again have a body of your own," Mystra murmured among El's racing thoughts. She was reading them, of course, and—

"In the meantime," the goddess whispered, "I can aid the one you have. You have been sorely wounded in my service."

The silver-blue fires changed, and in the mind they were sharing, Amarune recoiled in fear.

The floating eyes flared larger, brighter . . . and nearer.

"Embrace me," Mystra commanded.

Somewhat warily, with Amarune on the verge of whimpering at the back of their shared mind—an image of her fearful staring eyes flaring to outshine Mystra's huge orbs—Elminster stepped forward and spread his arms wide.

The shield-sized eyes of silver-blue drifted together, merging in smooth silence right in front of him, and flaring into silver lightning that shocked through him. His arms flew apart convulsively, and then tightened again around the lightning as if it were something solid he could crush. Not that Elminster was thinking of crushing anything.

Or thinking at all.

He was too busy screaming in pain.

The high, throat-stripping shriek of a young female dancer lost in agony and horror spat out of him into the night, as lightning slammed through him, his every hair standing on end like a straining dagger, snapped back out of him, then roared back into him again. It was as if a thousand spears thrust through him, tore back out, and then thrust right back in repeatedly through the same gaping wounds.

Elminster was dimly aware of falling to his knees and shuddering helplessly. He was caught on the bright spears of lightning, unable to collapse onto his face . . . unable to do anything.

Every time the lightnings snarled out of him, they took life with them, vitality that was not returned when they stormed in again.

Amarune was sobbing, or trying to, but her body could not breathe, could no longer make a sound. Her brain was awash in roaring silver fire, flames of power that thundered through her mind and might well have destroyed it had Elminster not been grimly fighting to stay himself, to cling to what was Elminster of Shadowdale amid the hungry fires of a goddess.

Around him, blue fire was being beaten back by silver flames, flames that circled him—and then darted into him.

Elminster tried to scream, but all that came out was a strangled squeak.

Mystra—if it was Mystra—had drained much energy from his borrowed body but was now at work on steadying his mind, forcing back the roiling blue fires that had lurked there for nigh a hundred years.

"There, my champion," Mystra whispered as tenderly as any mother. "Go forth renewed. Greater and more magic you can now work without madness coming upon you, but not an unlimited amount. I cannot do more. Go now, until next we meet."

Silver fire left him then, leaving only chill darkness.

Elminster stood forlorn, blind in the darkness.

Something soft and tender stroked his face and arm, turning him and leading him back. Out and up, stumbling over unseen things underfoot, once more into the moonlight.

Weak and dazed, reeling, with Amarune cowering in mute terror in a corner of their shared mind, Elminster shivered in the night.

Bare and chilled, feeling sick and empty—kiss of Mystra, half of Rune's energy must be gone—he staggered up rises and down slopes, through countless trees. The way was not long, but he would have been lost had a tiny silver star not guided him until the dark bulk of the little lodge loomed out of the night.

He leaned against its front wall beside the door, shuddering, until he could master his breathing enough to stand upright and square his—her—shoulders.

Amarune was still drawn into herself, but El could put the pain and horror of the lightning firmly behind him and take satisfaction in the healing that had been done to him.

By his goddess.

His Mystra.

Aye, Mystra was alive and in the realms still.

A part of him wanted to shout that to the stars above, to bellow it until folk came awake in their beds in Suzail to sit up listening.

And a part of him wanted to keep it so secret that not even the young nobleman inside the hut would begin to suspect it.

Let alone Manshoon or any other wizard of power.

Elminster threw back his head, drew in a deep breath—and smiled at the tiny silver flash of farewell that winked out in the darkness above his nose. Then he eased open the door with a fingertip and stepped inside as quietly as he could.

The hearth was dim, almost out, but someone had lit the brazier tray fixed in its spark-shield frame behind the door. Its dancing glow fell upon blankets frozen in the usual twisted chaos left behind when sleepers arise—

And it fell upon Storm Silverhand, her shirt-clad body bent back in a graceful bow on the floor. Someone had hogtied her to a leg of the table and her hair was over her face. She lay unmoving. Dead or senseless.

She'd been bound with Arclath's belt.

The door slammed behind Elminster. He spun around, managing to quell Rune's instinctive urge to leap back and away. He might need to be close.

As he'd expected, he faced a half-dressed Lord Arclath Delcastle, who waved his sword threateningly. Behind its bright edge—and above the burning brazier—the young nobleman held the coffer in which Storm had been carrying Elminster's ashes.

Arclath's eyes, as he glared at El, were like two dagger points.

"Luckily for my Amarune's sake," he snapped, "you seem unaware that even fine, upstanding nobles of Cormyr learn a few tawdry secrets of the realm—and lack scruples in exploiting them. The uses of darfly-sting essence, for instance. It brings on instant, topple-on-your-face sleep at the slightest scratch and can be found on the heads of the takedown arrows that Highknights of Cormyr hide in the same spot in every royal hunting lodge across the realm. Sleep that takes even legendary silver-haired bards blessed by the gods, it seems."

Elminster sighed and shook his head, and then he lunged back as the bright tip of Arclath's sword hissed past his throat.

Inside the mind they shared, El threw all his exasperation at Amarune, who spasmed like a speared fish, sent fury back at him, and stared at Arclath.

"Your ashes!" the nobleman hissed, shaking the coffer. "I'll destroy them if you don't surrender Amarune to me."

He bent into a lunge that kept his sword up and menacing Elminster as he lowered the box into the flames of the brazier. They flared up and crackled, right on cue.

"Wizard, get out of her *right now!* Or you die!"

He flicked his blade so its tip pointed at Storm's throat, where she lay with her head on the floor, silver hair fallen across her face.

"And so does she!"

Chapter
TWO

The Word of a Nobleman

In all my long years of pomp and splendor
Of revels and feasts and grand High Court balls,
I've found little that's worth more than a good back rub
And nothing that's worth less than the word of a nobleman.

Marchioness Althea Bleth,
One Old Crone's Simperings: Seventy Seasons at Court
published in the Year of Lurking Death

Amarune found to her astonishment that Elminster sat silently idle in her mind, all of his control over her body gone. She was free to speak and act just as she pleased.

After a moment of startlement, she burst out, "Arclath, what're you doing? You idiot!"

"Elminster," the young noble snapped, glaring at her, "don't try to trick me! I know it's you speaking, not my Rune! Let her go! Get out of her, and stay out! Or I'll destroy all that's left of you!" He waved the coffer menacingly.

Elminster took control again, so swiftly that all Rune could do was blink.

"Oh," he made her body reply, this time in the unmistakable drawl of the Sage of Shadowdale when he was being curious. "How?"

"I'll burn these ashes in the . . . fire."

Arclath's voice fell as his anger faltered into confusion.

"And? They're ashes, dolt! What do they teach nobles of Cormyr these days, I wonder?" El replied, now sounding for all the world like an arch and mincing marchioness of elder years.

"I—" Arclath's blade wavered back and forth and then thrust toward Storm. "Well, I can still . . ."

Amarune strode forward to plant herself right in front of the nobleman's face, her hands on her hips. He winced and flushed.

"Arclath," she spat, her voice very much her own again and full of all the disappointment she felt, "you broke your word, didn't you? You swore as a Delcastle, did you not?"

"I . . . I did. My word is my honor and that of House Delcastle. But, my lady, I discovered something here this night. I—"

"What could you possibly discover," she said, eyes flaring in anger, "that excuses breaking your word?"

Arclath reddened even more but he kept his gaze steady on hers. "I discovered," he replied, "that when you are endangered, I will sacrifice my honor—and everything else, by all the gods—in an instant. I did this for you."

Amarune trembled, tears welling up, and before her voice might fail her, she rushed out the words, "You struck down one friend so you could better threaten the other? Why? Are you mad?"

"I—perhaps I am. I know not what to do. I don't know if I'm talking to my beloved or to Elminster holding you captive in your own head . . . or facing something more sinister. Shapechangers once infested the Wheloon lands, and the war wizards never got them all."

Amarune sighed out fresh frustration and took a step back. "I am myself, thank you, Arclath. Though I have no idea how I'll be able to prove it to you."

She started to pace, and then she stopped and flung back at him over one bare shoulder, "Can you take nothing on trust?"

The young lord gave her a crooked smile. "Evidently not."

She took an imploring step back toward him, reaching out—but he raised his sword again, adding in a growl, "I dare not."

Rune glared at him, tears spilling over, and whispered, "So what will you have me do, Arclath?"

They stared at each other for what seemed a long time, as the brazier crackled.

"And what," Rune whispered, tears running down her face, "will you be able to do, to make me ever trust you again, Lord Delcastle? Answer me that!"

The shop doorbell tinkled merrily as the heavily scented merchant's wife sailed out, pleased with her purchase.

The alchemist sat back with a sigh, glad to see the back of her. Sixteen vials sampled, none chosen, and an ointment that had been buried on a high back shelf beneath three seasons' dust preferred instead. By a woman who seemed to think it was highsun and not the middle of the night when weary men must be roused from their beds to serve her. Gods-cursed highnoses ...

He set to work tidying up. "If I didn't need so stlarned much coin just to live in this noble-infested city ..."

A sympathetic chuckle from behind the curtain over his shoulder reminded Sraunter that he wasn't alone.

The fear that never left him reminded him that this particular guest was never to be kept waiting. He hastened off his stool and through the curtain.

"S-sorry, lord," he stammered. "I—"

"I know you are, Sraunter. No matter, and no apology needed. Commerce must come first. Not to mention the damage to your trade if Nechelseiya Sammartael thought you'd slighted her. Word of it would be all over Suzail before sunrise."

"Ah, indeed," Sraunter agreed, leading the way past the man who'd conquered his mind so easily three nights back, to reveal what until then had been his greatest secret.

Alchemists were more feared than loved, and if they desired long careers, they needed powerful secret weapons. These were to be his latest—if he ever learned some manner of commanding them. Until then, they could at least serve as a deadly trap against thieves. Or so he'd schemed, before Manshoon had stepped into his life.

In his fearful haste, Sraunter had some trouble with the locks, fumbling with the chains and the dummy padlock. Twice he dropped the key that opened the hidden coffer that held the real key.

Manshoon smiled an easy smile. "There's no particular haste, diligent alchemist. Unless, of course, Goodwife Sammartael takes it into her head to return for something else."

That horrible thought made Sraunter drop the padlock on his toe.

His involuntary roar and hopping ended as swiftly as he could master himself. He was still wincing, teeth clenched, as he put his shoulder to the door and flung it wide in a loud rattle of chains.

His guest stayed right where he was.

"There's no particular need to move them, is there?"

"N-no, lord. None at all."

Sraunter hastened into his strongroom and across to the cage Manshoon had come to see. His guest could take his home and shop and everything in it—blackfire, his very mind!—whenever the whim took him, after all.

Face it, he was a slave already, and slaves enjoyed better lives when their masters were content.

Sraunter undid his special knot and drew back the nearest half of the hide cover. The five occupants of the cage flew in smooth unison to its revealed front, the better to hover there and peer out through the bars.

Five little spheres, each the size of a blacksmith's fist. Beholderkin, their tiny eyestalks like so many writhing worms, eager to gaze upon something and do it harm, hissing in malevolence.

And falling silent as the smiling man just beyond the doorway thrust his mind into all of theirs at once, overwhelming them as easily as he'd humbled Sraunter.

That terrible smile grew.

"Acceptable, Sraunter, most acceptable. Five little flying steeds, whenever I need them. Release them."

"R-release them?"

"At once. Give them the freedom of your strongroom. What with all the locks and chains, you use it seldom, do you not?"

"Well, yes, but—"

Sraunter found that the objection he'd been going to raise had vanished from his mind, and his astonished anger with it. A malicious glee rose in him, twisting his dour face into a grin that sought to mirror the smile on his guest's face.

Oh, Watching Gods Above, what will become of me? he thought.

"The time for all 'buts' is long past, Sraunter," Manshoon purred. "You'll see the coming sunrise in as much health as you enjoy now, believe me—and you can believe me. I am no courtier of Cormyr nor yet one of its noblemen. My word means something."

He pointed past the cage with a languid hand. "Yon window opens readily? No? Ah, but I see its panes can be broken should I ever have need of haste. Good. My steeds can get out that way if need be."

"Need of haste?"

"Such a need is, I'll grant, doubtful, now that Elminster's dead; but, one never knows, good saer alchemist, one never knows. During my overlong lives these realms have taught me that much, at least."

"Overlong lives?"

"You make an admirable echo, good Sraunter, but someone—nay, several someones—have espied your lit lamps and approach your shop entrance. So open the cage and close this door. Now."

The next few moments were a whirlwind of panting activity for Immaero Sraunter, and his accustomed feelings of grim superiority and darkly sinister accomplishment had quite vanished by the time he found himself puffing and panting his way back through the curtain to blink at the customers shuffling into the gloom of his shop.

Manshoon had vanished sometime during that whirlwind, Sraunter knew not quite where, but he was uncomfortably aware that five beholderkin that could slay him or almost any Suzailan with casual ease roamed free in his strongroom—where he kept his poisons, his best drinkables, and most of his coin.

Not that this undesirable state of affairs would continue for long, if his suspicions were correct. And when it came to matters of personal misfortune for Immaero Sraunter, they usually were.

The boldest shopper's request struck his ears, then, and he heard himself answering it with the ease of long habit.

"Dragonmere eel essence, Goodwife? Well, there's not a lot of call for that, particularly at this time of night, but—"

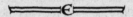

Arclath's face hardened. "Trust? Trust? Hah, you don't fool me, wizard! It's you in there, Elminster, and you have my lady ruined or bound silent. She's a mask you put on when you seek to deceive me!"

He sliced the air with his sword, weaving a glittering wall of steel as he took two slow, menacing steps forward, forcing his beloved back.

She looked so hurt, through her tears . . .

He scowled, reminding himself that this was really Elminster, just using his Amarune's body. "You must cease this evil of riding living folk! Right now!"

"Or you'll—what?" Rune asked, regarding him sidelong. "Carve me up, Arclath? Kill me, the mask dancer you call your lady and say you're doing all of this for? And when you've butchered me, and I'm lying hewn apart in my blood all over this floor, what then? How will you stop the wizard you so misjudge then?"

Baffled anger was rising in the heir of House Delcastle. She was right, Dragon take it! How could he strike at the wizard without harming Rune?

Arclath realized, as she reached the far wall of the hut's lone room and sidestepped along it, that his advance had taken him far from the brazier. Hastily he shuffled back the way he'd come, trying not to stumble in the abandoned bedding as he retreated, without taking his gaze off her for a moment.

Spell, she might cast a spell . . . he needed something to throw and another hand to throw it with. Ah, his dagger, of course, but—

Oh, damn and blast! Why was life always so difficult?

"These endless complications are irksome, but then, complications are what give life its interest," Manshoon murmured aloud as he strolled along one of the quieter streets of Suzail's Windmarket neighborhood, hired lamp boys before and behind.

"Irksome, did you say, saer?" a Purple Dragon swordcaptain asked, passing at the head of his watch patrol.

Manshoon gave the man an easy smile. "Minor annoyances, I assure you. The cut and thrust of mercantile trade brings obstacles to the most prudent investments and stratagems. I'll be happier when the Council is past, and matters have, ah, settled down somewhat."

The watchman smiled back. "You and me both, saer. You and me both."

They traded nods and continued on their separate ways, the patrol in the direction of the distant docks, and Manshoon bound for the walled compounds and grander towers where the wealthiest and most noble citizens dwelt.

Yes, Sraunter would prove useful indeed. The man's shop was in a central—yet not overly popular—location. Manshoon's collection of bases across Suzail was certainly growing quickly.

As he walked, Manshoon reached up and slapped himself on the cheek. "I must stop talking to myself. A bad habit, acquired during too many long, dark years of scheming, and all of that is almost behind me now, with Cormyr practically in my grasp."

He gave a bright smile to a surly carter sweating along under the weight of a full keg, received an astonished stare in return, and sauntered on with a light heart.

Elminster dead. By his own hand, thorough and certain. Yes.

That extermination opened so many doors and made so many perilous trails safer and easier. Though it did mean some rethinking of strategy.

With his need for haste gone, it was now imperative to delay this Council of the Dragon. With Stormserpent and his fellow young hotheads down, he needed time—another day should suffice—to replenish the ranks of noblemen serving him.

When the Council inevitably turned into a bloodbath, he wanted particular royalty, courtiers, and nobles slaughtered, not mere random murders.

Tailored bloodletting saved so much time.

Elminster quelled a sigh. Lord Delcastle was growing wild-eyed, apt to do nigh anything—and becoming truly dangerous.

Oh, Rune's body was agile enough to snatch up furs and blankets to trammel the blade the young fool was waving around, or even fling them over his head to blind him, and smite him cold—but Rune was naked, and Storm might as well be, and that sword was sharp. Someone was going to get hurt.

And it was all so unnecessary.

The coffer young Arclath was threatening him with was empty, until El departed Amarune—and Storm could just as easily store his ashes down the toes of her boots, or for that matter, scoop ashes that weren't him at all from yon hearth for the angry young lordling to destroy to his heart's content . . .

Ah, Storm was awake, throwing off the effects of the darfly. Through her glossy fall of silver hair, El saw the gleam of one eye opening a trifle, for just a moment.

Which made his role clear. He had to keep Arclath talking and all the lordling's attention on him.

"Arclath," he said in his best imitation of Amarune's gravely earnest manner, going to his knees and spreading his arms wide, "what can I do to convince you? I am your Rune, and . . . and you're frightening me. I don't know how to prove anything to you!"

He had to keep his eyes from straying to Storm and drawing Arclath's attention to her—but at the back of the mind they were sharing, Amarune had seen that eye open, too, and had instantly become interested in watching her.

Unthinkingly she reached for control of her eyes. They tussled mentally for a silent moment, until El brutally won that battle by shaking the dancer's head violently and making her look away and down at the blanket-littered floor.

"Arclath?" he sobbed, not daring to let Amarune look up.

"Rune," Arclath snarled, "if you are Rune and not the wizard, please believe me when I tell you I'm just as scared. And baffled about how to be sure you are . . . well, you."

El managed not to smirk. Would he have been any more eloquent, at Delcastle's age? Likely not . . .

Behind the young lord, Storm had set about freeing herself. Arclath knew his work. His belt was stretched tight, cutting deep grooves in her arms. Storm stretched like a great cat, arched herself even further, then relaxed, having tested the limits of her bonds. Which weren't much.

Yet it seemed she'd learned enough to decide what to do next, without any hesitation at all. As El fought not to watch, with Amarune providing no help at all, Storm made her move.

"And I don't know how to prove to you that I am Amarune. Elminster can't control me for long, but . . . well, he's not the monster you make him out to be."

"Hah! That must be you, mage! My Rune would never submit to tyranny without fighting and shouting about it every moment she could draw breath!"

Behind the angry lordling, Amarune and Elminster saw Storm dislocate one of her shoulders with a twisting thrust and a grimace of pain. That loosened the swordbelt enough that she could wriggle in painful silence, pull and slide out of Arclath's tight strapping, leaving the belt clinging to the shirt she left behind.

She rolled over with slow, infinite care, as bare as the day she was born and in utter silence, keeping her injured shoulder from harm. She kept rolling, across the furs and blankets to the hearth.

Elminster tried again—and this time felt Amarune in full agreement with him. He let her take over her voice midword, hoping he wouldn't regret it.

"Arclath Delcastle," he began severely, "how do you"—she took over so smoothly that there wasn't the slightest hitch in the angry sentence—"know what I would do? I pleasure men for a living, remember? I do so because I need to eat, and to keep from freezing in Suzailan winters; I've never been able to afford the principles you cloak me with!"

At the hearth, Storm wasn't reaching for any weapon nor doing anything at all to cover herself or tend to her shoulder. She was—El had to quell Rune's disbelieving stare—making tea.

"You're not my Rune," Arclath snapped. "Fancy words for a mask dancer, wizard! You'll have to do better than that!"

In their shared mind, Amarune's anger flared. She tugged at El for control of all her body, and he yielded it. This should be good.

"Arclath, are you truly so foolish? Or just too angry to think? Do you really believe a glib tongue, cogent arguments, and cultured words belong only to the highborn and a few courtiers? Are we beasts to you, barely able to do more than grunt and snort? We unwashed citizens who are your dupes, your servants, your slaves? For that matter, have you any idea what mask dancers—gods spit, what any two-coin pleasure lass—get to overhear, in any given season? I am Amarune Whitewave!"

Still on her knees, she wrapped her arms around herself and snapped, "And this body is mine! I'm not some old wizard pretending to be your Rune; I am your Rune! Get that through your thick head, Lord Highnose Delcastle—if you can!"

Arclath blinked. "Uh—ah—but Rune, how can I be sure? I—"

"You can't, Lord Delcastle! None of us can! All of us must trust in others in life or shun them completely and wander the wilderlands alone—until the first prowling wolf or hungry bear gets us! I have to trust you; you have to trust me; and we both have to trust others—the bard and wizard with us, for instance. Now, let me tell you something!"

Arclath blinked at her, then—wisely, El thought—nodded. And refrained from pointing out that Rune had been doing just that.

Good lad. Ye might live through this, after all.

"I am hurt, Arclath. I have just met a goddess. Face-to-face—stlarn it, and she touched me! It was terrible, and it was wonderful. I was lost in awe and wanted nothing more than to come back here and tell you how utterly magnificent it was. The most shining moment in my life thus far, possibly the finest happening I'll ever know. And you've ruined it, Arclath, utterly ruined it! I need to share it with you; I need you to understand it; and what do I find? You're waving a sword around as if that will solve everything! How typically noble! Gah!"

"B-but Rune, he's stolen your body!"

Amarune exploded up off the floor and marched right up to Arclath, slapping his sword aside with the flat of one hand, angry eyes glittering. "Now you listen to me, Lord Delcastle! Elminster—my ancestor, and don't you high Houses set much store by your bloodlines and hallowed forebearers, hey?—has borrowed my body. With many misgivings and no intention of keeping it, and I have seen that in his mind. We share my head, remember? I've seen his thoughts, and I know. Him I need not trust, because I know what he thinks and feels."

She halted right in front of Arclath, chin to chin, not quite pressed against him, and said fiercely, her breath on his face hot with anger, "And hear me well, Arclath Delcastle—that borrowing is fine with me. So, if you care about my feelings and my freedom at all, it should also be fine with you."

Arclath stared into her eyes, going pale, his sword sinking forgotten in his hand.

"If you can't accept that," his Rune added, "perhaps you'd better instead accept that none of this is really your business at all."

The young noble lord studied her face, and then he shook his head and backed away, sword coming up again.

"No," he said. "No. You're not my Rune. These words are coming from Elminster, seeking to trick me. Wizard, what have you done to my lady?"

Amarune clenched her fists at her sides and leaned forward to let out a shriek of frustration.

Arclath fell into a fighting stance, sword up. "You'll have to do better than that!"

"Why?" asked a gentle voice from just behind his right ear. "Can't we all calm down and sit by the fire to chat about this? I've made some tea."

Storm Silverhand! How had she—?

Arclath spun around, sword slicing the air to lash out—

And came to a sudden halt, shaking and aghast.

Not only had he almost struck down a naked, unarmed woman, but during his whirling turn, fingers like iron fangs had come out of seemingly nowhere and done something to his wrist to make his sword fly free, then taken his sword arm in a grip he very much doubted he could break.

Storm was stronger than he was. Not to mention much more beautiful than he'd ever be, and pressed against him.

"Applying a binding over clothing won't keep captive someone willing to shed her garments," she murmured. "You might with advantage remember that, Lord Delcastle."

She added a friendly smile, and it was as if the sun had risen in the hut. Silver tresses rose, seemingly on their own, to stroke his cheek and trace the line of his chin.

Arclath stared at her, fighting to keep his eyes on her face. Gods, but she was stunningly good-looking! He—he—it was hard not to stare at all of her or refrain from taking a half-step forward and feeling all of her. If they struggled now, their contact would be both vigorous and . . . intimate.

"I—I know not what to do," he blurted, feeling a soft hand (Rune's, and stlarn it, she was unclad, too!) slide around his waist from behind.

He sighed and gave up. "Where's that tea?"

Chapter
THREE

I Have a Little Plan

So once more our kingdom totters, foes on every hand, and
Every lord a traitor! Who can save the Bright Throne now?
(The cry goes up once more.)
Worry not, my lords, for I have a little plan.

> Old Lord Sneel, in Act I, Scene III of the play
> *The Bright Throne Shattered* by Baerlus Merlond of
> Athkatla, first staged in the Year of the Black Blazon

Two steps into the room above the shop of Immaero
Sraunter, Understeward Corleth Fentable came to a
sudden halt, his eyes going very wide. "I—I—"

The smiling man seated down the far end of the table, at
Sraunter's elbow, waved an airy hand.

"Ah, Fentable, you remember me? Favorably, I hope."

Fentable was too busy sinking into shocked horror to
manage a reply—a state of mind he saw mirrored in the eyes of
the third man at the table.

Wizard of War Rorskryn Mreldrake looked as if he'd swallowed a fatal dose of poison, and only just realized it.

They were all the mind-slaves of the man at the end of the
table. The handsome, amused man whose dark eyes devoured
Fentable.

Under their thrall, he sat down in the last empty chair,
barely noticing he was doing so.

He, Sraunter, and Mreldrake had been pawns of the
dark-eyed man until some brief time before yestereve,
when he'd withdrawn from them and made them forget
all about him.

Now he was back, to begin their servitude anew.

"I *know* we all know each other," Manshoon said, "though I'll admit I'd not intended us all to ever meet like this. Yet, circumstances change, and my paramount needs with them. So, gentlesirs, hear and heed attentively." He gave them a soft, sharklike smile and added, "as I *know* you will."

"Pull," Storm commanded, turning away from him. A trifle gingerly, Arclath obeyed.

"Harder," she added. Setting his jaw, he put his strength into it.

Suddenly, her arm moved sickeningly in his grasp. The silver-haired woman grunted like one of his guards taking a dagger thrust, reeled a little under his hands, and gasped, "Good. Back where it should be."

Disengaging her arm, she turned to face him and growled with mock severity, "Now *don't* make me have to do that again."

Arclath drew in a deep and somewhat unsteady breath and then let it out again before he dared to reply, "I'll try not to, Lady Immerdusk."

Storm rolled her eyes. "Just 'Storm,' *please*. Whenever I hear that title, I feel several centuries older." She reached for his tankard with the arm he'd just put back into its socket. "More tea?"

Arclath nodded, glanced at Amarune, and looked back at Storm. "I'm . . . ah, sorry to the both of you. To all three of you, rather, but Rune most of all. I—this is still going to take some getting used to, for me."

"You're not alone," Amarune told him. "Raise the door bar again, and let's get some sleep. I'm not just tired now; I'm cold."

Storm proffered tea with one hand and a sleeping fur with the other. Then she leaned between the two Suzailans, long and sleek and shapely, to blow out the smoldering brazier.

"Let's snuggle up. Elminster can keep watch."

Arclath's head came up. He gave her his best frown, and then peered all around the hut's lone room . . . but saw only the two women. When his gaze came back to Storm, she looked amused.

"Try to get a little *more* used to it," she said. "Start now."

Arclath sighed, sketched a parody of a court bow, and sank down among the blankets. His life had changed dramatically in a bare handful of days, and the changes still seemed to be coming—and coming faster.

He hoped he'd manage to stay in his saddle during the wild ride ahead.

Manshoon favored the three frightened faces around the table with an affable smile.

He was indulging himself like the most overblown nobles, he knew, with all of these leering, airy utterances and glee—but by the kiss of Bane himself, it was so utterly *fun* playing a dastardly villain to the hilt. And after all, why not? Who was to stop him now?

With Elminster dead, a blithely unaware and scarcely defended Cormyr was a certain Manshoon's for the taking, if he set no foot wrong in overeagerness.

So call this jauntiness a reward, richly won foolery that, after all, had more than a century of accomplishment behind it—unlike the empty, sneering strutting and peacock-screeching of this kingdom's young nobility.

Why *shouldn't* he?

Yet he'd missed chances and marred perfect schemes before. Elminster or no Elminster, this realm was still a prize.

A prize yet unconquered which had rebuffed formidable foes before.

Moreover, it had too many mages—however lacking in spells, prudence, and cunning—propping up its throne to dismiss its taming as an idle day's undertaking.

Chortlingly manipulating or not, he must keep to his plan. Part of which held that he must not, under any circumstances, publicly announce his presence or even existence for some time to come. He must *always* work through others. Overboldness and impatience had been his besetting flaws in the past; hereafter, he was determined not to repeat them.

"New flaws for old," he murmured to himself. "That's my road . . ."

"L-Lord?" Sraunter dared to ask. With a smirk, Manshoon waved the question away.

He had planned all along to cause an uprising at the Council—not a hard thing to achieve, after all—in hopes of bringing about a few deaths. An Obarskyr or two and a handful of nobles. Particular nobles. That should eliminate some of the stubborn stalwarts in his path and push Cormyr to the verge of war.

At least three different Sembian cabals sought the same ends but, hopefully, were as of yet unaware of his presence. So, too, were some rather foolishly overambitious merchants of Westgate, and of course the Shadovar.

If this ignorance was genuine and continued long enough, these other players might unwittingly help make this Council of the Dragon a blood-drenched disaster. If he managed matters properly, they would remain ignorant of Manshoon for a tenday or more . . . which should be time enough.

The upheaval of violence and a failed Council would of course afford a chance to move his pawns higher in the court hierarchy, and "his" nobles into favor.

Yet there was a problem.

And why not? There was *always* a problem. Usually a host of them.

This particular problem was rooted in Elminster's meddling, of course. One last gift from his hated foe.

With Stormserpent's treason exposed and most of that expendable lordling's callow young noble allies wounded and abed—and so unable to attend the Council—Emperor-to-be Manshoon lacked time to reach and influence replacements for his cause, new nobles he could manipulate into furthering his schemes at the Council and thereafter.

The ghostly Princess Alusair had hounded him out of the palace, but faded rapidly once outside its walls, so he'd eluded her and set about founding another base nearby in Suzail. Enter handy Sraunter . . .

He hadn't planned to awaken Fentable and Mreldrake as his agents again so soon after withdrawing from their minds, and doing so was a trifle clumsy, but changed circumstances forced new strategies—and they *were* the most efficient agents he could bring to bear.

Hence this little meeting.

"For the good of the realm," he purred, "the Council must be delayed. By a day, no more."

Fentable and Mreldrake relaxed visibly. The frowns didn't leave their faces—achieving even a day's delay would entail much work and unpleasantness—but it was far less perilous than some of the things they'd obviously been fearing he would say, and a postponed Council did have one or two advantages . . .

"That is . . . good," Fentable said cautiously. "The last Dragon reports have six or seven lords still on the road, journeying to Suzail. They might well not have arrived in time, and that in itself might have done grave harm to peace among the nobility."

Mreldrake looked dubious. "At the cost of peace among those already here, who are restless enough. With another day and night to work mischief, what with all the drinking, the harbored feuds, and the armed bullyblades they've all brought with them . . ."

Manshoon shrugged. "So much was on your platter already."

Sraunter cleared his throat. The other three all looked at him.

He stared back, flustered by the sudden attention, and then stammered, "B-but delay the Council *how?*"

"Well, as to that," Manshoon said, "I have a little plan."

That made it his turn to be stared at.

He smiled back, not discomfited in the slightest. "In fact," he purred, "it's why I arranged this little meeting. You three will cause the Council of the Dragon to begin a day late— though fear not, no one outside this room will know who worked the delay. If, that is, you play your parts according to my instructions."

He leaned back in his chair. "If any of you get, ah, *creative*, on the other hand, the consequences could well be disastrous. Yet, we've worked well together in the past. I know none of you remember that, but then, that's the beauty of it. If the days ahead go smoothly, I'll see that you forget all about them—and need never fear a prying Highknight or wizard of war tricking something out of your mind. You'll be able to—in all innocence—swear you know nothing at all about it. Because, you see, you won't."

He smiled, laced his fingertips together, and sent his brightest smile around the table, giving them time to shiver and then recover themselves.

Informed slaves are obedient slaves . . .

Lord Arclath Delcastle came awake very suddenly, alert and tense, and far from his usual slow, languid surfacing amid warmth and silky, soft bedsheets. He had a feeling that he was rousing at his customary time, near dawn. His skylight was nowhere to be seen, though, and his face was quite cold. He felt badly cured fur against his cheek, and from around him came the smells of wood smoke and damp duskwood and—

And someone bare and warm and shapely was pressed against him, with her arms around him.

"R-rune?" he whispered, his eyes flying open.

He found himself staring into the face of his beloved. Amarune was holding him as they lay on their sides, legs entwined and arms around each other, noses almost touching. Her eyes were closed and stayed that way, her breathing soft, slow, and regular. Asleep.

Arclath remembered everything then, and hastily twisted up onto one elbow to look around the cabin. The brazier was out, but the hearth was lit, the teapot sitting atop the soot-blackened grate. He saw no sign of Storm.

Good. For the moment, at least, he and Rune were alone. He could speak freely.

He kissed her, gently but insistently. Her eyes snapped open; she'd obviously been feigning slumber.

"Mmmm?" she purred.

"Ah, Rune," he whispered, "I—ah—love you very much and want to talk to you. Right now. While it's just the two of us."

"Ah," Amarune told him with an impish smile, in the gruff tones of Elminster. "Ye young lordlings don't waste your chances, do ye? Well enough, because I want to talk to ye, too. So, start spouting words, lad. 'Tis a new day, but growing older fast!"

Arclath tensed but managed to quell his urge to thrust the warm and curvaceous body away from him.

"Ah—uh—damn you, wizard! Can't I talk to my Rune without you stepping between us?"

"Lad," the wizard's growl answered him, Amarune's eyes fixed on him, "ye can. Hopefully—with but a very few exceptions—ye will. Ye see, I'll be using thy lass as little as possible and seeking a suitable replacement to ride. Ye have my word on that."

"Your word?" Arclath said bitterly. "And what is that worth? My own has been . . . somewhat devalued."

"Lad, I like this as little as ye do, and thy lady's not exactly blissful about it, either. She's my descendant, mind, and I want her unhurt in body and mind, so I'll try to take very good care of her. I say 'unhurt' because she is, after all, in here with me and aware of everything. That I have violated her as few have been violated, I grant. I've tried to apologize for what there can be no proper apology for, and failed, but she's seen my need and reasons in my thoughts and accepts them. She'll tell ye so, though ye're just going to have to accept her word when she tells ye it's her speaking and not me. If ye do not, I see her soon bidding ye begone, noble name and wealth or not. Now, can there be peace between us?"

Arclath stared thoughtfully into the eyes of the mask dancer so close to his. The woman he'd come to love, so swiftly and deeply that he was still a little disbelieving. Had the wizard used a little love magic? But no, he'd been nowhere around when . . . or had he?

Shards and stars, did any of that matter? He *did* love his Rune, more than he'd ever loved anyone before, and—and what *could* he do to thwart this Old Mage, anyhail?

Nothing. Nothing at all, but be there for his Amarune and hope she won clear of Elminster soon, unharmed. Or as unscathed as possible.

Which meant making common cause with the Sage of Shadowdale was the only prudent thing to do.

"Aye," he said aloud, awkwardly. "There can be. Peace between us, I mean."

Amarune's slender-fingered hand clasped his as firmly as any warrior's, and a bright smile spread across her face.

"Good, glad that's done," El growled then, causing her to roll away and fling back the furs. "Rune's bladder is bursting!"

Understeward Corleth Fentable was in none-too-pleasant a mood, but even if the fearful shadow of Lord Manshoon hadn't loomed everpresent in his thoughts, Fentable's displeasure so early in the morning was hardly surprising.

Unless ordered on duty by Palace Steward Rorstil Hallowdant, he seldom saw the dawn or much of the bright and chill early morning that followed it.

He was here on Hallowdant's orders, curt and stiff, snapping commands at half a dozen war wizards and twice that many Purple Dragons. More soldiers were standing guard in all the crimson-carpeted passages that led to the newly refitted Hall of Justice, where the Council of the Dragon was to be held. They were making certain all maids, doorjacks, and everyone else stayed well away.

Fentable's superior would probably have delegated this duty to him regardless, but the understeward had the minor satisfaction—if it could in truth be deemed that—of knowing it was no accident that Hallowdant had suddenly fallen ill. He was doubtless groaning away in his garderobe, enduring the effects of whatever Sraunter had provided for a servant—another of Lord Manshoon's pawns—to slip into the decanter Hallowdant was wont to sip from whenever he awakened at night.

Manshoon left no detail unattended. As he'd reminded them all to frighten them into utter loyalty.

Fentable's tight mouth became a thin line of fury.

"The search, saer, is done," a young war wizard reported. "The chamber is now clear."

"It wasn't?" he snapped.

The mage (what was his name, now? Darmuth? Tarmuth?) sighed audibly before replying, "Two mice, a dozen ants and beetles, and a manycrawl. All dead now, and removed. Four miceholes, blocked. We *are* wizards of war, saer."

And sensitive indeed about taking orders from mere courtiers, for once, though they weren't quite certain if they dared defy the understeward, in the absence of Royal Magician Ganrahast and Lord Warder Vainrence to tell them all what to do.

Fentable kept the grim smile he felt like wearing off his face and nodded, lifting his eyes to direct the briefest of glances past the mage's shoulder at Mreldrake, whose answering nod was almost imperceptible.

"Now ward it," Fentable ordered, "and close and lock the doors—or lock them first—or—well, do those things in whatever order you need to, to make the Council chamber secure!"

He turned away. The moment the war wizards withdrew, guards would be posted outside all doors into the chamber, so the entire palace—and inevitably, given Suzailan gossip, most of the city, ere highsun—would know the room was secured.

Not that it truly would be. Not with Mreldrake as one of the warders, who would then know the precise details of the ward spell and so be able to modify the many-person teleportation he would later cast in secret at Lord Manshoon's command, to bypass the wards.

Oh, this was going to be a memorable Council, to be sure.

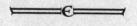

Amarune made it to her feet and managed two unsteady steps through the tangled furs and blankets before reeling and starting to topple.

Arclath scrambled up to catch her, knowing even as he tried that he was strides away from where he needed to be.

"*Rune!*" he cried, vainly reaching for her. Amarune flung out a hand, kicked her feet free of the bedding underfoot, and staggered in an off-balance run sideways until she fetched up against the cabin wall and slid down it.

The door had banged open by then, and Storm—clad in her worn leathers, with fresh kindling in her arms—had burst through it, flung the wood at one wall, and launched herself across the room.

Arclath got there first.

"Rune," he pleaded, putting his arms around her, "are you all right? Be well!"

"No, I'm *not* all right," his lady muttered—and it was her voice, thank the gods, not Elminster's!

"That wizard is draining the life out of you, somehow," Arclath snarled, helping her to her feet. "We've *got* to get you to a mage we can trust, to do something about this!"

"No," Amarune said, turning to look into his eyes, their noses bumping. "No, 'twasn't El. The goddess took it. Mystra."

Arclath gaped at her, and then frowned in anger and worry. He turned to look at Storm—and was frightened to see her even more concerned than he was.

CHAPTER
FOUR

DARK VILLAINY AGAIN

Ah, but there's one familiar stink my nose tastes not,
Something missing that is always there. Ah! There,
I catch a whiff! Friends, 'tis here, and we can begin!
Aye, that's the reek unmistakeable! Dark villainy again.

> Old Grauthum the Gravedigger, in Act I, Scene IV of
> the play *Burying Three Kings* by Aumraerus Fethurmyr
> first performed in the Year of the Wrathful Eye

Th-that's the last!" the carter panted through the curtain
of sweat streaming down his large, reddened face. He
backed hastily away from the silent men who'd been catching
every hay bale he'd tossed, stowing them somewhere in the
darkness beyond the alchemist's alley door.

Panting even harder, he almost fell twice in his feverish
haste to get around to the front of his wagon and whip his
dozing drays into motion, to race away from Sraunter's.

It was as if the carter expected death to reach after him. But
Manshoon merely favored the dwindling, rattling wagon with
a lopsided smile, straightened from his indolent lean against
the wall, and sent the slack-faced men he'd been dominating
into tossing hay bales back to the alleys. The spells he'd cast on
them would slay them—and the carter, too—when he uttered
a certain word. He'd do that well before highsun, long before
any inquisitive Purple Dragon might think to get around to
questioning them about anything.

If matters unfolded as planned, the good soldiers of
Cormyr would be rather too busy for inquisitions when the
sun rose over Suzail in the morning.

Manshoon closed and barred the alley door. Then he
strolled into the littered chamber Sraunter was pleased to call

his "concoction room," where the alchemist was still feverishly busy at his task.

Under the lash of Manshoon's spell, Sraunter was muttering and scuttling over his stained and scarred worktables, dancing and dashing across the room time and again to check and recheck various bubbling, glowing bowls.

Those hay bales had to be doused with *something* that would produce poisonous, oily, clinging smoke when they were set afire, and they had to be doused very soon.

But Manshoon trusted that Sraunter knew his work. He had three different mixtures curing, any of which should be enough to clear the Council chamber in frantic haste—and turn anyone stubborn enough to linger into a corpse. Three dooms should be enough to foil any single spell cast to quell smoke, and if the courtiers had ever heard of prudence (and what courtier hadn't?) the mixtures should also be more than enough to make the courtiers delay holding the Council until they'd made sure no other perils were lurking.

Manshoon managed to keep himself from rubbing his hands in glee, but a fierce grin spread across his face. Ah, with his old foe gone, dark villainy was truly *fun* again!

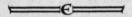

"What *is* that? Smoke?" Amarune pointed at the chill wisps drifting and coiling in the deepest shade, where the trees stood dark and thick.

"Ground mist," Storm and Arclath replied in unison. The young noble chuckled and gestured grandly at Storm to continue.

With a smile, she obliged. "What sailors call 'fog' when it's near the docks or at sea. Found here most mornings. 'Tis the damp rising as the day warms."

"Huh," the dancer replied, hunched against the cold under the trees. "Doesn't *feel* very warm yet."

"Agreed," Storm replied, cocking her head at a faint rustling in the distance. Fox, or the like, heading home.

All around the three humans, creatures of the woodland day were awakening; the King's Forest was astir. El was back in her boots for now; Rune was herself again; and Arclath was leading them north, keeping to the forest but following the road.

It wasn't far off to their right, and Storm had been expecting to see patrolling foresters for some time. The cabin was well behind them, but the cozy, private Delcastle hunting lodge Arclath had promised stood, according to him, more than a day's brisk walk northward.

The nobleman came up beside her, Amarune on his arm. "Suppose," he began conversationally, "you unfold to us just a little more of the, ah, life you and Elminster have been leading hereabouts these last few seasons. Our wizards of war seem to regard you as great foes of Cormyr."

"That view of us appears to be gaining popularity among them," Storm agreed. "As the passing years take from us older, wiser war wizards and elder courtiers, there is a growing ignorance of us and of She whom we serve—Mystra—in the wake of the great tumult that befell the Art. El and I find this somewhat annoying, given the centuries of work we've put into guarding Cormyr so that it's still here for these magelings to strut about in."

She smiled, shrugged, and added, " 'Tis true each new youngling must be taught, but we're getting older and clashing with arrogant idiots is less and less enjoyable."

Arclath grinned. "Arrogant idiots like me, for instance?"

Storm shook her head. "You're no idiot, Arclath Delcastle. Wizard of War Rorskryn Mreldrake or Palace Steward Rorstil Hallowdant—*those* are idiots. Neither believe we are anything more than common thieves who've seen some threescore summers and spent some of those seasons worming our ways into the royal palace."

Arclath rolled his eyes. "Come, now. You're not expecting me to believe all those tales about you being thousands of years old, rearing Azoun the Great, tutoring dread Vangerdahast, and suchlike, are you?"

Storm lifted an eyebrow. Arclath rushed on.

"Oh, you've borrowed grand reputations from folk out of legend, I'll grant, but there are no war wizards standing here to impress now. I've heard tell you're really Stornara Rhauligan, and Elminster's really Elgorn Rhauligan, your father? Older brother? Grandsire? The two of you are supposedly longtime lowly palace servants who were caught stealing magic items and dismissed for it. Some say you're Harpers or spies for Westgate or Sembia. I . . . well, I don't know *what* to think. It's just the three of us out here, so let's have truth, shall we?"

Storm Silverhand stopped and turned to face him, her hair stirring around her like dozens of restless snakes, and her eyes two silver flames. "I don't *expect* you to believe anything at all, Lord Delcastle. I've noticed your opinion of us changes like the weather, but I hope you're wise enough to arrive at shrewd judgments of folk, given enough time. So now that we're together, you'll watch and listen to us and draw your own conclusions accordingly."

Arclath came to a stop, too, and faced her. On his arm, Amarune looked from one of them to the other, frowning.

"Very well," he said calmly. "In the interest of mutual trust, let us assume that the answer you're about to give me is utter truth and that I'll believe it. So who are you, really? You and the cloud of slithering ashes who calls himself Elminster?"

"I am Storm Silverhand. Some ninety summers ago, I was the Bard of Shadowdale. Elminster is . . . Elminster. The Sage of Shadowdale, the Old Mage of legend. We were—are—both Chosen of Mystra, the goddess of magic. Her servants. Her Highknights, if you will."

"Mystra. A dead goddess, who once ruled—corrupted, some say—all magic."

"That Mystra," Storm said calmly, silver tresses still playing around her shoulders like serpents. "Yes."

"You're not going to tell me she's still alive? And that she has some secret, sacred mission for Rune?"

"No," Storm replied. "I don't have to."

Arclath arched one eyebrow. "Oh? Why not?"

"Because *I* know she's alive and can tell you myself," Amarune interrupted firmly. "I've met her. And if she has some secret task for me, she's said nothing about it."

"Yet," Arclath told her darkly.

Storm smiled. "Good," she said briskly, starting to walk north again. "You know who El and I are and as much about Mystra as any mortal dare trust in. We can cover the rest whenever we've time to waste talking. As we trudge toward this family hunting lodge of yours, for example."

Arclath frowned. "Lady . . . Immerdusk, do you prefer? I don't believe we've quite finished establishing where we stand. Elminster steps into the mind of my beloved whenever he pleases, and is forcing her to . . ." He felt a sharp tug on his arm.

"*Lord* Delcastle," Amarune said sharply, "you will refrain from making assumptions about me, and from thinking I'm some sort of cow or pet snail, docile and brainless, whom you can discuss as if I'm not here."

"Forgive me, Rune, but that's just it," the young nobleman said earnestly, staring into her eyes. "I don't know if your brain *is* your own, right now, or if that old wizard is inside your mind forcing you to think one way or another and even keeping you from knowing it!"

"Oh, don't be ridiculous!" Amarune flared. "Do you think for one momen—"

"Easy, lass," Storm murmured, reaching out a hand to the dancer. "He can't know. He hasn't shared his mind with Elminster or anyone, and so can't feel what it's like, or—"

"I'm not letting—!" Arclath roared.

Storm's slap to his codpiece startled him into silence mid-snarl, leaving him staring at her.

"No one is suggesting you'll have to," she told him gently. "I was merely soothing Rune by pointing out to her that you have no way of knowing what it's like when El is in your head. Let me tell the both of you right now that I'm deeply unhappy about his entering Rune's mind, and I would have fought him to try to prevent it had I not thought it was necessary. His . . . ah, invasion makes it very hard for us to trust each other . . . but that's all we can do now. Plead with you, is perhaps a better way to put it. Trust us. Please. Or this is going to end badly for us all, and soon."

Arclath was astonished to see tears glistening in her eyes.

Storm smiled wryly and added, "Lord Delcastle, you should thank us. A tenday back you were bored and wandering through the days, chafing at the meaninglessness of your existence and desperate to find some purpose in your life. We've taken care of all of that. Welcome to the grandest life of all. Welcome to saving the world."

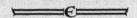

Manshoon realized he was smiling again.

The alchemist must be almost done, now. Sraunter had already nodded at one mixture, frowned and stood back, and slowly let himself smile at the second, before carefully shifting it off the heat of the small fire in his grate, Now he devoted his complete attention to the third.

Since forcing the man into nightlong brewing—if that was what alchemists called it—Manshoon had kept himself out of Sraunter's mind, not wanting to distract him at a crucial moment, or frighten him any further.

Instead, the future emperor of Cormyr had kept back in the shadows, idly examining the alchemist's shelves for substances that might prove useful in the future, and thinking.

The moment he had effective control over Cormyr—open and absolute command or several steps short of that—he'd set the Dragons of the realm to hunting down Storm Silverhand.

She must be taken alive, with her wits undamaged.

Interrogating her at leisure should yield to him much he desired to know. Secrets of the Chosen, where magic was hidden, and the whereabouts of The Simbul—the onetime Queen of Aglarond, whose Art had been mightier than Elminster's own. Mad and far too magically powerful for anyone's safety, that one must be destroyed.

Sraunter turned and nodded eagerly, sweat dripping from his chin. "Ready. All three, ready."

Manshoon let his smile widen. "Good man. You have saved Cormyr from itself."

Horns blew a fanfare that the cool morning breeze carried far across Suzail, summoning the invited—the nobility—to the Council of Dragons.

Mreldrake hardly needed the arrival of the hurrying palace doorjack, and Manshoon's surge from that man's dark and knowing eyes into his own mind, to know it was time to begin his castings.

Manshoon's mind was already sharing a crisply clear vision of the soaked and ready hay bales that Sraunter was igniting.

Few mages could translocate fiery materials without troubles, but Mreldrake's mind was filled, overwhelmed, and steadied by Manshoon's own, and the hay bales were only just beginning to burn.

Mreldrake caught a glimpse—briefly, before Manshoon firmly sealed that sight away and forced him back to full concentration on the complex spells he was working—of someone else Manshoon was scrying.

It was a noblewoman, unfamiliar to Mreldrake, who had long since risen and checked her appearance in her mirrors more than once already. The fanfare had brought her out onto a balcony to peer excitedly between towers and over grand roofs and the leafy tops of trees at the soaring royal palace of Suzail.

Coaches were already rumbling along the streets, and from her highest window the lady could see some nobles on foot, too, walking in their finery.

Dressed in her best, she hurried down into the streets to join them.

Then she was gone, and Manshoon's dark amusement was all Mreldrake could see ... that and flames rising and crackling from hay bales as Sraunter carefully set each one alight with the burning brand in his hand.

Then Mreldrake could discern something else through the heavy dark weight of Manshoon's mind. Shouting and the pounding of feet. A bobbing view of a grand palace passage—through the eyes of the same servant who'd brought Manshoon to him—and thick, acrid smoke, its coils a deep, menacing blue warring with a greasy, baleful green, billowing out around the closed doors of the Council chamber.

Hay bale after hay bale his spells plucked from the dim crowding of Sraunter's back room to the smooth oval of hitherto-empty flagstones at the heart of the Hall of Justice, with its rising tiers of empty, glossy, dark wooden benches all around, until . . . the work was done. All the little fires had been sent.

The alchemist's shop went away, and Mreldrake was plunged into a strange, multiple-eyes view of hurrying Purple Dragons, various guards and war wizards being overcome as they arrived to try to investigate . . . a confused chaos of falling, staggering, then more shouting and barked orders and booted guards scrambling. Name of the Dragon, but Manshoon must have command over the minds of a dozen courtiers or more!

One scene swam nearer, of a palace passage with an angry woman storming along it, a wizard of war he knew all too well . . .

"No more fanfares!" Glathra called furiously down the passage.

"Lady Glathra?"

"You heard me!"

On the heels of that furious bellow, Wizard of War Glathra Barcantle spun around to part a curtain and say in a far gentler voice, "Your Majesty, I fear the Council cannot proceed. This day, at least. Not unless you want to die—and all the senior nobility of the realm with you."

"Understood," came the calm reply from the alcove behind the curtain. "There are some who would welcome that particular extermination, but I can't count myself among them. I take it you'd prefer I withdraw, bodyguards and all, to the royal wing? Right now?"

"Your wisdom is as swift and keen as ever, Majesty."

"Would that your flattery were shining truth," came the affectionate, rather sad murmur. "We go."

"Good," Glathra breathed, letting the curtain fall and spinning around again to glare at a Purple Dragon lionar who was stumbling up to her, coughing hard, his face gray. He waved a hand, fighting to speak but failing.

A swordcaptain behind the lionar tried to speak in his stead, only to be plunged into helpless coughing and retching. "I—I—"

"Fools!" Glathra snapped. "Keep clear of the smoke! Close the doors across the passages by the Hall of Victories and by Queen Alvandira's bower—open all windows and doors hard by us, here! We must get rid of the smoke!"

Catching sight of a wizard hurrying up from the other direction, she pointed at him and ordered, "Tracegar, strip all wizards of war from their assigned guardposts and *get* into the Hall of Justice and *get rid of* whatever's causing this!"

"B-but—"

"There'll be no Council this day! Do it!"

She turned back the other way, saw a young mage she recognized peering anxiously out of one of the rooms along the passage, and snapped, "Tarmuth, go after the king's bodyguard, and make sure *all* of them put on night helms to keep them from being traced or influenced by spells! Hurry!"

Tarmuth nodded hastily and ran, but someone else was shouting at Glathra, and his voice was not friendly.

"Glathra," an older mage called, appearing through a door with a handful of fellow senior war wizards behind him, "I don't recall you being named lord warder! Surely—"

"Surely *someone* must guard the king before all else, Raeldar! Seeking to do anything less courts treason, does it not?"

"But why call off the Council?" another of the mages growled as they hastened up to her. Courtiers were appearing now, too, fleeing the smoke or appearing out of various chambers, drawn by the shouting. "The king will be less than pleased!"

"I have spoken with the king," Glathra roared, her voice as deep and clear as many a burly Dragon swordcaptain's, "and he saw in a moment what you have not: that the fires are not normal—hence magic is involved—and there must therefore be a traitor among the wizards of war, unless someone read our minds and so knew how to defeat our wards without alerting us or breaking them. Now, where does that compel *your* thinking, Brandaeril?"

The older wizard regarded her soberly, nodding as he considered and then announced, "Glathra is right. We have no choice but to delay the Council while we investigate. To do aught else could well be to doom King Foril and imperil the peace of the realm."

"Aye," Raeldar agreed reluctantly. "Ganrahast and Vainrence, if they were here, could hardly act differently. We must quell the smoke, learn all we can, cleanse the room, and cast new wards around it, then cry a new time for the Council across the city."

Manshoon tightened his grip on Mreldrake's mind, thrusting like iron-hard talons, and the suddenly mute, helpless wizard of war felt himself torn away from the scrying that had been showing him Glathra. In bewildering haste, his limbs not his own, he threw open his chamber door and hurried to the passage where everyone was gathering around her, to offer his obedient services.

It was too much to hope she'd be careless enough to let anyone who had a hand in crafting the first set of wards also work on the second, but a loyal war wizard would eagerly make the offer, so . . .

As he flung open the door and stepped into the crowded passage, Manshoon abruptly left Mreldrake's mind. Entirely.

Which could only mean Mreldrake wasn't expected to succeed in trying to be a part of the new wards.

He could grasp that much, no matter how dazed and shaking he was. Wiping sweat from his face and gulping to calm his panting, Mreldrake tried vainly to relax.

"You thought your work was done? Ah, but no, brave master of alchemy!"

Manshoon's smile was gentle, but Sraunter broke into help-less shivering, chilled anew by sudden sheer terror. What *now*?

"We've merely begun," Manshoon murmured, bursting into the alchemist's mind before the man could even whimper. "We're going for a little ride, you and I. You've done so well with the hay bales that you deserve good food and better drink, not to mention some laughter and a chance to restock your sadly depleted larder, in a score or more of the best—and worst—clubs, taverns, and shops across this fair city. Places in which you'll oh-so-slyly spread rumors of various wild and mysteri-ous attacks upon the palace."

"But—but I don't know what to say!"

"Ah, as to that, lose all fear. I'll guide your tongue, and I've done this a time or two before. Rulers must learn to hear and steer rumors, or they soon run out of time to learn anything at all."

CHAPTER
FIUE

TRAITORS, TRAITORS EVERYWHERE

It has always been the curse of this realm
And many another: traitors, traitors everywhere
Against scarce enough loyal folk to be worth
Drawing swords to slay.

> Old Duke Steeljaws, in Act II, Scene III of the play
> *Darth Thorn Horn* by Mydantha "Ladyminstrel"
> Marlest first performed in the Year of the Risen Elfkin

A Purple Dragon horn call rose into the air.

"Gods, *again?*" The veteran Dragon lionar was running out of profanities. He spun away from the table of drunkards he'd been about to glower down at, and strode hastily back out of the tavern. His men, some of them groaning, followed him in a weary thunder of hurrying boots.

Manshoon drifted out of the shadows to watch them, not quite smiling. Tension had been rising in the city all day; skirmishes had erupted between various nobles' bodyguards in clubs, taverns, and then the streets, and not long past highsun the "to arms" had been sounded, calling all Dragons out of barracks to establish order.

The Council of the Dragon had been proclaimed to begin not this day but on the morrow—and Suzail was not taking the news well.

Rumors were racing from table to table and along the alleys. Of course. Some had King Foril dead, and others swore a dozen nobles had been hunted down and butchered by royal command, though no two tales seemed to agree on just which lords had met their bloody ends. Still others said tombs in the royal crypt had burst open and the dead kings of Cormyr were stalking the palace, furious at Foril for even thinking of curtailing royal powers—and rending servants, courtiers, and wizards of war alike limb from limb in their displeasure.

Vangerdahast had returned from the grave, transformed into a horrid skull-headed monster, one particularly gruesome tale insisted, and was demanding noblewomen be brought to him "to breed a new line to warm the Dragon Throne."

Manshoon had chuckled aloud at that one. It sounded so unlike that old fool Vangerdahast—and so much like something Elminster might have tried.

Yes, he was going to *enjoy* blaming things on Elminster. Why, he might be able to keep that useful line of besmirchment going for decades, and use it to cloak all manner of wayward butchery . . .

Not that he had overmuch time to spare for such pleasant musings just now. Not with half a dozen new blackhearted traitors to recruit from among the ambitious lesser nobility. The young Houses, those lowly highborn so hungry for more power that they'd do almost anything. They were here to gain anything they could and would listen to a certain sort of whispering.

A handful of them might be capable enough to prove useful, and Manshoon would seek out these few.

He smoothly thrust aside a curtain and stepped to the elbow of one of the useful few. "Lord Andolphyn?"

A sharp-featured man looked up with a doubtful frown from the splendid decanter he'd been about to unstopper, the twin daggers of his forked chin-beard glistening with the scented wax that kept them teased into two points. "Do I know you, sirrah? How did you get in here?"

"Your guards are . . . mere swordswingers, Naeryk. No match for a wizard of war."

A gasp came from the men clustered around Andolphyn in this back tavern alcove, but Manshoon gave them all a soft smile and added, "And still less of a match for me."

After a moment of uncertain silence, many of the men cast swift glances at their master, seeking guidance with hands hovering near blade hilts.

Lord Naeryk Andolphyn seemed to be having some sort of silent seizure; he'd gone stiffly upright in his chair and trembled violently, his eyes rolled up in his head. Then, quite suddenly, he'd relaxed. His face went smooth, his eyes reappeared, and a smile swam onto his face.

"At ease, all," he said huskily. "I . . . remember this man. An old friend. A very old friend."

Manshoon clapped the lord's shoulder gently. "Until next time, then," he murmured and slipped back through the curtain.

One mind invaded and conquered; one man now his. If all of them had such paltry magical protections, all six were going to be that easy. Yes, six should be enough—though it would be *far* too much to hope that six lordlings, even minor ones, would lack enough magic to prevent such unsubtle assaults.

Andolphyn down, Blacksilver not far ahead . . .

Smiling his gentle smile, Manshoon strolled on.

"You are here," Wizard of War Glathra Barcantle said earnestly, leaning forward to stare into the faces of the handful of courtiers in the room, "because the Crown trusts you most deeply, and seeks your counsel."

"Thank you, Glathra," King Foril said quietly. "Very well put."

The four courtiers facing the monarch and the lady wizard refrained from pointing out that the "most deep" trust just mentioned couldn't be all that deep, given the two mountainous knights in full plate armor kneeling in front of the king, and the three stone-faced wizards of war standing behind him with powerful-looking magical scepters in their hands . . . but then, they *were* senior courtiers.

The palace steward was notably absent. In his place sat the palace understeward, Corleth Fentable. The head Highknight Eskrel Starbridge was also missing, gone from the city on a secret mission, but his immediate underling, the well-spoken clerk of vigilance, Sir Talonar Winter, was present in his stead. Next to Winter sat the old, gruff, and very capable Steward of the Regalia Langreth Ironhorn, his towering height and ample girth settled in the stoutest seat, the two sticks he tottered around on gathered into the crook of one of his massive arms. In the last seat, which she'd hitched a hand's breadth or two away from the others, was Lady of Graces Jalessa Windstone, every bone of her a prim, disapproving perfectionist. Palace protocol was "her charge and her only child," it was said about Windstone.

"You are here," Glathra added, "because we are frantically trying to learn the identity of the traitor who introduced the deadly smoke into the Hall of Justice—or at least hit upon some way of finding out who that traitor is." She watched Fentable's gaze move to the three mages behind the king, and added quietly, "We are using all the spells we can think of, never fear. We are hoping one of you can think of some other means we might employ, to make sure that—"

Sir Winter gasped, shivered, and reeled in his seat.

Even before anyone could react, they all saw the cause. A ghostly, translucent figure had stepped through the wall behind Winter's seat and then through the courtier himself to stand facing King Foril Obarskyr.

"Majesty," she greeted him gravely, ignoring the swords the knights snatched out to thrust at her, "your traitor is Wizard of War Rorskryn Mreldrake. He's working with others, I believe, but the spells that brought the hay into the palace were his. He couldn't resist bringing himself into the room to check, just for an instant, after sending in the third burning bale. I saw him."

"Who are you?" Fentable snapped furiously—as the Lady of Graces fainted dead away and old Ironhorn leaned forward with a delighted chuckle.

The Princess Alusair favored the palace understeward with a look of scorn. "You know very well who I am, Fentable. We've seen each other often enough—and I've seen rather more of your doings than you'd like me to have witnessed, I'm sure."

Three scepters were now leveled at the ghostly figure, but Glathra held up a warning hand to keep the mages from unleashing magic just yet. Drawing a wand from her belt to menace the princess, she told Alusair curtly, "I'm not sure we should even listen to a ghost, let alone believe anything you have to say."

The longtime Steel Regent kept her eyes on those of the king as she shook her head sadly, sparing Glathra not even the briefest of glances.

"Foril," she sighed, "it seems you're surrounded by fools. If you'd like a larger one, I can fetch Vangerdahast—or what's left of him."

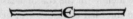

Lord Danthalus Blacksilver proved to be a tall, mellifluous dunderhead. He and the effete, oh-so-sophisticated Lord Lyrannus Tantorn were as easily subverted as Andolphyn had been.

Rather more easily, as both were straining for any chance to win greater influence and respect in a Suzail teeming with wealthier, more arrogant, and far more powerful nobles.

However, Manshoon felt his smile fading when he found Lord Melder Crownrood hunched over a gleaming platter of skewered roast quail at the best table in the Merdragon. Two steely-eyed hired wizards were seated on either side of the nobleman, wands ready in their hands as they stared watchfully at the diners all around. One shifted his scrutiny to Manshoon and sharpened it into a baleful challenge.

Servers hovered nervously in distant doorways, and no wonder. This was the most exclusive and expensive room of one of the haughtiest and most overpriced clubs in the city, the Rearing Merdragon, and those wands were menacing some of the wealthiest citizens of Suzail. Any misunderstanding could mean disaster.

"Come no closer," one of the wizards told Manshoon in tones of soft menace.

The advancing future emperor took no notice of the man; his slow, deliberate stride continued without hesitation, and his urbane, slightly bored expression never changed.

"Crownrood," he asked in the gentle purr an indulgent lover might use, as he bent over the quail-chewing lord, "are these lackspells yours? I was unaware they allowed pets in the Merdragon."

"As they seem to tolerate walking bones in here," Crownrood replied without looking up, "I suppose they'll put up with hired mages."

His tone was dismissive, even bored, but Manshoon noticed the man was clutching his just-emptied skewer like a dagger. A ring on the lord's dagger hand had begun to glow fitfully.

Ah, Crownrood's means of knowing his undeath.

Manshoon sighed, sat down in the vacant chair across from Crownrood, and murmured, "I'd like to discuss a little treason with you. Profitable treason, mind."

A sharp singing, tinkling sound marked a wizard's point-blank use of his wand—and the twisting of whatever magic it had unleashed into otherwhere, along a silvery astral conduit. Manshoon felt one of his rings crumble to dust in the wake of that defending, its fading taking the wizard's deadly magic with it, and he quelled a flare of irritation. Such defenses were expensive these days, not swiftly or easily replaced.

"You are refreshingly direct, undead stranger," Crownrood muttered, turning to meet Manshoon's gaze for the first time. "Suppose you convince me why I shouldn't be just as direct with this skewer. Quickly."

The wizard on Crownrood's far side glared at Manshoon and then looked away again, surveying the room for other perils. Such as accomplices.

Manshoon bit down on the dried pea he'd been carrying in one cheek, let its cargo of acrid dust fill his mouth, then turned and blew it in the face of the wizard right beside him, who'd just used his wand and was hauling out another one.

The wizard started to cough helplessly, unable to breathe. Not a surprising result, given what the dust was, and that he wasn't a vampire.

Manshoon went back to ignoring him. Crownrood chose to do so, too, but lifted the skewer meaningfully.

"I have plans for the future rulership of Cormyr that include you, Melder Crownrood. As chancellor of the realm, you will oversee the Purple Dragons and directly command the wizards of war," Manshoon told him.

"A splendid dream," Crownrood drawled, though not before a flash of his eyes betrayed his excitement. "And you are, O granter of dreams—?"

"Your master," Manshoon purred. He leaned forward until they were almost nose-to-nose, and launched the spell that wrapped around his mind, and hurled it into Crownrood's.

The skewer started to thrust . . . then fell back. The nobleman shuddered and spun around in his seat to slap aside the wand the alarmed wizard behind him was trying to aim. "Dolt! D'you want to ruin everything?"

"You're doing something to the Lord Crownrood!" that mage snarled at Manshoon, springing up from his chair to back hastily away and aiming his wand again. "*You're* doing it, undead thing!"

The man's voice rose, and heads turned at nearby tables. Manshoon smiled crookedly, shook his head, and made Crownrood turn to him and do the same, and cast a swift and simple spell.

The wizard's head burst in a welter of spattering gore. Even before the screams started, Manshoon rose from his chair, drew a knife from his sleeve, and sliced delicately across the throat of the still-coughing wizard, and strode away.

If he'd been wearing his own face, being seen by so many of Cormyr's high and mighty would have been a grave mistake.

As it was, Crownrood's mind was his, now. And it was the mind of an accomplished schemer and lawbreaker, who had already been thinking much treason without any help from visiting Manshoon at all.

As he smiled at a server and made the man flinch back out of his way in stammering fear, Manshoon started to hurry. Not out of any fear of lawkeepers; he'd be long gone before any Dragons arrived.

No, there were still two nobles he wanted to recruit—and with Suzail crowded with ambitious feuding nobility and their already-roused bodyguards, finding and reaching his quarries was going to take time.

Lord Jassur Dragonwood and Lord Relgadrar Loroun. Bane and blasphemy, but they even *sounded* like arrogant idiots . . .

"Your Majesty," Glathra said quickly and a trifle sharper than she intended to, "should we place any trust in the words of a ghost, or even listen to them? My experience has been that undead understand little of the changing world around them, clinging instead to what they knew in life, and that they can appear as anyone they please! This might well be an image sent by a hostile mage sitting in Sembia, or the ghost of an exiled traitor noble just *pretending* to be the Steel Regent, and—"

"Your 'experience' has been?" Alusair's eyes flashed. "Glathra Barcantle, just *what* experience have you had, treating with ghosts? You always seek to ignore me when you see me around the palace, and frankly, it shouldn't matter if I'm the lowliest chambermaid or passing street urchin! The moment you hear the slightest hint of possible treachery on the part of any wizard of war, you *must* investigate—or the House of Obarskyr, and Cormyr as anything other than a wizard-ruled land, is doomed!"

Glathra gave the ghostly princess an angry glare. "A *ghost* telling me my business? Why, next you'll be—"

"Holding your peace," King Foril Obarskyr said firmly, giving Glathra a glare that outshone her own in ferocity. He glowered at her for a long breath before turning to favor Fentable with the same quelling look, slowing the understeward to fumbling uncertainty as he clawed some sort of talisman or magical token out of a belt pouch.

"Ironhorn," the king of Cormyr added gently, "I believe the Lady of Graces needs reviving. Please?"

Then he turned to face Alusair directly, nodded to her as an equal, and said gravely, "Your Majesty, we thank you for your counsel."

The ghostly face drifted closer to his and acquired a smile. "Majesty, you do me honor. I'm a 'Highness,' and no more. I never ruled as queen, only as regent."

Foril waved a grey-haired hand. "To me, anyone who defended the Dragon Throne and the realm, when she could have taken both, is a *true* monarch of Cormyr. Your Majesty."

Fentable sputtered.

The king rounded on him and said sternly, "*My* decision, faithful understeward, and *my* judgment. This royal princess knew the burden and took it on, without enjoying the reward. She served the realm long and well, and made many of our nobles more loyal to the Crown than they had ever been. So slight her not, in my presence or behind my back. Oh, and it is high time that you and many of your fellow courtiers—to say nothing of others in the realm—ceased to mistake my customary reserve and politeness for weakness and vacillation of mind and purpose."

"Well said," Ironhorn and Alusair murmured in unintentional unison—and the king astonished everyone in the room by flashing, just for a moment, a boyish grin by way of reply.

Then he turned to Glathra and said politely, "Lady Glathra, I command that Wizard of War Rorskryn Mreldrake be taken into custody and questioned with spells, priestly assistance, and everything else short of mind-reaming. Search his rooms here in the palace. And set tax-scribes to turn up any properties he may own in or near Suzail, that *they* may be searched without delay. If we wrong him, I'll tender my apologies."

Foril looked back at Alusair grimly and added, "Yet, I very much doubt that we will."

Fentable, face flushed and downcast in the wake of his rebuke, was behind Foril Obarskyr, hidden from the others in the room by the king's body. That was a good thing for Foril, because it kept the other members of the court from seeing him stiffen, his face change, and his eyes flash with momentary fire—highly unusual behavior for Fentable or, for that matter, any prudent understeward of any high House.

A moment later, Fentable was his usual urbane, almost expressionless self again, but the mind behind those thoughtful eyes was once more crowded, as Fentable's own sentience quailed and cringed beneath the cold weight of Manshoon's mind. He had returned to the understeward's mind in haste and in none-too-good a temper, after conquering the mind of Lord Jassur Dragonwood just in time to hear Mreldrake denounced as a traitor.

Manshoon made Fentable turn away and pass his hand over his eyes to conceal any grimace or eye-flash his swift departure might cause. He had to get to Mreldrake without delay.

"Traitors, traitors everywhere," he said sardonically, so those were the words the understeward mumbled, in his wake.

The words that made everyone else in the room—save for Lady of Graces Jalessa Windstone, who was still blearily drifting her way back to full awareness—nod grimly.

It was a sentiment every one of them had heard before.

Wizard of War Rorskryn Mreldrake had just risen from the seat of his favorite garderobe in the palace, adjusted his garments, inspected the inside of his nose with a practiced finger, and reached for the door when Manshoon burst into his mind like a dark thunderbolt.

Mreldrake stiffened, swayed in midair with his fingers not quite close enough to the door bellpull to close on it, then lunged for the door in pounding haste.

He had to get across the upper floor of the palace, down the far stair to the easternmost of the tunnels that linked the palace with the sprawling pile of the royal court, traverse that underway, ascend from the court's uppermost cellar to a certain nondescript linen-cupboard in the southeasternmost corner of the court's ground floor, and pass through the portal that was hidden there. Without being seen, if possible—as himself, at least—and without raising any sort of cry.

The portal would take him to the fortress of the king's tower in Marsember, and hopefully buy him time enough to get aboard a ship bound for somewhere more distant than Westgate, before he was traced.

Mind-reaming is not a pleasant death.

He was sprinting along a passage when Manshoon again gripped his mind, flooding him with his master's growing disgust at his frightened flight, and Mreldrake was forced to slow to a normal walk, open the next door he came to, calmly step into the vacant guestroom beyond that door, and work a magic that would alter his appearance.

A few long, calming breaths later, a rather stocky, plain, middle-aged female wizard of war stepped out of the guestroom, carefully closed its door, and trudged along the passage as if bored and tired, rather than in a hurry to go anywhere at all.

She felt a bit dazed but remembered she had to get to Marsember and take a ship for Turmish or some other distant place, without anyone in the palace knowing. She was on a mission so secret that it would be revealed to her only when she was safely on the waves. Her name was . . . was Mythandra, but she had to fight to remember that—and it was a fight that brought to her a confused, whirling half-memory of a very powerful and coldly malicious mind departing hers in haste, searing many memories as it went.

Mythandra's head hurt. She growled wordless displeasure and plodded toward the door that opened into the far stair.

"Traitors, traitors everywhere," she mumbled—then paused, lifting her head with a frown. Now where had *that* come from?

Chapter Six

Stormbreak

I feel it coming, heavy and thunderous, rising like
menacing war-drums to that moment when
Death is loosed, a thousand warriors shrieking
As war bursts its bonds, and the realm knows stormbreak.

Halavar Thentle, Bard of Wheloon
War, Stormbreak, and Tears from the chapbook
RoarRiven published in the Year of the Mages in Amber

Wizard of War Ellard Gauntur was young, callow, full of self-importance, and zealous. At the moment, he was decidedly *not* full of sufficient breath.

He was gasping with excitement and exertion, having just sprinted the length of the royal court with five Purple Dragons in full armor puffing and clanging along in his wake. He skidded to a stop in front of a door that needed his hand and a whispered password to open, exulting as he flung it wide.

He *finally* had a chance to do something important, to get noticed—to be a hero!

Oh, and do true service for Cormyr, too . . .

"There's one portal that usually gets forgotten!" he'd shouted. "He probably won't go that way—but if he does, we can be there to prevent him!"

His heart had leaped up like lit torchwood when he'd seen the Dragons nod. There'd been approval on the veterans' faces! Clear in Narbrace's expression, and Hethel's!

Now they were through the door and pounding along the dim and narrow passage behind him, around this last corner and—

Someone was standing at the closet door. Someone in wizards' robes!

"Mreldrake!" Gauntur shouted. "Hold!"

The wizard at the open closet turned to look at him—then rushed into it, leaving behind only the soundless flash of light that meant the portal had taken her.

Yes, *her*. It had been a woman, not Mreldrake!

A woman he'd never seen before.

In robes that—

"It's him! 'Twas a trick! Those were Mreldrake's robes!" Gauntur snarled over his shoulder at Narbrace. "With that food stain down the front by the—"

He reached the open closet door, caught hold of the frame, and swung himself in and right at the dancing glow of the portal, then skidded to a stop and caught his breath in sudden apprehension—

Whereupon Narbrace shoved him hard in the back and growled jovially, "*Lead us*, gallant Gauntur!"

And the portal's glow claimed him.

"As per orders, saer," the Dragon puffed, "after Narbrace, Hethel, and the rest all followed him through, I came back to you to report. Mreldrake's gone to Marsember, if the lad's to be believed, and—and I knew you needed to know this, without delay!"

"Very proper, Swordcaptain Troon, and well done," Fentable agreed, nodding. "Go now—catch your wind first, there's not *that* much need for frantic haste—and catch up to Narbrace and your fellows. I'll inform the wizards of war." He clapped the breathless soldier on one armor-plated shoulder and hurried away.

Troon nodded, gasping for breath, and staggered to a garderobe door. His bladder was *bursting* . . .

Not long after a distant door had shut behind the hastening understeward, and Troon had found relief behind a much closer door, a streaking shadow came racing down the corridor.

It halted for a moment to rise up and glare around, and then it plunged through a wall and was gone again.

Once a Steel Regent, always a Steel Regent. That Fentable was every whit as rotten as Mreldrake—but when had he got that way? Who had gotten to him?

Sometimes, Alusair thought, she still existed only because of her abiding rage.

The court weren't such a sorry, corrupt lot in my day!

Were they?

Targrael awakened in the chill darkness of the crypt with a pounding headache. She hadn't known death knights could *have* pounding headaches.

The reason for her mind-pain was clear, even through her glee at being loosed once more to dance with the living. Manshoon, as he jabbed her back to awareness with vicious mental thrusts that shattered the cloaks over many of her memories, was in a seething rage.

That arrogant beast Mreldrake had been seen departing the palace through the main magical gate to Marsember—the king's tower portal—by a shining-eyed young war wizard and a handful of Dragons. Who must now be slain, every last one of them, in a hurry. With the bodies hidden to prevent swift and easy priestly questioning.

All to hide Mreldrake's trail. Manshoon must find him very useful.

To the slaughter, then, Wizard of War Ellard Gauntur and Purple Dragon veterans Ilstan Narbrace, Gorloun Hethel, Mandron Saldar, Berent Thallowood, and Unstrarr Troon. You served the realm in life, but your swift and sure deaths are now required for Cormyr's greater service . . .

Targrael set the coffin lid carefully back into place, glided through the darkness like a chill breeze, and departed the crypt in a swift, gathering gale.

Manshoon was with her, but riding her mind lightly, most of his attention elsewhere. She was a hasty, brute-force solution to a problem that had arisen just at the moment when he'd have preferred to enjoy something else. Just what that "something else" was, she knew not, nor cared.

She was awake again, and that was enough.

The royal palace and royal court were her home; she knew both buildings better than anyone else. Every last damp and long-forgotten cellar corner, every nook with an outside window—ah, it was just after nightfall—and every secret passage. So it was ease itself to flit unnoticed, a tall and silent shadow among so many pillars, to the passage that led to a certain closet.

She approached cautiously. The guard who ought to be standing sentinel had power enough to destroy her with ease.

The door that led into the passage stood ajar, and no one stood guard at it . . . or anywhere within sight.

She used her sword to thrust the door open and tiptoed into the passage.

Where the silence held.

Everything was deserted.

Peering around a corner, she felt her eyebrows rise.

She was more than a little surprised to find the closet door open and the portal completely unguarded—after all, it was a way in and out of the heart of Cormyr's power, and restoring it to safe reliability after the Spellplague had cost at least seven war wizards' lives—but Targrael wasted no time in speculation or tarrying to wait for trouble. She strode fearlessly into the portal's glow.

The far end of the portal—a cold, humid, and dark upper room of the king's tower in Marsember that she remembered from long, long ago—was also deserted.

Well, now. The surprise deepens steadily, she thought.

There was the uncomfortable stool provided for the guard, and yonder the lidded chamberpot, the three lanterns hung on their hooks, and . . .

The mirror. Ah, yes, and didn't the last true Highknight of the realm look lovely that night? Black armor and silver-edged black sword, bareheaded with her long, wild hair more white than gray. Framing a fine-boned face that had dead white skin to match, though there was a patch of mold growing on her cheek ...

Targrael shrugged, giving her reflection a smile. Yes, mold or not, it was as cruel a face as ever.

She preened for a moment longer, her hand on her hip, to see if Manshoon's anger would flare.

Yet he seemed not to notice, his attention even fainter. Whatever else he was seeing to was far more important to him, it seemed.

Which just might afford her the chance she needed ...

Sword in hand, Targrael ducked through the open archway she knew young Gauntur would have taken, wondering if she could get to Ildool's Veil before Manshoon realized what she was up to.

"But he's one of our *wizards*," a soldier growled under his breath, somewhere up ahead. "He'd go up to the spell chambers where they keep the magic, wouldn't he? Not down to the docks like a sneak thief!"

"That's why young Gauntur's running back and forth like a chased chicken," another Dragon replied. "He left us here to make sure Mreldrake doesn't just fetch something and come right back to the portal, to get back to the palace."

"Huh! The *last* place I'd run to, with Glathra after me! Still, splitting up your forces is nigh as foolish, so perhaps they don't teach wizards of war basic sense ..."

"Oh, well said, soldier," Targrael murmured as her sword whipped across his throat. "I almost regret having to kill you. Yet—as you both know well—orders *are* orders."

As she shoved the reeling, dying warrior away and slashed at his fellow Dragon, she saw the frightened face of her newest foe for an instant, on the far side of the sparks that flew as his desperate parry met her blade.

"So who are you, loyal Dragon?" she greeted him regally. "Saldar or Thallowood?"

The soldier gaped at her. "You know—?"

"Far too much, I'm afraid," Targrael replied, driving his warsteel aside with her own and chopping his throat with the edge of her free hand.

The man sobbed for breath as he fell. She slammed down atop him, both knees to his belly, and chopped ruthlessly with her steel. His blade was easily sent flying from his numbed sword hand, and she brought her sword back in under his chin as she leaned forward, bringing them face-to-face. "Your *name?*"

"S-Saldar," he gasped.

She smiled like a playful lover, kissed the end of his nose, and purred, "And what was the name of your friend, whom I dallied with first?"

"Thallowood," he gulped.

Targrael slit his throat.

Heedless of how much of his blood drenched her, she sprang up and ran on. The king's tower—what luck!

Now, if young Gauntur had been kind enough to have headed higher in the fortress, to the loftier rooms where wizards of war kept their trinkets and luxurious sleeping quarters . . . not to mention a certain old Crown secret known as Ildool's Veil . . .

He had. Exulting, Targrael raced up the stairs after a young and panting Purple Dragon who was trying to catch up to at least two more. Gauntur would be with the foremost pair, to be sure, unless he was even more of a reckless young fool than she suspected. Even Highknights knew better than to challenge renegade wizards of war alone, when loyal and ready sword-swingers were at hand.

Just two floors higher was the Veil, icy cold and endlessly whispering. A curtain black as night and everpresent, it was a field of magical force created long ago by Thayan mages hired by the villainous Lord Ildool, and deemed too useful to destroy.

Useful because those who ventured into its chill darkness and tarried there long enough were freed of all scrying, tracing, and prying-from-afar magics . . .

Ah! Of course! Much magic was kept in the chamber next to the Veil, and young Gauntur was no doubt eager to get in there and use most of it. Notably a scrying sphere that might help him find Mreldrake if his quarry had been truly stupid and not cloaked himself from it . . .

At the next landing Targrael caught up to Troon. Tapping the young Dragon on the shoulder, she easily caught his sword as he spun around to gape at her, and dragged him down until their lips met. Stifling any cry he might make, she drove her blade up under his chin.

He convulsed in her embrace and spat blood helplessly into her mouth. Targrael enjoyed its iron tang as she held him through brief and violent death spasms. When he sagged, she let him sprawl on the steps, and continued on.

The two remaining Dragons were veterans whose names she'd recognized; she would not overcome them so easily. Yet defeat them she must—the trick was to do it either without Gauntur knowing, or in a way that made them shields against the young fool's magic, until she could get within sword's reach of him . . .

"What's through this door?" a man snapped. "Perhaps he went in here!"

Watching Gods Above! One of the Dragons was heading to the Veil!

Targrael swarmed up the last flight of stairs so swiftly she generated her own wind; its chill made Narbrace turn to face her as she reached the head of the stair. It was simplicity itself to thrust the tip of her sword through the open front of his helm—huh, he was the first of those she was hunting wise enough to *wear* a helm—and into his face.

Narbrace gurgled out his lifeblood as she stalked forward, twisting her sword and thrusting upward at the same time to make sure he died. That noise was enough to make Gauntur, who was on the far side of the half-open wizards' armory door, call, "Narbrace? Is aught awry?"

Targrael smiled a brittle smile and moved to the wall beside the armory door, letting the dying Dragon slide off her gore-spattered sword.

Gauntur stuck his head out of the door at about the same time that the last Dragon—Hethel—emerged from the room with the Veil, saying, "There's something in there that you'd best see, saer mage—"

The Dragon broke off to gape as he saw Gauntur staggering forward, clutching his slashed throat in a vain attempt to keep blood from spraying all over the stair he was about to topple down.

His tall, sleek slayer left his side, and stalked toward Hethel with a wide and gleeful smile on her face.

Her dead face.

The Purple Dragon backed away, starting to swear. Then he frowned in thought and glanced over his shoulder, obviously deciding it would be good to stand and defend the doorway of the room he'd just stepped out of, if he ducked back through it and—

Targrael gave him no more time to think of tactics or curses.

Thrust, parried, ducked low for a lunge that became a parry and forced the Dragon's sword high, flung herself at his ankles in a roll, used the edge of her hand against the back of one knee as she pivoted around his ankle in a swift scuttling that left his sword biting only flagstones behind her, hacked up at his face and made him lose all balance in a wild parry, then tripped him over backward, over her.

He landed in a heavy, bouncing crash, and she pounced. Throat sliced open then up, up and sprinting for the Veil before he began his last choke.

I'm not betraying you, Master, I'm just carrying out my orders. Still busy killing the six you sent me after . . .

The Veil's cold was like a welcoming caress. She was always cold, but this whispering left her skin tingling—alive, as she'd not felt in many a year—and her mind suddenly empty of Manshoon and all else.

Targrael shuddered, as if in the highest throes of lovemaking.

Free at last.

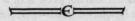

The magic crashed into Manshoon's mind—and his waiting wards. He felt a shrieking, clawing instant of swirling chaos, of magic clawing vainly at magic, that for a moment gave him the feeling of an icy tingling, then swirling, veil-like darkness, and loss . . .

Manshoon blinked reflexively, unharmed and with an unwavering smile on his face, in the wake of what was Lord Relgadrar Loroun's most powerful magic.

The old noble was retreating from him with reluctant defeat all over his face, letting fall the hand that bore hissing streamers of smoke where an ornate ring had been.

"*That* was the defense you were trusting in?" Manshoon asked incredulously. "Dear, dear."

And he struck. Plunging through a pitiful excuse for a ward and into Loroun's undefended mind, making it his with ruthless speed.

It was a dark and twisted mind, a place that felt almost welcoming. As with Crownrood—whom Loroun detested as a rival but measured as at least enough of a man to have the wits to *be* a rival—Manshoon was now master of a lord who plotted treason with eager gusto and fell intentions.

As his hold over Loroun deepened, he watched a slight smile to match his own slowly spread across the noble's face.

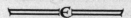

A sudden storm broke over Marsember with an ear-splitting crash, the sky splitting in bright lightning that stabbed past the highest windows of the king's tower. Then the rain came, hammering against the double-thick panes loudly enough to drown out anything less than a shout.

All of which suited Targrael just fine. The guards came down the stair from the roof in a drenched and cursing rush, charging right past the spattered blood without seeing it in the dark, lightning-shot wetness as their boots, cloaks, and scabbards all shed streams of rainwater.

Targrael stood still and silent behind the door that was only just ajar, listening to them pound past. The heavy trap door slammed down behind the last of them, two miserable men who spat water out of their mustaches to trade friendly insults and fervent desires to get "down below, to the fires" and warm themselves.

The death knight wished them every comfort, so long as they kept well away from these upper rooms until she was done searching them. The bodies of the six she'd been sent to slay were heaped against a back wall in the concealing darkness of the Veil, and unless any betraying ribbons of blood ran out from them to alert more diligent Dragons, or someone came along with a lantern and saw that some of the seas of water now adorning the tower flagstones were dark red, nothing looked amiss.

"I care not!" a man's gruff voice floated up to her as a door banged open several floors below. "A far worse storm than this one will hit Suzail if we don't keep vigilant, Swordcaptain! I want—"

Another door banged, taking whatever the Dragon officer wanted well beyond the reach of her ears.

Targrael smiled, willed the storm to rage on all night, and set about searching the rooms of the uppermost level. What she was seeking was old, dark, heavy, and decidedly unflattering. A one-piece warrior's helm of oiled metal that bore no device or ornamentation, except a whimsical little etching of a wizard's tall hat above the eyeslit.

A night helm. Or perhaps *the* Night Helm.

The tales said the legendary meddling mage Elminster had only given one to the Highknights of Cormyr. Perhaps he'd made the thing himself, though she'd never heard of him doing smithy work.

A "last defense" for an Obarskyr heir on the run, he'd termed it. The thing cloaked the mind of its wearer from all magic, so he—or she—couldn't be magically found or influenced by wizards of war or anyone else.

Vangerdahast had hated the very idea, of course, and had tried to confiscate the thing and outlaw its possession or acquisition—but Caladnei had held a different view, and he had instead advocated making many night helms, to be held in secret, guarded storage until need arose.

Targrael knew not if any such helms had been made, but palace lore insisted Elminster's gift had not been destroyed nor had any curse cast on it, but rather had been hidden away somewhere "well out of Suzail." In Marsember, most rumors suggested. At the top of the king's tower in the damp and often rebellious port, one whisper specified.

Targrael very much hoped that particular whisperer had been right, and the helm was here, so it could hide her from Manshoon henceforth. And of paramount importance, hide her from his scrying spells *before* he came looking for her.

She flung open a door and started searching. The gods smiled upon her thrice in this; first, the king's tower was old and massive, made of stonework that did not hide new construction well, and hadn't been built with hideaways in the first place. Secondly, Cormyrean armories, magical ones in particular, were strongholds where items were carefully crated, shielded from each other by stone half walls or even full walls with stout doors, and everything was tidy. Lastly, as a Highknight, she knew how most Cormyrean seneschals and garrison commanders liked to arrange things—and that they did *not* like to face nasty trap spells or alarms when snatching up arms in an emergency. Such spells would be found lower in the tower, commanding the stair up to the top levels, not on the upper levels themselves.

Unless, of course, even more idiocy than she'd thought had crept into the minds of the upper ranks of Cormyr's wizards, soldiers, and her fellow Highknights in the long years when she'd been resting in that tomb.

The Night Helm was nowhere to be found in the first chamber or the second, though she did acquire a useful trio of daggers in forearm and ankle sheaths—but it was the first thing to strike her eye in the third room.

She peered around swiftly for traps, alarms, or paralyzing-bite spider guardians, saw none—and picked up the helm.

Nothing happened.

With tense excitement, Targrael examined the helm carefully to make sure nothing was inside, like a blade set to snap across the wearer's throat, or any sharp inner points coated with suspicious substances. None.

She hadn't needed to breathe for over a century, but as she lifted the helm, she realized she was trying to hold her breath.

In sudden impatience, she hauled it down over her head, settled it in place, and peered out of its eyeslit at the room around her.

Nothing happened. Silence.

Utter silence, that is. The ever-so-faint, everpresent singing sound that had been in her head since Manshoon's first trampling invasion was gone.

Gone.

She was free.

Truly free.

Unleashed and with the leash torn away, let loose to follow her own desires. To serve Cormyr properly once more.

Free to hunt Manshoon down. And do the same to Elminster the meddler and the incumbent fools of the court, the current courtiers and wizards of war—from the doorjacks on up, most of them were incompetent traitors and fools who endangered Cormyr by their very presence.

Yes, she was free to be herself again. No archwizard's slave, but the guardian of Cormyr.

The guardian of Cormyr. Its sole true bannermaster. Her every thought and moment once more devoted to calculated deeds that would advance Cormyr to new greatness. Unmoved by sentiment and misplaced loyalties to traditions or the House of Obarskyr or anything else. She would be the clearheaded, dispassionate agent of the Forest Kingdom.

Unless, of course, she ran into that bitch Alusair again.

Chapter
SEVEN

Let It Begin

My life has been long; I've had my share of victories
And revenges, and tasted more than my share of disasters, too.
This is a good sword, and I'm ready to greet the gods,
So cry the charge, draw steel, and let it begin.

> attributed to Azoun II of Cormyr on the morn
> of the last battle that retook besieged Arabel
> fought in the Year of the Keening Gale

It had been, Elminster decided, a very long day.

This young lass whose body he was riding was more fit
and supple than he'd ever been, but right now she was footsore
and weary.

Her legs groaned at every step; she'd long since reached
the stumbling stage; and if her life suddenly depended on
sprinting somewhere farther off than, say, yon tree . . . well,
Amarune Whitewave's life would come to an end right
then.

He had a new appreciation for the views of upcountry
Cormyreans who said the King's Forest went on forever.

El knew better, having walked across it a time or two and
magically whisked himself over it or translocated from end to
end of it often. But, traversed this way, step after clambering
step in the deep brush flanking the Way of the Dragon trade
road, it certainly *seemed* endless.

The cozy, private Delcastle hunting lodge Arclath had
promised them was still half a day's trudge north, then a good
walk west from the road along a grassy track straight into the
deep heart of the forest. A walk that would happen on the
morrow, being as night had fallen while they were tarrying in

one of the roadside camping glades, debating whether or not they should push on to the next one.

"Clean jakes," Storm reported crisply, in a tone that made it clear she'd decided they would stop there for the night.

Arclath gave her a sour look that swung around to include El. "So you've decided, have you?"

"Look ye, young lord," Elminster replied, waving at the trees ahead. "Can *ye* see clearly, to avoid missteps? Or to always find room enough to swing thy blade in a good clear sweep, so as to slash a wolf off its feet and away from thy throat? Because I've been hacking at wolves in forests for far more than a thousand years longer than ye have—and I know *I* can't, when nightgloom gets this deep."

"Well, of course not now, in your dotage," Arclath muttered, but bit off his next words with a sigh, shrugged, and spread his hands. "You're right. We camp here."

Storm chuckled. "Well, we can go on arguing about the life El and I lead—and our fell attempts to ensnare Rune in it—just as well here, around a fire, as we can stumbling on blindly through the forest in the dark."

Arclath gave her a look.

All day long, as they had trudged along beside the road, they'd debated the ethics and merits of the life in service to Mystra that El and Storm had led for the better part of the last century. Arclath was obviously more interested in what they'd done than he cared to admit, but he held several reservations about his Amarune joining in that life, not to mention dragging him along with her.

"Couldn't we just have stayed in Suzail to fight Windstag and his ilk barehanded?" he asked. "Or taken on those blue-flame ghosts, with us naked and blindfolded? Wouldn't that have been *safer*?"

Storm smiled. "Safety is most often a matter of how one feels, rather than true security. Ask your Amarune about Talane, and see if she feels so eager to return to Suzail."

"I *can't* ask her," Arclath pointed out bitterly as they went to the glade's little roofed stand of ready firewood to take what they needed for a small fire. "Not with old Leatherjaws in residence."

From the far side of the clearing came Elminster's dry chuckle, higher pitched than it should have been thanks to Amarune's younger throat. "I may be ancient, lad, but there's nothing at all wrong with this splendid young body's hearing. Speaking of which, I should be returning it to her so the two of ye can kiss and cuddle and try to pretend ye're alone."

Arclath gave El a hard look, or tried to. He found it difficult to favor his beloved with a properly withering scornful glare, even when she was wearing the lopsided grin El liked to adorn her face with.

The noble gave up trying, sighed again, and went to his knees by the firepit to set down his wood for Storm to build the fire. Firetending was something Delcastles left to servants; he knew only enough about it to be certain you didn't just pile the wood in a heap and try to get it going.

"I believe I'll be more accepting of this," he told the silver-haired lady, "when I know who—or what—Mystra really is. To me, she's little more than a name from the past. The dead goddess who once ruled or corrupted all magic."

"You have much to learn," Storm replied softly.

Arclath nodded. "That, I freely grant." He held out some of the smaller split logs to her. "Yet I hinted as much earlier as we walked, and instead we talked more about the current politics of Cormyr."

Rune joined them, still speaking with Elminster's voice. "Well, such concerns matter more to ye and to the lass, right now. Talk of gods—and ethics—can take lifetimes."

She bent down and embraced Storm, breast to breast. Arclath watched, fascinated, as ashes suddenly flowed from Rune's mouth, ears, and nose, flowing like purposeful lines of ants down Storm's cheek and neck, to vanish into her bodice.

Then he looked away. It seemed somehow . . . obscene. "Done yet?"

"Well, El's out of me," Rune murmured in her own voice, reaching out for him, "if that's what you mean. Is there anything to eat?"

Storm smiled. "Trust me. Where foresters make these camping spots, Harpers hide food nearby. And despite what you may have heard, there *are* still Harpers in the world."

Arclath nodded skeptically. "Can you name me one, who's here in Cormyr?"

"Certainly." Storm gave him a wink. "Me."

Under her hands, the fire flared up then, with an eager crackle. She fed it carefully, calmly moving a flaming twig to three different spots before letting it fall into the rising flames, then she rose to her feet.

"I'll be right back. Or I can take some time returning, if you two would prefer."

"If—? Oh." To her surprise, Rune found herself blushing.

"*Oh*," Arclath added, catching on more slowly. He gave Rune a swift glance and added, "Uh, no. Not this night. Not ... out here, under the trees."

Storm nodded and walked away, moving almost soundlessly into the deepening darkness where the clearing ended.

Arclath watched her go but was astonished at how quickly he lost sight of her amid the trees. He thought he saw movement, but ... no, he could no longer be certain where she was.

Suddenly, his intent peering was interrupted by Amarune's face, bobbing up right in front of his, nose to nose.

"You *could* give me a kiss," she suggested in a whisper, offering her lips. "Lord Delcastle."

"But of course," he murmured airily. "Where *are* my manners?"

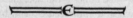

Manshoon leaned back in his chair, a stylish goblet of Lord Relgadrar Loroun's best wine in his hand, and regarded his host.

Loroun sat across the table staring past him, rendered dumb and immobile by Manshoon's grip on his mind.

That mind was a dark and fascinating place. Loroun was another Crownrood, only more so. The lord had dabbled in half a dozen intrigues against the Crown and knew of thrice that many. Most were fledgling, stillborn attempts at small, sneaking treasons, more angry talk in back rooms and minor deceptions against Crown inspectors than matters of swords-out or real harm. But a few had gone as far as specific plans for killings and seizures of keeps and bridges once the hated wizards of war were dealt with.

That did not surprise Manshoon at all. If there were no mages spying for the Dragon Throne and hurling spells at any sign of insurrection, this land would have been drenched in the blood of civil strife long ago—many times over.

What *was* a surprise was what had driven him to pour a second glass of wine and spend far more time than he'd intended sorting through Loroun's thoughts, searching for more. Loroun knew a surprising amount about the foremost Sembian-sponsored treason afoot in Suzail.

Most folk believed a mind held thoughts like some sort of gigantic ledger or written tome: ordered sentences that stayed in one spot and could easily be consulted time and again. Most folk were fools.

Even the simplest mind held thoughts as images—fading, overlapping, confusingly melded images that swam around in endless rearrangements, clinging to favorite linkages but apt to move, links and all, anywhere in the shifting murk.

It was enough to drive a man—even an accomplished arch-wizard gone vampire—mad.

Manshoon smirked. *More* mad, as Elminster might have said.

He was thankful that he no longer had to contend with that particular old menace, or have any regard at all for the ancient fool's views.

These Sembian intrigues, now . . .

Manshoon was no Cormyrean, and what he knew of Suzail's streets came from the relatively few citizens whose minds he'd plundered. Though some of those minds had known much, "Andranth Glarvreth" was not a name he'd ever heard before.

Apparently, Glarvreth was a successful, established merchant dealing in imports of ironmongery and glasspane. "Respectable" in the eyes of the city, a merchant who supplied shops, rather than a shopkeeper himself. Suzailan-born and grown quite wealthy, he was one of the growing number of successful citizens who wanted to be nobles but hadn't yet been admitted to the titled ranks. A rebuff that festered behind their well-fed smiles.

It certainly did behind Glarvreth's. Enough that the man had scorned Loroun in private twice, rather than accept his friendship and common cause in certain plots against the Crown. Glarvreth wanted to carve his own way to a title, not accept the help of any noble of Cormyr.

The importer's intended road to nobility, Loroun's spies had long ago learned, lay through Sembia. Glarvreth headed the strongest Sembian-backed scheme to bring down or enthrall the Dragon Throne, and had assembled a sizeable armory hidden right in the heart of Suzail.

Sipping wine in growing amusement, Manshoon settled down to learn all he could about Andranth Glarvreth from Lord Loroun's sour, resentful mind.

Loroun went right on staring. Dust was beginning to settle on his frozen, glaring eyeballs.

Manshoon discovered the goblet in his hand had somehow become empty and started to rise.

Then he sat back and compelled his newfound servant to fetch the decanter for him. It was more fun to make the stiffly staggering Loroun do the work.

Clumsy servant though he was.

Yes, *servant.* "Slave" was such an ugly word.

"Will it bother you much to leave Suzail behind?"

"I . . . know not, yet. I don't think so, but I don't *know* so," Arclath replied thoughtfully, staring into the hot orange coals of the fire that warmed their faces.

He and Rune were talking together after a meal of astonishingly tasty forest roots and leaves, flavored with a meaty paste that Arclath strongly suspected had been made from freshly scooped snails.

The cook was standing watch a few strides away, on the far side of a large tree, leaning against the trunk facing out into the night. If Arclath leaned and peered, he could just see the side of one of Storm's boots, but she hadn't moved a muscle, so far as he could tell, or made a sound, for . . .

Well, a long time.

He quelled a yawn. Just how late was it? Night had fallen a good long time ago, and rustlings arose in the brush here and there, well beyond the light of the fire. He hadn't seen eyes peering out of the darkness, yet, but—

"Good even, foresters. If you *are* foresters," Storm said suddenly, her voice calm, firm, and loud. "Will you share our fire?"

Her challenge floated out into the night. After what seemed a long time, some sudden cracklings and twig-snappings arose . . . and seven foresters with bows in their hands and daggers at their belts stepped out of the dark forest and approached the fire. They formed a wide arc that almost encircled the camping glade; the only gap in their line was toward the road.

The elder foresters had impressive beards and hard, weathered faces to match. They regarded Storm expressionlessly, and one who looked to be the oldest said, "We *are* foresters. The king's foresters on patrol. And who would you be?"

"Nobles of Cormyr who have been vastly entertained by your attempts to stealthily encircle us," Storm replied gently.

"Nobles, hey? You, lad, what might your title be?"

As he flung that question, the oldest forester strode forward, drawing his dagger. Behind him, others strung their bows.

Arclath stood up and put his hand to his sword. "I am Lord Arclath Delcastle, and this is Lady Delcastle. The lady you've just spoken with is the Marchioness Immerdusk."

"Not noble Houses *I've* heard of," another forester growled, as the ring of men in leather and homespun tightened around the fire.

The oldest forester came to a stop facing Arclath and held up his hand in a wave that might have meant "stop" or might have meant "halt, let us have peace."

"Well, then, Lord Delcastle," he asked, "is this all of you? Three afoot? I've never seen a noble out here without a horse and several servants. Are you running from something?" Two foresters fitted shafts to their bows.

Two more reached swiftly for arrows after Storm stepped away from her tree to face them, her long, silver hair winding about her shoulders like a nest of restless snakes.

The old forester eyed her for a moment, and then looked back at Arclath.

"Well, noble lord? You have my questions; have you any answers for me?"

Manshoon sat back, frowning. His exploration of Loroun's mind was done, and the noble's wits and tongue had been restored to him. He was sitting there in his sweat, glowering at Manshoon as much as he dared to and reaching for the wine.

Loroun knew a lot—but much of it was hints, gossip, and reports from men he paid to spy but trusted little. Suzail could be a seething snakepit of men just aching to erupt into widespread treason . . . or it could be a nobles' den of arrogant malcontents, a few of whom had dreams and a few more of whom had loud, unguarded tongues.

Which made it not much different from anywhere else that had nobles.

Westgate, Zhentil Keep, Sembia . . . he'd tasted them all and found them very much the same in this respect. True traitors seldom made much noise. Those too fearful to ever do anything, unless carried away in the heat and blood of someone else's tumult, did most of the blustering and taunting and making of grand doom promises. Loroun was at least shrewd enough to know he was dealing with shadows more than things that could be held and trusted, which put him above many of the young fools Manshoon had encountered in this city these last two nights, as nobles gathered to attend this Council.

"I have a question or two, Lord Manshoon," Loroun said, his voice polite, "and I believe that in a world that knows any shred of fairness, it is more than my turn for answers, if you have them."

Surprised, Manshoon unfolded one hand palm upward, in a silent signal to proceed.

"What's become of these blueflame ghosts? Are they a war-wizard weapon, soon to be sent out to hunt down nobles? Or, are they a sword wielded by a noble? Or, do they instead obey a Sembian or some other outlander foe of Cormyr? Or, are they the tools of someone who wants to be noble and is determined to butcher lords until so many titles and holdings are vacant that the Crown may well ennoble him seeking to fill them?"

"Good questions, all," Manshoon replied. "So good that I can answer none of them." He raised a swift forefinger and added soothingly, "Yet I *am* trying to find out."

Whereupon Loroun glared at him with narrowing eyes and demanded, "Or is it *you?*"

Manshoon shook his head. "If it were, Loroun, do you think I'd waste my time befriending you? Hmmm?"

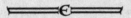

"We are . . . serving the Crown in a matter we cannot discuss," Arclath improvised, glancing at Storm to see if she approved. She gave him a solemn wink, strolled over to Amarune, and put her arm around the dancer's shoulders.

"El?" Rune whispered.

"Not yet," Storm murmured. "Only if need be."

The foresters had been cautiously drawing closer and peering closely at the three by the fire.

"No axes," one reported.

"Nor snares," said another.

"I give you my word," Storm told the oldest forester, "that we have no intention of hunting, woodcutting, or setting fires outside this firepit. We are traveling, no more and no less. We are *not* fugitives from justice."

The oldest forester nodded. "I believe you. Yet one matter remains that I find most curious of all: Lord Delcastle, why aren't you at the Council?"

Arclath opened his mouth slowly, not knowing what to say—and heard Storm reply smoothly, "The elder Lord Delcastle is attending Council, as head of House Delcastle. He instructed his son here to take the two of us"—her arm tightened around Amarune's shoulders—"well away from the roving eyes of, ah, certain nobles to avoid any unpleasantness arising. Due to past entanglements."

Several foresters nodded, and something that might have been the beginnings of a grin rose onto the oldest forester's face—until his head snapped around, just an instant after Storm turned hers.

Then everyone heard it: the faint, irregular thunder of hooves from the north. Many horses, ridden hard.

Conversation and confrontation forgotten, everyone hastened to the road.

They reached the near ditch beside the Way of the Dragon in time to see many coach lamps bobbing in the distance. This was unheard of in deep night, when coaches so often overturned or slid off roads. All the foresters readied bows, except the oldest, who flung out both arms to bar anyone from stepping up onto the road.

What came sweeping down on them was a contingent of two dozen riders or more, galloping south as fast as their snorting, half-frightened horses could take them.

Purple Dragons in full armor—though lacking the banners and spears of a formal ride—swept past, three abreast and filling the road, hard-eyed and intent.

Then the watchers in the ditch caught sight of wizards bouncing uncomfortably on saddles in the midst of the soldiers. Wizards of war, being escorted south at speed, almost certainly traveling from Arabel to Suzail.

They could see the rear of the hurrying force, or thought they could. There were no coaches or wagons; the lights they'd taken for coach lamps were torches on poles, guttering wildly in glass spark shields. This was truly out of character. Such contrivances were used only in slow, stately wedding and funeral processions. What was going *on*?

Arclath and Storm were frowning openly in concern, and the oldest forester had seen enough. He scrambled up the bank with astonishing speed for a man of his years, flung up his arms, and cried, "What news?"

Horses shied and reared, riders cursed and fought with reins to keep their seats and lessen the inevitable collisions, and one of the wizards promptly fell off.

Some of the rearguard Dragons slowed their mounts and made for the forester, drawing their swords—as all the rest thundered on past, heading south and leaving only road dust and the fading din of their passage behind.

"Who are you?" a Dragon officer demanded, drawing a blade that shone with light, and pointing it so its glowing beam played across the foresters and Storm, Arclath, and Amarune. Seeing all the ready bows, he cursed under his breath and barked, "King's men?"

"Of course," the head forester replied gruffly, bending to help the groaning wizard to his feet. A Dragon had caught the riderless horse a little ways along the road and was calming the snorting, stamping gelding to bring it back.

"Got any fresh horses we can have?" the Dragon constal asked, not too hopefully.

The oldest forester shook his head. "No, I walk *my* patrols. As for yours—where to, in such haste?"

The wincing and bruised wizard under his hands growled grimly, "The Council down in Suzail has been disrupted; there's uproar in the city, and some are saying it even looks like war, and—"

Arclath turned to Storm, towing Amarune like a startled pet. "I *must* return there. Take Rune to Eveningstar; there's a barrelwright there who owes the Delcastles a lot of coin. Keep her safe until I retur—"

"*Oh*, no," Storm and Amarune both snapped back at him, in unintended unison. "We're coming with you!"

Chapter
EIGHT

Untidy Arrivals

Behold, my lord! More untidy arrivals!
Yet not much is broken, yet,
And this is fair entertainment.

> said by Marauntra the Maid in Act I, Scene IV of the
> play *The Night the Gods Cursed* by Rustarn Horhalloran
> first performed in the Year of the Black Blazon

In front of Burrath, his master stopped and peered up past the gate of watchful stone lion head, to the tiers of lit, many-paned windows rising into the night above.

"This is our destination?" he asked quietly.

The guide Glarvreth had sent to fetch his exalted guest merely nodded and rapped a complicated rhythm on a little panel in a recess set into the stone just beside the gate doors.

Lord Oldbridle stepped back, giving Burrath a swift "be ready" glance. Nothing in his master's face suggested that Olgarth Oldbridle was impressed in the slightest by the Suzailan mansion of Andranth Glarvreth, wealthy and successful ironmongery and glasspane merchant—but then, these days, the jaded and cynical head of House Oldbridle was very seldom impressed by anything.

Inside Burrath's quivering and defeated mind, Manshoon smiled, awaiting the entertainment soon to come. If anything in this part of the world was more haughtily ridiculous than a Cormyrean noble, it was a rising newcoin personage who hungrily sought to join the ranks of that nobility.

Like this man Glarvreth, who'd invited Oldbridle to dinner. Seeking his support, no doubt, which meant this meal should be an enjoyable feed rather than an agonized and ultimately fatal nightmare of poisoning.

The gates opened, servants bowed, and they passed within. Burrath held his peace, offering no challenges to the retainers who glared at him as he followed his master, striding along just behind Oldbridle's right shoulder. They offered no open insult, for if a noble had been limited to just one bodyguard, that guardian should be considered extremely capable, well equipped, and dangerous.

Manshoon waited until the polite greetings were done and Glarvreth had politely asked if, as he fondly hoped, this evening found Lord Oldbridle in the fairest of health.

That was when Burrath leaned forward to murmur in his master's ear, loudly enough for everyone nearby to hear, "My Lord Oldbridle, twice in the streets I caught sight of men I believe were following us. It is only right that Lord Glarvreth should know."

If his master was annoyed at his bodyguard's boldness or at Burrath's referring to their host as if the man had achieved the nobility he so hungrily craved, he did not show it. For his part, Glarvreth flushed with pleasure at the honorific and gave a silent hand signal to his retainers. Burrath did not appear to even glance at their movements, but Manshoon knew how many departed and that they were armed with daggers and bowguns no doubt treated with venom.

They slipped out into the streets to hunt no one at all. Manshoon had invented the followers he'd made Burrath speak of, but he was certain Glarvreth's zealous agents would find some. Slaughter was coming to the streets of Suzail, giving Emperor Manshoon something to crack down on.

Burrath knew only a little of what his master suspected— but Manshoon was well aware, from visiting certain minds in the palace, that Andranth Glarvreth headed a long-established covert Sembian presence in Suzail that had been patiently awaiting a good chance to seize power for years.

This Council seemed increasingly likely to provide a superb opportunity. Of course, Glarvreth's cabal would have to thwart some rival undercover factions seeking to accomplish the same thing—such as the one headed by Kormoroth of Westgate. And if open civil strife broke out, they would have to be very careful as to which Cormyrean nobles they backed and whom they'd slay, betray, or thwart.

Some nobles wanted a return to elder days in Cormyr, when a handful of wealthy and powerful oldcoin noble Houses ran the realm and kept a puppet Obarskyr on the throne, with a royal magician who served the foremost Houses as the royal leash, And any wizards of war the kingdom might suffer to exist would be mere hedge-wizards who patrolled with the lowliest Dragons and did the bidding of swordcaptains. Newer and more minor noble families could be swept into graves at the earliest pretext, shopkeepers and farmers firmly reminded of their proper places underfoot. And Sembia taught a sharp, swift lesson in a war that would loot their coffers and restore the Bleths, Cormaerils, and the rest to staggering wealth and whimsical lives of ordering matters in cities and realms far away. Lord Alsevir and Lord Huntcrown led that faction, but there were some hints that each man was preparing to oust the other, if ever he got power and opportunity enough.

Then there were two smaller groups of oldcoin nobles who wanted the Obarskyrs gone and a new royal House on the Dragon Throne.

The schemers led by Lord Crownrood, on the other hand, wanted "the old rot" of all the long-prominent families swept from the kingdom. The likes of the Illances, Crownsilvers, and Huntcrownsuch would be exiled or exterminated, so past excesses and treacheries would never be repeated as the realm flourished anew under the wise and benevolent rule of King Melder Crownrood, of course. Manshoon could barely suppress a snort just thinking of those arguments.

The schemers led by the Goldfeathers and the Emmarasks wanted a ruling council of six lords—unsurprisingly led by House Goldfeather and House Emmarask—to choose a king to do their bidding, after which all the large and wealthy noble families not on the Council, old and new, would be stripped of wealth and titles and turned out of the realm by order of that stern new king. Just how the six ruling lords intended to manage that, Manshoon hadn't yet heard ... and he doubted they'd prepared any proper plan for carrying out that grand scouring, or could, when the time came, accomplish anything set forth in any plan at all.

The younger and more minor Houses understandably wanted no part of oldcoin rule. Manshoon had heard of factions led by Lords Halvaeron and Torchmore but hadn't yet identified who really supported them or what plans and preparations—if any—they had made.

He *had* heard whispers galore among the nobility gathered in Suzail that someone was meddling in nobles' minds—must be, to make the timid act so boldly and stalwart oldcoats abandon their long-nursed feuds so swiftly and completely—but there was no agreement at all as to who was doing it, and how.

Well, the "how" was magic, of *course*, but cast by whom? Hired outlander mages, or wizards of war playing their own games or serving the Crown in some dark set-nobles-against-nobles scheme—the identity of the caster was something titled Cormyreans could not agree on. Not even to decide if the mage who'd so emboldened and advised the young fool Stormserpent was the same spellhurler who must be hiding the commander of the blueflame ghosts from all the house wizards—and palace mages, too—seeking the ghost-wielder.

Manshoon suppressed a smile. It was nice to have one's meddlings noticed and feared, even if no one knew who was behind them, yet. Ah, but the time for that would come ...

They were being led into a high-beamed, splendid feasting hall. One of its walls was covered in magnificent relief carvings of hunting scenes, the opposite wall pierced by an impressive row of toweringly, narrow, arched windows. Polished platters gleamed back the reflections of many candles hanging in sconces, which also mirrored flickering flames all along the row of windows.

Glarvreth turned with a smile. "Be welcome to my table, Lord Oldbridle! Let us—"

The rest of his words were lost in a series of nigh deafening, shrieking crashes, as several of the windows burst into the room, shattering into countless tumbling shards under the boots of heavily armed men swinging on stout ropes. The men landed hard, staggering as they whipped out swords and hand axes, then set to work hacking and hewing anyone who moved.

Glarvreth shouted and fled, his guest forgotten.

Guards streamed into the hall, but the invaders ignored them. They raced after Glarvreth as the merchant wrenched open a secret door in the hunting-scene wall and plunged through it.

Lord Oldbridle tried to follow—but got chopped to the floor by the foremost armed intruder.

Burrath drove his sword over the dying lord and right down the throat of Oldbridle's slayer. Then he sprang free and crashed through the door, shoulder first, before Glarvreth could shove it closed.

Flung backward by the door, the merchant promptly fled.

"Close it! *Close it!*" he shrieked over his shoulder as he disappeared down a dark and narrow passage that ran along behind the carved wall.

Burrath did so as fast as he could, hacking at an intruder trying to burst through, until the man fell back. The door slammed. Finding a bar and stout cradles to hold it, he barred the door for good measure.

Heavy blows promptly fell upon the closed door. He did not tarry to see how long it would hold.

"Who's your foe?" he shouted, running after Glarvreth.

"Kormoroth of Westgate!" a shout came back. "Didn't you recognize him? You just killed him!"

A heavy, metallic crash followed those words as some sort of portcullis slammed down across the passage in front of Burrath, separating him from the fleeing Glarvreth.

The bodyguard stopped, shrugged, and retreated down the passage past the barred door. Enthusiastically wielded axes started to bite through it, but it was stout and thick; he should have ample time to find another way out of Glarvreth's mansion.

In the other direction, the passage ended at a door that opened into a back pantry. Cooks and maids scurried and screamed; his arrival sent them dashing headlong into rooms beyond.

Manshoon took his borrowed body after them, confident they'd take a back way out—kitchen slops must go somewhere, and almost always through a handy rear exit—and he could follow them to somewhere far from murderous cabals from Westgate.

Not that this night had been wasted. Far from it. Andranth Glarvreth was a badly frightened man, and the struggle for Cormyr's future was now short one ambitious adventurer-merchant outlander. Ah, well, no doubt the butchery would manage to stumble along without him.

"Here," Amarune said suddenly, ducking into a gate. "This is private enough!" She dragged Storm into the gateway with her and flung her arms around the taller woman.

"Rune," Arclath hissed, still panting from having just jumped down from the saddle of a hurrying horse, wrestled the same winded and upset mount to a pawing, bucking halt, then plucked his white-knuckled lady down from that same saddle, "What're you *doing*? This is the royal *gardens!* They're guarded at night, and—"

"No harm done, lord, if your lasses come no farther in," the calm growl of a veteran Purple Dragon came out of the darkness on the far side of the gate. "Unless—ahem—ye're in need of some trifling assistance in, ah, *handling* them—"

"That *won't* be necessary," Arclath snapped, tugging a little tentatively at the two embracing women. He had hold, he discovered, of Storm's elbow. In response to his pulling she made an ardent moaning sound, setting Rune to helpless giggling.

He let his hand fall, knowing without looking that ashes would be streaming from the tall Harper to his beloved. His Amarune was surrendering to Elminster.

Again.

"Damn you, wizard," he said under his breath, catching himself just in time to avoid announcing to the guard—and all the Dragon's unseen fellows; they never stood guard alone—that a mage was involved in this.

"The palace is still open to those announcing their belated arrival for the Council, I suppose?" he asked more loudly.

"No, lord," came the firm reply, out of the night. "There's been . . . trouble. The Council's put off until morning, and palace and court both locked up tight now, under full guard. Were I you, I'd take yourselves well away from here until you hear the three horncalls on the morrow. If you or anyone tries to get in before then, we've orders to resist. Forcibly."

"Ah. I quite see. My thanks, loyal sword."

"Fair even to you, lord," came the friendly reply.

Arclath sighed and tugged at Storm's elbow again. This time she and Amarune came willingly back into the street with him.

"You have warm bathwater at Delcastle Manor, I presume?" the silver-haired Harper asked sweetly.

"We do," Arclath replied curtly, setting a brisk pace down the Promenade toward the brightly lit stretch where it swept around the imposing front of the royal court. "And while you splash, Lady Immerdusk, I have some words I'd like to exchange with a certain Elminster."

"Ye're saving them, lad?" Rune muttered in Elminster's voice. "Are ye now short of words, for some reason? I hadn't noticed any lack of them!"

By highsun the next day, the bodyguard of a murdered noble might be a hunted man in Suzail—or might be far beneath the notice of local lawkeepers, if the Council went the way he expected it to. Manshoon took no chances. Burrath scaled the taller shop next to the alchemist's and made the dangerous leap down onto Sraunter's roof, landing with a teeth-rattling, roof-shaking thud that roused the reelingly exhausted Sraunter from his bed. Saving Burrath the trouble of shaking him awake.

Manshoon had the alchemist give Burrath something to drink that would send him right down into slumber and keep him there for a good long time, then forced the long-suffering Sraunter to yield up his own bed to the man.

Sraunter was too falling-down weary to argue. He fell asleep in the next room after scrabbling up the blanket he wanted from a seldom-opened chest.

Manshoon left him that way and rode one of the five beholderkin out into the night. There were dozens of little touches that still needed seeing to, if the Council was to be the splendid success—or, to those who liked Cormyr's present ways and stability, the utter disaster—he intended it to be.

"These realms," he murmured, causing the beholderkin to emit a hissing hum, "belong to those who care to shape them to their will. Until I eliminate all others who dare such shapings, of course."

Arclath had firmly shut the door on the carefully expressionless faces of the servants who'd pumped the hot water up from the kitchen kettles, leaving them to think whatever thoughts they wanted to about the younger Lord Delcastle sharing the manor's best bathing chamber with a mask dancer and an unfamiliar silver-haired woman.

Storm plunged into the large, pink, marble bath his mother liked to soak in, even before Arclath got himself turned around to offer her a robe. He suddenly faced a swiftly disrobing Rune, who promptly perched on the edge of the bath and told him, in Elminster's growl, "Ye *know* this Council is going to fall into bloodshed and civil strife, don't ye? With Foril slain right then and there, if Tymora smiles not *and* we don't fight hard and well?"

"What?" Arclath snapped back at him. "Even with the mighty Elminster standing guard over it?"

Elminster shrugged. "How so?" He waved one of Rune's arms down at her bare and shapely self—even as Storm rose like a striding sea devil from the bath, gesturing to Rune that the waters were all hers—and told the young noble sourly, "*This* body won't even get me through the doors."

Arclath's mouth clamped down into a thin, hard line, and his stare became a murderous glare.

"Oh, no," he spat. "*No.* I am *not* letting you into my head. I'm sure you can use some spell or other to force your way in and burn away my hold over my own body in mere moments— but I'll fight you. I will *never* surrender my body, nor let House Delcastle's vote and voice be stolen by . . . by a wizard I can't trust, who could in truth be *anyone*, who . . . who . . ."

He ran out of words and clawed the air furiously, in an exasperated "away with you!" gesture.

Storm ducked under his flailing arm and plucked up a robe, leaving Rune to reply, as she in turn sank down in the warm, scented water, "I won't be forcing my way into thy mind, lad. 'Tis not necessary. Yet. I'm merely warning ye to expect the worst. I can see it ahead, and I'm nigh powerless to stand against it."

"So you're not the legendary, all-powerful Elminster?"

"I was never all-powerful. Not even close. I was at best a scurrying, none-too-organized, overworked castle errand-boy. Aye, that's the best way for ye to view what I did and was. I'm a lot less than that now. And, yes, there's precious little I can do to stave off disaster at the Council."

" 'Precious little'?" Arclath flung back at him bitterly. "So why do you always act as if you can take care of everything?"

El wagged a wise old finger in a way Amarune would never have done, and said mildly, "That master-of-all-things act accomplishes much, lad. All by itself. Try it; ye'll see."

"Gah!" Arclath burst out, words failing him again.

Storm tapped him on the shoulder. "After all that tramping through the forest, you need a bath," she said gently. "And while you're in there, sluice off a little of that seething anger and give us back the jaunty, debonair Fair Flower of House Delcastle that all Suzail is so used to seeing sporting airily about the streets."

Arclath glared at her, trying—and succeeding—to keep his eyes above her chin and not straying down to the rest of her, which she was casually using the panels of the open robe to rub dry.

"And with Cormyr about to plunge into blood-drenched disaster, what good will *that* do?" he snapped.

"Entertain us all far more than your seething anger," she replied gently.

"Gah!" Elminster supplied helpfully, before Arclath could find the breath he needed to make that very same comment again.

Arclath stared at him—or rather, at Amarune's bare, wet body, as she stepped out of the bath to take the robe Storm was offering her—then turned and hurled himself into the bath in a great angry dive that sent its waters crashing against walls and ceilings.

Somehow, as bubbles roared past his ears and the half-dissolved scented soaps in the water made his eyes start to sting, he felt a little better.

He might be heading into the worst noble-slaughtering bloodbath Cormyr had ever seen, but at least he'd be clean and smell sweet.

Chapter
NINE

In Stately Conclave Met

And so our just and beneficent ruler smiles
On proudest lords in stately conclave met
Seeing no little deceit, no shortage of wiles
Though they work no open regicide. Yet.

> Sarauntra Tynorora, "The She-Bard"
> from the ballad *The Dance of Kings*
> first performed in the Year of the Queen's Honor

Horns blew a fanfare that the cool morning air carried far across Suzail, summoning the invited heads of noble Houses to the Council of Dragons.

Arclath's rising had awakened Amarune, though he'd dressed and dashed from Delcastle Manor without a word to either of his guests.

Storm quietly opened Rune's door, the coverlet wrapped around herself in a clumsy way, and wordlessly had handed her a bundle of clothes. They all proved to be magnificent gowns. Borrowed from Lady Delcastle's wardrobes, Rune guessed, but decided not to ask. Storm had vanished again, anyhail.

Amarune found something dark, long, and simple that more or less fit her. It was too ample for her taste but could be drawn tightly around her waist with a sash, and Storm had provided several beautiful ones. She put on her own clout and boots under it, looked at herself in the guest chamber mirror, winced, then shrugged and flung open the door.

Storm was leaning against the passage wall outside, also in her own worn boots—full of Elminster's ashes, of course—but above them wore a splendid gown Rune was sure Lady Delcastle *would* miss.

"Come," Storm said softly. "We're off to storm the palace."

They hurried out of the Delcastle mansion, nodding to servants without slowing, and hastened through the grounds.

Coaches rumbled along the streets, and once through the gates they saw some nobles on foot, too, walking in their finery.

Hand in hand, Storm and Rune set off down the street to join them.

Another fanfare rang out across the city.

"That's the second," a wealthy merchant who hoped to be soon ennobled declared to one of the nobles converging on the palace, Beckoning banners flapped above the gates. "The third won't sound until we're all seated, to let the city know the talking's about to begin. Brought your belt flask, I hope, for the boring bits?"

The noble ignored him, striding on without pause or reply.

Citizens came out onto their balconies and peered from their windows and the doors of shops to watch the nobles stroll past.

There was that young fop, Lord Arclath Delcastle, and yonder quiet old Lord Adarl Summerstar ("A proper gentlesir, him!"), and beyond them, in an open carriage and wearing a magnificent hat, the Lady Deleira Truesilver ("Didn't she take to her bed, not long ago? Looks well enough, now!")

Those on the Promenade, or whose vantage points were close enough, could see watchful lines of war wizards at the gates.

None of the watchers were close enough to hear one of the older guards flanking the inner doors tell his junior partner—inexperienced, but a swifter runner than the veteran—that the visible war wizards were the least powerful, there largely for show.

"The truly powerful are already inside, peering into minds and watching and listening like owls a-hunting."

"I'll be glad when this day's done," was the muttered reply.

"You and me both, lad," the older guard replied. "The third fanfare's when all the fun begins—the actual start of the Council."

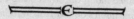

The strong, cloyingly sweet tropical blossoms that scented the wax Lord Naeryk Andolphyn had used to freshly shape the two chin-spikes of his forked beard was making Lord Danthalus Blacksilver feel faintly ill, but Blacksilver forebore from saying so. If his sharp-featured newfound friend hadn't offered him a ride to the palace gates, he'd have been reduced to walking.

Their coach rumbled over some loose cobbles, then clottered past many a walking lord as the two spent the ride trading opinions of newly discovered wines and superior cheeses from far lands. Idle chatter was something Lord Danthalus Blacksilver considered himself rather good at.

"Oh, *gods*," his host exclaimed, breaking off in mid-rhapsody over Sembian soft sharpnip and looking behind them. "Wouldn't you know it? I thought only the ladies indulged in that sort of nonsense!"

"What?" Blacksilver asked and then saw. "Oh. Oh, I see. I quite see."

Behind them on the Promenade were large, ornate coaches drawn by matching teams of splendid horses, each conveyance bearing a lone lord, seemed to need a score of horses to pull him along. In the far distance, even grander wagons appeared—one looked like a ship hauled up out of the harbor onto a massive cart, and another appeared to have *balconies*—all moving toward the palace.

In this, as in most other matters, the nobles of Cormyr were seeking to outdo each other.

Blacksilver peered at a coach team with a peculiar slinking gait. "Are those . . . *lions?*"

"Yes," Andolphyn said shortly. "Must be using a hired wizard to keep 'em under the whip. Hope no one casts any mischief."

Something that seemed to be drawn by dragons came into view, and Andolphyn shook his head in fresh disbelief. "Oxen cloaked by illusions, must be. Those *can't* be real."

Blacksilver chuckled uneasily as their coach slowed, nearing the cluster in front of the gates. "If I know anything about war wizards, their fury soon will be, though."

In this, he was correct. Two coaches rounded the curve of the Promenade in the far distance, escorted by shining-armored outriders whose mounts, long banner lances, and splendid armor outshone those of the best Purple Dragon honor guards. A rather *large* number of outriders.

"Someone's brought along his own army," a gruff old lord in a nearby open carriage commented—as wizards of war stormed past, hastening on foot from the palace toward the still-distant outriders. Onlookers in windows and shop doorways were murmuring, having caught sight of the unauthorized military might on display.

Andolphyn and Blacksilver saw the hurrying Crown mages stop just long enough to work spells then hasten sternly on. A tense breath or two later the outriders were all trotting briskly past, on down the line of coaches and right past the palace. Trotting at the exact same pace, despite some spur-kicking and hauling on reins by their surprised-looking riders.

One outrider even fell off, and his empty-saddled mount continued right on. He ran after it, caught hold of the reins, and pulled hard; it dragged him, slowing not in the least.

On the riders went, up the Promenade to the Eastgate and out through it, some of them yelling for help or cursing.

Andolphyn laughed. "Willing to wager Dragons are waiting outside the gates with a camp set up to gather those dolts in?"

Blacksilver shook his head. "I'll not take that wager. I'm sure they are."

He looked again at the lions. "I hope they've enough war wizards to quell battles, or . . ."

"Yes," Andolphyn agreed. "'Or,' indeed."

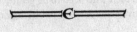

The name of Lord Arclath Delcastle held no weight at the gates; the Dragons there looked her up and down and shook their heads.

Amarune looked past them, hoping—in vain—to see Arclath.

"I'm expected!" she said almost pleadingly. "Lord Delcastle will be escorting me on from here!"

The guards merely laughed, shook their heads, and said firmly, "Not today, lass."

Whereupon Storm Silverhand took her hand and led her around the Dragons toward the watchful line of war wizards, telling the guards smoothly, "The lady *is* expected, saers."

As they stared at her in surprise, she added, "Please come with me, Lady Amarune. Lord Delcastle is being kept busy by some of his more, ah, *demanding* fellow lords, and sent me to bring you to him."

She swept a startled Amarune into the palace, mouthing the words "Ganrahast tells me the falcon is dark" to the nearest war wizard.

Startled at being given the passphrase by someone he didn't recognize, he blinked and yielded way, murmuring, "Who *are* you?"

Storm gave him a smile so warm he blushed, and with little stars of promise shining in her eyes, replied, "Someone in disguise."

"No doubt," came a cold and familiar voice from just inside the palace door. "Wherefore you can turn right around, both of you, and depart this place. Go far. We're much too busy today to entertain mask dancers and thieves."

"Why, Glathra, dear," Storm replied mockingly, "doesn't Foril need you at his side right now, far more than we do?"

"Speak the king's name with more respect, if you dare utter it at all!" Glathra spat, waving at the guards beside her to move Storm and Rune away. "Get them gone," she ordered. "Now."

Faces hardening, the Dragons advanced. "You heard her," the foremost snapped. "Go—or be taken!"

"If they resist, there's no need to be gentle," Glathra added, turning away to give some arriving nobles a glare.

Storm took Amarune's hand again and strode off down the street too quickly for the guards to bother to follow far.

"Now what?" Rune murmured. "Are we giving up?"

"Of course not. There are scores of ways into the palace," Storm whispered back. "Right here, for instance."

She ducked into an exclusive-looking shop, gave the proprietress a wave that incorporated some sort of subtle signal, then ducked through a side door in the shop showroom and down a dark and narrow flight of stairs . . . only to come to a halt in front of a spearpoint that had a hard-faced Purple Dragon behind it. Beyond him was a lantern, and beyond that more guards and a war wizard.

"The palace," the half-seen mage intoned flatly, "is closed. Return tomorrow."

Without a word Storm went back up the stair and out into the street, with Rune hurrying to catch up.

"They'll have every way guarded," the dancer sighed.

And it soon seemed that they had. The stable gates were closed and manned by a row of alert Dragons with spears. The next two secret shop-tunnels Storm tried were also guarded. And the door of the high house behind the stables was answered not by the usual beautiful chatelaine, but by a sour-looking wizard of war who said firmly, "No bedwarmer-lasses are wanted in the palace this day or night, thank you," and closed the door in their faces.

"The royal gardens are full of guards, too," Rune commented, looking past Storm's shoulder. "Was that the last way in?"

"No," Storm replied, "but I was hoping to avoid the slow and unpleasant ones. Or we may reach the Council chamber too late to be of any use." Putting a finger to her lips for silence, she strolled along the ivy-cloaked wall of the high house they'd just been shut out of, turned the corner to continue along the side wall, and let herself through a narrow swinging gate into the house garden.

She was just reaching for a particular section of the ivy-drenched wall ahead when the hidden door she was seeking in it opened. The same wizard glared out at her, wand in hand, and said, "You're far more persistent than a mere coinlass would be. I think we'll just—"

The pot that struck the back of his head then made a solid *thlangg* sound, and the mage's eyes rolled up in his head before he collapsed in a heavy, untidy heap on the doorsill.

A bewhiskered old face grinned out at Storm and Rune over the hairy hand that held the pot.

"Well met, lasses! Storm, ye got me into the palace, an' the food an' drink I've been scrounging since have been splendid, so 'tis my turn to do ye a favor! Let me drag this lard-sack out of the way, then come in and be welcome!"

"Mirt!" Storm greeted him happily, "I could kiss you!"

He took her up on her offer, promptly and enthusiastically, and she responded so warmly that Amarune, squeezing past them, murmured in her ear, "You *sure* you haven't spent time mask dancing?"

Storm chuckled and broke free of Mirt's lips.

"Later, old lecher," she told him fondly. "We're in some haste right now. We've got a kingdom to save."

"What, another one? Which one is it this time?"

Hiding watchfully behind the darting eyes of the young and excited Lord Jassur Dragonwood, Manshoon listened hard to comments from all around as noble lords jostled and glared, laughed and waved . . . and shuffled through one of the doorways into the Hall of Justice. From what he was hearing, no goading would be necessary; these lords were spoiling for a chance to rebuke the king.

He'd prejudged matters rightly, which is why he was well away from the minds of Crownrood and Loroun and had left all memories of him heavily cloaked from them. Freed from his influence, they could better be themselves—and as they were as expendable as every other titled lord and lady of the Forest Kingdom, any recklessnesses they indulged in were just fine with him.

So long as *someone* dragged out a sword and disrupted this Council, or Foril was forced to turn tyrant to keep order, causing most of the nobles to end up seething at him, the future Emperor of Cormyr and Beyond would be well content.

Now, had the palace dolts been foolish enough to try to dictate seating? No, it seemed not, aside from a small royal area.

Ah, well, *that* sort of blunder would have made things *too* easy.

In the crowd of nobles outside another door into the Hall of Justice, Arclath glanced back down the long, crimson-carpeted palace passage he'd just traversed, wondering if he'd ever see its splendors so unbesmirched, and its guards standing quite so peacefully again. To do so, he had to peer past the shoulder of Lord Braelbane—year in and year out, still a tiresome old windhorn—and was startled to see a superbly gowned Amarune Whitewave halfway down that passage, walking toward him.

Dodging past Braelbane without a word, he strode to meet her. "You got in? *How?*"

A nearby guard turned his head sharply to give Amarune a hard look, and she laughed, replying, "Why, Arclath, what better chance to see the palace and try to decide if I'd like it here, without a lot of questions being asked by bored guards and courtiers and war wizards and highnoses . . . ah, *other* highnoses?"

"Nobles," he corrected her.

"Nobles," she echoed.

Arclath drew her close, giving the guard a "none of your affair" frown, and murmured, "But . . . but how'd you get in, Rune? Past the guards and all?"

"Mirt let us in," Amarune replied. "Storm and me, that is—"

She turned to indicate Storm and found she was gesturing at empty air. Storm Silverhand was nowhere to be seen.

Above and around them, thunderously, the third fanfare sounded.

The anteroom off the crimson-carpeted passage was small, dusty, luxuriously furnished, and occupied only by a silver-haired woman talking to herself.

Or rather, arguing with a swirling cloud of ashes.

I must get into that Council. So either we conquer some poor, unfortunate, high-ranking courtier or a much-less-poor noble, or I go back into your boots and you march right in there. At least get me to the open doorway, so I can drift away to find a suitable victim, while you distract the guards.

Storm sighed. "No, El. It won't work. Not with all the wizards, Highknights, and Dragons they've gathered around that room."

Show them your bitebolds, Stormy One. That usually works.

Storm shook her head. "I don't mind in the slightest trying that, but I just don't think it'll work. Not this day. There are handfuls of war wizards at every door, all with wands in their hands, orders to use them without hesitation, and worry and excitement all over their faces. They'll blast you."

I'm already dead or bodiless; what can they do to me?

"That's just it," Storm hissed. "We *don't know!* They could destroy you! And it'll all end right here—Mystra's dreams, your promises, and all—over a bunch of nobles fighting over the Dragon Throne, something that's been going on ever since there first *was* a Dragon Throne. El, use your *head!*"

Haven't got one any more, came the inevitable reply.

"Then use mine, and see sense!"

Nay, nay, lass, I've got ye to do that for me. When I behave like a madwits, that's when things go best, remember?

"My memory, Old Mage, is rather less selective than yours!"

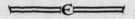

Amarune and Arclath turned together to the nearest doors that opened into the Hall of Justice, but at its doors many stern war wizards and Purple Dragons denied Amarune passage.

"Now, listen here!" Arclath began sternly. "I'm Lord Delcastle, and I—"

"No bodyguards or companions of any sort," the oldest wizard told him sternly. "We'll *not* bend this clear royal decree, so if you want to avoid unpleasantness, lord, you'll be best advised to—"

"Do not presume to give me advice, man," Arclath began but broke off as Amarune dug steel-like fingers into his thigh.

"Lord Delcastle, you have a duty to your family and to the realm," she hissed in his ear. "Get to your seat. You can tell me how it all unfolded afterward!"

And before he could reply she turned away, leaving him staring into the wizard's face and watching the man do a masterful demonstration of smirking at a noble lord without *quite* smirking.

Chin high, Arclath strode past and into the Hall of Justice.

Storm was gone, and of course Elminster with her. They were up to something, and Amarune's own part in it—for now—was done.

So, in small and modest ways, mask dancers can help save kingdoms after all.

Marching back down the crimson-carpeted hall, Amarune Whitewave did not see the oldest wizard of war direct three others to follow her.

At the third fanfare of warhorns, servants were dismissed from the chamber, and most of the war wizards and Dragons moved to stand guard outside its doors. As Arclath hastened up to the nearest vacant seat in the great oval tiers of nobles, the only non-nobility he could still see in the room were a pair of armored bodyguards and two scribes around the king. Probably everyone present knew or guessed they were really Highknights and war wizards.

The older scribe rose, his abrupt movement lessening the din of chatter, and struck a little bell. Silence fell. The Council of Dragons had begun.

King Foril rose to address the nobles, looking more calm than impassioned. Was there a hint of sadness about him?

Arclath devoted himself to listening hard and gazing all over the chamber, watching the expressions riding the faces of his fellow nobles. Most, like Harkuldragon yonder, held open contempt.

Foril wanted all the peers to swear binding "blood oaths" before the attending wizards. Meaning those mages would formally take vials of their blood, upon which to work magics if the sworn nobles were disloyal in the future. These would further be oaths of loyalty to Crown Prince Irvel—who sat impassively to the left of the king: vows to serve him and keep his person safe to ascend the Dragon Throne, and then rule as rightful king of Cormyr.

In return, King Foril expressed his willingness to restore "some" rights and privileges trammeled by the Writ—if the assembled nobles could convince him that doing so wouldn't harm the lives of Cormyreans not born with titles.

"I have heard your anger, directly and by report of what you have said aloud but not to my face. Remember that I must rule justly over *all* Cormyreans, high and low. I am prepared to dispense with evasions, long speeches, and insults, and deal plainly, here and now. So, what rights and privileges are you, good lords of the realm all, most concerned with?"

The king spread his hands in query and resumed his seat. Which, Arclath noticed, was no throne but identical to all other chairs in the chamber.

After a short, uncertain silence, it began. Old Kreskur Mountwyrm was bold enough to rise first. Noble after noble followed suit, each rising to speak of what he wanted restored.

Which, when those who liked to flap their tongues—Arclath not among them—were done, was everything.

Few of them were unreasonable or wanted all that much, but put together, all their demands would not just gut the Writ, it would grant them more power than ever before, leaving the king of Cormyr little more than a figurehead.

In other words, just about what Arclath had expected.

Now the *real* fun would begin.

And if everyone in this room was more fortunate than they probably deserved to be, they might—just *might*—still have a kingdom come next morning.

CHAPTER
TEN

I Foresaw All This

Believe me, lords, when I tell thee it gives me no smug comfort
When I remind every last one of ye that I foresaw all this.
So if I may ask one bitter question: have ye learned to listen to me yet?

said by Baeron Tanthor, Lord of Waterdeep
to the nobles of Waterdeep at the Restoration of the
Lords in the Year of the Wagon

A slight sound behind her—the scuff of a swift striding boot on carpet—made Amarune glance back.

Far down the passage were three men in robes. War wizards. They were heading after her, their forbidding eyes locked on her.

They were coming for her.

Rune quickened her pace and looked back again. The mages, wearing tight smiles, were gaining on her.

Sighing in mingled fear and anger, she came to a right-angled bend, strode around that corner—and discovered she was trapped.

The passage ahead was long, straight, and ended in closed double doors that were visibly locked and barred. There were other, lesser doors along the passage but all were closed and probably locked, too. She tried the nearest one.

Yes. Locked.

Rune set off down the passage, moving very briskly as the three wizards turned the corner behind her.

A sudden, unseen force shoved and clawed at her knees and ankles, and she stumbled and fell. *Magic.*

Scrambling up again, she found the Crown mages almost upon her.

"Surrender, woman," one commanded, "in the name of the king! You're suspected of treason against the Crown, and—"

"What do you want with me?" she snapped.

In her fine garb, she was weaponless and stood still, panting from her fall and from rising fear as they surrounded her.

"Your obedience," another mage replied grimly, "which every loyal citizen owes the Crown, I remind you! If you're innocent, you've nothing to fear. A few swift spells will tell us what's in your mind, and—"

"And I'll go *mad!*" Amarune snarled. "A barking, drooling madwoman I'll be, and—"

"Ah," the third war wizard said soothingly, "but you'll be a *loyal* one, and—"

A door behind them opened, and a storm of ashes swirled out of it, spinning up to the height of their heads.

Amarune ducked down hastily as the wizards shouted in alarm and started casting spells. Through watering eyes she saw them staggering around as someone else came through that door.

Could she flee?

No, this new arrival seemed to know just where she was, and was striding toward her, reaching out . . .

It was Storm!

A spell worked by a war wizard took effect, lashing Storm with lightning. She staggered but caught Amarune by the arm and started towing her toward the still-open door.

Another spell struck, and as Storm moaned in pain, Rune felt a flare of searing heat in her shoulder and down her back. She ducked low and flung herself into the room beyond the door, leaving Storm reeling behind her.

Ashes were still whirling around the cursing mages' heads. Looking back through swimming eyes, Rune saw Storm, her gown aflame, collapse into the arms of the nearest wizard.

He grappled with her as she snatched a wand from his belt and used it on his two fellows.

They toppled, and she twisted, served him the same fate. The roiling ash seemed to thrust her away and hurry her to

Amarune, who reached out and hauled a gasping Storm into the room.

"Help me with the door bar," she hissed at Rune, smoke rising from her smoldering gown. "Hurry!"

As they barred the door together, they could hear distant shouting from the Hall of Justice. The shouts rose into full-throated roaring.

Arclath had been wrong; his fellow nobles were *not* done. Emboldened now, they were falling over each other to stand and shout for more. Lord Landrar Dathcloake had gone so far as to demand that a "Council of Regents—heads of noble Houses, all—should have clear governance over the war wizards, the armies of Cormyr, *and* all matters of royal succession, including Irvel's. So the Council will choose, whenever a ruling Obarskyr dies or becomes unfit to rule, who—Obarskyr or non-Obarskyr—will next ascend the Dragon Throne!"

There were roars of approval, and many shouts of disbelief and disapproval, too, as Dathcloake sat down with an air of triumph.

The king was on his feet. "Now that," he said sternly, "I *cannot* agree to. The only reason to have a royal line at all is to give the realm some measure of stability. If a Council can choose *anyone* to rule, that is all lost, and Cormyr will become an endless battleground of factions vying to put their people on Council and to destroy those councillors whose views they decry."

Many nobles rose to shout responses to that, but one angrily overrode them all: Obraerl Foulweather.

"An easy doom to proclaim," Foulweather declaimed. "We can *all* call down darkness and disaster in our imaginations, Your Majesty! Yet we do not see the Council as the strife-ridden, shallow thing you paint it. Elder nobles have at least as much sense—and regard for the realm—as most of your courtiers."

There arose a general roar of agreement.

"Ah," the king responded mildly. "Well, then, if so, it should be simplicity itself for everyone here to calmly and swiftly agree on just which nobles should sit on this Council, and which should not. So name your roster, lords, that all may judge your wisdom and prudence." He looked up at the tiers of seats in clear challenge and repeated, "Name it."

Uproar ensued, of course, with Arclath grinning in wry silence as it raged, until one leather-lunged noble—Lord Mulcaster Emmarask—prevailed with repeated shouts of "Hear me! Hear me!"

When the chamber quieted, Emmarask advanced a plan for an eleven-person Council, formed of members of specific oldcoin families such as Emmarask and Illance, but *not* including the Obarskyrs, Crownsilvers, or Truesilvers. Further, he claimed that this was the will of the last regent of the realm, the widely revered, heroic Princess Alusair, and was approved by her, her mother, the Dowager Queen Filfaeril, and the royal magician of the day, Caladnei!

This falsehood proved to be one blatant fabrication too much for one lurking witness in the room to stomach.

The glowing figure of Alusair Obarskyr appeared in midair above them all, pointing at Emmarask angrily and shouting, "You lie, Emmarask! Twist my words at your peril! As regent of the realm I advocated an advisory-*only* council of eleven citizens, to be named by the monarch or a surviving Obarskyr, and *not* to have members drawn from specific, set families, noble or otherwise. *That* was what my mother and Caladnei supported. But all the senior courtiers *and* nobles of the day hated it and said so, your father being one of those who openly threatened that the founding of such a Council would be immediate cause for rebellion; so, it came to nothing! Cleave to the truth, noble lords, or Cormyr is surely doomed!"

Lord Mulcaster Emmarask sneered at the ghostly princess. "What war wizard trickery are you?" he asked. Without waiting for a reply, he looked around the tiers of seats and said loudly, "The falcons are certainly flying this season."

About a dozen older nobles seated all over the room rose as one. Arclath, as most others there, peered around, trying to mark all of them; the two nearest were Lathlance Goldfeather and Corladror Silversword.

Emmarask pointed at Alusair. "Begone, false and lying apparition! You're not the Steel Princess of legend; you're some young chit of a war wizard, saying and doing what Ganrahast tells you to! Begone!"

That enraged Alusair, who plunged down through the air as nobles gasped and ducked away and rushed right *through* Mulcaster Emmarask. He clutched at his heart and fell to shivering, bent in pain and frozen into silence. Swirling, she swooped and did likewise to all the nobles standing in support of him, one after another.

Leaving them terrified and chilled, shaking—and furious.

Other nobles were struck to anger, too. The scribes laid aside their quills and rose to defend King Foril with their wands. Whereupon many nobles promptly and loudly accused them, as war wizards, of "meddling in the lawful debate" of the Council.

In a trice, ceremonial swords and daggers flashed out of scabbards and sheaths all over the room; the Highknights made ready to hustle the king out to safety. And nobles rushed from their seats to surround the king and prevent him escaping anywhere.

Arclath Delcastle sighed as he drew his sword. This was all so *predictable*.

War wizards and Purple Dragons traded worried frowns as the shouting they heard coming through the closed and guarded doors rose to a full-throated roar, like unto battle. Should they go in? Were they needed to prevent bloodshed? Regicide?

At that moment Storm Silverhand, in a scorched ruin of a gown, with Amarune right behind her, came marching up to them.

"You cannot pass, by order of the king," a Dragon said automatically, barring their way.

"The king," the silver-haired woman snarled, "has been poisoned. We've only just uncovered the plot! He'll very soon fall on his face, dead. Let me through this door! Do I *look* like I have any weapons?"

She spread her hands, showing what was left of her once-magnificent gown clinging to her shapely figure, to reveal that she wore nothing much beneath. Involuntarily, the wizards and guards blinked at her.

Then they stared at each other, worry and doubt on every face.

"What if they're Marsembian agents? Or Sembians? Or from *Westgate*?" one mage snapped, waving at the two women.

"Can't be," one of the youngest Dragons replied, pointing at Amarune. "Seen that one before, dancing at the Dragonriders'—an' if she's some sort of secret agent, I'll eat my cods!"

From inside the Council chamber came the ring of steel and shouts.

"Oh, *farruk!*" snarled the senior war wizard. He turned and flung open the doors.

"Sit *down!*" Lord Summerstar, Lord Delcastle, and other nobles bellowed, but many nobles clearly intended to menace the throats of the crown prince and the king, and were already crossing swords with the Highknights.

In moments, a pitched battle was raging around the two royals. A war wizard reeled, clutching his slit throat; a Highknight went down under a dozen stabbing nobles; and someone managed to stab Irvel—only to discover that his dagger plunged through a royal midriff as if the prince weren't really there; although, the hard punches Irvel was landing told him the struggling Obarskyr was present and very solid, to boot.

"Ironguard!" that murderous lord cried and clawed at the prince's gorget—which was popularly rumored to confer such protection—to tear it off.

A Highknight's desperate leap took the lord away from Irvel and down to the floor with a heavy crash. The landing proved fatal for the lord, as both the dagger and sword of a writhing, groaning noble he landed on burst through him.

Startled shouts and gasps rose all over the Hall of Justice as a woman in archaic fluted armor appeared out of thin air in the empty uppermost tier of seats. A pair of hooked and curved swords—blades like something out of Calimshan or far Raurin—gleamed in her hands.

As nobles stared, she vaulted two tiers down and ran both blades through Lord Barelder, who was wrestling with another noble from behind.

He arched, shrieked, and fell limp. Kicking him off her swords, she sprang down to the next tier of seats, ducked past a shouting dagger-wielding noble, and pounced on Lord Ambrival, hacking ruthlessly.

He managed to half-turn to face her amid that storm of sharp steel before she slashed out his throat. As he toppled, head flopping loosely amid a fountain of pumping blood, she spun away and leaped down another tier of seats.

The unknown swordswoman was seeking specific targets, moving like lightning as she hunted—lunging and slashing with eerie speed through nobles, wizards, and guards alike. But what awakened fear in the brawling Cormyreans wasn't her deadly swordplay. It was the aura of cold blue flames that wreathed her, igniting nothing but leaving those they touched wincing and moaning with chill.

"Blueflame ghost! A blueflame ghost—a new one! Right here!" Lord Mountwyrm shouted hoarsely.

"Get her!" a young lord bawled. "If we all strike at her, we can have her down before she slaughters every last one of us!"

As he shouted those words, the flaming figure reached a tall, aging lord—Foulweather—and hewed him bloodily to the floor.

Then blue flames flashed brightly—and were gone.

The ghost had disappeared as suddenly as she'd arrived.

Oaths filled the air. The nobles of Cormyr might be many things, but few of them were slow or stupid men. What they'd just seen . . . aye, it had been real enough; there was Foulweather lying butchered, and up there Ambrival was draped over the seats with his throat still spewing gore. It meant that someone in the room, a noble attending Council, had a blueflame item and knew how to use it.

Curses faltered in that grim realization—until a lord thrust his belt dagger into the face of a longtime rival, and the chamber erupted in wild battle again.

So much Arclath saw as he fought his way along the seats toward the Obarskyrs, to defend them—before someone he knew sprang out of nowhere, so close their noses bumped. A face grinned at him as he stared in dumbfounded astonishment.

Amarune Whitewave stopped smiling long enough to kiss him on the nose and vaulted past him onto the nearest seat.

Standing tall on it, she shouted in a rough old male voice that rang across the chamber thanks to magic, "I, Vangerdahast, order you all to stand away from the king and crown prince! *All of you!*"

In the wake of that thunderous shout, as everyone turned to stare, she smiled with sad, old eyes.

Her hands wove a spell, and as nobles began to shout derision, seeing only a young woman instead of a wizard, she unleashed her magic.

It was a spell Elminster had perfected centuries before. A horrible spell.

As it flooded the chamber, it tore bones out of noble bodies, killing this lord and that, but leaving others untouched, taking down only those who were charging at the royals. As the shrieking deaths mounted, dumbfounded Highknights, war wizards, and Obarskyrs stood back, untouched.

The clash of steel died as those who remained stared at the boneless, blood-drenched things, whose screams fell into dying burblings.

Amarune reeled and slumped, starting to gibber.

Shocked and frightened, Arclath reached out to catch her before she fell. Storm Silverhand already had hold of Rune's other arm and was whispering, "Oh, *El!*"

Doors burst open all around the chamber, and more war wizards and Dragons came storming in. Servants entered after them, and the uproar arose again as hasty misunderstandings reigned, spells were hurled, and servants dashed the wine they were ready to serve into noble faces. Meanwhile, the Obarskyrs were hustled out.

As Storm slumped into a seat as Rune abruptly stopped gibbering and instructed Arclath in her own voice, "Come!"

Looking at her, then down at Storm in bewilderment, Arclath found the wrist of his free hand captured in Amarune's firm grip. She guided it to Storm's waist.

"Carry her!" Rune snapped. "Hurry!"

Arclath blinked, nodded, hauled Storm up against his hip, and took one awkward step, waving his sword for balance.

A war wizard promptly loomed up in front of them. "Halt, in the name of the king! Surrend—"

Amarune's leaping kick hurled the man's wand high into the air, shattered the fingers that had held it, and burst through them to the mage's chin. He went over backward without a sound, out cold.

As Amarune landed like a cat, two gleaming-armored Dragons raced up to confront them, but gave way before Arclath's wildly swung sword and her desperate snarl, "Harm us and you are both traitors! We serve the king!"

When the Dragons' blades came up in reply, Arclath hacked them aside. Rune flung herself at the guards' boots in a roll that swept them off their feet with a wild clangor of blades and armor, leaving Arclath's path to the door clear.

He ran, dragging Storm, with Rune gasping, "I'm right behind you! *Hurry!*"

A few frantic moments later they raced out of the palace together, into a bright and sunny morning.

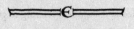

Palace Understeward Corleth Fentable had spent much time being angry these last few days, but he was *really* angry now. War wizards and countless Dragons rushed this way and that, and not one of them would stay still long enough to hear his orders. He wanted some to seek the Lord Arclath Delcastle, others to find a young lass who'd been admitted into the palace that day but shouldn't have been, and—

He was just about to let loose a great bellow of rage and hit someone with something when a familiar, faintly glowing shadow that looked very much like the portrait of Alusair Nacacia Obarskyr, the Steel Princess, that hung in the High Hall of Heroes—strode up to him and snapped, "I have orders for *you*, Fentable. Do none of those things you're gabbling about, and instead apply yourself to something *important*, for once. Namely, getting down to the Hall of Justice with mages enough to put the worst belligerents to sleep. Then disarm everyone, summon healers from the temples, and set yourself to calming all surviving nobles who attended Council, before some of them—possibly several cabals of them—decide making war on the fair family of Obarskyr will bring a brighter future to Cormyr!"

"Nobles always think that," Fentable snapped before he could stop to ask himself why he was bothering to talk to a ghost. "Why should I do anything about *your* silly fears?"

"Because some of those nobles can't wait to execute every last war wizard—or courtier—they can find," Alusair told him calmly, "and because *your* silly fears are about to include *this.*"

She stepped right into the same space his body was occupying—plunging the understeward into an unbearable cold that drove him into uncontrollable, gray-faced shivering, his teeth chattering wildly.

Just as everything started to go dark and he fell, she stepped back, looked down at his gasping body, and said briskly, "Now get up so I can do that again, Saer Fentable. You aren't sick enough of it yet. You aren't *pleading.*"

CHAPTER
ELEVEN

BLOOD ON THE WHIRLWIND

As rebels and traitors have learned before, once laws are dashed
Down and folk know fear, as you've flung aside graces and let
Masks slip, then all beasts are loosed and any man may go down;
there's blood on the whirlwind, and no safety to be found.
Be proud of your achievement, butchers. Be proud.

Grauth the Old Warrior, in Act III, Scene I of the play
Daunthan Laid Waste by Dunsul Blaklam "the Black
Bard" first performed in the Year of the Sceptered One

To Arclath's astonishment, Amarune steered him along
the outside of the palace to the stable gates, where they
found the row of guards gone and only one worried-looking
hostler and a lone young Purple Dragon left on duty.

"What's *happening?*" the Dragon asked them sharply.

"Fighting at Council," Arclath replied grimly, holding up
his sword to show the bright blood on it.

The young soldier stared at it and looked a little ill. His
spear trembled as it came up to menace Arclath. "I'll be needing
you to surrender that, lord, and—"

"*I'll* be needing *you* to stop trying such foolishness,
and get yourself to the Hall of Justice as fast as you can
run," Arclath snarled. "They tried to kill the *king!* And
the crown prince, too. Some of the old lords, that is, and
they're all still loose in the palace right now, most of them
waving swords. *Go!*"

The young Dragon gave him a frightened stare—and went.

Leaving the gates unguarded, their way into the royal
stables clear. The hostler had taken to his heels at his first sight
of Arclath's blade.

Rune strode into the stableyard. "We'll be needing a horse. Storm won't be able to walk for some time."

"You're Elminster, aren't you?" Arclath asked, struggling along in her wake with Storm draped over his back. "What have you done with Amarune?"

Rune turned, found the point of his blade at her throat, and smiled a little sadly at him.

"No, Arclath, it's me." She shook her head wearily. "Even if it was the old wizard, if you kill your Amarune—well, you kill your Amarune, don't you?"

With a growl, Arclath took his blade away.

Together they went into the warm, dimly lit stables. Horses occupied every stall, but Arclath and Rune found no guards and surprisingly few hostlers—and the handfuls they did see were whispering excitedly in various corners.

None paid them any heed as Arclath shifted Storm's limp body onto his shoulder and let Amarune guide him deeper amid the stalls.

When she started to stride too swiftly, he flung out a hand and caught hold of her wrist. "I'm *not* leaving your side. Come what may to House Delcastle or the Dragon Throne, whether that was Vangerdahast or Elminster or the ghost of the fourth Azoun himself speaking through you in that chamber, when you stood and shouted, I—I—all gods damn it, Amarune, I love you!"

Eyes shining, Rune spun, flung her arms around him, kissed him as if she wanted to take his entire body into her mouth, and gasped, "And I love you, so *hurry!*"

They hurried.

"So," Arclath puffed as they hastened past stall after stall, "are—are you really *you* right now, Rune? How can I tell?"

His lady gave him a wink. "Trust, Lord Delcastle. *Trust.* Believe me when I assure you it was truly Amarune Whitewave, whose dances you've enjoyed so often, who kissed you just now—and professed my love in return. I do still have *some* scruples."

She pointed at Storm's slack face and gaping mouth, within which she knew ashes were roiling in merry madness. "Him, I'm not so sure about."

"It was you? That's, ah, good," Arclath replied uneasily. "Tell me, Rune, what sort of horse are we seeking?"

"Anything good and sturdy that will carry her and not go wild on us," she said a little helplessly. "I don't know horses."

"Ah," said Arclath, turning her about. "Back here. We'll take the most suitable of the ready mounts—those that by standing order are kept saddled and bridled, in shifts."

He chose an older, sleepy-looking beast and used a long leading rein to lash Storm's body onto its saddle. The horse stood still as he worked, so he deemed it acceptable and led it out of the stables.

At the gates they encountered a fresh and rather breathless handful of guards and war wizards, who gave them—and Storm's bound body, scorched gown and all—rather startled looks, but Amarune told them brightly, "Another of her fits—too much excitement. She once took an evil spell meant for the king and has suffered from *these* ever since, poor thing. They know what to do, down at the temple, to stop her from sliding into even *worse* shape."

They waved a farewell and led the horse out into the busy Promenade before anyone thought to stop them or ask more. Such as *which* temple.

"That did *not* go well," King Foril Obarskyr said grimly, accepting the goblet of flamewine Glathra—after sniffing it suspiciously and taking a tiny sip—passed him.

"Your Majesty has a peerless gift for diplomatic understatement," Glathra replied curtly and turned to give the priests working on Crown Prince Irvel another glare. "How is he?"

"Only a few bruises now," one replied soothingly. "There were three cuts, none of them deep. Our healing has made them disappear completely."

"How many lords were lost?" the prince muttered sleepily, from somewhere beneath the attentive clergy.

Glathra was about to ignore the question but caught the look Foril gave her, an unspoken command to provide a full and honest reply.

"We know not. For one thing, there's still fighting going on, as some seek to settle old scores. For another, some lords were sorely wounded—at least, so all the spilled blood tells us—but fled the palace. Whether they'll reach healing in time . . ." She shrugged.

"There *were* deaths," the king said heavily.

Glathra nodded. "The bodies of the Lords Dragonwood, Ambrival, Foulweather, Barelder, Tantorn, Hardivyper, Ravenhill, and Briarbroke have been identified and taken to the Chapel of the Valiant, where they lie under guard." She started to pace. "I can't find Sir Winter, yet, nor my fellow wizards of war Blamreld and Lareikaun, but I want all three to examine the bodies before priests or kin get to them."

Running a hand over her weary eyes, she added, "Most of all, I want the wielder of our new blueflame ghost identified and found! Right after young Lord Stormserpent, who commands the two who have caused so much butchery in the city already, is taken into custody—alive, if we can manage it—and the items he uses to control his ghosts seized by us and put somewhere secure."

"Busy days," Irvel murmured, from the drawling edge of slumber.

Glathra stiffened, then quelled the angry reply that rose to her lips. One does not rebuke princes. Over trifles, at least.

She sighed instead, looked at the king, and told him bluntly, "If the nobles set to fighting each other and the commoners and our Dragons, in the streets, we'll be hard pressed to hold the palace. We'll have to call on every ally, from Alusair's ghost to the Sage of Shadowdale—when he inevitably reappears. Even that self-proclaimed Lord of Waterdeep who's skulking around our halls stealing food and wine as if he were eating for a dozen. I hate to trust any of them, but right now we must. We need them—or at least need them not to be our foes."

"And later?" one of the king's Highknight bodyguards asked with a bleak smile.

"Later," Glathra said viciously, "we'll take their measures and settle scores accordingly. When the Dragon Throne is safe again."

"Do what you must," King Foril said wearily, looking at the soundly sleeping prince, "but don't presume I'll hide forever. My place is leading my kingdom, not vanishing because the palace—or the city or the realm—is deemed unsafe."

"Majesty," Glathra said hastily, "I would never presume—"

"Glathra, you do nothing else," Foril told her with a wry smile. "I know. I've been watching you. Don't turn into another Vangerdahast on me, now."

Before she could stop herself, Glathra spat out an oath that made the priests wince and the Highknights all grin.

Then, mortified, she bent low to add, "Of *course* not, Your Majesty," then spun around and fled without meeting the king's gaze.

After she was gone, he sighed, reached for more flamewine, and murmured, "Busy days, indeed."

Outside the guarded chamber, as if on cue, there was a muffled crash.

"The king is dead! They killed King Foril and chopped him up into so many butchers' roasts!"

"Who killed him?"

"All the highnoses—the high Lords of Waterdeep, what met with him in this Council and all! Went for him, every last one of them!"

"Well, *I* heard he's alive and well, and brought in hire-swords to carve up the lords before they could lay a finger on him!"

"Get out of it, the both of you! 'Twas no regicide, nor nothing to do with the royals! It was noble knifing noble—and they're still at it, right across the city!"

So went the excited shouting as patrons rushed into The Goose of Doom, a dockside tavern not known for its loyal support of House Obarskyr or the lowliest Purple Dragon.

No sooner were they hunched around the tables with tankards in their hands, arguing excitedly about who'd been seen dead and who'd done the slaying, when the loudest and proudest of the Goose's regulars, the fat, retired Dragon swordcaptain Brorn Roril, stumbled through the front doors, wild-eyed and streaming blood.

"The Obarskyrs are dead!" he panted, "and it's civil war, saers! Lock up your daughters, or get out of Cormyr, as fast as you can! The Forest Kingdom is at war!"

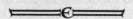

The Delcastle stablemaster took one look at the horse Arclath was leading into the stables and sneered. "Where, lord, did you get *that*? I hope you won the wager rather than losing it!"

"This was the most docile ready mount in the royal stables, Burtland," Arclath replied crisply, "and it's soon returning there. However, I find myself in need of a short stretch of privacy, here and now, so if you'd like to take yourself off to the kitchens for an early feasting, and tell them I sent you . . ."

The stablemaster rubbed his hands a trifle cleaner on his belt linen, looked Amarune up and down, and gave the younger Lord Delcastle a broad wink. "But of *course*, young master! I know—"

"Burtland," Arclath snapped, "you will *apologize* to the Lady Amarune for what you were just about to say, and amend your thinking. Regard this sorely wounded lady, here on the horse! We must tend to her and discuss her future and ours. So banish all thoughts of, ah, trysting from your head, and—"

The stablemaster surveyed the scorched and unconscious Storm—who chose that moment to open one bleary eye, notice him, and give him a wan smile and a solemn wink—bound to the horse. Bending to examine her bindings, he looked back at Arclath, then at Amarune, at Storm again, and back at Arclath.

And winked.

"*Indeed*, young master!" he boomed. "I wronged you dearly, that I did! Only one maid was I thinking of, and here you have *two* willing wenches! Not to mention bonda—"

"Burtland!" Arclath roared. "Go! Not another word out of you! Just go!"

The stablemaster went, hastily, but wasn't quite swift enough to get out of earshot before he started chuckling.

Amarune watched him dwindle across the gardens. "Aroused old goat," she commented flatly.

"I—ah, my apologies!" Arclath said hastily. "That was unforgivable! I—"

"Should think nothing of it," Storm told him, twisting around as much as she could in the bindings, "because you haven't *time*. El is . . . badly overstretched and likely to be wandering half-witted this next little while. I'm not much better. So you're more or less on your own."

She squirmed against the leather looped around her. "Get me free of this, will you?"

"Sorry," Arclath said hastily, leaping forward. "I—" He fumbled with the knots briefly, then hissed in exasperation and started slashing with his belt knife. Storm rolled weakly over—and thumped to the straw-strewn stable floor.

"Oh, gods, *sorry!*" the young lord burst out, reaching for her. Amarune smothered a sudden attack of giggles.

Storm chuckled, too, as Arclath helped her into a sitting position. She looked down at herself. "Your mother's going to be none too pleased with me," she said, surveying the ruined gown without apparent concern for how much of her was now on display. Then she looked up sharply. "Is the realm at war yet?"

Arclath shrugged. "We've been a bit too busy getting you out of the palace to survey matters. Yet, I've seen no smoke and heard no warhorns . . ." He looked at Rune.

Who shook her head. "A few men running, shouting about this or that doom. No clash of arms that I saw, but Storm, we *were* busy. Folk are upset, all right."

"Then we need to get to the palace," Storm decreed. "Quickly."

"The palace? We just got you *out* of there!" Arclath protested, aware that his debonair façade was long gone and he was increasingly sounding like a naïve village idiot aggrieved by his status—and aggrieved anew by each new thing that happened to him.

"And I thank you for it. You didn't find it necessary to kill *too* many annoying wizards or obstructionist guards, I trust? In circumstances where there were witnesses?"

"No, but—"

"Then back we go. *Now.* Tell your servants to arm themselves and guard your mother as if an invading army is about to sweep down on Delcastle Manor; get me my own leathers back—this gown is melted *into* me in spots and hurts like the Nine Hells—and let's go find Mirt and Alusair and what's left of Vangerdahast, before all of us seek out Glathra. We've got to rally Crown and court and try to prevent some of the more gleefully enthusiastic rebel nobles from riding the kingdom right into civil war."

"But I thought we were turning our backs on all of this, and—"

"We were, but things have turned bad enough that Cormyr's needs now outweigh ours."

Rune frowned. "Talk to Glathra about what, exactly?"

"Taking Marlin Stormserpent into custody," Arclath said grimly, "and getting our—that is, the Crown's—hands on the Blade and Chalice that give him control over his two slayers. The blueflame ghosts that murdered Seszgar Huntcrown and everyone with him."

"No, you were right when you said 'our,'" Storm said firmly. "Glathra's no more to be trusted with the ghosts than young Stormserpent. They're too powerful for her—or anyone at the palace—to resist. However, she doesn't need to know I feel that way about her just yet, or that we don't intend to get both Blade and Chalice straight into her hands."

Rune rolled her eyes. "And just how is what I'm now hearing different from what nobles do, that you and Glathra and everyone else of Crown and court thunderously denounce as treason?"

Storm smiled. "That's easy. They're blackhearted villains—whereas, we're good folk, with nothing but heroism and shining intentions in our hearts."

Manshoon's head hurt.

Or rather, his mind throbbed with aches brought on by strain, and sagged with weariness, and that made whatever head he inhabited at the moment hurt, too.

However, he was still on the scene.

Others had not been so fortunate. Lord Lyrannus Tantorn and Lord Jassur Dragonwood were both down and lost, slain in the brawls that had raged through the Hall of Justice.

He'd had to flee Dragonwood's dying, dimming brain precipitously, bursting into the nearest mind he'd already conquered—which had happened to be that of Lord Melder Crownrood.

His arrival had saved Crownrood's life by making the overwhelmed noble reel and fall—down behind some seats that shielded him from the vicious hackings two longtime rivals had been trying to deliver to the back of his head. As they leaned down from the tier above to get at Crownrood, and overbalanced when his body collapsed down out of sight as they were in mid-swing, their blades had lodged in seat backs—and doomed them, as nearby lords who'd mistaken themselves for the targets of those attacks retaliated bloodily.

Though he was almost certainly still alive because his sprawled position underfoot had kept him out of the furious fighting that had thereafter raged so closely above him, Crownrood was far from grateful. His bruised mind had plunged into a nasty headache and had birthed its own swift black rage at his unwelcome rider.

For his part, Manshoon cared not a whit what Crownrood thought. The man's body could run—and for that matter, crawl and stagger, too—well enough, and had served to get Manshoon out of the royal palace of Suzail and away, back to the home and shop of the alchemist Sraunter.

Through streets where nobles' bodyguards had glowered, exchanged sharp words, and threatened each other with half-drawn swords, men had fled the palace shouting all manner of dire overblown dooms, and some fearful citizens had hastened to shutter their shops.

Yes, it was all very satisfactory.

King Foril still lived; wherefore, no one had a good excuse for mustering armies for open war over an empty Dragon Throne. Yet, confusion ruled the city, and fearful folk everywhere were reaching for swords and daggers.

Which meant a certain deft villain known as Manshoon could start to work violence openly, a killing here and a disappearance there, amid the wider fighting that was sure to erupt—and if the Crown clamped down on such bloodshed with the full might of the Dragons, the populace would grow angry at such tyranny. Angrier. Weakening this weak king still more, and giving the future emperor more room to do what needed to be done.

Yes, Crownrood could stew. On a cot in an otherwise empty room, safely locked away in a corner of Sraunter's cellar. If the man had any sense at all, he'd get some sleep—but then, heads of noble Houses in the Forest Kingdom weren't noted for their abundant sense. Low cunning, yes. Arrogant schemes and the notion that the world owed them everything and the gods smiled on them, indeed. Common sense, more rarely, and in far more paltry supply.

Crownrood's handy little prison was actually the alchemist's wood room, but its current lack of firewood bothered Manshoon not at all. By the time cold weather came again, he'd be enjoying the comforts of the royal palace—and if for any reason he wasn't, and the alchemist remained too useful to let the cold claim him, there would be time enough then to seize or steal someone else's firewood.

Right now, more important matters beckoned. Manshoon needed to discover which noble commanded this new blue-flame ghost, in a hurry.

Right after he checked on the ghost-commanding noble he was already familiar with, to make sure Stormserpent still had his life, freedom, and possession of the Flying Blade and the Wyverntongue Chalice.

So it was that the largest room of Sraunter's cellar was flooded with the eerie glows of freshly conjured scrying eyes, and a darkly handsome future emperor was strolling among the floating, glowing, spherical scenes, peering hard.

The Promenade in front of the palace was seething. Someone—was that Dathcloake?—was trying to get back into the palace within a moving wedge of his bodyguards, and learning that Purple Dragons not only could not be ordered, blustered, threatened, or shoved out of the way, but that they had procured crossbows from the armories and were sternly threatening to use them if the coldly furious lord didn't cease his attempts to storm the palace and didn't return to his lodgings, peacefully and promptly.

It was tempting to tarry and watch that fun unfold, but the death of Elminster didn't mean this particular incipient emperor was *entirely* without foes . . .

In this darker sphere, one scene demanded his immediate attention: Lord Marlin Stormserpent was badly scared and pacing in an upper bedchamber of Stormserpent Towers, not knowing where to run, or how. Clearly visible out the room's window were the Crown's hounds, coming for him: half a dozen wizards of war with two dozen Purple Dragons, most in full armor, and a few of their fellows wearing lesser war-harnesses, but bearing crossbows.

The Flying Blade scabbarded at his belt and the Wyvern-tongue Chalice clutched to his chest, a sweating Stormserpent mumbled fearful possibilities to himself.

His two ghosts could easily slaughter mere Dragons—but *six* wizards, now, could likely deal with his blueflame slayers in a trice. Teleporting the ghosts halfway across Cormyr rather than destroying them would still seal Marlin Stormserpent's doom.

Wizards of war without their lord warder or some cool-headed Highknights or a battle-axe like the Lady Glathra to lead them were proving to be cautious, prudent men. The Crown force was still carefully encircling the walls of Stormserpent Towers, not yet ready to thunder upon the doors of the Stormserpent mansion and demand entry—let alone force it.

That gave Manshoon all the time he needed.

He turned. The alchemist sat uncertainly on a barrel amid heaped packing crates and coffers along one wall of his cellar, watching Manshoon—who obligingly gave Sraunter his best softly menacing smile.

"Faithful alchemist, fetch whatever you need that can make enough poisonous smoke to quickly fill Stormserpent Towers. That 'whatever' should be something you can easily carry, that you can have back down here less than ten breaths from now."

Sraunter gaped at him, so Manshoon added cheerfully, "Hurry. Or I'll spend your eleventh breath summoning enough boring worms to eat your body apart while you lie watching them, paralyzed and screaming."

The alchemist swallowed.

"Go," Manshoon prompted him gently—and with a speed hitherto unseen in Immaero Sraunter, the alchemist sprinted up the cellar stairs.

Manshoon chuckled and sent the unleashed beholderkin soaring after the man, to keep an eye on him.

Vampire lords might not need to breathe, but explosions and acids could hurt them well enough . . . and do harm to what was filling the third room of the alchemist's cellar.

The beholders he'd be needing very soon.

CHAPTER
TWELVE

GOING TOO FAR

'Tis never a question if she'll go too far. 'Tis always an asking
of how soon, and how much wreckage will ensue. Gentlesirs,
I'd rather kiss a spike-studded viper than ally with such a one.
Yet, lords, you must suit yourselves—after all, you might love pain.

Nahlvur the Bowman, in Act II, Scene II of the play
Black Blades of the Barons by Tarla Semmurt, Bard of
Yhaunn, first staged in the Year of the True Omens

Mirt sat himself down on the window seat, in the
smooth-worn dip in the stone where thousands of
predecessors had done the very same thing, and peered out
over the bright, awakening spring splendors of the royal
gardens. He was . . . happy.

He now knew where the treasuries were, the main kitchens
and the royal ones, several bedchambers no one ever seemed to
check on, the cheese and sausage pantries, and where the duty
warder who always dozed off hung his spare keys.

He'd located a better dagger than he'd ever owned in all
his life—safely stored away where it had lain, wrapped in oiled
cloth to keep the rust off, for years. So, it wouldn't be missed.
Nor would the rusty little sphere stored in the same drawer,
twin to one he'd once used in Waterdeep Castle, used to bind a
creature. A handy little magic, that; it would ride happily with
him when the time came to take himself elsewhere.

He even knew where to get his next roast, after the smoked
leg of lamb he'd purloined and was now devouring bite by
greasy bite was gone.

The fat, old lord let out a loud, ripping belch, settled down
across the window and propped his dusty booted feet against

the far side of the window frame, patted his stomach, and sat back to devote himself to making it more rotund.

All in all, he was quite content. This wasn't home, but it *was* a palace. Its servants a little on both the tense and pompous sides for his tastes, but—

"Mirt? Mirt of Waterdeep?"

The voice was a woman's, sharp and imperious. Holding not the slightest hint of friendliness.

Mirt sighed, hefting the lamb in his fist to see how well it might serve him as a club. Or perhaps a hurl-cudgel, if it came to that. He put a smile on his face before turning from the pleasant garden view. "Aye?"

He hadn't expected his questioner to be alone, and she wasn't. Carefully arranged to block off any escape was a small crowd of folk, all staring at him.

Foremost stood a woman in plain, dark, wizardly robes, feet planted apart and hands on hips. Huh. One of *those*.

She had a pair of mages a step behind each shoulder—subservient to her, all four of them—bookended by a dozen-some armored and impassive Purple Dragons, armed with spears as well as all the usual warsteel.

"I am Lady Glathra, a wizard of war here in Cormyr. I do not recall you ever being invited within these walls as a guest of the realm, saer, and I have a few questions for you."

Mirt waved the leg of lamb at her. "Ah, good. I've some for ye, too." He took another bite.

"I've been told you are a famous man, a lord of your city. I've also been told that you ... *flourished*, if that's the right word, about a century ago."

Mirt chewed calmly, offering no comment. Glathra sighed. "Is this true?"

Mirt nodded unconcernedly and took another bite.

Some of the guards grinned openly, behind the lady wizard's back. By the expression on her face, she could feel those grins. Mirt went on chewing.

"So, you are over a century old?" Glathra put a biting edge of incredulity on that question.

Mirt nodded again.

"So, how came you to live so long? And how is it that a Lord of Waterdeep appears in the royal palace of Suzail?"

Mirt swallowed, raised the lamb like a scholar's finger, wagged it, and gave her a broad and greasy grin. "Magic."

Glathra was unamused. "*Whose* magic?"

Mirt shrugged. "I'm no loremaster when it comes to the Art, lass, but the jack who brought me here by some spell or other was an insolent young pup by the name of Marlin Stormserpent. *Lord* Marlin Stormserpent, I'm told."

"Told? Told by *whom?*"

"Quite a few folk. Two of yer fellow Crown mages among them."

"And did he say anything at all about why he, ah, summoned you here?"

Mirt turned the leg, choosing the best spot for his next hearty bite. "Wanted a third flame ghost to go with two he already had. Got me instead. Wasn't best pleased. We parted company swiftly."

"A *third flame ghost?* Would these be blueflame ghosts?"

Mirt nodded, bit into the lamb, and devoted himself to chewing. He looked out the window again.

Glathra's mouth tightened, and she took a step closer to the fat man in the window seat. "And did you witness him commanding these ghosts? Calling them forth?"

"No," Mirt said sweetly, turning back to deliver his reply through a mouthful of half-chewed lamb. "And, no."

Glathra took another step closer. "In Cormyr," she informed him flatly, "most folk have the prudent sense to speak to a wizard of war with something closer to respect."

Mirt shifted his current mouthful into one cheek, and past its bulge replied, "And in Waterdeep, I'm accustomed to interviewing angry lasses when we're both comfortably unclad and sharing a bed, some wine, and a full meal. On my earlier visits to Cormyr, good old Azoun was in the habit of handing me a bottle or six, and sharing a good hot meal while we talked, boots on the table. But, I understand the realm may have slid a bit since his death, and all backward upcountry places cherish their own quaint customs, and so I am making allowances. Ye, too?"

Some muffled chuckles wafted up from behind Glathra. She did not turn to see whom they'd come from.

"I could imprison, slay, or enspell you to servitude right now," she pointed out calmly.

Mirt raised a greasy finger. "Correction, lass. Ye could *try*."

He swallowed the lamb in his mouth, inspected the much-reduced leg for the best site for his next assault, and added mildly, "I'm the jack who defeated two angry young noble lords of Cormyr, in the mansion o' one of 'em—despite two blueflame ghosts and the admittedly small heaps of enchanted items they were wearing and waving about. Ye might want to remember that."

"Oh, I will," Glathra said softly, signaling the wizards behind her to advance.

Mirt favored her with a disgusted look. "I'm *eating*, lass. Where were ye raised? In a stable?"

Glathra froze for a moment and then trembled in real rage as she drew herself up tall.

Mirt eyed her with interest. Well, now, it seemed she *had* been reared in a stable, and was sensitive about it, too.

This should be good.

If he survived.

"You really think they won't have someone new guarding the door by now?" Rune asked curiously.

Storm shrugged. "You have a better plan?"

Rune winced. "Your hit strikes home."

"I take it you, ah, took care of the guard here last time?" Arclath murmured. At their nods, he added cautiously, "Things *might* go differently. Being as the Council is . . . well, not being held right now, and I'm with you, and am heir of a noble House."

"I'd not count on a friendly welcome," Storm warned, "given all the lords running about waving swords and snarling treason hereabouts, not so long ago. Granted, we don't look like hairy, surly bodyguards, but . . ."

Despite her wary words, her stroll was the height of ease and unconcern as she approached the door of the high house behind the royal stables. It was too small a place to be deemed a mansion, unlike the three homes that flanked it, all backing onto the stables, but its front door was solid and imposing enough to deny entry if no one answered her knock.

No one did, so Storm led the way she'd taken before, around into the garden to the side door. It was closed, but it opened when she turned its ring, admitting them into the same stately, deserted quiet they'd seen before. This time there was no struck-senseless wizard decorating the floor or Mirt grinning at them over him, but the pot he'd used to fell the war wizard was sitting mutely on the table at the end of the hall.

Storm held up a hand for silence and stood still, listening hard. After a few long, patient breaths, she stepped over the threshold and stopped to listen again.

Silence. She strode briskly forward and took the stairs down, heading for the back cellar and the tunnel under the stableyard that led into the palace.

"They could still have alarm or spying spells in place," Arclath warned, "even if we hear and see nothing amiss."

Storm nodded. "They usually do. Which is why we're going to start hurrying, right . . . *now*."

Amarune and Arclath obeyed. Storm led them along dim tunnels, through doors in darkness, down stairs beyond those doors, and out into the faint glows of the palace cellars. She seemed to know exactly where she was going, and they never saw another person, though she was obviously taking detours around well-lit areas where servants and courtiers were presumably at work.

"Where are you taking us?" Arclath murmured at her shoulder as she stopped to peer around a corner.

"The royal crypt."

Arclath frowned. "Why?"

"She knows it'll attract my attention, that's why," a soft voice that wasn't Rune's murmured in Arclath's other ear, from a space that should have been too narrow for anyone to stand in.

He flinched, badly startled. Clapping hand to sword, he started to turn—and stared into a ghostly face floating in the air right in front of his nose. As Arclath gaped, feeling a chill emanating from that apparition, it gained apparent substance, the suggestion of a body starting to appear below it.

"Princess Alusair Obarskyr, sometime regent of the realm," the face told him politely. "Well met, Lord Delcastle."

The ghost's gaze went to Amarune. "Lady," she greeted the dancer gravely.

Then she turned to Storm. "Well? What?"

"You know what befell at the Council," the Harper said gently. "We're rallying your kin and the loyal courtiers to hold the palace and help restore order before things get more out of hand."

"'We'? You three?"

"With you and Vangey and Mirt, if you can get us all together, before we try to talk to Glathra."

"Huh," Alusair said dismissively, "*that* one. She's up in the east wing trying to sink her claws into Mirt right now."

"Then Vangey can wait," Storm replied, "though he'll be far from pleased. Let's get to Glathra before she goes too far."

"You're several seasons too late for that," Alusair retorted, growing even more solid. They could see the sword at her hip, now, and the long and graceful leg below it. "This way, stalwarts of Cormyr!"

Manshoon glanced at the two death tyrants. His two sturdiest, their bodies almost entirely intact, were almost good enough to pass for being alive, and in far better shape than his worst undead beholders. "Putrid in some spots, mummified or just crumbled away and *gone* in others," Sraunter had judged those lesser death tyrants a day back, and Manshoon thought that description put matters very well.

The tyrants floated like limp, sleeping things at that moment, of course, lacking any direction from him. Yet, he'd just tested them both, fleetingly, and they'd turned and lashed out with gratifying speed. No longer needing to breathe, they should take no harm from Sraunter's poisonous smoke.

So all that remained was Sraunter himself, with concoctions in hand . . .

The future emperor of Cormyr yawned. For a long time he'd thought vampires never got weary, but they felt mental strain every bit as much as living humans—or at least, this one did.

Yes, it had been a tiring day, and its ever-more-crowded parade of excitements showed no signs of being anywhere near over, yet—and why *did* things all happen at once? Was it the whim of the gods, their way of deriving maximum entertainment from mortal desperation? Manshoon looked again into his scrying spheres.

Three of the floating glows showed him the outside of Stormserpent Towers. The Crown force thundered on the doors and loudly demanded entrance, their encirclement of the walled mansion complete. Onward—or rather, inward—brave stalwarts of Cormyr! Take that collective stride too far . . .

Manshoon turned to his newest sphere. In its depths, Lady Narmitra Stormserpent lay on her favorite lounge, sweets in one hand and slender flagon in the other. She was in a savage rage at the temerity of these unwelcome guests. And so she had summoned servants to hiss vicious threats about their fates if they let the "barbaric intruders" in, and to give them grand orders to defend the mansion and defy all who tried to gain entrance, up to and including the king himself.

Manshoon caught himself smiling. *Such* a she-viper! A trifle shallow and old for his tastes, but if she'd come into his life a good century ago . . .

But what of her son?

Manshoon looked into his oldest sphere and saw just what he'd expected to see.

Up in his tower, Marlin Stormserpent was pacing in rising fear, faster than before, almost dashing from room to deserted room. Feeling the jaws of the trap around him, no doubt, and seeing no way out.

Manshoon didn't have to go into the lordling's mind to know what the young fool was thinking.

No escape but a desperate fight through the house, using the ghosts and their ability to drift through solid walls to make them stealthy slayers-from-behind. Yet, they did not obey him absolutely, and he didn't—couldn't—trust them to keep him safe. They'd let him be captured or enspelled or even—

"I-I'm ready, Lord Manshoon," Sraunter stammered, from behind the vampire.

The future emperor of Cormyr turned, his soft smile broadening. At last.

The alchemist was pale with fear. He stood uncertainly holding a trio of emerald-liquid-filled glass flasks in each hand.

"One from each hand broken together produces killing smoke?" Manshoon asked. "Is there a defense or cure?"

"N-no, lord. None short of powerful temple magic."

"Good. Worry not; I'll send you *and* bring you back alive. Just try to stay out of your smoke as you cause it, hmm?"

Sraunter nodded fervently. He was still bobbing his head like an idiot when Manshoon's teleporting spell deposited him a few paces behind the frightened servants in the forehall behind the closed and barred front doors of Stormserpent Towers.

In the scrying sphere, Manshoon saw Sraunter grimace at the sight of the servants, bend down, and carefully set his flasks on the floor. Smashing one, he dashed another into its wreckage, snatched up the remaining flasks, and fled.

Smoke billowed up, and Manshoon's second spell—the one he'd cast on the sprinting alchemist before the teleport, not that his dupe had noticed he was doing three castings rather than one—took effect, birthing a strong wind from Sraunter's back that slowed the servants pursuing him, swept the smoke against the doors that the war wizards outside were casting spells at, then swirled around the forehall. All over the room, coughing and staggering servants fell.

The wind blew on, spreading smoke with astonishing speed. Sraunter was dashing deeper into the mansion, the flasks tucked close to his body, heading for the central feasting hall. Good man; he was too frightened to think for himself or dare to betray his mind-master.

Sraunter reached that lofty hall and broke two more flasks. A fresh cloud of smoke arose.

The alchemist stumbled on, through deserted passages. Winded now, he was moving more slowly, but he was following Manshoon's orders, seeking the small back hall at the rear of the mansion. Where the disused towers had their roots, it was the hub of the rooms where most of the servants dwelt and worked. Every mouth silenced was one less source of talk about Storm-serpent's little conspiracy that the Crown might find useful.

Which reminded Manshoon to look back at his newest sphere. Farewell, Lady Stormserpent . . .

The front doors of Stormserpent Towers gave way, blasted and melted by war wizard spells, and Purple Dragons plunged headlong into the waiting smoke.

Manshoon's smile grew. Served them right, overzealous hands of tyranny, for bursting unbidden into the private home of a respected noble family of the realm.

Sraunter shattered his last pair of flasks, and Manshoon awakened the last of the three castings on the man. The gasping alchemist was snatched away from the doom he'd been spreading, across some of the richest streets in Suzail in a trice—to arrive on the other side of yon door, in the locked cellar room where Crownrood was brooding.

He hoped the two of them would have sense enough not to kill each other while he was busy in Stormserpent Towers.

Soldiers of Cormyr were coughing and falling in the mansion forehall, and war wizards were lurching back outside, choking and cursing.

Manshoon chuckled and cast the spell that would put him into what was left of the decaying mind of the nearest death tyrant.

It took hold, and the cellar around him seemed to lurch and sway. Then he gazed out of darker, multiple eyes and watched his handsome human body stagger under the mental weight of seeing out of two bodies at once, of controlling a living host and an undead one.

Then he drew his human body upright, smiled, and cast the spell again.

Plunging himself into the mind of the second death tyrant, too.

The cellar swam around him—Bane *forfend*, but he was tired!—then slowly steadied.

Very slowly.

Manshoon's human host sighed.

When things had stopped swimming and swaying, he made his human self go to a wall and slide down it to a sitting position, where he could see the scrying spheres and hope to come to no harm.

From there he cast the greater translocation that would take both undead beholders to a tower room two floors below the frantic Marlin Stormserpent.

Then he cast it again, this second incantation a delayed working that would snatch the tyrants—and their burdens— back to the cellar again when he willed it to take effect.

The cellar went away, and all of his many eyes saw swirling smoke.

Manshoon shuddered as everything swam again. He *was* tired.

Drifting back to clarity, he saw that all around his two floating selves, the ground floor of Stormserpent Towers was a dim and silent labyrinth of slumped servants and darkly roiling drifts of smoke.

Death tyrants couldn't smile any more than the frozen curves of their wide and crooked maws, but Manshoon tried to smile.

Before the idiot war wizards managed to deal with this smoke, the future Emperor of Cormyr and Beyond should have more than enough time to snatch away young Lord Stormserpent and his two precious ghost-commanding items.

Lady Shout-at-Everything Glathra would be *so* displeased.

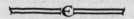

"Lady Glathra!" Storm shouted, seeing at a glance that there was no time at all left for politeness. Only for a swift and desperate lie. "The king wants you!"

"Not *now*," Glathra started to snarl, flames of orange and purple already whirling around her raised hands as she stalked toward the fat man in the window.

Then she sighed and lowered her burning hands. "Who calls?"

Most of the war wizards and Dragons had already spun to face the door had that banged open and dashed the luckless soldier leaning against it to the floor. They all stared at a young noble, the dancer he seemed to go everywhere with, a tall and strikingly beautiful silver-haired woman . . . and the ghost of the Princess Alusair.

"We do," Storm replied quietly.

Glathra glared at her. "The king wants me *why*? What message?"

"The king wants you to treat his guest, a visiting Lord of Waterdeep, with rather *more* respect and *less* deadly magic," Alusair snapped, sweeping through the assembled Cormyreans like a cold breeze to float facing the war wizard.

Who let the flames fade around her hands and asked coldly, "Your Highness, is there no end to your meddling?"

Alusair's ghostly nose was suddenly almost touching Glathra's living one.

"When an Obarskyr engages in ruling Cormyr, dear," she said softly, "it is anything but 'meddling.' Courtiers who fail to grasp this may well find themselves swiftly replaced."

Chilled and shivering, the wizard of war drew back a step. "But you're *dead*, Princess! Dead! And—"

"Glathra," Storm interrupted sternly, "hear us! Lord Marlin Stormserpent is the master of the two blueflame ghosts who murdered young Lord Huntcrown at The Bold Archer! He holds the Wyverntongue Chalice that commands one, and a Stormserpent family treasure, the Flying Blade, that controls the other. You should be accosting *him*, not this Lord of Waterdeep!"

Glathra stiffened. "Other loyal Crown agents are doing so, right now. As His Majesty knows full well. Why are you four getting involved?"

"We're here to help," Arclath spoke up.

"Help with *what*? Driving me madwits?"

"No, that's been done already," Alusair told the lady mage, flying around her in a tight spiral. "We six loyal Cormyreans are here to help you and your fellow mages and Highknights and Dragons to defend the palace and try to keep order in Suzail."

"*Are* you, now?" Glathra asked cuttingly. "Six? I mark four—who else?"

"The Royal Magician Vangerdahast," Alusair replied, "who's not with us now, and the man you were just about to scorch."

Glathra stared at her incredulously then swung around to favor Mirt with the same look.

He unfolded himself from the window seat with a wheeze, stamped his boots, and struck a swordsman's pose with the greasy lamb bone.

"Well," he grunted, with a friendly leer, "if ye'll have me."

CHAPTER
THIRTEEN

SOON AFTER WHENEVER

War comes soon after whenever good men stop trying to prevent it.
Getting it to depart again takes a lot more than the striving
Of good men—if any survive.

Filfaeril Selazair Obarskyr, Dowager Dragon Queen
of Cormyr, *Thoughts from a Throne*
first published in the Year of the Lost Keep

It took Glathra a moment or two to gather her breath and her temper. When she gained mastery over both, she let fly.

"Have you? *Have* you? I'll have you chained to the wall in our deepest, dampest dungeon, I will!"

Mirt gave her a wide-eyed, innocent grin. "Is that a yes?"

Glathra shrieked out wordless rage, then dashed her hands down to her sides, drew in a deep breath, and said icily, "I have no *time* for this. The realm stands in peril."

She took three swift strides away, then whirled and marched back again. "I hope all of you are loyal to the Dragon Throne, and I value your assistance. However, I really *cannot* welcome four or five or six self-styled heroes wandering around this palace or Suzail outside these walls doing just as *they* please, without any obedience to royal commands or lawfully delegated authority—such as the orders I give."

"Loyal wizard," Alusair asked gently, "may we speak to you in private?"

Glathra looked at her, then around the room. "You want me to dismiss these good Dragons and my fellow Crown mages? Sorry, but no. You might very well try to overwhelm me. You may even succeed."

"A poor reason," the ghostly princess replied, "being as we could easily do that right now."

"Is that a threat?" Glathra flared.

"It's a statement of fact," Alusair replied flatly. "If you'd like, I could make it a promise."

"Heh," Mirt chuckled, "I'd've thought ye'd have started to learn some lessons by now, Lady Glathra. Thick-skulled courtiers seldom rise to high office, or last long if given it."

"*You,*" the war wizard snarled, rounding on him, "be silent! You are my prisoner, and—"

"Ah, no, lass, that I'm not. I'm King Foril Obarskyr's honored guest—and, as it happens, the senior lord of a city that can buy and sell all Cormyr with ease in a day, if ever for any madwits reason we decided to do so. I admire yer force of character but not yer judgment. Ye're being offered aid that embattled courtiers should leap to embrace, and yer spurning it. Idiot."

Glathra sputtered wordlessly, then clamped her lips into a thin, hard line.

"You may be right in all you say," she said curtly, "but *I* am in charge here."

Alusair sighed, but Glathra raised her voice and went on. "Wherefore hear my orders, all of you! You, who when alive I would have obeyed"—she faced the ghost of Alusair unflinchingly—"are to go out and play sheephound, rounding up all the nobles and bringing them back here. *Without* their bodyguards."

The princess stared at her, something close to grief on her ghostly face. So the talk might well be true, Glathra realized; these were orders Alusair couldn't fulfill if she wanted to . . . probably she *did* fade away to no more than a whispering wind if she moved farther from the palace than halfway across the Promenade. Well, if so, she could swallow her royal pride and stlarned well admit that.

Glathra turned and pointed at Amarune. "*You* shall surrender yourself into the custody of the Dragons here with me, to keep out of trouble."

"And be a hostage to ensure Arclath's loyalty," Rune hissed under her breath, glaring at the war wizard—who pretended not to hear, having already turned to Arclath.

"Lord Delcastle, you are to report to Sir Winter, to receive assignment to the ranks of the Purple Dragons, who are in pressing need of battlefront officers—especially if we face open rebellion."

Arclath cocked an incredulous eyebrow. His expression put his thoughts clearly enough. Nobles took no orders from courtiers in matters of military service to the Crown. Did this mage think herself regent of the realm?

"Get over it, lordling," Glathra muttered at him. "I've no time for arguments. None at all."

She turned to Mirt. "Your opinion of me is baseless, and I repudiate it. I repeat: you are my prisoner. Resist or try to escape, and you'll face deadly force."

She looked to Storm.

"You," she told the silver-haired woman crisply, "stay with me. I need you to tell me everything you and other Harpers are up to in Cormyr right now—along with all you know about what nobles we can trust, which are eager traitors, and who's just following the strongest passing lion."

Storm met Glathra's stare expressionlessly, then turned and looked at Rune, Arclath, Alusair, and then Mirt.

Silent agreement was reached.

Glathra glared. Were they giving in? Or deciding that whatever their loyalties to the Crown of Cormyr, they could not accept her conditions?

Storm calmly stepped around Glathra and headed for the door she'd come in by. Mirt fell into step behind her.

Glathra grabbed for the wands at her belt and sidestepped to block the fat Waterdhavian's path.

Storm whirled. Glathra started to turn, but iron-strong fingers caught her shoulder and flung her off balance into a helpless stumble across the room.

"Stop them!" Glathra snapped at the Dragons and mages, but Amarune and Arclath darted for the door as Alusair swooped through one man after another, chilling their hearts and leaving them gasping.

Glathra caught her balance just shy of ramming a wall, set herself facing the backs of her fleeing prisoners and their allies, and reached for her wands.

Her fingers closed on nothing. They had all been plucked away and strewn across the room! Stumbling boots were trampling them underfoot.

Yes, stumbling. The ghost of Alusair was racing repeatedly through them like a savage wind, leaving a weak, momentarily frozen and clumsy crowd of Dragons and fellow war wizards to carry out her orders.

Glathra fought for calm and began to cast a spell. Whereupon Storm Silverhand turned at the door in a swirl of silver tresses, plucked the nearest war wizard bodily off his feet, and flung him through the air.

Straight at Glathra.

A looming, helplessly shouting weight, all clawing arms and legs.

Who proved heavy, impossible to avoid, and *very* solid.

Glathra was slammed to the floor, bruised and winded. The mage who'd just felled her had thankfully rolled on past. Though not before ruining her spell, helplessly driving sharp knees and elbows into her . . . and giving the fleeing five time to get out the door.

As she fought to get her breath back, Glathra saw her fellow wizards on their knees clutching chests and throats, with Alusair curling up from them in ghostly triumph to dart out the door, calling, "To me, friends! I'll take you to a place in this house of mine where no one will trace or follow you!"

"Don't bet on that," Glathra hissed furiously, struggling to her knees. "This particular thick-skulled idiot doesn't embrace defeat so willingly."

Something swirled in the dark passage beyond the door— and Alusair blazed back into the room like an arrow, straight at the war wizard's head.

Only to stop right in Glathra's face.

"Glathra Barcantle," the ghost hissed, "Cormyr stands in peril! The realm needs you to *grow up*, right now. Think on that."

Then the princess was gone, leaving nothing but empty air in front of Glathra's nose.

And beyond it, a lot of sheepish men in robes or armor, awkwardly avoiding meeting her gaze as they wincingly found their feet.

Unexpectedly, Glathra found herself on the trembling verge of tears.

"No!" Marlin Stormserpent shrieked, slashing at the death tyrant in wide-eyed terror. The Flying Blade flashed and bit, sinking into rotten plates that in life would have been as hard as Purple Dragon armor.

Each blow shook the beholder, jostling Manshoon's many overlapping visions as its eyes danced and writhed.

Momentarily everything blurred, and a pounding pain arose in his mind. Blackfire, but he was tired!

His vision steadied, sliding back into focus again. The second death tyrant had hold of the Chalice, and had just slammed into the struggling noble from behind. The room was too small for the beholders to battle effectively—

Yet the clumsy strike worked; the sword tumbled from Stormserpent's hand. Manshoon used the tyrant that had hold of him to shove him back, pinning the lordling when he went limp and tried to slip to the floor and crawl to his blade. The other tyrant snatched the sword up.

Back now, out of Stormserpent Towers, to me.

To Sraunter's cellar . . . so tired . . .

Had the smoke somehow come with the tyrants? No . . . What, then, was this purple-gray, heaving mist that swirled in his mind? The rising *pain* . . .

Manshoon was vaguely aware he'd lost control over one tyrant. It was drifting limply near the cellar wall. He was seeing it from the floor, a floor that lurched beneath him, slowly, like the deck of a ship he'd been on, long years ago, fighting slow, rolling waves in the Moonsea . . .

Too much. He'd tried controlling too many minds at once. Sraunter's roiling fear, the dark, cold dead weights of the two undead beholders, all while keeping his scrying spheres going as he cast multiple teleports, holding some in hanging abeyance . . . too much. Stormserpent's flood of terror had defeated him, had put the noble's mind beyond his mastery this time, exhausting him . . .

Bile of Bane, but he had limitations after all.

"Sark and lurruk," he cursed in a weary whisper, watching the ceiling spin above him. Stormserpent was on the move.

The lordling had torn free of the tyrant holding him, but Manshoon still had a tenuous hold over it. If Stormserpent tried to harm Manshoon's human body, he could slam the beholder into the man, or interpose it between angry young lord and exhausted vampire lord . . .

Or, he could take mist form to escape destruction if he had to—but the last time he'd done that, as Orbakh of Westgate, *so* many of his bindings and mental holds over others had faded away that he'd spent the better part of seven seasons restoring a little more than half of them; the others were gone for good.

So that was very much a last resort.

Ohhh, his *head* . . .

The sword and the chalice lay on the cellar floor beneath the other, limply floating tyrant. Through swimming eyes Manshoon saw the young noble snatch them up.

Blade in hand, Marlin Stormserpent turned a pale, frightened face in Manshoon's direction for a moment, then turned and bolted for the cellar stairs.

Manshoon lay on cold stone, listening to the thunder of the noble's boots die away. He was too drained and near senseless to prevent Stormserpent's flight.

Silence descended in the shop overhead. No smashings, no smoke . . . just stillness.

So his pawn had escaped—for now—and the two blue-flame items with him.

Manshoon sighed. Undeniably, the future emperor of Cormyr had overreached himself.

He let slip his control over the last tyrant and watched it drift, eyestalks drooping. If the pain would only *fade*, sark it …

From overhead came the faint slam of a door and the tinkling of the shop's bell.

Then an imperious female voice, a little breathless but with shrill volume to make up for that, coming nearer.

"Shopkeeper? Alchemist! Master Surontur, or whatever your name is! Yoohoo! Is anyone here? Service! Ser-*vice!*"

From behind the door of the corner cellar room where an alchemist and a noble lord of Cormyr were confined arose the muffled thunder of Immaero Sraunter trying to get the locked door open.

Manshoon's lips twisted in wry amusement. Of course. The alchemist knew all too well that Nechelseiya Sammartael didn't like to be kept waiting.

"Th-they're saying it everywhere, saer! Rumors always run wild, aye, but they're *all* crying it! Noble lords butchered, and King Foril dead, and the realm now at war!"

Lord Irlin Stonestable shook his head. "Surely not *all* of this can be true! Broryn, is this steward of yours a drinker?"

From the far side of the decanter-crowded table in the front parlor of Staghaven House, his grim-faced host shook his head.

"Aereld here is one of the oldest and most trusted Windstag servants," he announced almost fiercely. "Shrewd, prudent, and utterly trustworthy. If he tells us all the city's saying so, then you may trust that all the city's saying so!"

"Well, haularake! If this doesn't naed all!" Stonestable swore, draining his flagon and sitting back to stare at the steward as if the man were a shapechanging monster growing jaws and claws before his eyes.

Windstag suddenly rounded on the old steward, in one of his abrupt changes of mood.

"At war?" he bellowed into the man's frightened face. "Are you *sure?*"

"Yon trusty may or may not be," a familiar voice gasped, before the stammering Aereld could say a clear word in reply, "but *I* sure as the Purple Dragon am!"

Lord Mellast Ormblade, red faced and puffing for breath, staggered past the steward to crash down into a vacant seat at the table and gasp, "Truth, all of it! *Many* nobles butchered—by a barepelt club dancer, seemingly possessed by the ghost of the legendary Vangerdahast! The king clings to life despite three or four swords through him, I think—and Handragon's alive, for sure—but many of the oldbloods are frightened or enraged enough that we may already *be* at war!"

A clatter of hooves and the loud neighing of a protesting horse came from outside. Before anyone could go to see the cause, Lord Sacrast Handragon came striding in.

"Butchery at the palace, a score of oldblood lords dead, and the rest all crying rebellion, and worse news!" he said grimly.

"Worse?" Windstag growled in disbelief. "How so?"

Handragon snatched up a decanter and drank deeply, not bothering with a flagon.

"Just now I almost rode down some Stormserpent family servants," he replied, slamming what was left of the wine down on the table. "They're running through the streets saying Lord Marlin Stormserpent and most of his household have been slaughtered in Stormserpent Towers, by unknown hands!"

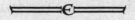

"Where are we, exactly?" Mirt growled.

"Deep in the haunted wing," Alusair replied. "Where the old enchantments are so thick that none of the wizards of war who serve the realm now can scry us or even find us with certainty."

"They'll guess we're here," Storm said dryly, and they were all treated to the sight of a ghost shrugging.

"Let them," the princess replied. "What boots it? I trust we can agree on some things before Glathra can assemble enough Dragons, priests, and mages to dare to march this far in. So start arguing."

Arclath smiled. "You know us well."

Alusair smiled back. "You *are* a noble of Cormyr, Lord Delcastle."

"And although known well for your debonair lack of concern over anything at all," Storm said gravely, "you have been anything *but* unconcerned—or even approaching calm—these last few days. I feel your mistrust. 'Tis high time we talked."

Arclath flushed, let out a gusty sigh, leaned back against a pillar, and folded his arms across his chest. "It is. Though we haven't had much opportunity for leisurely discussion of anything. Nor have I quite dared to say what I think, with Rune justifiably furious if we talk about her rather than to her, and with, well . . . my fear of you, Lady Storm, and he whom you carry."

"True fear? Or just wariness?" Storm asked quietly.

"*Real* fear, Storm. You are . . . a figure out of legend. And so is *he*."

"Elminster," Mirt and the ghost said together.

"Elminster," Arclath confirmed. "Servants of a goddess, hurlers of magic that can shatter castles and level mountains and all of that; I've heard the tales. At many a revel, late at night over flagons, there's talk of you, Lady Storm. It's said you lead whatever Harpers are left in Cormyr, or recruit new Harpers, or both. I grew up hearing about you. Now I've met you and come to care for Rune—and now I fear Elminster wants my Rune, body and soul, to be his thrall."

"And if he did?" Storm asked gently. "Wouldn't that make her the best-guarded woman in all the realms?"

"Not if he can take over anyone he wants to. That makes Rune or anyone he rides something to be used up or abandoned when harmed, tossed aside like a cracked flagon. Moreover, long before the flagon gets cracked, my Rune could be gone forever. This has been my fear. That if ever I leave you, Lady

Storm, alone with Rune, Elminster will enter and conquer her utterly, keeping her body and making all that's left of the real Amarune I love fade away!"

Rune started to say something, then closed her mouth firmly and shot Storm a look of challenge.

The silver-haired woman looked back at them, saw Mirt and Alusair gazing at her with just as much interest, and let out a sigh.

"Fair enough, Arclath. Hear the truth: Elminster can only take over bodies I prepare for him, or have previously prepared. Right now, that means just one person in all the world: Amarune."

Storm took a step forward and stared right into Arclath's eyes. "He cannot take over your body unless you choose to let him—willingly."

"I don't believe you," Arclath whispered.

"Yes, and that's the problem that's been hovering like a shadow between us," Storm agreed sadly. "A shadow I'd love to be rid of."

She strode a few steps away through the dusty gloom, then turned back to face him. "I can prove the truth of what I say, Arclath, by going mind-to-mind with you—but I no longer have magic enough to do that without help."

"*Whose* help?" Arclath asked sharply.

"There's a certain enchanted item on display in this palace . . . clear across it, as it happens. Right now, with the Dragons roused and Glathra after us, the trip to fetch it will hold some danger, but—"

"No," Arclath said flatly. "You're carrying Elminster with you, right now. If our minds are, ah, touching, El could come right into mine and overpower me."

"Not so."

"So *you* say. Yet, how do I know Elminster isn't controlling you right now, forcing you to speak—"

"Enough of this," Alusair snapped, soaring over their heads. "You, Lord Delcastle, hold an opinion of the Sage of Shadowdale that's far from how I see him, and I've known him for—gods help me!—more than a century, now. Hear this, my royal command: Stop refusing all offers to show you truth, and accept one of them. Cormyr needs wise nobles not just stubborn ones!"

Arclath gazed up at her. "Your royal command? I'm sorry, Princess, but as Glathra said, you're dead. Your time for giving commands is past."

"Is it now? Well," Alusair announced, her voice suddenly as sharp as a sword, "my time for keeping my royal patience is certainly at an end!"

She plunged down out of the dimness like a vengeful arrow, straight into Arclath—and stayed there.

As they all watched, Lord Arclath Delcastle gasped, stiffened, and started to shiver.

Chapter
FOURTEEN

Sunderings and Wild Chases

Some lead boring, humdrum lives of drudgery groaned about,
taxes, and bitterness, as we watch the daring and glittering
rise and fall, entertaining us. Yet for the few, life is far from
routine, nor yet safety. Hearts pounding, nerves afire—
for them, it's all shouting, sunderings, and wild chases.

Roryndrel Tanroun, Sage of Athkatla
Lives Are Falling Leaves
published in the Year of the Quill

The *cold*, the clawing *cold* . . .

Arclath fought to breathe, struggled to stay on his feet,
tried to speak . . .

And lost all battles.

Sinking down, everything going gray, he was only vaguely
aware of Rune shrieking and clutching at him.

Her fingers were warm, but everything else was colder,
darker. A deadly chill that had a cutting edge of fury cruised
angrily through his innards, searing his mind with a pride and
grief greater than anything he'd ever felt.

So, that's what it feels like, to be the ghost of a princess.

You have no *idea, naïve lordling,* came a snarl from the
depths of his mind.

He was sliding down the pillar, his limbs as heavy as stone,
and had reached his knees, his mouth slack and his head hanging,
before the ghost of Alusair Obarskyr curled out of his chest like
a wisp of smoke and snapped, "Helpless, yet? I want you broken,
Delcastle, if that's what it'll take to have you let Storm or Elminster
enter your head and *show* you what it's like—and that El has no
intention of keeping Amarune's body or destroying her mind."

"You . . . *tyrant*," Arclath managed to hiss, glaring at her.

"Yes, I am that," the face floating in front of him agreed bleakly. "I had to be. They called me the *Steel* Regent for a *reason*, Arclath. I accept your judgment."

She drifted closer, her chill taking the last color from his face. "Yet, hear my judgment of you: 'tis time for you to be wiser, Lord Delcastle. Your friends need you to be, and the realm needs this, too."

She backed away—the gods granting a small mercy—and Arclath could move again.

He looked at Mirt. "And what's *your* judgment of me, Lord of Waterdeep? Am I the stubborn, callow fool these elder folk think I am?"

"Of *course* ye are, lad. Ye're a noble of Cormyr! Stubborn, callow fools is what most nobles are—and stay, unless someone gives them a boot up the behind. Ye just got one. Will it work, I wonder?"

Arclath looked at Amarune, whose arms were still around him. "You, Rune? Do you think I'm a fool?"

Her eyes were two banners of love. Two sad, proud pools.

"I think you're a tower of strength who refuses to surrender," she replied quietly. "But unlike the many bullies among your fellow lords—that Windstag, for one—you prefer to hide your strength, rather than use it as a daily weapon. I love you for that. My Lord Fool."

Arclath blinked at her then slowly grinned. "I . . . see. And as you see so much more swiftly and clearly than I do, I put my fate in your hands. School me, Rune. Even if you use Elminster to do so."

Amarune looked at Storm.

Who shrugged. "I know not if El's recovered enough to do or say anything."

Slipping off one of her boots, she reached inside. When she withdrew her arm, it was cloaked in clinging ashes up to the elbow.

Rune reached out, Storm clasped the dancer's hand, and ashes raced along their joined arms like lightning.

They watched Amarune shudder, arch backward, and roll her eyes up until only the whites showed. She swayed.

Arclath caught her to guard against falling, and watched her give Alusair a glare before rasping in Elminster's voice, "Is this wise? When ye crowd young lordlings, 'tis my experience most respond wildly, doing much harm. I'm not in the disaster business."

"El?" Storm asked cautiously. "How are you?"

"Dreadful. Ye?"

Storm smiled. "I've been better."

"Huh. I suppose all of us here can say as much." Rune looked at Mirt. "Well met again, old thief."

"Ho, ancient destroyer," Mirt responded cheerfully. "Ye seem to surround yerself with fine lasses."

" 'Tis what I do. Until I've trained replacements, at least. Which reminds me . . ."

Rune turned to Arclath and sank against him in their mutual embrace. "Kiss me," she growled into his face, in Elminster's incongruous voice.

Arclath winced. "You're . . . coming into my mind?"

"Aye. Not eagerly, lad, not as any sort of a conqueror—but now that Luse has forced us into this, I may as well. Just as soon as I prepare you,"

Arclath frowned but shook his head in surrender. And kissed the woman in his arms.

As their lips parted, Arclath's face changed subtly. He stiffened, gently pushed Rune away, and strode off down the passage.

After he went a few pillars distant, well into the gloom and with Alusair gliding after him to make sure no skeletons were lurking, he turned and came back.

"Right," he said slowly. "I've seen your truth. I believe you."

He backed himself against a wall. "You really don't intend to conquer Rune or me, or keep our bodies overlong. Just borrow them briefly when you think it truly needful." He drew his sword. "Yet know this, Elminster of Shadowdale—I'll resist you still."

He held his blade up and ready. "I want to like you. I want to trust you. Yet, your mind is like a mighty mountain, where mine is a small stone."

He hefted his sword, looking steadily into Amarune's eyes over it. "I believe a mind *that* much more powerful than mine, belonging to a mage who's had a thousand years and more to practice deception, can lie to me. Not just with words as any man does, but mind-to-mind."

He looked at Storm, then back at Amarune. "Is this not true?"

"It is," Elminster admitted, "yet there's another truth you should be aware of, Lord Delcastle. Such a deception can't succeed when other minds share in the contact and don't want to deceive. Storm? Alusair?"

The ghost and the silver-haired woman both nodded and started toward Arclath, but the young noble held up a warning hand.

"Don't bother. I'll grant I've been told truth, a princess and a centuries-old Harper attesting to it. It matters not. There's still nothing that you can say, any of you, to make me agree to let you take over my body. I *hate* that you can do that to Rune, and even more that she agrees to it, but you can—so isn't that, before all the gods, *enough*? The rest of us have to make do with one body in life! If it's torn apart, we die. Why must you take over her and me and then someone else, building your own army of mind-slaves? Hey?"

"To save the world," El whispered, "and never an army."

"Sage of Shadowdale, forgive me," Arclath replied curtly, "but I still don't believe you. I saw in your mind that you must recruit Cormyr's war wizards. Are they not an army?"

"A question, Lord Delcastle," Storm asked softly. "You swear you'll never let Elminster into your head or let him ride your body. If Cormyr's survival hung in the balance, or Amarune's life, or the continuance of House Delcastle . . . would you trust *me* to enter your mind and control your body?"

Arclath stared at her, feeling his face going hot. He was aroused by the idea and ashamed of being so; could they tell that? Could they *all* tell that?

Storm always looked so wise; Elminster always seemed two strides ahead of whatever he thought . . . and the Princess Alusair had done much, years and years ago . . .

He couldn't take this. Fool or not, he *could* not—

He had to get away, off by himself to think. Away even from Rune.

Slamming his fist against the wall, Arclath spun away from it and ran, swinging his sword as he sprinted as if the empty air were foe upon foe that had to be slashed open and slain.

No one called his name or ran after him. No one at all.

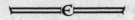

Lord Broryn Windstag looked up from the nearly empty decanter and scowled.

"Back again? Aereld, I told you to leave us alone! We've important matters to discuss—"

The old steward bowed very low. "Y-yes, Lord Master! Please believe me when I say I interrupt you with the greatest of reluctance! You have a visitor, a lord who was a great friend of your father and always welcome in this house, who tells me he comes on a matter of great urgency!"

Windstag grimaced. The priests had healed him, but somehow the pain lingered—and he *hated* surprises.

"Well," he snarled testily, "announce him, then!"

The steward bobbed even lower then scurried away, returning before Windstag could finish trading "What *now?*" looks with his frightened cronies Stonestable, Ormblade, and Handragon. Had the Crown killed Marlin? Were they next? And who was this unexpected—

"The Lord Traevyn Illance," Aereld declaimed grandly, bowing low.

The white-haired lord gave the steward a tight smile and strode into the room. He bore a black walking stick and wore a half-cloak, in the old fashion. His boots were so old and smoothworn that they fitted him like a lady's elbow-length gloves.

"Broryn," he asked gently, "how are you? Word reached my ears that you'd been wounded."

Lord Windstag grinned up at him in genuine pleasure. Illance had been a longtime friend and creditor of his father, and was the one man Broryn had been reared to trust.

Traevyn's sneering son, Rothgar, was no friend to Windstag, Stormserpent, and the others at this parlor table, but the elder Lord Illance was a different sort of man.

"Lord Illance," Broryn said eagerly, rising to offer his hand, "be welcome! I've paid priests and been healed, and count myself fortunate not to have been at this Council, where I might have taken worse harm!"

"That's good to hear," Illance replied, espying an empty chair against the wall and reaching for it. Aereld got there first.

As Illance sat and looked wordless thanks at the steward, he made a swift hand signal that sent the old servant racing from the room. Windstag's eyes narrowed.

"Will you take wine, lord?" he asked, but Illance waved the offered flagon aside.

"I'm not here to drink, lad." He looked around the table. "Forgive my bluntness, but what has befallen this day forces swiftness upon me. These gallant young lords with you—do you trust them?"

"With my life," Windstag said slowly. "Why?"

Illance picked up the nigh-empty decanter, held it up to catch the light, and told it, "I have heard Lord Broryn Windstag makes common cause with Lord Marlin Stormserpent—and others. Are these men all numbered among those others?"

Around the table faces tightened into wary expressionlessness, and hands stole to daggers.

"Yes," Broryn Windstag admitted. "Again, lord, I ask you: why?"

Illance set the decanter down. "Our brave kingdom is plunging into a time of . . . strife. Sides will be taken, and those who try to avoid declaring their loyalties will suffer. Here I find myself greeting what some might term a 'faction.' I happen to represent an older and more numerous faction that sees itself as too small to prevail in most struggles. Wherefore, I seek to recruit like-minded nobles, joining factions into a larger alliance that might succeed in both saving and reshaping bright Cormyr."

"I confess myself interested, lord," Handragon murmured. "A faction that seeks what, exactly?"

"You are wise enough to seek no names. A test passed." Illance let a fleeting ghost of a smile touch his lips. "Know that certain lords of this land believe our good but often misguided King Foril should be, ah, *protected* by a group of nobles—ourselves and those who join with us. We will hire outland wizards to advise the king—'control' is such an ugly word—as we employ mages, mercenaries, and loyal Cormyreans who cleave to our cause, to hunt down and exterminate those foul subverters of the throne, the wizards of war."

He sat back and looked into the eyes of the young lords around the table, watching them relax in relief . . . then lean forward in excitement.

Good. The ring on his finger that could slay them all would not be needed. Yet.

Lord Windstag could read faces, too. "I think I speak for all of us," he said eagerly, "when I say we are *most* interested in—"

The door banged open without benefit of steward or announcement, and a panting, wide-eyed arrival was in the room before a single dagger could be drawn.

"Save me!" Marlin Stormserpent gasped, almost collapsing onto the table. "You've *got* to hide me!"

"From whom?" Handragon snapped.

"Who's after you?" Lord Illance asked sharply, twisting a ring on his finger until it glowed.

Stormserpent's eyes were wide with terror as he waved a heavy chalice in one hand and a bright-bladed sword in the other.

"He bursts into your *mind*," he hissed in Illance's face, "and hunts you with beholders!"

Everyone was on his feet, talking at once. Decanters toppled, rolled, and shattered unnoticed.

"What *happened*, Marl?" Ormblade demanded, his voice louder than the rest. "Who's after you—"

"*Hold!*" Handragon shouted, drowning out the rest of the question. "Who's *this*?"

He was pointing at the door.

Which stood open again. Framed in it stood the wincing steward, with a man whose stance and garb suggested he was a house servant, but of another household.

"Osbur? What news?" Illance barked, before adding to the rest of the room, "This man can be trusted!"

The man bowed then announced huskily, "I am sent by Lord Elbert Oldbridle with a mess—"

"*Elbert?* What of your master, Lord Olgarth Oldbridle?"

"Dead, Lord Illance. Slain by . . . others, led by a man of Westgate. Lord Olgarth's last orders to me were to pass on a specific warning to his son, if he fell. I did this, and his son—my master, now—bade me seek you out and give you the warning, too."

"Do so."

" 'Competing cabals from Sembia and from Westgate are seeking to subvert senior courtiers of Cormyr during this unrest, so as to either influence or outright rule the Forest Kingdom. Beware Kormoroth and Yestrel and the Lhendreths of Saerloon.' Those were his exact words, Lord Illance."

"Thank you, faithful Osbur. Take yourself back to Lord Elbert, and convey my sympathies for his father's demise. Tell two of my men—the warriors in red you passed, outside the gates—that they're to accompany you, on my orders, for a safe return to your new master. With the city in an uproar, some nobles may see messengers as targets."

The servant bowed low, gave thanks, and departed, the steward going out with him and firmly closing the door.

Stonestable raised his flagon to Illance. "Lord Oldbridle—the unfortunately deceased elder—was of your faction, I take it?"

"Father and son both," Illance replied calmly, guiding the still-panting Stormserpent to a chair. "Olgarth will be missed, for his fellowship and his prudence. This last news he sent,

I'm afraid, surprises me not in the slightest. Lords, we stand squarely at the heart of . . . interesting times for us all."

Marlin Stormserpent made a confused, almost sobbing sound, and all eyes went to him.

"The realm at war . . . what have I done?" he quavered, staring around at their frowning faces. "What have we all done?"

Many young nobles of Cormyr might be languid do-nothings, but there was nothing at all wrong with Arclath Delcastle's legs or lungs. He was racing like a harbor-gale wind, dwindling into the dark and echoing distances of the haunted wing with impressive speed.

With a sigh that would have done any exasperated mother proud, the ghost of Alusair Obarskyr sped after him.

"What's she going to do to him?" Amarune demanded, trying to see where the fleeing noble went. Her voice was that of an angry, frightened young mask dancer, not the rougher tones of the Old Mage.

"Protect him," Storm replied. "This is the haunted wing, remember? Spells, traps, even a few walking skeletons . . ."

"Elminster," Rune said fiercely, "I require the use of my body. *Now.*"

"So ye can pursue him, too? Catch and comfort him? Of course," the wizard within her said—and was gone, falling from her in a thick, momentarily blinding cloud.

"Thank you!" Amarune gasped. And sprinted off into the gloom.

"By the gods," Mirt growled, "but the lass can run! They'll have to be swift spells, traps, and skeletons, to do aught to—"

"Thank you for that cheery thought, Lord Moneylender," Storm told him tartly, as ashes flowed up her legs in an eerie rustling stream, into the tops of her boots.

The moment the stream had ended, she started to run, too.

Mirt sighed gustily, shrugged, and lurched after her, his ragged old boots flapping.

"Rather than tarry alone, I may as well join the parade," he growled aloud, hurling himself along passages and across cobweb-hung chambers. "See Cormyr, dance with its skeletons, leave my mark. Or find my grave at last."

Unseen, behind him, a spider as large as the puffing Waterdhavian's head descended on a thread of its own making, to survey the spot all the noisy humans had just departed.

Torn remnants of its web hung everywhere; there was much work to do. As always.

Chapter
FIFTEEN

The Happy Reign of Chaos

Lords and ladies, hear me now, as I unfold this splendid tale
Of love and murder, betrayal and heroes; it befalls in a kingdom
Splendid and near, that has not known, for many a year
The happy reign of chaos.

> Gulkyn the Jester, the opening of *The Throne
> of Three Kings* by Delmur the Bold Bard
> first staged in the Year of the Dauntless Dwarves

The last of the smoke is gone," the young mage—Caldor
Raventree, a keen-to-prove-himself lad from Arabel—
reported, throwing his shoulders back like a Purple Dragon
on parade. "Sixteen spells it took us, to make sure."

"Good," Wizard of War Yarjack Blamreld replied curtly.
"So, who's been found?"

He had Dragon officers trotting up to keep him apprised of
that throughout the cautious search of Stormserpent Towers,
but he was interested to see if Raventree was a "do my job
and pay no attention to anything else" sort, like the last eager
youngling he'd been saddled with . . . or someone who just
might turn out, after some firm training, to be halfway useful.

"Names, I know not, but I saw the Lady Stormserpent
and twoscore others, all of them garbed as house servants. I've
heard nothing of Lord Marlin Stormserpent being found, yet."

"How many dead?"

"Six or seven, but the priests say more may die. There's
much coughing among the revived, and none can walk yet."

Absently Blamreld caught hold of his scraggly beard, tore a
fistful of loose hair out of it, and flung it away into the breeze.
He always did, when thinking hard.

So, who got into a noble mansion undetected—through a cordon of Dragons and Crown mages, himself among them, yet—and caused poisoned smoke to rise from smashed vials throughout the place, before vanishing again? Sending a beholder, or perhaps the illusion of one?

"You can entrust the questioning of the pris . . . er, survivors, to me," said Raventree. "Ah, overseeing it, that is. Of *course*, all of our fellow Crown mages will be—"

"Of course they will. And so long as they remember as well as you do that these good Stormserpent folk are blameless citizens and not prisoners, I have every confidence I can leave this in your hands. The count of the dead is now—?"

"Ah, still seven, Yar—ah, Saer Blamreld."

"Just 'Blamreld,' Raventree. We're all wizards of war here!"

"Uh, yes, sae . . . er, Blamreld."

Blamreld scratched his bulbous, unlovely nose. "Search the place again. Loose floorboards, bookcases that move, any wall that looks thick enough to hold a hidden passage . . . seek not just young Stormserpent but every last sword and chalice, goblet, flagon, or loft-stemmed metal bowl. Oh, and *any* concealed coin, gems, or weapons. Bring them all here to me. Our fox has probably fled, but if he has a den here, I want it found."

Raventree managed to hide his sigh of exasperation with a curt nod before he raced off into the mansion again.

Yarjack Blamreld strode away, passing the steady stream of underpriests arriving to help tend the still-coughing folk of Stormserpent Towers. Lady Stormserpent had been safely whisked to the palace, apparently healthy, and safely away from the clumsy interrogations of young Raventree. That was what mattered.

That, and the beholders, of course. If those terrors were real and not illusory. Glathra and all the veterans had to hear about them, at once.

Out on the Promenade, an air of worry and excitement prevailed—and *everyone* was talking, in a din that made Blamreld wince more than once. Many commoners with hastily loaded carts seemed to be in a hurry to leave the city, and servants in a riot of liveries seldom all seen at once under the open sky in Suzail were milling about trading gossip about the war at Council.

Interestingly, although watchful Dragons were much in evidence, there was no sign at all of nobles or their bodyguards, nor any fighting in the streets.

The talk around Blamreld as he strode purposefully back to the palace was in agreement on one matter, though: Cormyr was heading for civil war. Fast.

"I'm getting too old for this," he muttered to himself, tearing out another generous handful of beard.

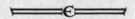

Wizard of War Welwyn Tracegar shook his head grimly. "They're saying Foulweather was killed, and Briarbroke, too. Not that either's much loss, but if the realm is plunged into war ..."

"Barelder and Tantorn, I heard," his fellow Crown mage Joreld Nurennanthur replied, as they strode along Battlebanners Passage paying no attention at all to its familiar and seemingly endless succession of faded trophies. They were headed for a moot with the Lady Glathra that neither was eager to attend. "Not worth anyone fighting for, wouldn't you say?"

"Huh. I'm thinking some lords'll fight over anything at all, right now, and that's what Glathra and the rest are so worried about. I just hope her worry doesn't mean she gets to screeching and cuts our pay or sets us to guarding dung heaps in the stables, or some such. She's a right battlebrand when she gets going!"

"I wish she *would* get going, somewhere far from here! Then the rest of us could sit down over wine and good cheeses and the best palace cooking, king and every last lord, and sort it all out. Or just sit feasting and arguing for a year or more, while we go on living our lives with nary a hint of war! Why—"

Someone burst out of a door and raced across the long passage, far ahead. One person. A man with a sword.

Tracegar and Nurennanthur traded looks, then shrugged in unison. Such a sight would be cause for full and instant alarm at any other time, but since the disaster at Council, the palace seemed bursting with scurrying servants and messengers, and clanking Purple Dragons, too.

Those Dragons waved shields and spears wherever they went, and though this hadn't been a Dragon in armor, and he'd had a sword and not a spear, it *was* just one man.

They strode on and looked left and right when they reached the spot where the running man had crossed the passage. The door he'd come through and the one he'd left by both stood ajar. The narrow passages beyond both were empty and dimly lit. As usual.

They exchanged glances again, then hastened on their way. Being tardy in appearing before Glathra would *not* be wise.

"So which lord was trying hardest to slice up the king, anyhail?" Tracegar asked. "I came to the west doors, staring straight into twoscore brawling lords, and couldn't see a thing befalling the royals!"

Nurennanthur snorted. "Well, that's a matter of some dispute, as old Hallowdant is fond of saying. I got there too late to—"

Engrossed in this exciting discussion, both men entirely missed the beautiful young woman who sprinted across the passage right behind them, her hair streaming behind her, following the same route the man with the sword had taken.

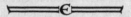

An ambitious young wizard of war, whom both Tracegar and Nurennanthur held a low opinion of, could hardly miss her, however—being as she ran into and right over him as he stepped out of a room with his head down, intent on the scroll he'd just selected.

The scroll went flying; he crashed to the flagstones fighting for breath and feeling decidedly bruised; and his assailant raced on without a moment's hesitation.

Toward the well-lit Loyal Maid's Hall, as it happened, so Wizard of War Surgol Velard could watch her gale-swift sprint.

To his mind, an unfamiliar young woman running through the palace could only mean trouble. She must be a thief—or worse.

Having regained his feet and his breath, Surgol Velard raised his hands grandly, aimed his wand with his usual unnecessary but satisfying flourish—and sent her to sleep.

Velard walked over and blinked down at the fallen woman. Crown and Throne, but she was *beautiful!* Not much older than he was, if that. This was one interrogation he'd handle himself.

His first, and overdue. Veteran war wizards seemed to think him unready for such duties, but thankfully—during this brief reign of chaos—there were no older Crown mages around to order him about, finding fault with what he said and did, or to step in and sweep him aside.

"Guards!" he called hopefully, excitement rising in him. "Guards!"

Two duty Dragons were always stationed in Loyal Maid's Hall, and he was pleased when they came trotting, respectful frowns on their faces just as if he were the lord warder, or Lady Glathra in full roar.

"Manacle this captive," he ordered sternly, "and secure her by the throat to a wall ring in the Mages' Dutychamber off the Long Passage. The keys here in my hand, the moment you're done."

"Of course, saer," they murmured, plucking up the limp woman as if she were a rag doll. A beautiful rag doll that needed handling as gentle as it was thorough.

"What're you doing to her?" Velard snapped.

"Orders, saer. All captives to be searched for weapons, saer."

"Unless *I* countermand such *standing* orders, loyal blades! Stop pawing her, and get her to the dutychamber!"

"Yes, saer."

Was that unison reply sullen? Well, no matter. As long as they obeyed.

"Bear up, Lord Stormserpent," Illance said sternly. "You can't expect to prod the sleeping lion and then quail when it awakens with a roar."

"B-but they've been waiting for this," Marlin hissed at him, eyes wild. "The man with the beholders, the one who takes over minds! He's of the palace!"

"A courtier?" Illance asked sharply. "How do you know this?"

"He's been in my head," came the snarled reply, accompanied by a trembling grab for the nearest decanter.

After a long, deep swig—amid the gasps that greeted his latest words—Stormserpent added, "I know not his name or face, but he's someone of rank who gives orders. Not a maid or cook or doorjack—someone who *matters*."

"These beholders," Lord Illance snapped. "Were they alive—or did they look dead or wounded, perhaps rotting? Think hard, now. Try to remember how they looked."

Marlin stared at him then blinked. Frowned, and blinked again.

"They *did* look rotten, here and there," he said slowly. "Yes ..."

Lord Illance nodded and sat back, looking around the table. "Some of the older, more madwits wizards of war were working with such foul things. Your mindworm must be one of them. If they're after you now, these Crown renegades, we've no time to waste."

Three lordlings started to speak at once, but Illance held up a hand, and silence fell in an instant. He leaned forward to peer into Marlin's eyes.

"Hear me well, Lord Stormserpent," he said, in a voice that was soft yet had a hard, sharp edge to it. "The only way to avoid being hunted down and butchered as a traitor is to use your pair of blueflame ghosts—"

A sudden tension filled the air, a bristling around the table. Illance held up his other hand to quell it and continued.

"Oh yes, lord, your mastery of them has been noticed by more than a few lords of this land, believe me. No courtiers yet, I hope, save perhaps this traitor with the death tyrants— but *your* only hope is to trust that he dare not reveal himself yet. Use your ghosts, just as soon as you can, to seize King Foril."

The tension this time came with amazed oaths, but Lord Illance had run out of hands with which to quell.

"Then," he continued, his eyes still locked on Marlin Stormserpent's, "you must deceive our aging Obarskyr into thinking you are daringly rescuing him from the ghosts, in a staged battle. Which all of us around this table must help you plan, without delay."

Marlin stared at him, eyes brightening as he saw the way out of certain doom before him.

"Yes!" he shouted, bringing an eager fist down on the table, which made the decanters dance. "By all the gods, *yes!* Brilliant, Lord Illance! Simply *brilliant!*"

For so it was. Most nobles knew King Foril Obarskyr was a lot less than the kindly and just man the commoners thought him to be. He was a deluded, out-of-touch old fool.

So this "rescue" of him from fell ghosts was almost certain to succeed.

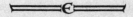

Storm paused at the open door, seeing the door opposite standing open as well. Then she strode across the grand passage as if she were a queen.

A queen managing very regally to utterly ignore the fat, wheezing old man in floppy boots who was following her.

What she saw three steps down the next stretch of narrow passage made her stiffen, then glide to one wall and freeze there, waving at Mirt to do the same.

With a sigh that should have been soundless but wasn't, he obeyed. Not that he could see past Storm's curves to learn what had alarmed her.

Storm cared not; she was too busy intently watching two Purple Dragons carrying a limp, senseless Amarune Whitewave off in the direction of the Long Passage, with a self-important young war wizard preening in their wake.

"Can you proceed very, *very* quietly from here on?" she whispered over her shoulder.

"I believe so," Mirt growled amiably, not much louder than a husky whisper.

Storm nodded and stalked forward in utter silence.

He followed, just a trifle more noisily.

Which meant the two curtly dismissed Dragons, returning to their posts in Loyal Maid's Hall with mingled regret and resentment, didn't hear either of them.

Storm hoped that the door she chose to bypass the guards and reach the Long Passage unnoticed would lead to a deserted chamber.

She and her wheezing shadow reached one door of what she knew was a war wizards' dutychamber, in time to hear a faint rattle of chain.

Unashamedly, she put her ear to that door.

"They didn't find any weapons," a nasal young voice mused, "but I stopped their search, didn't I? Which means it's only prudent, before I awaken this intruder, to search her myself. Now how does this undo, I wonder?"

Storm turned, met Mirt's questioning gaze, and moved back to where she could whisper into his ear. "Go along the passage to the other side of this room, and very noisily bang open its far door. Take care to keep behind the door, in case he casts a spell."

Mirt grinned, nodded, and lurched off to obey.

The moment she heard that far door bang, Storm wrenched open the door in front of her and launched herself at the back of the young wizard's neck.

He heard her and was starting to turn—

But "starting" was more than a breath too late.

To the floor he went, struck senseless, keys rattling out of his hand.

Storm closed the door she'd come through, then went to the other door and looked out. There was no sign of Mirt. After peering up and down a deserted passage, she frowned, shrugged, and closed the door.

The young mage had a wand at his belt, a slender coin purse, and a knife so small and blunt it could only see practical use spreading pastes and jams. She took the wand, knowing the symbols painted at its ends; this end gave sleep, and that one awakened.

She touched Amarune with "that" end, then slid the lone ring from the wizard's finger. By its design, it had to be one of the spell-reflecting bands Caladnei had enchanted, and betimes loaned to certain Harpers.

Donning it, Storm caught up the keys and freed Amarune. Ankles in a walking chain, wrists to a chain passed around her back, and a throat collar chained to a wall-ring with a length of links short enough to keep her standing—or she'd strangle. Such restraints might prove useful later, but she had no place to hide them and no quiet way to carry them, so she let them be.

"S-storm?" Rune asked quietly, staring around the room and feeling her throat. "What happened to me? One moment I was running, starting to lose my breath, and then—"

"This bright young wizard cast a spell of sleep on you," Storm told her. "Which means time enough has passed—being as I've heard no great tumult in *that* direction—that Arclath must have got out of the palace without dispute or alarm, and clean away into the city."

"Meaning?"

"There's no use chasing him. We'll seek him at Delcastle Manor later, but right now I'm *hungry*, and by the rumblings your innards have been making, you are, too. So, kitchens first. Then we'd best have a little talk with Lady Glathra, if we don't want wizards chasing us every time we turn a corner in this palace."

Rune opened her mouth to protest, then sighed and shut it again. She *was* hungry. And weary, too.

Once again, the wisest thing Amarune Whitewave could do was give in.

Thank the gods, the Sammartael woman had gone away again without daring the dimness of Sraunter's back room—let alone the darkness of his cellar.

The alchemist was back at work in his shop, having slipped Crownrood a few sips of wine tainted with something harmless that had sent him to sleep. Manshoon, sitting alone on the alchemist's best chair—which didn't say much for the man's taste in comfortable furniture—felt much better.

He would just have to be mindful from now on that he *did* have limits. No more than two minds at once, and only one if it was strong and hostile.

His scrying globes had all burst or faded while he'd been fighting to stay conscious, leaving the cellar very dark.

As he needed no light, he didn't bother seeking any. Instead, he worked a spell to reach out to the mind of Wizard of War Rorskryn Mreldrake.

And waited, sitting in the darkness, a very long time as surprise gave way to irritation, then anger . . . and then resignation.

His spell had failed.

Mreldrake was well shielded, dead, or his own newfound limitations were greater than he'd thought.

Manshoon cast the spell again, this time seeking the mind of Lady Highknight Targrael.

Again, a long time later, he was forced to admit failure.

Future emperor or not, he had limitations, all right. Which meant he should behave accordingly.

Time to think again as a mortal, living man. Wary, prepared for battle, and hunted by alert foes.

His beholders would be better scattered. One death tyrant and a beholderkin hidden—separately—in the palace, another pair in Sraunter's attic, and the rest elsewhere, in some more defensible stronghold than this shop . . .

Was it time to reawaken Talane? Probably, but given the

happy reign of chaos at the palace, he had to know what was going on there. So, Fentable first . . .

"There's *always* soup, hot biscuits, garlic butter, and sausages in the end kitchen," Storm explained, "for servants who must eat at full scurry. These covered tankards aren't for ale; they're for soup."

"I'll try to bear that in mind," Amarune replied, feeling full and much better for it, "the next time I storm the palace."

Storm chuckled as she went to a small, worn old door at the end of the room.

Rune sighed. "Whither *now*?"

"A particular pantry."

"Where the rarest dragon meat's curing?"

"No, it's all crocks of jam and pickles."

"Then why—?"

"It has a loose stone."

"I . . . see." Then a thought struck Rune. "A stone Harpers know about?"

"Precisely."

Evening was coming down outside as they hastened past a small window into a maze of passages and pantry doors. Storm seemed to know where she was going, and soon enough snatched a glowstone from its wire rack, flung open a nearby door, and stepped into a dark, low-ceilinged room crammed with large crocks and smelling faintly of brine.

"It's been threescore summers since I last set foot in here," she murmured.

"Oh, surely not," Rune began, but her words faltered when the silver-haired woman turned eyes as old as kingdoms on her.

"It wasn't until I went into the inner kitchen, just now, that I remembered this place," Storm said. And sighed. "El has the same problem. Doors open in our minds unexpectedly—doors we often didn't know were there. Sometimes what's revealed is neither safe nor comfortable, and we rarely have time to deal with it properly, no matter what it is." She smiled crookedly. "As my sister still says from time to time, at least it's never dull, being mad."

Amarune stared at her, not knowing what to say.

Storm gave her a wink and turned to a particular fat crock on the floor, under a shelf. Moving it out into the room, she pushed on one end of a stone that had been beneath it. The stone shifted a trifle, and she thrust a finger into the revealed crevice and flipped the stone up into her hand. The recess under the stone was small, and she drew out something that looked like a scrap of chainmail. A purse?

"What's that?" Rune asked.

Storm put a finger to her lips for silence, replaced stone and crock, then fished inside the chainmail for something and held it out to Rune.

It was a plain iron finger ring.

"Put this on."

"It's magical?"

"Yes. Ironguard. Doesn't affect any metal you carry, but unenchanted metal coming at you goes right through you as if you're made of smoke. There are four other rings just like it in this—which is a paralyzing glove that I don't think works, anymore. All of these are old Harper items the Crown mages won't readily be able to trace. Tell no one about this."

"And I'll be needing this why, exactly?"

Storm gave Rune a sad look. "I rather think, Amarune, that we're going to war."

CHAPTER
SIXTEEN
FRIEND AND FOE

Masked, all our lies we spend as changing winds of fortune blow
The trick that fails many in the end is in time enough coming to know
Who is staunch, trustworthy friend—and who, behind smiles, is foe.

from the ballad *The Long and Deadly Dance*
by Marlarra the Kissing Minstrel
first performed in the Year of the Lost Ships

S ir Winter shook his head.
"A few lords have traveled the streets from club to club,
or from lodgings or their city mansions to various eateries," he
replied, "ringed by well-armed bodyguards, of course. But as
for pitched battles in the streets, or signs of armed men gathering anywhere for an assault—nothing. None at all. Thus far, at
least. We remain watchful."

Glathra pursed her lips. "Perhaps the lords of this land are
more sensible than I judged them to be," she muttered.

She nodded a farewell to Winter, who returned her nod and
hurried away. A steady stream of reports was reaching his office,
and it would be tragic to miss something crucial because he was
busy relaying "no troubles at all" to a demanding wizard of war.

"Thornatar?" she barked.

"Here, Lady Glathra. We've restored order in the palace.
The wounded nobility have all been tended, questioned, and
removed to their own lodgings. Three listening spells cast on
them have abruptly been ended, we presume by hired mages,
but the rest remain in force and have thus far turned up
nothing of interest."

"Good. I am particularly interested in anything involving
Lords Emmarask and Halvaeron. If even the slightest *possibly*

useful or cryptic utterance is heard, my ears are to be apprised of it without delay, no matter the time or circumstances."

"As you decree," Thornatar replied, bowing as low as if Glathra had been an Obarskyr.

She grimaced, shook her head, and turned to look for Menziphur, the court alchemist. The man could creep around as silently as a spider! *Where*, by all the—

Her eyes fell on two faces in the crowd patiently standing around her—faces that should not have been there.

Storm Silverhand and the young mask dancer, Amarune Whitewave.

Biting back a curse, she snapped, "And what are the two of *you* doing here?"

"Well met, Glathra," Storm said dryly. "We'd like to meet with King Foril Obarskyr. Soon, if that's at all possible."

Glathra stared at her, guilt and rage rising in her with almost choking speed, emotions she'd thought she was done with, and—and—

"Absolutely not," she heard herself snap. "Your powers, Storm, are no doubt exaggerated by legend, yet remain mysterious. I could be dooming His Majesty by letting you within two *rooms* of him, for all I know. As for mask dancers, King Foril's standards have always been rather higher than that—and though she's young and there's but one of her, she's a mystery, too. For all I know she could be full of poison and sent to work regicide by foes of the Obarskyrs."

The courtiers, Dragons, and war wizards around her were silently bristling, all now facing Storm and the dancer—and drawing back from them.

Glathra went on, wanting them all to hear her every word, so they'd know to watch over these two when she wasn't around to give them direct orders.

"Nor are there just the two of you, whatever your protests to the contrary," she said. "Princess Alusair, Vangerdahast, and Elminster walk with you, whether we can see them or not."

She raised her voice and pointed at Storm and Amarune dramatically. "I would consider it treason on my part even to let you get close to our king, when for all I know you'd promptly try to take over his wits somehow and rule Cormyr from the grave."

The two women stood alone, now, in a circle of frowning, hard-staring men. Glathra gave them a triumphant smile.

"Tracegar? Nurennanthur? Wands out, and capture these two for me. Work no magic that can harm the rest of us, and slay them not, but short of that, do anything needful to take them dow—"

Sudden light flared out of empty air right in front of Glathra's face, and from out of it a voice she knew cried, "Glathra? Lady Glathra! Lord Delcastle broke through our post here! We—our Dragons wounded him, but he cut a few of them, too!"

Glathra felt her temper start to slip, and ground her teeth. "And how is it, Harbrow," she asked sharply, "that *one* lone noble is able to fight his way through a guardpost of eight Dragons and no fewer than *five* wizards of war, you among them? Answer me that!"

"Delcastle wasn't alone, lady! The ghost of Alusair defended him and froze us all, one after another. She—we could not stand against her. She . . . stopped us from capturing him."

"My Arclath!" Rune burst out. "Where is he? How badly did you hurt him?"

"Lady?" the distant war wizard asked, obviously puzzled at who was crying these questions at him.

"*Thank* you for your report, Harbrow," Glathra told him firmly. "Defend your post until I order you to do otherwise, or else send relief."

"Lady, I hear and obey," came the reply before the light winked out.

Amarune strode toward Glathra. "Where is he?"

Glathra ignored her. "Tracegar!" the wizard of war snapped, turning away. "*Deal* with these two! The rest of you—"

Something slammed into her ankles, and Glathra toppled helplessly, letting out a startled shriek—a cry that ended abruptly as she lost her breath against unyielding flagstones.

Hard fingers clawed their way along her—the mask dancer, who was—

A flash and a ringing sound rose into a second shriek, this one singingly magical, as Tracegar's wand blast struck the invisible protection conferred by Glathra's ward-ring and rebounded at him. Only for the spell to be turned back by his lesser ward, and die in a harmless cacophony as it reached Glathra again.

Almost snarling in fresh fury, Glathra Barcantle found her feet and spun to face the mask dancer.

Only to hurtle to the floor again, with even more bruising force.

Storm had tripped her! The bitch had got herself *right* behind Glathra, somehow, and was now grabbing at the dancer's shoulder and hissing, "Come! Harbrow was guarding the Hall of Victories—*this* way!"

The dancer dashed down the indicated passage without hesitation, Storm right behind her.

"Intruders! Villains! *Traitors!*" Glathra shouted furiously, struggling to her feet with her hair all over her face and her temper in an utter shambles. "Halt! Halt and surrender! I *forbid* you to flee!"

Storm slowed and looked back. "Glathra," she replied crisply, "I think you'd better get used to having your commands ignored by those you have no authority over—or *should* have no authority over. I see neither the royal magician here nor any Obarskyr, and as a noble of this kingdom for centuries, I recall that, except when obeying the direct orders of either royals or the royal magician, wizards of war have very little legal authority. You *pretend* to have the right to order everyone about, but that's a very different matter. I, the Marchioness Immerdusk, defy you, disloyal servant!"

Glathra opened her mouth—and choked on more anger than she'd ever in her life felt before. All words failed her. Utterly.

When they returned, an incoherently snarling string of moments later, she spat a single "Bitch!" in the direction of the swirling silver hair dwindling down the passage, and hurled slumber at the two fleeing women.

Less than a breath later, her own magic got flung back at her, staggering Glathra for an instant as it lit up her ward.

The Silverhand woman could reflect spells back whence they'd come.

Even as Glathra glared after Storm, seething, the two fleeing women turned a distant corner and were gone.

Clenching her fists, Glathra tossed back her head to clear the tangled hair from her face and drew in a deep breath, fighting for calm.

Acutely aware of all the silent men watching her.

Be regal. Your authority is absolute, whatever that lying bitch says. Cloak yourself in it, and serve Cormyr. *Be* Cormyr.

She worked a swift and simple spell, and said into the glow that kindled in the air in front of her, "Harbrow? Two women are coming your way. One of them tall, with long silver hair that moves around her shoulders as if alive; the other one younger, a mask dancer. Storm Silverhand and Amarune Whitewave. Storm—she of the silver hair—can reflect spells back at their casters. The dancer should have no magic at all. You are to capture both, by any means necessary short of slaying them."

She listened to Harbrow's "hear and obey" and ended her spell, smiling grimly.

She shouldn't have to wait long for his report, and it should recount success, now that she'd warned them about Storm.

After all, it wasn't just Harbrow, embarrassed by his failure to stop Delcastle and eager to make up for it. He *did* have four other wizards of war with him.

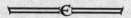

Mirt strolled out the side door of the house behind the stables as if he hadn't a care in the world, the sack of coins purloined from the palace treasury reassuringly heavy on his shoulder.

And why not? He was leaving the merry chaos of the ruling fortress of Cormyr behind, and its rushing guards and wand-waving mages *were* his chief cares in this new world of nigh on a hundred summers since he'd last lorded it in Waterdeep.

Those guardians were busy at various doors and gates trying to keep nobles out, so *this* noble was going to do just that—get out.

He would take rooms at one of the upscale inns along the Promenade, under a false name. "Aghairon Mizzrym" had a certain ring to it. There he'd sip wine and sit awhile and decide what sort of new life to forge for himself.

His first instinct was to flee from the land where at least two young nobles wanted him dead. Flight should be easy, considering Suzail was a port and had always had hidden magical ways that those with coin enough could readily buy the use of, linking it with Marsember, a seedier port where inquisitive Crown authorities seldom received straight answers . . .

Yet he *liked* the feel of Cormyr, turmoil and all.

Haularake, he wanted to stay!

Storm was a damned fine woman, and he liked young Delcastle and his lass, too, but their battles were not his. Save in this wise: if the thick-skulled nobles of this land *did* rise up, they could well shatter the Cormyr he prized—but then again, troubled times offered shrewd merchants wonderful opportunities to establish a profitable business or seize a position of power at court . . . or perhaps even marry into a powerful noble family . . .

Mirt looked down at his food-stained paunch, chuckled, and shook his head.

Well, mayhap there were a few powerful matriarchs, sitting all alone because they were uglier than goats or the hind ends of draft horses, or had tempers to match those of a pain-maddened bull, who might have grown desperate enough to entertain the blandishments of such an old wolf.

Had he patience enough left to endure the less pleasant sides, though, to gain the luxuries that might come from tethering himself to a matriarch? Boredom had never been his friend. Hmmm.

Thinking on this would undoubtedly unfold better if he were in a good chair, with his feet up and a decanter of something splendid to hand.

First, find the right inn . . .

All that was left of the Princess Alusair glided to a reluctant stop in midair, little more than a thin wisp of shadowy air, a dozen strides outside the palace. Arclath Delcastle was gone, vanished along one of the streets on the far side of the Promenade, and she could follow him no farther.

It was time to return to Storm and Amarune and Mirt. She might as well, for she had few enough friends left in the world, and knowing Glathra and how upset all the palace-guarding mages and Dragons were, the three might well need her help, and—

"Hold!" a man's voice rose excitedly, from four rooms deep inside the palace. "You, there! Halt! Lass—woman—you! I'm speaking to you! Halt! Halt or I'll—"

A brief scuffle followed, other men shouted various things at once, and Alusair flew into their midst in time to see a hard-running Amarune Whitewave wobble, lurch, stumble, and fall, head lolling and arms limp. Asleep on her racing feet.

The five Crown mages flanked by two bristling-with-weapons Dragons made no move to catch her. They just watched, a few smirking, as she crashed to the stone floor in a loose, heavy heap.

Alusair swirled up behind them, growing more solid. She could chill all of these cruel swaggerers by plunging through their bodies, but this time she was angry enough that she wanted to slap one of them—Harbrow, who was chuckling heartily down at his spellwork—across the face first, and spit her royal displeasure into his face.

It took a lot of effort to achieve any sort of solidity, even very briefly, and she was still straining to when Storm Silverhand came striding down the passage, long silver hair coiling and slithering about her shoulders like a nest of angry serpents.

"That was *not* well done, Saer Mage," she snapped. "Since when do Cormyr's wizards of war strike down any blameless citizen they see?"

"Since they are ordered to smite particular miscreants and espy two of them," Baern Harbrow told her triumphantly. "This mask dancer—and *you!*"

The wand in his hand spat magic at Storm.

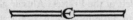

Mirt stared around the luxuriously appointed room—hah-hum, *nice* four-poster; pity he'd no one to share it with—and took a sip of Berduskan Dark.

Then, frowning, he took another.

Frown deepening, he held the glass up to the light.

This was the wine he'd remembered as so special? Either he'd been off his head, this inn was playing him false, or the drink that went by that name these days was poor swill compared to the vintages he'd tasted all those years ago.

He downed the whole goblet in one great gulp, to see if that improved matters. It didn't, and the servant who'd just brought it winced visibly.

Mirt gave the man a hard and heavy look.

After the man started to back away, the Waterdhavian asked gently, "Have you a better wine to recommend to me?"

"N-no, saer. That *is* our best."

"I see," said Mirt, and sat down heavily in the great chair. It groaned under his weight but held up. Well, at least the gods granted some small mercies.

"Bring more," he commanded, and he sat back to commence thinking.

Harbrow's sleep wand struck at Storm Silverhand at the same moment that two of his fellow mages made the mistake of deciding to join in the fun.

Storm smiled.

Caladnei of Cormyr had become her good friend, and they'd worked together for years. She'd shown the silver-haired Harper how to use the ring Storm now wore to do more than simply turn back spells. When more than one magic struck the ring at a time, its wearer could decide where to redirect some or all of those magics.

Storm sent the sleep spells that struck her from three sides all at Harbrow.

Whose feeble defenses bought him just time enough to look surprised before he collapsed to the floor, joining Rune in slumber.

The other four wizards shouted in alarm and scattered, throwing back their sleeves and preparing to hurl *real* battle magics at this obviously dangerous foe. Alusair promptly plunged through the nearest one, to spoil his casting—and was *just* solid enough to give his heart and lungs a good bruising that sent him to his knees, gasping in pain and terror.

Storm didn't wait for anyone to blast her with anything. She sprang at the nearest mage, punched aside his feeble grapplings, took him hard by the throat, and spun him around to serve as a shield as she throttled him.

He tried to shriek and managed to get out a gargling wail— as Storm ran him hard back into the nearest wall, knocking him cold against its stone carvings. As he started to sag in her arms, she took him by one elbow and the opposing thigh and flung him into the next wizard.

By which time the last wizard had gone gray and toppled to the floor, as Alusair hovered in his chest, freezing his heart. Behind him, the mage she'd chilled just before that was crawling away down the passage as fast as he could, with the one whose innards she'd bruised sobbing in terror and feebly trying to follow.

Alusair sped to where she could grin into Storm's still-angry face. "Want me to fell the fleeing?"

Storm frowned. "Just long enough for me to get their rings and wands off them."

"Glathra and the other senior war wizards can readily trace Crown-enchanted items from afar," the ghost warned.

Storm nodded. "If we can put, say, a ring into the keeping of Marlin Stormserpent without his knowing it—in his clothing or belt—it'll draw them to him. Or we can use the wands as lures, if we hide them in places we want war wizards to find."

Alusair gave a low laugh of agreement as she swooped down the passage. A moment later, the most distant fleeing mage moaned in pain and fear as she plunged into him.

Storm watched her sport with the two crawling men for a moment, then relieved Harbrow and the other two nearby mages of their rings and wands.

"El," she murmured, pulling off a boot, "I need you to take over Rune's body and walk her out of here. The war wizards slept her."

Where is "here"? Are we escaping the palace?

"Yes," Storm told the briskly flowing ashes. "Again."

Well, 'tisn't as if we haven't done it before. Glathra still furious with us?

"You could say that," Storm replied dryly.

Good. So long as a wizard of war is enraged at us, we're doing something right.

Chapter
SEVENTEEN
A City Cursed

Castles fall, fires rise, and worse!
We all now dwell in a city cursed!

> from the ballad *This City, Our City*
> by Ondrel Ammandreth, the Minstrel of Castle Ward
> first performed in the Year of the Queen's Honor

Mirt tossed the empty decanter onto the empty bed, glared down at both, and let out a growl.

It was no use. He was as restless as a prowling cat with the flea-itch.

As he'd always been, when it came to ponderings. He always mulled over matters better while he was striding somewhere, *doing* something, rather than sitting idle and alone in luxury . . . and ever-deepening boredom.

Night had fallen, but no matter. If he could walk Dock Ward in Waterdeep and bring his unlovely old hide home more or less intact, he could stroll the well-lit Promenade of Suzail and have a better-than-fair chance of returning to this tarted-up rental hovel in one piece, too.

The coins were hidden where only a strong and determined thief could hope to take them from, flattened behind a wardrobe it would take two strong men—or one sweating, straining, snarling, fat, old Waterdhavian lord—to shift. He had his blades; the desk would mind his key; there was enough loose coin down his boot to buy a cuddle with a dancer if his wandering feet took him past such a place . . .

"Moneylenders aren't alive if they aren't finding trouble," Mirt muttered aloud, "and if ye wander a city, trouble generally soon finds ye. Aye."

Down the sweeping, dark-carpeted stairs he went, under the soft light of many ornate hanging lamps, and wheezed his way out into the street.

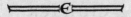

Marlin Stormserpent strode along the shuttered shop-fronts, his darkest cloak swirling around him in the wind of his own haste. His oldest, quietest boots made little sound as he hurried through the night.

He was so excited he was almost choking, and a small worm of fear was rising in his throat, blossoming swiftly now. Illance's plan had seemed so gods-sent, so *right*, back at Staghaven House, but now . . .

Well ahead of him, two blue flames moved quickly in the deepening darkness, side by side. His ghosts were heading straight to the palace.

To imperil the king.

Either the nobles were taking their time mustering warriors and buffing their boots so as to look their best when they broke into rebellion, or the Dragons had done a *very* thorough job of scouring the city—well, this part of it, at least—of armed and excited folk in the streets.

The Promenade, under its usual warm and plentiful lamps, was but lightly traveled in its long sweep around the soaring, imposing bulks of the vast, many-windowed royal court and the older, more castlelike royal palace. Oh, there were people about, aye, all of them afoot—not a cart or wagon to be seen—but no one was shouting or waving a sword or anything else. Most folk were walking alone or in pairs or trios; the only larger group Mirt could see was a watch patrol—Dragons with a war wizard, talking quietly and looking far from excited.

Yet out of lifelong habit, Mirt looked back fairly often as he walked. His first glance was to fix his inn in his mind, the way it looked by night, so he could readily find it again. His second was to mark anyone who might be following him, who'd been in the street at his first glance and seemed to have moved since in a way that suggested Mirt of Waterdeep might be of interest to them.

None such rose to his notice.

Well, hardly surprising, that. He was, after all, no one at all to anyone but a handful of folk currently alive, in this time so long after he'd expected a waiting grave to find him. Living for centuries was for archwizards or god-tainted priests, not fat old moneylenders with smart mouths, who liked to provoke people who thought themselves powerful or important. Why—

Mirt looked back a third time and revised his thinking in an instant.

"Talandor! Caztul! Caztul *caztul!*" he exploded.

There was no mistaking the two men wreathed in ceaseless bright blue flames. Walking purposefully toward him, with drawn swords in their hands.

"Kelstyn, gelkor, and hrasting sabruin!" he added to surrounding Suzail, as he started to hurry, rushing along with his battered old boots—the same footwear that had made the inn's grandly garbed seneschal visibly wince—flapping loudly.

If they were giving chase, there was only one halfway-safe place for him. The damned *palace*. Again.

"This city is cursed—or I am!" Mirt growled as he picked up speed, lurching from side to side in his loudly wheezing haste to be elsewhere.

"I'm too old for this," he muttered. "Damned deadly magics! Why don't these rats-underfoot war wizards police them, hey?"

He hoped to lead the two slayers into the midst of those same Crown mages; if he could dart through or into the detaining arms of war wizards, mayhap his flaming pursuers would come right after him—and the Dragon Throne's tame mages would destroy them.

He cast another swift look back and pushed himself to lurch along faster.

Aye, the wizards were his best hope.

Provided, of course, he reached the palace before the ghosts caught him.

Manshoon had managed to forget how irritating the mind of Understeward Fentable could be.

The trouble lay in Fentable's character; the man was moderately cunning, had learned the arts of deft manipulation and subtle misdirection, and derived real enjoyment from intrigue and the cut and thrust of palace diplomacy.

However, he was only about a fifth as clever as he thought himself to be, and so shallowly gleeful in his petty chasings after *this* chance to browbeat a lowly courtier or *that* opportunity to emphasize his superior rank in dealings with someone just a little below him in court standing that it left Manshoon seething.

"Tiresome" was a polite way of putting it. Wherefore, Manshoon rode Corleth Fentable's mind with a savage, impatient edge to his control. He'd thought it imperative to learn the state of things inside the palace—but wished he hadn't bothered.

The king was in hiding, heavily guarded, and the ever-ambitious Glathra was kinging it as ably as her tireless bullying would reach. While chaos reigned, minor courtiers traded whispered rumors behind closed doors, and higher-ranking court officers cowered in various unexpected chambers, well away from their offices and usual posts, so Glathra's scurrying messengers couldn't readily find them.

According to palace protocol, the—still missing—royal magician and the lord warder could both give orders to the palace understeward; whereas, all other wizards of war, except in times of declared war, could not. Yet, it seemed Glathra called on custom and protocol when they suited her, and blithely ignored them when they did not.

Just as Understeward Fentable blithely ignored the six successive sets of orders she'd had messengers deliver to him. He'd taken care to inform the palace heralds that the Lady Glathra Barcantle had been declared a traitor to the Crown, so her orders were to be ignored. He'd omitted to mention that the declaration of her status was his alone, not a royal one, but the heralds had winked expressionlessly, informing him without a word that they were well aware of that. They knew he was carrying out this empty gesture to preempt Glathra's inevitable move to declare *him* a traitor, the moment she discovered him missing and her orders not carried out.

However, even the lowliest Dragon on guard at court or palace would have found it odd that the palace understeward had departed the palace, at a time when his superior, Palace Steward Hallowdant, was abed and snoring.

It was even more unusual for Fentable to slip out alone, without grand pronouncements and orders, a messenger or three in case a need for them arose, a scribe to capture the most crucial-to-the-realm of his passing thoughts, and a bodyguard or two to emphasize his importance.

Manshoon would have sent him out naked and covered in dung, if it had suited his purposes.

However, on this occasion, it—and anything else that might attract attention—did not. He was riding Fentable forth to meet with certain nobles. Ostensibly to try to arrange a noble cabal to keep the peace and protect both the royal family and all Suzailan courtiers, in the event civil war broke out. In truth, Manshoon intended to use his magic to covertly read the minds of all nobles he got close enough to, to learn who could be used, and how. Fentable's cabal would become Manshoon's power base of allied nobles when he took the throne.

Moreover, there was a chance—admittedly small, but a chance nonetheless—that he might get close enough to the right noble to discover who controlled the blueflame ghost that had appeared at the Council.

It was also high time to begin spreading rumors that would cause public suspicion of the priests of all popular faiths in the kingdom. Thefts, murders, deceptions, baby-devourings . . . the lot. Priests were a peril to vampires, and he wanted them kept busy in his new empire or at least hampered by public resistance and suspicion, not free to work mischief or try to step into the present chaos and restore order, seizing power and influence for themselves in the process.

The most private way out of the palace that didn't involve a damp tunnel and lots of stairs up into this or that tavern or shop along the Promenade was the house behind the stables. Fentable took that route but was barely a block from the palace when he saw an unmistakable wheezing, lurching figure hurrying toward him along the Promenade, casting many swift glances back over his shoulder.

Mirt of Waterdeep, making for . . . the palace?

And right behind him—Fentable came to an abrupt halt, almost before Manshoon felt astonished—were Marlin Stormserpent's pair of blueflame ghosts, rushing along vengefully after the old Lord of Waterdeep.

Manshoon backed Fentable into a doorway to watch the slaughter.

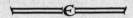

El shook himself and waved his arms—Amarune's slender, shapely young arms—in satisfaction. Gods, but it felt good inside a body this young, strong, and Mystra-kissed *supple*. Why—

"If you're finished enjoying Rune's general health, I'd like to remind you that it won't continue if we tarry here," Storm warned, plucking at his arm.

Obediently El joined her in a sprint down the narrow passage she was heading along. He recognized it; ahead was a door that led to an alcove that was a guardpost presiding over one of the smaller, less important palace doors.

"Why can't matters be as tavern tales have them, for once?" he asked idly as they ran. "No guards at their posts—that sort of thing?"

Storm chuckled and banged open the door to the alcove.

Several startled Purple Dragons cursed and went for their swords, but she marched straight through them with the crisp words, "At ease, loyal Dragons! I'm Lady Glathra, testing a new spell with Wizard of War Tracegar here. If we both look like rather striking women, me with silver hair and him the very image of a certain mask dancer some of you may have seen a time or two, our spells are working. We're off to the Dragon and the Lion, to test our guises on harsh critics."

"I—uh—fair fortune, lady!" the highest-ranking Dragon said hastily, throwing wide the door just as Storm reached for it. She thanked him with a bright smile, stepped out into the night—and stopped, so suddenly that only Amarune's grace and balance kept Elminster from walking right into her.

Mirt the Moneylender was coming down the Promenade, hustling hard and groaning for breath, making for their door just as fast as he could lurch. Behind him, Storm could see the reason for his haste.

Two blueflame ghosts were right on his heels, swords out, with unpleasant grins on their faces.

"A rescue!" Mirt gasped. "A rescue, stlarn it!"

"Of course," Storm said, running to him and taking the winded lord by one shoulder. "*Rune!*"

Elminster took the Waterdhavian's other arm, and they hustled him back through the door.

"Change of plan!" Storm barked at the frowning guards. "Fetch all the Crown mages you can find here, at once!"

They gaped at her.

"*Now!*" she roared, trying to sound just like Glathra. "Go! Run as you've never run before! *Run!*"

The guards ran—three of the youngest right away, the others as Storm gave them glares and finally let go of the panting old lord and advanced on them, snarling like an angry wolf.

"They're right behind us," El murmured, kicking the door shut and swinging Mirt around against the passage wall.

Storm sprang to bar the door. "I'm hoping Luse—"

Two blades burst through the door and bit into the door bar in her hands.

She tugged, even as the blueflame slayers pulled, freeing and withdrawing their swords. Storm hastily barred the door.

A moment later, the wards alongside it flared into sudden visibility, bulging and glowing as the ghosts sought to walk right through the thick stone palace wall.

"There's no time to wait for Alusair," Elminster growled. "If I go wild-witted, Stormy One . . ."

"Of course," Storm replied, readying her blade.

The ward went blinding white, flared into wild, spitting lightning in front of Elminster, spat forth an angry shower of sparks—and a glowing blue sword burst through that radiance, its wielder right behind it.

Elminster smiled, sidestepped the sword, and gently said a spell right into the ghost's face.

All sound went away in an instant, or so it seemed—but swirling dust and racing cracks across nearby plaster wall adornments told El he'd just been deafened. The ghost's blue light winked out, leaving behind an immobile, blackened skeleton holding a sword, and the palace ward shrank away, retreating along the passage in both directions like two racing grassfires.

Only to roil in the distance momentarily—and come rushing back.

The blue flames rekindled, the motionless skeleton was once more a solid-looking man on the move—that the wards slammed into from both sides.

Whereupon Elminster's sight went away, too. He was briefly aware of flying helplessly through the air, then encountering something smooth, flat, and very hard.

Only to rebound back off it, to walk forward blindly on legs that suddenly seemed made of rubber or perhaps of string . . .

"They could build palaces, in those days," he observed brightly, or thought he did, before lightning stabbed him in thousands of places and took all Suzail away.

The blast smote Fentable's ears like a hard-swung kitchen skillet, its bright flare slashing the night as if the darkness were a smooth-stretched cloak that could be sliced with a knife.

Cringing in the doorway with hands clapped to his ears, Fentable blinked at the sudden brightness, but clearly saw the old and massive palace door blown high into the air and flung across the Promenade to smash hard into the stone front of a grand shop-below-and-clubs-above building, then crash to the ground in splintered ruin, raising dust.

Right behind the whirling door tumbled a figure wreathed in flickering blue flames.

It struck the shop front lower down, on a central pillar flanked by the shuttered shop windows, and slid limply down the unyielding stone to the ground.

Fentable might have been terrified, but Manshoon was merely astonished.

He stared at the felled host, then at the gaping doorway whence the door had come.

Framed in it was the mask dancer, Amarune Whitewave, reeling unsteadily as she stared out into the street, arms raised and flung wide, lightning playing angrily around her hands.

She'd just blasted down a blueflame ghost?

Just what had happened to this hitherto unskilled-at-Art young mask dancer, descendant of Elminster, to make her an archwizard in ... what, days?

Manshoon's eyes narrowed.

The very cobbles underfoot shook as the door burst out of its frame and went flying.

Pressed hard against the Promenade side of the palace wall right beside that door, a blueflame ghost watched another blueflame ghost hurtle past.

Then, not even looking to see what befell that fellow slayer, and caring less, it ducked through the gaping doorway into the palace.

Right past a reeling, drooling, empty-eyed lass in the grip of snarling lightning it raced, and a groaning, also-reeling, silver-haired woman beyond, to pursue a fat man stumbling along a narrow passage that led deeper into the palace, trailing a muttered sea of curses.

The ghost smiled gleefully as it ran and raised its sword.

Mirt saw the blue reflections of its flames looming up close behind him and turned grimly to give battle.

The ghost's grin widened. One slash at most this might take, two for sport, and then—

A sword that was more ghostly shadow than steel slashed at blue flames—and sliced them into dark nothingness.

The running ghost faltered in sheer astonishment.

And found itself staring into a smile as full of grim glee as its own, adorning the floating face of a ghostly woman in leather half-armor, her helmless hair flowing free as she stood in midair like a shield, barring the way to the panting, wheezing old lord.

"Dare to come into *my* palace to slay a man, against *my* laws, in *my* kingdom?" the ghost of Alusair Obarskyr whispered, that terrible smile still on her lips. "Prepare to pay my price."

Amarune staggered out of the palace and started to topple into the street—but silver tresses caught her, and a strong, shapely arm swept her upright again.

"Easy, El!" Storm murmured, embracing the dazed dancer from behind and holding her upright. "Easy!"

El?

Manshoon stared in disbelief at the two women across the street for one moment.

In the next moment, riding a soundless shriek of fear and rage, he departed Corleth Fentable in reckless haste, leaving the understeward drooling and staggering as badly as the mask dancer. With no Storm Silverhand to catch him, Fentable promptly collapsed on his face on the cobbles.

An instant after, a beholder the size of a child's head burst out of his robes and darted off into the night.

Jaws dropped, and men shouted at that, and Manshoon had the vague recollection that some Purple Dragons hastened along the street to investigate the blast.

Bah! Right now, he cared not if all the world knew that the palace understeward carried a beholderkin in his armpit.

Elminster of Shadowdale *was alive!*

It took him surprisingly little time to race across streets lined with mansions, past spires, towers, and domes, to a particular open-for-breezes window of Truesilver House.

The Lady Deleira Truesilver caught sight of the hovering beholderkin before her maids did, and abruptly ordered everyone from the room. If any of them saw her pluck a particular pendant up out of the open coffer on her sidetable, or draw a dagger from a sheath affixed to the underside of that same table, they gave no sign of it.

In the space of two quick breaths, the room was empty and its door closed in their wake.

Manshoon ignored dagger and pendant and wasted no time in niceties. "Talane," he ordered, "find the wizard Elminster, who is alive and using bodies not his own. Slay anybody he inhabits—destroy him utterly. Make *very* sure he is dead, then call on me to make certain. Hurry!"

"How will I know him?" she asked, tossing down both pendant and dagger.

The beholderkin darted at her like an oversized wasp, its eyestalks writhing.

She almost managed not to flinch as eyestalks slid greasily into her nostrils and ears, clinging for the fleeting moment Manshoon needed.

He thrust an image of Amarune Whitewave—reeling unsteadily in a doorway, staring at nothing with lightning playing around her upflung hands—into Talane's mind, then stripped away the lightning from that vision.

"This is the guise he's hiding in right now."

The beholderkin drew back far enough to give the Lady Deleira Truesilver a menacing glare. "Find Storm Silverhand, and force her to reveal who is Elminster and who is not. Don't slay her until you are certain. Kill her, too, but after. Foremost and above all, your task is to *bury Elminster deep!*"

CHAPTER
EIGHTEEN
I Go Now to Hunt

Bother me not with treaties, embassies, delegations, grand offers
Of brides to be, or bribes in hand, the surpassing peace
of smiling gods, or eternal youth and bodily vigor!
I am grave-tired with niggling responsibilities, and go now to hunt.

> said by King Olosar of Tethyr, in open court,
> to his advisors
> The 22nd of Mirtul in the Year of the
> Wandering Wyrm

Storm staggered, sobbing in pain. Magic was surging out of the body in her arms, clashing snarlingly with the palace wards.

Where Elminster's magic struck at the wards and the wards struck back, energies were loosed. They swirled around Storm and Amarune, feeling first like fire and acid, then more like a slaver's salted lash she'd felt long ago ... or the whirling, ruthlessly slicing edges of a priest's conjured barrier of many blades ...

To keep them both alive, she shoved Amarune out into the night, away from the wards. Back into the Promenade, both of them seared and hurting, where she fell heavily to her knees, Amarune a limp weight in her arms.

Suddenly swords ringed her, their deadly tips pointed down in a glittering circle.

"Surrender!" a Purple Dragon barked. "Show us empty hands, and declare yourselves."

Storm looked up at him, panting, and forced down pain enough to gasp, "We're wizards of war, soldier! Burning inside from wild magic! For your own safety, *keep back* from us and from yon doorway, all of you!"

Soldiers went pale and gave ground. Wincing, Storm wrapped her arms around Rune and rolled, taking them both farther out into the street. Two Dragons stalked suspiciously alongside them but were called away by their swordcaptain.

Gritting her teeth, Storm stood up, hauling the still-blind, dazed Amarune with her, and walked the dancer slowly away into the night.

"El?" she hissed, as they reached the mouth of a side street on the far side of the Promenade.

The only reply she got was a wordless, feeble moan.

Far down the side street she caught sight of a hunched-over, stumbling man fleeing away from her. He was wreathed in dim, feebly flickering blue flames.

"Ghost brought low," Storm hissed aloud.

As she said that, the distant figure turned a corner and was gone.

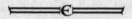

Unimpressed by her eager smile, the blueflame ghost attacked fearlessly, a sneer on its face and confidence in its almost careless slash.

Alusair deftly struck its sword aside with her own ghostly blade and in the same twisting slash cut deep into its side, flying as she did so to keep herself close to the bright blue aura and her blade hitting home, slicing up and over its torso, the tip bouncing on rib after rib, heading for its throat.

Blue flames shrank from the silver-gray mist of her sword, parting and darkening, laying bare the man beneath. Alusair soared up out of reach of his frantic backswing and hacked at the back of his sword arm, just above the elbow, as she passed.

The blueflame ghost's sword clanged to the palace floor, and Alusair whirled and came back at him in a slicing pass. She didn't quite dare to try a hard thrust through him, or a beheading, because every touch of the ghost's flaming aura to her sword—which was part of her, solidified by her will out of the same spectral essence that made up the rest of her—ate at her undeath.

It would be folly to slay this intruder at the cost of her own existence, and leave her beloved palace evermore unguarded.

So she contented herself with great slashes, slicing body and arms, looping around the ghost in a relentless weaving of sharp steel that reduced it to cowering in a heap around its blade, growing dimmer and dimmer.

Abruptly it sprang up and fled with a wail of pain and fear, heading at a frantic run right back out of the palace, waving its sword wildly to try to shield itself against Alusair's blade.

"Greatly weakened, at least," the ghostly princess told the empty passage in satisfaction, halting just in front of the roiling chaos of the violated ward seeking to knit itself together again, to watch the ghost dwindle across the Promenade. It fled into the mouth of a side street and kept going, fast.

Outside, Dragons were assisting a reeling, mumbling Palace Understeward Fentable to his feet. He looked confused or drunk, and the soldiers holding him up were talking excitedly about a "beholder, like in the tales, but only the size of a child's chamberpot!"

One of them was keeping the tip of his sword near Fentable's throat. "Beholderkin, I think such are called. Heard one of old Dhargust's sagely lectures about eye tyrants, two summers back. He says there're still some of them hiding in the heart of the Hullack, just waiting their chance to conquer the realm!"

"Well, I've heard some have been seen right here in Suzail!" an older Dragon growled. "Never mind about distant forests we should all stay well out of, we've got—"

Alusair leaned forward to hear better, frowning in interest.

Which was when something hard and sharp burst right through her from behind, thrusting her forward into the seething energies of the wards.

Coldly scornful laughter accompanied that ruthless blow, and as Alusair writhed in helpless agony, torn by the full fury of the wards, she was dimly aware of a sword being pulled roughly back out of her, spinning her misty body around.

A blade that had burst right through her.

A sword that sliced ghosts as readily as the living.

Floating near the floor, awash in pain, Alusair stared up at her assailant.

Who was standing in the open doorway just beyond the roiling wards, the sword in her hand and a cruel smile on her face.

It was the death knight Targrael, the crazed Highknight. Lady Dark Armor.

Who hissed down at her, "I guard the Forest Kingdom and care for it, not you, wasted and foolish old bitch of a failed regent! I go now to hunt down a great foe of Cormyr—but when I've time to spare, I'll be back to finish you! Depend upon it."

Manshoon was gone, leaving Talane excited.

She was, yes, *delighted* she'd been ordered to hunt down Amarune.

So, the lass was really Elminster? If she'd known that, she'd not have been quite so bold at her first meeting with the Whitewave wench—but no matter. If he'd ever been the towering spellhurler of all those wild tales, the Sage of Shadowdale must now be a weak husk of his former self for Manshoon to entrust this slaying to her. Castles shattered and blown into the clouds, dragons tamed or slaughtered in the skies, archwizards dueled and left as smoking heaps of ash ...

Grand tales, to be sure. Yet, perhaps that's all they'd ever been.

Talane looked down at her shapely self, crisscrossed by broad belts of leather festooned with no fewer than nine scabbarded daggers—all razor sharp and finely balanced for throwing, even the one she'd hurled into a cheating Sembian merchant's eye not all that long ago—and pronounced herself ready.

Which was a good thing, considering Manshoon's burning desire for urgency in this matter.

She checked her hollow right boot heel for keys to certain doors in her mansion and found them right where they should be. Then she shifted her sword belt one last time to make certain it caught on none of the crisscrossing baldrics.

Good. Time to be hunting.

Talane caught up a magnificent ankle-length shimmer-weave nightcloak—the sort of frippery worn to show everyone Truesilvers could casually outspend any dozen lesser noble Houses, every bright shopping morning—and pulled it around herself to conceal her leathers from any servants who might witness her departure. Taking a last look around her bedchamber to ensure things that should be hidden were, she stepped out onto her balcony.

Where the climbing cord she kept secured behind the stone griffon carving at the east end of the balcony was waiting. One kick off the wall and a swift plunge down onto the softest mosses of her gardens later, she would be on her way to her back garden door and the night-shrouded city beyond.

"Amarune Whitewave," she whispered to the night, as the black cord hissed past her chin, "you are one dead mage."

"She was right there, Lady Barcantle!" a hoarse-voiced man shouted down the passage, pointing. "Right where the fat man is!"

Mirt had regained his breath, rubbed his sore feet—he *was* getting a mite old for running for his life on hard cobbles across far too much of a city—and restored his clothing to rights. Then, with a sinking feeling, he peered in the direction of that shout and beheld fully helmed and armored Purple Dragons. Lots of them. With more than a few wizards behind them.

They were coming toward him fast, with swords and spears out, and were looking his way in a decidedly unfriendly manner.

"Aye, right where the—naed of the Dragon! The door! The stlarning *door's* gone!"

A voice Mirt knew rang out. *"Mirt!* Mirt of Waterdeep! Stand and surrender, you miscreant, or your very life is forfeit!" Lady Glathra sounded furious.

"Ooops," Mirt growled, turning hastily and lurching in the direction of the doorway. Which, he thought to himself as he started to run again, gathering speed as he wheezed his way across the Promenade, was a rather grand word for "gaping hole where a good stout door recently was, and still ought to be."

Wizards. 'Twas always wizards that brought the real trouble. Them and yer fell creatures of the night with their elder magic.

Aye. Now, feet fail me not . . .

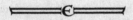

Mystra, fail me not . . . Ohhh, the pain.

Elminster was vaguely aware that he was out under a night sky, hurrying over damp, faintly foul-smelling cobbles, with a fainter sea smell under the dung and rotting refuse, and the familiar strong, curved warmth of Storm was pressed against him and carrying him along.

"Him" meaning Amarune, of course. Who still seemed to have all her limbs and the usual manner of moving them, though her vision was a tear-filled blur and her ears rang and echoed in ceaseless cacophony.

That could have been worse, he told himself dully, through the splitting agony in his head. He'd been caught in a wild backlash he should have anticipated, standing right in the wards. Like any fumbling first-time hedge wizard . . .

"S-storm?" he managed to mumble. He couldn't mindspeak her, even pressed together as they were. That part of his head was all churning, roiling dark fire.

"El," Storm said soothingly, shifting her grip on him to something slightly more comfortable, "I'm here. I'll heal you when we get somewhere safer. Don't try to talk or mindspeak unless you *really* must."

Good old Storm. Good lass. She knew what it was like, the roughness and pain of hurling magic.

She knew what it was like to have Mystra and then lose her.

"Storm!" Mirt called hoarsely, fighting for breath. "Silverhand! Hey, lass—here! Wait for me a breath or two!"

Storm had just ducked into an alley, dragging the limp Rune with her. She stuck her head back around the corner, saw Mirt, and grinned.

"Get in here," she ordered. "You can stand guard."

"What?" Mirt wheezed, joining her. "Ye have to let fly, then?"

Storm rolled her eyes. "No, I have to try to get Elminster's mind back closer to what it should be."

Mirt nodded and dragged out his dagger. "Glathra's after me," he warned, turning to plant himself in the alley. "With a whole lot of Dragons'n'magelings. Don't they ever sleep?"

"Not if we don't let them," Storm replied, kneeling over the slumped Amarune and touching their foreheads together. "It's all part of our clever plan for conquering all Cormyr."

"Huh," Mirt growled, "it strikes me there's far too many folk in this city busy hatching clever plans for conquering all Cormyr."

A shuttered window swung open beside him, revealing the head and shoulders of a bored-looking maid. Without really looking, she tossed a basinful of dirty wash water out into the alley.

Mirt ducked. As the water-hurler reached out to close the shutter, he came up grinning into her startled face, waving his dagger. "Are ye one of them?"

Accompanied by a startled scream, the window slammed hastily shut again.

"He's getting better," Storm reported, "but that's mainly due to Rune being young and strong. I need peace and quiet lasting long enough to really heal him."

"Then let's be up and staggering again before Glathra's hounds get here," Mirt growled. "If we cut through this alley to the next street south, double back the way we've come and up that second lane along, we'll get to the damnably expensive inn I've taken a room at, and can spend the night there."

He gave her a hopeful leer and added, "Two lasses, one a mask dancer and the other with silver hair that moves by itself? 'Twill do wonders for my reputation."

Storm gave him a look. "Mirt, your reputation needs something a little larger. Conquering a kingdom, fathering dragons . . . that sort of thing."

Mirt drew himself up and gave her his best grin. "It does? Well, now . . . just whereabouts in this bright realm do ye keep yer dragons?"

The most powerful-at-Art wizard in all Suzail was also the wealthiest, but had not become so by ignoring credible requests for his hire.

Even requests that came after full night had fallen.

So it was that by invoking his name, rank, and family wealth, Lord Arclath Delcastle won admittance past an expressionless porter.

Who led him along a passage lined with two dozen rows of magnificent and identical armored warriors who turned in perfect unison and utter silence to regard him after he passed—and whom he strongly suspected were recently created helmed horrors, the sort of guardians a handful of the oldest and wealthiest noble Houses boasted a single one of, each.

The passage opened into a lofty hall dominated by two curving staircases ascending into unseen gloom. It was lit by the pale, silver-blue glow of an endlessly cycling mobile of floating swords, daggers, and stranger pointed and barbed weapons that hung in the air above the center of the chamber.

The porter led Arclath straight across the room and under the weapons, without paying them any attention.

Arclath noted bloodstains on the floor—old and faint, but unmistakable, and more than a few—under the silently flashing and gleaming blades.

Seeing them, Arclath could not help but look up at the whirling storm of steel. At least until he was safely out from underneath it.

Whereupon, his eyes fell upon a new menace. It seemed Larak Dardulkyn liked to impress, or rather intimidate, his guests.

Only after the visitor tore his gaze from the whirling scimitars and falchions did he notice four direhelms, the smoothly flying armored guardians that looked like armored men, brandishing two swords each. Men, that is, who were simply missing from the waist down.

One floated watchfully above each of the visible doors out of the chamber. Their heads turned smoothly to follow Arclath's progress across the room.

The porter led Arclath to the door across from the one he'd entered by, opened it, and wordlessly waved the Fragrant Flower of House Delcastle through.

Into a gloomy, high-ceilinged audience chamber of black-painted paneling adorned with strange-looking symbols Arclath strongly suspected were for show, having no real meaning or use at all.

Unless, that is, they were examples of the recent fashion among archwizards to enspell drawings or painted runes. Magic unleashed at a touch, or if the drawn device was damaged.

Yes, that was likely, wasn't it?

The room held a simple black table, with two chairs facing each other down its sleek length.

Arclath made no move to go near them but strolled slowly around the room, peering at the runes and glyphs—or impressive-looking, mock-mystical nonsense symbols, if that's what they were—as he passed. No other door was visible in the room except the one that had been firmly closed behind him, but of course any of these panels might open. Or the floor or ceiling, both of which had their own symbols. Their faint glows were the only lights in the room.

Arclath strolled, and no one came.

On his third slow circuit of the room, he thought one of the symbols had changed behind his back to a new configuration, but he could not be certain.

Impressive. Or trying hard to be.

Time stretched. Arclath waited alone in the dusty silence for an audience that, it started to seem as unmeasured time unfolded, might not befall until morning.

Upon reflection, he found that this bothered him not at all. Here, deep in this fortresslike mansion that shouted out the fell arcane power of its owner everywhere one looked, he was—or at least felt—safe from Elminster and Storm, Glathra and all her wizards of war, Stormserpent's blueflame ghosts, the third ghost and whoever was controlling it, and all other mages ambitious nobles might hire.

As a wizard for hire, Larak Dardulkyn had a reputation for being both coldly impolite and very expensive, so if Arclath was going to succeed in enlisting his services against Elminster, to keep Amarune—and his own mind, too—safe, he had best be patient and polite.

Idly he tried to figure out what he could of the layout of this floor of the mansion. He was probably slightly more than the height of a tall man above the streets that surrounded the place on three sides, judging by the number of steps he'd ascended to the front door, and . . . well, unless the tales about wizard's houses being larger inside than they were on the outside were true, he'd walked pretty much clear across the width of the building. There should be a street on the far side of *that* wall.

This had once been old Raskival Rhendever's house—a crabbed old merchant Arclath could *just* remember from his youth, a hunched-over man with two canes. Before that it had belonged to Lord Sarlival, last of his line, who'd kept a mistress there with the full knowledge—and abiding fury—of his wife. Or so the tales—

Soundlessly one of the panels opened, and a tall, rather homely man with unpleasantly glittering black eyes stepped into the room, his high-collared black robes swirling.

Ah, yes. Menacing archwizard; must look the part.

"Lord Delcastle," Dardulkyn said coldly. "What do you want?"

"To hire you to protect me and another person I am fond of from a mage who wants to control our minds."

Dardulkyn raised one eyebrow and indicated one of the chairs with an abrupt thrust of his hand. "Sit."

Only after they were both seated did he ask, "Who is this mage you believe imperils you?"

"He's . . . Elminster. Elminster of Shadowdale. *The* Elminster."

Dardulkyn snorted, sending an icy look down the table. "Lord Delcastle, you'll have to do better than that."

CHAPTER
NINETEEN

FEARING WORSE, I FLED

And when the gates were burst, and the foe rode in
And did their murderous worst, to all my bleeding kin
Leaving the fortunate ones dead; then, ladies and saers,
Ah, then, fearing worse, I fled.

Thormar Daern, Minstrel of Amn
from *The Ballad of Baerin Boldblade*
first performed in the Year of the Walking Trees

N o," Arclath said patiently, "I am neither mad nor—I
believe—mistaken. I *do* mean Elminster."

"Did he call himself that?"

"He did, and others did, too. Including the Lady Glathra,
a silver-haired woman who calls herself Storm Silverhand and
certainly looks like the Storm Silverhand of legend, and—"

Dardulkyn waved a dismissive hand. "Tall, imperious or
rude, strikingly beautiful, long silver hair that moves by itself?
I can make you look like that, or myself, for that matter, with
a simple spell. You have been deceived, young lord. Threats
to invade the mind are usually just that: threats. The magic
is simple enough, but there are dangers to the caster that far
outweigh any benefits. *Competent* workers of Art don't splash
in such waters."

"Saer Dardulkyn," Arclath said carefully, "I find myself not
caring much if I am imperiled by an incompetent madwits or a
competent archmage of peerless power. I have heard his voice
come out of my beloved's throat, have had conversations with
him—her, that is, but with him in her head—that I could not
have had with . . . my lady were he not present, and he has
pressed me to let him into my mind. After what I've seen and

heard, I know he can do this, whether he is truly Elminster or not. I also care not if he's taken the name Elminster to impress me or half Faerûn—it's what I've seen him do that impresses me, not the name he uses."

Dardulkyn leaned forward. "And just what have you seen him do?"

"Well," Arclath began, "I . . . uh . . ."

Dardulkyn made a grimace that might have been meant as a smile. "Precisely. Lord Delcastle, it seems to me that you are wasting my time. Yet, you are determined to try to hire me?"

Arclath sighed. "Yes. I must say you hardly seem eager to take my coin!"

"I'm not." Dardulkyn turned one of the rings adorning his fingers, and there was a sudden singing in the air between them. "Come no closer to me, or you will be harmed."

"What? Saer mage, I assure you—"

"No, Lord Delcastle, I will assure *you* of something, now. You are my prisoner and will remain so until it suits my purposes to let you go."

"*Whaaat?*"

Arclath sprang to his feet, the chair toppling, and snatched out his sword.

"Behold the usual response of arrogant nobility to anything they dislike. Hence the shielding magic I just raised."

"But—but *why* are you doing this? Are you in league with Elminster?"

"There is no such person, anymore. The real Elminster is long dead, with his goddess. Oh, there may well be any number of lackspell charlatans using that name, trusting in the Elminster of legend to frighten those they fleece. I'm not interested in such buffoons. I am, however, interested in *you*, Lord Delcastle."

"Why?" Arclath snapped. "Am I an attractive prisoner?"

Dardulkyn tapped his fingertips together thoughtfully as a small, wintry smile rose onto his face. It hovered there for a moment, as if uncomfortable to find itself in such an unaccustomed spot, and swiftly faded away again.

"Not in yourself, no. Don't flatter yourself, Delcastle—though I know most of you younger lordlings do nothing else."

The wizard rose and strolled across the room. Arclath felt a sudden pressure in front of him, shoving him back. Dardulkyn's shield moved with its caster.

"No," the wizard drawled, gazing idly around at the symbols painted on the black walls, "I believe you are the leading envoy of one more faction of scheming nobles, of the various factions circling like vultures around the fading days of old Foril's reign. This 'Elminster' business is just your less-than-candid way of hiring me and so binding my services to your faction. Which in turn means you can be a valuable captive in any bargains I may need or want to make with your faction. If they deem you disposable, I'll at least have weakened your little cabal by the resources of one member—a wealthy one, at that."

"Wizard," Arclath asked sharply, "are you mad?"

"All wizards are mad, nobleman. Or seem so to thick-skulled clods like yourself, who see the world as a place of coins and willing wenches, swords and threats, and can never know the glories of the Art."

"I see." Arclath backed away. "And just whom do *you* work for? Yourself, I know, but what faction counts you as a member?"

"None of them. I stand apart from all this tiresome thronestrife. If representatives of other cabals visit in the days ahead, I may well capture them, too, and assemble a collection."

"To what end? Do you think you can bargain with every noble House in the land? All of whom have House wizards and can hire more mages, so you'll end up battling many spellhurlers at once?"

"Ah, spoken like a true noble. Power is something to be fought for and used to fight with, is it not?"

Arclath frowned. "Power is the art of getting what you want *without* the use of brute force."

Dardulkyn smiled again. It looked no healthier than the first time he'd tried it. "You surprise me. That's quite correct. I intend to fight for no one and against no one—unless someone is foolish enough to assault my home."

He strolled forward until his shield forced Arclath to retreat again. "I've decided to take no sides in the increasing chaos and strife, until the time comes when all surviving factions are eager to bid huge sums and concessions for my services." He spread his hands.

"I'll then accept the best deal, settling for no less than a peerage and court rank, and ideally, a position of real power behind the throne comparable to that enjoyed of old by Vangerdahast. Yet, without any of the responsibilities or need to obey royalty that accompanies the title of royal magician or court wizard."

He looked Arclath up and down and sneered. "I'll be a lord then, Delcastle—and, I suppose, on my way to being as low and brutish as you."

"I suppose I'm meant to feel insulted," Arclath replied, "but I find, rather, that I feel ill, Saer Dardulkyn. I came to find aid against Elminster and was prepared to pay well for it, but it now seems Elminster is a lesser evil than I'd thought him to be."

"Well, we all have to start learning about the world sometime." The archwizard sneered, taking another step forward.

Arclath gave ground then suddenly turned, vaulted over the table, and rushed along the wall toward the door he'd come in by.

The wizard sprinted across the room with astonishing speed to thrust Arclath back from that exit—when Arclath was a mere stride away.

"That," Dardulkyn said severely, breathing heavily, "was *not* wise. I will summon some of my guards to take you elsewhere."

"They're helmed horrors, aren't they?"

"Indeed. Of my own crafting. It would be *very* unwise to dispute with them."

Arclath nodded. So the door was unreachable—until the helmed horrors came through it, whereupon the wizard would step back, taking his shield with him, and leave the realm's favorite Delcastle sharing a wedge of the room with them. The panel Dardulkyn had come in by was likewise unreachable.

But what of the other panels? He turned and dashed across the room again, vaulting the table and slamming hard into one of the panels on what he'd thought might be an outside wall.

It gave a little, so he sprang at it again, putting his shoulder into it. The panel thundered, yielding more than a little this time.

Dardulkyn was raising his hands to cast something, an angry frown on his face, by the third time Arclath struck the panel.

It gave a groan and rebounded open like a sprung door— revealing a window beyond!

A large, clear window of bubble-free glass, of the most expensive sort that it took too many golden lions to buy. Framed by frilly, feminine draperies and a matching valence!

Arclath crossed his arms in front of his face and throat, clutching the pommel of his drawn sword foremost, and launched himself at the window, hoping it bore no strange spell or other that would hurl him back.

It didn't.

The crash was tremendous.

Arclath was vaguely aware of shards hurtling out in all directions, a strip of garden about as wide as the shoulders of a large man, a dark Suzailan street beyond it—and between garden and street, an ornate, many-curlicued, wrought-iron fence that looked quite sturdy.

It was.

He crashed into it and slid down it, trapped between stone mansion and fence. A fence that could no doubt spit lightning or extend iron claws if Dardulkyn had time enough to make it do so.

Snarling in frantic effort, Arclath leaped up, caught hold of the upper curlicues, and launched himself up and over, landing with a crash and the ringing clang of his dropped and bouncing sword.

A noise that should bring a watch patrol down on him in a trice, in a good neighborhood like this.

He rolled, snatched up his sword but didn't waste time trying to snatch his breath, found his feet, and started to run.

No patrol, of course—*why* were there never any blasted Dragons when you *needed* them?

"A rather frosty converse," he heard Dardulkyn announce calmly. "Late night bargainings seldom go well. However, I can't allow an energetic and talkative young noble to escape me, knowing what he now does. So, a simple spell will hold you, Arclath Delcastle, until my horrors collect you."

Arclath dashed to one side of the street, trying to hide himself from where the archwizard could see and aim. Did paralysis magic work like that? He couldn't remember; he had only heard it talked about twice, and—

"Oh, *hrast*," he cursed, feeling a sudden creeping lassitude, his limbs slowing. "Oh, no! No . . ." It was like trying to stride through a neck-deep pool of placid water.

He tried to fight his way onward but slowly became aware that, although his heart was pounding and his limbs were straining, his surroundings just weren't changing any longer.

He was standing still.

Oh, *naed*.

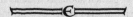

"Hold!" Mirt grunted. "A man was running our way, up ahead there—and he's just stopped."

"Awed at the sight of the famous Mirt the Moneylender, Lord of Waterdeep, no doubt," Storm replied from just behind him, as she towed the lolling and loose-limbed Amarune along. Rune could walk by herself, all weakness gone, but had to be led to keep her from falling.

"Nay, lass, not 'stopped' normal-like. Paralyzed by magic. I've seen it done often enough. Someone froze him midstride. An' damn me if he doesn't look familiar."

"What *sort* of familiar?" Storm asked warily, trying to see past the fat man's bulk.

"Arclath Delcastle sort of familiar," Mirt replied, a few lurching strides later. "By the looks of things, he just burst out yon window. The one with the dolt in evil wizard robes standing glaring out of it."

Storm clamped a hand on Mirt's shoulder to bring him to a stop, then peered around him as if he were a large, concealing boulder. "Oh, he *didn't*."

"Obviously he did," Mirt rumbled. "Didn't what?"

"Went to see the calmly ruthless Dardulkyn, wizard-for-hire most puissant of all Suzail, to hire himself some magic," Storm replied. "Means to ward away Elminster from certain minds, no doubt."

"And negotiations went poorly?"

"It seems so. Rumor declares Dardulkyn has a personal army of helmed horrors, so he's probably watching over Arclath until they can collect him."

"So, we collect him first," Mirt growled, lurching forward again and dragging Storm along with him, "and use Arclath as our shield against his spells, being as the lad's already frozen, hey?"

"Hey," Storm agreed ruefully, expecting something terrible to smite them at every step.

Mirt didn't look toward the window or walk warily. He simply tucked Storm under one arm to keep her on his far side from the wizard's mansion, lurched up to Arclath, thrust his free arm between two noble legs and up to catch hold of the back of Arclath's belt, boosted the frozen lord up onto his hip, and kept on walking.

The first spell struck them about six paces later, as Mirt was busily turning Arclath to keep him between them and the window.

It dashed them all down in hard-bouncing pain and sent lightning sizzling away across the cobbles.

As those snarling little bolts faded, Storm—who was chin-down on the cobbles, tingling everywhere she wasn't numb—looked over at Mirt, then at Amarune.

The fat merchant's hair was all on end, his face was smudged, and smoke curled up lazily from his jerkin. Or whatever that dirty, shapeless upper garment the old Lords of Waterdeep wore was called.

Rune's face was no longer teary and vacant. It was alert and angry.

"El?" Storm whispered.

"Who did that?" the Sage of Shadowdale's familiar voice snapped, out of Rune's beautiful mouth.

"Dardulkyn. The most powerful archwizard in Suzail, probably in all Cormyr. He's standing in yonder window."

"Is he, now? Well—"

The second spell struck then, a blast that plucked them up and hurled them like gale-driven leaves down the street, tumbling and helplessly cursing.

"Enough of this," Elminster spat, when they were all lying on the cobbles again. "Storm, heal me!"

"He's sending his helmed horrors after us—"

"Then start healing me *now*."

Storm turned her head. "Mirt, help me. We need to get around *that* corner, then find a doorway or an alcove for me to use, while you gallantly hold off all helmed horrors until I'm done restoring El."

Mirt gave her a wordless, wary "you'll be lucky" grunt, then started crawling. "I must warn ye," he growled as he wormed slowly past her, looking rather like a kitchen midden heap on the move, "that my vanquishing-helmed-horrors skills are a mite rusty. Piergeiron only has—er, *had*—two of 'em, and thought 'em too precious for us to really smite."

"All we need is for you to delay them long enough," Storm replied, crawling to where she could reach Arclath and roll his stiff body over. Reaching back, she tugged at Amarune to keep her crawling, too.

"Huh," Mirt growled, reaching out a hand to help roll the frozen young noble. "The older I get, the longer 'long enough' seems to get."

"I've noticed that, too," Storm agreed, scrambling forward to catch and cradle Arclath's head before it crashed down on a cobble. "I believe some call it 'progress.'"

"Oh? 'Some'? What do others call it?"

"The general decline of the realms, sliding ever faster and inevitably into the Abyss, crawling chaos, and eventual obliteration."

"Ah. So, I should make my coins now, hey?"

"Hey," Storm agreed, breaking into a smile.

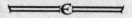

Broryn Windstag could not remember a time before Delasko Sornstern had been grinning at his elbow. They'd done nigh everything together for years; they still did almost everything together.

And in the wake of Stormserpent's vow to carry out Lord Illance's bold plan, they had wasted no time hastening to their favorite "private place," a certain shady back corner of the Sornstern family gardens, where they could talk things over without being overheard by anyone.

It would have dumbfounded them both—and plunged them into cold, despairing terror at the thought of all the treasons they'd so casually discussed—to learn their every jocular comment was being overheard and committed to memory by a Highknight of the Crown who'd been tailing Windstag for years. A certain Sir Talonar Winter, who looked *very* much like the better portraits of the great King Azoun, fourth of that name, and who was lounging above them on a bough of a mighty shadowtop at that moment.

A man who'd become so comfortable on that bough overhanging the bower where the two friends were wont to talk that he could arrive and depart soundlessly, even in utter darkness, tall and spike-topped Sornstern walls or no walls.

Yet the two lordlings remained blissfully unaware of their audience, and so spoke untrammeled by prudence. Just as they were discussing Marlin Stormserpent's chances just then.

"Yes, *straight* through the perimeter wall of Stormserpent Towers. Solid stone feet thick, mind, not where there was a gate or hidden door. Strode without stopping, blue flames and all, leaving not so much as a scorch mark."

"*Not* a secret door?" Windstag asked disbelievingly, a second time.

"Not," Sornstern confirmed. "He swore to this, insisting he was sober and had seen it all *very* clearly. The two of them stepped through a wall without muttering any sort of spell. In a spot where the stones were solid—he checked, just after. And Indur would never embellish or tell us false. He knows full well his neck would pay the price."

Windstag nodded. "So tell me about these blueflame ghosts."

Sornstern leaned back to look up at the night stars—what few of them he could see around the great dark canopy of the shadowtop looming overhead. Even if he'd had a glowstone on a pole to peer properly by, he had no chance of seeing the Highknight who was listening so intently, because the Highknight was not in the habit of handing such chances to others, even headstrong and idiotic young noble lordlings.

Not that Delasko Sornstern was looking for anyone. He was enjoying the moment, savoring this rare time when Windstag was listening to *him*.

"My father, Haedro," he began slowly, "has a hobby."

He paused then, just to see Broryn lean forward eagerly and acquire the first signs of impatience. Before it could flare into anger, he continued.

"He collects lore and relics of famous adventurers of the past. Years ago, he heard all about those famous adventurers, the Nine. Not the heroic tales bards and old tavern gossips like to tell, but *all* about the Nine. How they ended, to be specific."

"The Silverhair Sister—Lurl or Laeral or some such—fell under a god's curse, right? After she put on the Crown of Horns, and it ate her brain?"

Sornstern winced at Windstag's words. "Y-yes, you could put it that way. She went evil, at least until the Lord Archmage of Waterdeep, the Blackstaff, rescued her and took her as his wife—"

"Funny how that happens, hey? Off with that gown and behold my cure!" Windstag leered.

Out of long habit, Sornstern supplied the expected nod and enthusiastic grin. "Yes, I've noticed that, too! What we missed by not being born mighty wizards, hey?"

"Hey, indeed. So, she went mad and bad, and the Nine scattered, never to reunite," Windstag almost chanted. "See? I remember a *little* of what my tutors droned on about . . . see?"

Sornstern nodded and grinned again. "Well done, to have emerged from that flood of drivel with anything salvaged at all! You have it right, and some of the Nine were hired by a certain rich merchant of Athkatla. Unbeknownst to them, that merchant was under the influence of an archmage who desired to bind longevity and resilience into magic items by imprisoning the vitality of living beings within them, and—"

"Those Amnians! Sell their own left arms, they will! Can't trust them for half a trice or the scrapings off a copper coin!"

"Ah . . . well said, you can't indeed! Well, this wizard easily overcame the adventurers with spells and bound them into items of his making. Later, at least one, more likely two, of these enchanted things fell into the hands of the Stormserpents."

For the first time, Windstag stopped looking enthusiastic. An eye-narrowing thought had struck him. "Just how is it that you know *that?*"

"My father," Sornstern replied triumphantly, "and he had it from that infamous hot-breeches Old Mage the tales all tell about: Elminster of Shadowdale. In return for hiding the Sage of Shadowdale for a night and letting him drain a decanter of half-decent wine. The old fool thought he was getting Father's best."

The two lordlings snorted and sneered together for the thousand-thousandth time over the gullibility of the lower classes, ere Windstag stiffened as another thought struck him.

Leaning forward excitedly, he asked, "So just how many of the Nine were bound into items? How many does Marlin control?"

Sornstern shrugged. "I think just the two, but in truth I know not. I *did* notice that Marlin said nothing at all about blueflame ghosts to us, for a good long time after he was sending them out into the city."

Windstag smiled. "Would you, if you stood in his boots? They're his secret weapon against the Obarskyrs."

"Or us," Sornstern told his friend thoughtfully. "Or us."

CHAPTER
TWENTY

FEARFUL FOR GOOD REASON

Gellurt? Mraukhar? Gone, lords. Out yon door, shouting
Death was hard at their heels, to slice them and turn out
Their innards for passing flies, as it lately served their friends.
You do well to back away, for no one is here left alive but me
And I tell you, soft but true, that they fled fearful for good reason.

> Morold the Mad Knight, in Act III, Scene I of the
> play *Darth Thorn Horn* by Mydantha "Ladyminstrel"
> Marlest first performed in the Year of the Risen Elfkin

"I f ye can hurry, lass, now would be a fair good time to do
so," Mirt growled from the mouth of the alcove.

"Helmed horrors?" Storm asked, not moving from where
she lay pressed against Amarune, forehead to forehead. She
was so *close* . . .

"Aye. A dozen or more. Floating down the street as menacing as ye please. Striding on air."

Storm closed her eyes. "How far off?"

El was almost completely himself again. *Almost.*

"About ten strides. Nay, six now. Too stlarned *close—!*"

Mirt grunted that last word as the foremost empty suit of
armor descended onto the cobbles in front of him and swung
its greatsword, its baleful inner fire pulsing.

Steel rang on steel as Mirt parried, puffing. He dared not
duck aside with the lasses behind him needing to be shielded.
The horror swung again as a second one floated down to the
cobbles.

Mirt shook his head. The moment it walked up beside the
first one, he was a dead man. "Storm?" he growled. "Got any
miracle magic? I need it now!"

"Aye," came a familiar deeper, rougher man's voice from behind him. "I believe I do."

Mirt sighed with relief and lurched aside. As the horror promptly stepped forward into the spot where he'd stood, to swing its sword again, Elminster murmured something—and the night exploded in an angry emerald flame.

Or was it a bolt of something else? With a weird burbling sound that was part exulting song and part keening saw, it spiraled down the street in a slowly expanding, blazing cone, plucking the walking suits of armor up into itself as it went. Every last one of them.

Greatswords, gauntlets, and helms could be seen whirling around and around the moving, expanding glow, swept down it as it sputtered, darkened, sputtered again—and abruptly winked out.

Leaving the street dark and empty, save for one blackened, bouncing helm that clanged on the cobbles and fetched up beside Mirt's boots, ruby red internal fire still roiling inside it.

El reached down with one of Amarune's long-fingered, graceful hands, caught up the helm, and murmured something swift and simple over it that made its red fire shrink smoothly into an endlessly whirling sphere. Then he tossed it to Storm. "Keep this for healing later, when we need it."

He stalked along the street toward the corner. Mirt lurched along warily in his wake. Shapely young lass or not, she moved like Elminster when he was angry—and when Elminster was angry, things tended to get spectacular.

Dardulkyn was no longer at his window, and the panel inside was closed across the hole where Arclath had burst through it.

Elminster regarded the broken shards around the edge of the missing window for a long, silent breath, then lifted his arms and unhurriedly worked a spell.

The mansion wall vanished with a roar, laying bare the innards of half a dozen rooms and causing an overhang of suddenly unsupported roof-slates to groan, lean forward—and drop, one by one, to shatter loudly on the ornate iron fence below.

Mirt gaped, then winced.

As a door at the back of one of the shattered rooms flew open and an astonished Larak Dardulkyn stared at the sudden ruin of one end of his home.

He glared at the young mask dancer, who still stood with arms raised in the last gesture of her casting. Throwing up his own arms dramatically, he spat out an angry-sounding spell.

The air was suddenly full of flame, snarling spheres of it that expanded with frightening speed as they rushed through the air at Rune. Mirt cowered back around the corner, flinging out an arm to warn Storm, knowing even as he did so that he was too late to do anything, too late even to cling to life, as—

Above them, the highest of the fiery spheres came to an abrupt, shuddering stop in midair, as if it had struck an unseen wall. Its angry orange-red flames went blue, then green, then blue-silver—and fell away to nothing, plunging toward the cobbles like spilled sand but vanishing utterly before they landed.

Timidly, Mirt peeked around the corner again.

This time it was Dardulkyn who was gaping. His spell was gone as if it had never been—and he'd watched it shatter in midair, seen the angry young lass down the street foil one of his greatest battle magics in an instant.

She couldn't *do* that. No one could.

"Who—who *are* you?" he snarled, turning a ring in frantic haste to call up his strongest shielding magics. Without waiting for a reply, he ran across the riven, open-to-the-night room, heading for where his mightiest magical staff awaited, behind its own panel.

"The name," came the calm, almost insolent reply, "is Elminster."

Rune's nimble fingers moved again—and even as Dardulkyn wrenched open the panel and closed his hand triumphantly around the gleaming black grip of his most potent staff, feeling its power thrumming through him, Elminster's next spell struck.

The sound was like a thunderclap, despite the stormless night sky. This magic was no tidy vanishing, but a series of bursts that blew apart several deeper rooms of Dardulkyn's mansion, hurling their stones and plaster and all high and far into the night sky in the general direction of Jester's Green. Plucking the crackling, angrily pulsing, and ultimately exploding staff from the mage's hands in the midst of their punishing tumult, the bursts whirled it away across the night sky with the rest of the wreck . . . and left. As the last rolling echoes of the magic rebounded off nearby buildings, and dazed and bewildered folk started to thrust their heads out windows, a stunned and terrified Larak Dardulkyn clung to the edge of the opened panel amid the smoking ruins.

His grand black robes were shredded, and many busily winking motes of light appeared and disappeared up and down his body in mute memorial to the shielding and warding magics that had kept him alive but paid the price.

With a sound that began as a groan but ended as a sigh, a fanglike remnant of an interior wall toppled over into collapse.

Leaving Dardulkyn clinging to nothing at all.

He fell to the littered floor in a huddled heap, only his terrified stare telling Mirt that he was still alive.

Above the fallen wizard, his four direhelms hung in midair, a motionless square facing inward, guarding doors that were no longer there.

At the sight of them, Elminster sighed. Then he moved one hand in a swift, complicated spellweaving.

For many pounding heartbeats, nothing seemed to happen. Then, there came a single *clink*. Followed by another. And another.

Something fell.

Then, in a series of *clinks* and *clanks*, pieces of armor plate fell from all four floating menaces. More followed, in an ever-swifter sequence of plummeting. Until nothing was left floating at all, and heaps of metal festooned the floor around the quivering Dardulkyn.

Who could only watch, mewing in disbelieving fear from time to time, as the fallen metal started to rust before his eyes with uncanny speed.

By the time he'd swallowed twice or thrice, it had all crumbled to reddish brown powder. Even the sword hilts.

"You can cry now," Elminster told the huddled archwizard gently. "As wizards seem to be all too fond of saying, these days: We all have to start learning about the world sometime."

Marlin Stormserpent had hurried home groaning in fear. It had all gone *wrong!*

What to do now, what to do *now?*

Did he even *have* any blueflame ghosts at his command, anymore?

He couldn't get that sight of one of his ghosts being hurled across the Promenade out of his head. It had looked just like an ordinary hiresword, a man who could be killed as swiftly—and stlarn it, *easily*—as other men, a man with a sword who just happened to have some pretty blue flames around him. Why, a hedge wizard could conjure up such a look!

He'd thought himself so powerful, so important . . .

The ghosts had made short work of Huntcrown, but—but—

Were they anything more, now, than bright banners pointing him out as a traitor to anyone who cared to look?

Ganrahast, the royal magician? That snarling bitch, Lady Glathra? The *king?*

He had a brief, dreadful vision of a chopping block in the palace stableyard, and Crown Prince Irvel waiting beside it with a large, sharp sword and a ruthless smile—

Shaking his head to banish that imagining, Marlin strode across the room, bound for his favorite decanter. He'd made a proper mess of—

Oh, no.

Behind him, rich blue radiance had blossomed seemingly out of nowhere and glinted back reflections from all his decanters. Clapping one hand to the hilt of the Flying Blade and snatching up the Wyverntongue Chalice with the other, Marlin whirled around.

The ghost was smiling, of course. The blueflame ghosts always did. Wide, terrible smiles, malicious or madly gleeful, and obviously false.

At odds right now with the angry hiss Treth Halonter, who long ago had been the best warrior of the Nine, was giving Marlin as he strode through the wall. His worn and nondescript leather war harness looked torn and battered, some of the leather hanging in frayed tatters. In the heart of fainter, more flickering blue flames than usual, the warrior leaned forward threateningly.

"Sent us into the maw of mighty magics, you did," he whispered, as if wounded inside. "You pewling, prancing idiot."

Marlin somehow got himself around behind the table he'd grabbed the Chalice from, and from the skimpy shelter of its far side snapped fearfully, "You serve me! Remember?"

Drawing his sword in desperate haste, he held it up before him, with the Chalice, as if they were holy things that could ward off the furious ghost.

"I do. Oh, I do," Halonter replied, glowering over his wide smile. "In fact, lordling, I'll never forget."

"I—I'm sorry. I saw the—what happened to the door. Uh, and you. But I really couldn't have foreseen that any wizard of war would be so crazed as to destroy part of his own *palace* just to smite you! Could I?"

Still wearing that terrible grin, Halonter swung his sword in a deft arc that severed a row of fresh, unlit candles and the neck of one of Marlin's oldest decanters, slicing it without shattering the vessel or toppling it.

Marlin shivered at the thought of how sharp the ghost's blade must be.

"No, I couldn't," he answered himself shakily.

"No," Halonter hissed, "you couldn't."

He took a menacing step forward, until he was against the table and Marlin could smell Halonter's faint, acrid reek. Like soured wine and a mix of many spices.

"More fool you," the ghost added, shoving the table forward.

It might well have pinned Marlin painfully against his best sideboard, but fortunately for the noble, a stone replica of a figurehead of a long-ago Stormserpent ship flanked the piece, massive and solid and as immobile as the wall behind it. The table struck it and could be shoved no farther.

With a snarl the ghost spun around and stalked away, across the room.

"Relve!" he spat. "How did *he* fare?"

"I—I—"

Stammering in dread, Marlin had gotten no farther by the time the wall Halonter had come through glowed blue again—a dark, feeble blue—that became the hunched-over, staggering Relve Langral.

The second ghost's flames were weak, flickering shadows, and he looked as if he'd lost a brawl with a cleaver-wielding butcher. Or three.

"You," he snarled at Marlin, "sent me up against some sort of mighty phantom! A mistress of the blade, or lady master of the blade, or whatever the *tluin* one calls a woman who can make her sword dance and pirouette and pour stlarning wine for her! Her sword was part of her—its touch seared me! She could fly; she could fade away; it was all I could stlarned well do to parry! Send me no more to fight proud ghost princesses in their very palaces! Bah!"

He lashed out with his sword, but the slash that should have shattered a row of unopened, expensive bottles of vintages from afar sliced only empty air as his leg gave way. Langral staggered helplessly sideways and crashed to Marlin's carpet.

"I'm sorry, I'm sorry, I'm *sorry!*" Marlin gabbled desperately, rushing to help the fallen rogue—but halting abruptly as Halonter thrust out his blade warningly.

"What should I do?" he asked.

"Use us wisely," Halonter hissed. "Less often. And not soon. We both need time to heal."

"You can *heal* in—in here?" Marlin burst out, waving the Chalice.

Halonter gave him a long and silent look that clashed in its naked balefulness with his wide and tireless smile.

Marlin shrank back from him, then scuttled to the side door and through it into his robing room, hurriedly shoving a chair to block the closed door. From behind it, he began forcing the two blueflame ghosts back into their items.

Halonter said not a word but never stopped glaring. From the floor, Relve became hissingly, profanely hostile.

It was not until they both were gone, and Marlin was standing alone and drenched with sweat, that he realized what had frightened him most of all.

Both ghosts had been deeply scared.

Well, so was he.

"I must flee Suzail," he told the room around him, grimly. "Right now."

Kicking the chair aside, he strode back to the table, set the Chalice on it, then stormed around the room plucking up things he'd need.

"Weathercloak, lantern, coins in plenty, spare dagger, my old hunting boots rather than these stylish things . . ."

The King's Forest came into his head. Yes, that's where he'd go.

Even now, when all the lords who mattered were here in Suzail and the fate of the realm on a carving platter in their midst.

Yes, he was going.

Why? Because, stlarn it, he was afraid.

Lady Glathra's glare flashed before him, then Halonter's baleful look, then the weight of the dark and evil will that had ridden his mind so often . . .

"I'm stlarned well fearful for good reason," he snarled aloud, striding back to the table to stare down at what he'd accumulated.

Oh, he'd need a royal warrant to get the city gates opened, by night. Good thing his father had been of the generation who thought every noble House should bribe courtiers for a handful of the things, in case of future need.

The warrants were yonder, hidden in the drawer on the underside of the little Amnian table, with the—yes—poisoned daggers he'd probably also need.

Ah! He'd be lighting that lantern how, exactly? Flints and strikers, the ones that adorned their own tinderbox. After all, he'd have no servants to call on, out there in the forest.

The forest. *Where* in the forest?

He could hardly go to the Stormserpent hunting lodge. The moment Glathra's wolves found him missing from home, that's where they'd go looking.

No, it would have to be another lodge he knew, one where he'd be less likely to be found.

Which meant a place belonging to one of his admittedly few friends, his band of fellow traitors.

Windstag.

Given his wounds, the stain he'd brought on himself hunting the hand axe, and his vanity, Windstag wouldn't be setting foot barefaced outside the gates of Staghaven House for days. Which meant he wouldn't be using his lodge for some time, being as no other living Windstag had any stomach at all for hunting.

That's where he'd go.

But not alone. Not in those wild reaches. Not when the king's foresters might well treat him as badly as any desperate outlaw with a sharp knife.

He'd take three of his men, the best bodyguards left that he could trust.

As much as he could trust anyone, of course.

And wearing the wry and bitter grin that thought brought to his lips, Marlin hastened out of the room with his bundle, seeking saddlebags.

After all, he'd also be taking the four fastest horses.

"One spell too many," El muttered as Storm wearily lay down atop him again and took hold of his chin—Rune's smooth chin—in both hands to press and keep their foreheads together.

Their minds sank into each other in the familiar melting ... and the healing began anew. Neither of them wanted to notice how dark and tired Storm's mind was.

"Always the grand gesture," she hissed, her breath holding a hint of cinnamon. "The one last touch. The magic too far."

"'Tis *important*, Stormy One," he replied. "The right impression can save a dozen battles, or more. Cow thy enemies—"

"Yes, yes, I know." She sighed. "Just cow them with fewer castings next time, hey?"

"I will, love," he murmured. "Or ye'll be the one staggering and falling, I know."

Storm murmured something wordless and contented against him, her mind warming in a flare of pleasure.

El wondered very briefly what he'd said to cause that reaction . . . and then forgot it along with everything else, as the healing reached the stage where he always slid into oblivion.

Wonderful oblivion . . .

Chapter
TWENTY-ONE

Hiding and Seeking

Here we go again, hard at pursuits some seem to love
Though I, lords, am not one of them.
All this hiding and seeking gives me acute rectal pain.

> Halderand the Guardcaptain, Act I, Scene IV of the play
> *The Princess Denied* by Aldaerlon "Chapbooks" Palameir
> first performed in the Year of the Hidden Harp

Mirt lurched sideways, nearly turning an ankle on a broken cobble, and growled a curse.

A pace farther on he asked, "How much longer are we going to be carrying His Lordship, hey? He's not getting any lighter!"

"When the spell that's locked his limbs wears off," Storm replied, "or El decides he might not need to cast something more pressing."

"Huh. That'll be never, if I know mages," Mirt growled. "Why—"

Rune, carrying the other end of Arclath, turned her head sharply and hissed in Elminster's deep whisper, "Silence! Head down and look away yonder!"

A jerk of Amarune's head signaled the direction in which Mirt was to turn; the tone of El's voice made him obey unhesitatingly.

Two bare breaths later—time El spent murmuring something—four riders on fast horses burst past them, out of the night.

Looking up from under bushy brows, Mirt kept his eyes on the mask dancer's slender shoulders and was rewarded with the sight of her turning to point a finger at the second rider.

The sound of hooves died away.

"Someone's in a hurry to leave town," Mirt commented, "an' you know who, don't ye?"

"Young Lord Stormserpent," El replied shortly, "with some of his bullyblades. I cast a tracer on him."

"Wisely done," Storm said wearily, her silver tresses uncoiling themselves from around her head to bare her face again, "but if it lasts long, I'll be needing healing. Magic or a long and well-tended rest. Preferably both."

"With warm baths as often as ye desire, hey?"

"You know women well, Lord of Waterdeep."

"Better than I know magic. This tracer, it drains ye, the longer old Mightyspells here holds it on our fleeing lordling?"

"It does." Storm sighed, coming to a halt. They'd reached the gates of Stormserpent Towers. El had noticed they stood open in the wake of the four departed riders, and he stopped to peer in.

"No guards that I can see," he murmured. "Not even servants out to close the gates again. Come. The stables."

"And if someone confronts us?" Mirt growled. "We're a mite encumbered."

"We're playing a prank on Lord Stormserpent *and* Lord Delcastle, at Lord Windstag's request," El replied promptly. "If they don't seem to believe us, Storm and I—Rune, that is—will take our clothes off. *That* usually seems to distract most guards and pompous male servants."

"And what am *I* supposed to do?" Mirt growled.

"We'll need you if they're *female* guards or pompous servants," Storm said brightly.

No one challenged them or even showed a face from the Stormserpent mansion as they slipped into the darkened and deserted stables. El borrowed Storm's dagger, kindled the faint glowstone in its pommel, and went straight to a corner where an old carriage stood at such a lean that it was obviously not usable. Beneath it was a torn and huddled heap of rotten awnings, thick with dust and the litter of many mouse nests.

"We hide the magic that Glathra and her hounds can trace here," he announced in a whisper. "Then go."

They did that, in smooth haste. Storm gave both El and Mirt Harper ironguard rings to wear, and they were back out on the road with the still-paralyzed Arclath to continue their journey to Delcastle Manor in the space of a few breaths.

Mirt looked back seven times, but the Stormserpent gates never closed.

Targrael marched along the sweeping street as if she owned it. She was, after all, a Highknight of Cormyr—*the* senior Highknight of the realm, regardless of what the living thought—and watch patrols of this wealthy neighborhood of noble mansions were frequent and apt to pounce on skulkers. The haughty, however, they'd learned to treat with respect.

She'd already been several streets south, on the far side of the Promenade, seeking Manshoon—for if he found her before she found him, she'd be swiftly back into slavery. In her fist was a palace gem, a very old Obarskyr treasure. Gifted by elves, so the tales ran. Most of what it did had been forgotten, but it functioned as a keen detector of awakened Art, close by.

Manshoon was far from the only spellhurler apt to be busy this night, in this city crowded with nobles and afire with scheming intrigue, but Targrael knew his love for constant spying, and walked the streets hoping the gem would catch the steady flows of Art that attended multiple scrying eyes.

Yet she found none.

She'd become increasingly mindful that with every step she took she gave the old vampire more opportunity to notice her. And that the longer the gem was missing from where it should be, in Duar's Retiring Room, the greater the likelihood that wizards of war would come looking for her.

It was probably best to rethink this bold searching, return the gem, and hide herself in the haunted wing. Yet, she might as well pass Stormserpent Towers on her way back and try the gem there. Manshoon had spent much time riding the feckless Stormserpent lord recently, and even if the young fool had more than earned his own violent disposal, there remained the matter of the blueflame ghosts and his ownership of items that controlled them.

She'd have to be swift. The nobles' streets were well-nigh deserted—though she'd caught a distant glimpse of three revelers carrying a wounded or more likely drunken companion home—and Manshoon was as likely as anyone else to take an interest in the wealthy and powerful and the uses he could make of them.

Coming round the curve, she saw something that almost made her stop in surprise—and after a moment of hesitation, quicken her stride. The gates of Stormserpent Towers stood open.

Almost all of the grander mansions had high walls around their grounds to keep out thieves. Not to mention persistent hawkers or creditors and unwanted, garden-trampling gawkers. Those who had such expensive barriers tended to use them, especially by night. If a carriage or greatcoach wasn't about to enter or depart, gates would be firmly closed and locked. To see an unsecured entrance and no servants standing watchfully by the opened gates was unusual.

No watch patrol behind her, and none to be seen ahead. There were no side streets near, and the unbroken line of mansion walls afforded no cover for a patrol—or anyone else—to lurk, ready to pounce.

So with head held high and shoulders back, Targrael strode right up to the gates and into the grounds of Stormserpent Towers, as if the gates had been left open for her.

Six strides in along the deserted, night-shrouded carriageway, the gem in her hand warmed slightly. Not the flare of active spells nor the steady rise in temperature that heralded the nearness of always-functioning wards, but a sharper, smaller kindling.

There was *palace* magic here! A small amount of it, but nearby and very recently arrived . . .

Targrael frowned. Then she took a step to the left. Yes. Turning, she crossed the width of the carriageway, onto the lawn to the right. No, fainter, so back to the left.

The house rose straight ahead, though of course the carriageway reached it in a series of long, graceful curves. Off to the left, just past this stand of duskwoods, was ... the stables.

Targrael went into a crouch and turned sharply to the left, departing the carriageway for a stretch of lawn that would let her go around behind the duskwood bower, to reach the stables from the side or rear.

If a watch patrol or any inquisitive war wizards were lurking in the stables, she wanted to see them before they saw her.

Once behind the trees and closer to the stables—which loomed up dark, silent, and seemingly deserted—the gem in her hand grew warmer with every step she took.

Could Elminster be up to his old tricks, thieving palace magic? Or was this his cache of stolen enchantments? A walled noble compound wasn't the hiding place she would have chosen, but perhaps he intended that if his loot was discovered, the Stormserpents would be blamed.

For years he'd posed as old Elgorn Rhauligan, working at the palace with his sister—Storm Silverhand, his fellow refugee from the service of fallen Mystra. They were still working together, weren't they?

Aside from a few scurrying mice, the stables were deserted. The gem led Targrael straight to a small sack of rings and wands. Sleep wands, except for one that blasted and one that spat sticky webs. War wizard issue.

So unless a cabal of Crown mages was plotting something, these were stolen.

Most likely by Elminster and Storm, or some Stormserpent servant. Not by Marlin Stormserpent; *that* one would take them inside his walls and hide them somewhere in the mansion he thought was secure, behind all its wards and shieldings.

Frowning, Targrael put the sack back as she'd found it, covered it again with the long-decayed awning, and stood pondering. Should she seek Storm Silverhand around Suzail? Lush of figure, beautiful, and with that long silver hair, it was more likely a man would notice her than either Elminster or Manshoon—particularly if those wise old mages didn't want to be noticed.

Should she try to find such noticing persons and question them?

Or do the wiser thing, return to the palace, hide, and work on her patience?

"Bah!" she told the night loudly, turning on her heel.

The wiser, patient thing for once.

Huh. Undead or not, death knight or no, she *must* be getting old.

Manshoon slid eagerly back into his darkly handsome human body. Beholderkin were fine, better than drifting along ghostlike as vampires could, but he liked to be solid and in the sort of body he'd been born with, when it came time for serious thinking.

It was time right now, here in the cellar of the alchemist. A squalid place by some reckonings, and he'd certainly known more luxurious surroundings—he still missed the soaring gloom of his Tower High back in Zhentil Keep, even after all these years—but increasingly it was starting to feel like home.

His scrying globes glowed patiently as he sat up, ran his gaze over them all to make sure nothing really alarming was unfolding anywhere—nothing was—and sat back to ponder.

So his old foe was alive, or perhaps undead. Elminster was back in Suzail, back with Storm Silverhand. *Not* destroyed, after all.

And not, so far as he could tell, preparing to smite one Manshoon.

Which was odd; if Elminster had slain one of *his* clones and the next had awakened, it would do as he'd so often done—found some way to hit back, hard. Swiftly, too.

Not so boldly as to sacrifice yet another of his selves, but to make it very clear to Elminster that he hadn't been vanquished and was back undeterred.

So what, then, was Elminster now up to?

Well, meddling, of *course*. 'Twas what the Old Fool *did*. Trying to rule thrones from behind them, sway this lord into giving him food and a bed while he stole magic and coins from that lord, or in this case the royal family of Cormyr. Stay close to the rich and powerful, whisper in their ears, get them to do what he wanted them to do—just as he'd been doing for centuries.

Manshoon knew the lure of power himself. It was *the* elixir; there was nothing stronger.

Yet, he'd done it all himself, not ridden the skirts of Mystra the Mighty, never stolen into the heart—and bed—of a goddess to shelter in the warmth of her smile and fondness. He'd *earned* his might, where sly old Elminster had wormed it out of a doting goddess. Oh, that worming had worked, all right, and who could have foreseen that the great goddess of All Art, Our Lady of Mystery, *the* goddess, would fall?

Of greater importance now was this: with the Weave to call on at will, and all Mystra's servitors and other Chosen to use and abuse, Elminster had become lazy in his own Art. Had spent years doing this and doing that, for Mystra and for himself, but seldom honing greater Art, mastering more magic.

So the great Sage of Shadowdale, alone now with all his friends and easy power gone, was behind and beneath Manshoon the *truly* mighty.

Be he Orbakh of Westgate or Manshoon of the Zhentarim before that, he himself had worked the greater Art and had improved his skills through his own work, not by godly gifts or reliance on abundant ready aid. *He* was the better mage, the true archwizard.

Which in turn inevitably meant Elminster, the sly but lazy, could but follow in Art where Manshoon had led.

Was Elminster not seeking to steal all the magic he could? Oh, to feed his mad, chained-somewhere lover, yes, but did he not examine each enchanted item he took, to learn all he could before he took it to her?

So, while Emperor-to-be Manshoon rode the minds of all he chose, Elminster must be a step behind, doing what Manshoon had formerly done. Using many selves, clones awakened when their predecessors were destroyed.

Yes, that was it. Must be . . .

He *had* killed Elminster, had destroyed him. Burst right through his body, dismembered him, then burned him to ashes.

Accomplishing all of that quickly, leaving his foe unattended for not even an instant, all the while watching hard for the slightest sign of any escape. There had been none at all.

So somewhere, as Elminster had died, Elminster's next clone had awakened. Fearing to face death again at the hands of the one who'd so effortlessly slain him, he'd used magic to disguise himself as a young lass—the mask dancer who was his own descendant—and no doubt forced the real Amarune Whitewave into stasis, in some hidden cave or crypt, to await his future need.

Which would come when he mastered the Art of riding the minds of others, as Manshoon could now do, and took over his descendant's younger, stronger body for good.

In the meantime, there must be other clones of Elminster, hidden deep in Suzail.

And, whereas he could leave frustrating and foiling the current Elminster to his tools, finding and destroying the waiting selves, the clones, must now be Manshoon's foremost task.

Let his noble cabals scheme and slay; when highborn ranks were thinned he could return to *that* game and still seize the Dragon Throne, or decide who precisely would warm it until he deemed the time ripe for that puppet's disposal.

Before all, starting now, he would hunt down and destroy hidden Elminsters.

So, where in Suzail, if I were Elminster, would I hide my waiting selves?

Or . . . wait!

He himself had tasted death many times, often thanks to this same Elminster. He'd grown used to it, had become harder and stronger. Not so his slayer.

This hiding, this failure to strike out at Manshoon, might well mean that Elminster—the awakened clone—was cowering somewhere. That his death had plunged him into fear of Manshoon, so he remained in hiding, using spells to see and hear through a puppet Amarune Whitewave.

Which would mean the question should be, where, if I were Elminster, would I hide myself in Suzail?

Well, somewhere I could keep at least one clone near at hand. Somewhere servants couldn't stumble on it, nor the general public. Somewhere unlikely to be searched without warning by Purple Dragons or, more importantly, by wizards of war.

Yet, this was the thinking of Manshoon the accomplished ruler and war leader. How would *Elminster* see things and think?

The man is sly but lazy, thinks himself clever but often takes the easiest way. He's lasted for centuries and has been the favored servant of a goddess; the man has pride, *is* pride. And he seeks to be like me, the more successful archwizard, without rising to such dominance the hard way.

What better way to hide from the war wizards and live lazily, in luxury and wielding magic whenever he pleases, than to "hide" himself as a powerful wizard?

Yes!

Why if he was, say, Larak Dardulkyn, he could dwell in the heart of Suzail in a near-fortress, awash in luxuries, able to hurl spells at will without raising suspicion, and be fawned over, to boot!

Larak Dardulkyn . . .

The most powerful independent mage in Suzail. An ideal mask for an Elminster clone to wear.

Manshoon sprang from his chair and strode into the midst of his scrying spheres.

This one could readily be set to scry that haughty wizard's mansion, yes . . .

But when the picture of the mansion swam into view, Manshoon shook his head in astonishment. When had all of *this* befallen?

The tall mansion of Larak Dardulkyn was half gone, one side torn open to the sky, and in the rubble-heaped heart of the devastation he could see the archwizard huddled on the floor, with ten helmed horrors circling him in a troubled, uncertain floating dance.

Well, now! If this *was* Elminster, behold a Bane-sent opportunity! Slay him now, while he's laid low—but go in hard and fast and powerful, in case whoever humbled him is still around. If Dardulkyn wasn't Elminster, it was still the best chance he could hope to find for plundering the place or coercing the man into becoming another useful thrall.

Manshoon hurried across the cellar. His most powerful beholder would be best—of the living ones, not a death tyrant.

Yes, beholders remain impressive beasts, when it comes to forcing one's way in.

"There's no need to worry Arclath's mother," Storm told them. "His stricken self got us through the gate—that's enough. Set him down here."

They were on the grounds of Delcastle Manor, on a gently rolling grass slope, between a garden carefully planted to seem wild and a more formal terrace that fronted a boundary orchard.

"Too tired for fencing with noble matriarchs, hey?" Mirt grunted as they laid Arclath gently down.

"*More* than too tired for almost any nicety you care to name," Storm murmured, "and hoping Arclath can plunder some healing potions from his family vaults—if they hold such treasures—before I'm finished. El, try to do this quickly."

"Aye," Elminster replied, his voice still sounding incongruous from Amarune's young, shapely body. "Lie ye there, Storm, and I'll put myself between ye and the lad, and we can do this without ye having to even sit up."

"Healing him again?" Mirt asked, lending his arm for Storm to lower herself to the grass.

"Yes," Storm replied. "Holding him where he is while he works a spell, actually, but it's the same thing. I heal as he drains, to keep him stable."

"I'll stand back, yonder, and keep daggers at the ready," Mirt growled. "Seeing as ye haven't any spells to spare for making me young and thin and strong again. Or stopping my feet hurting."

Bending over, he peered at Arclath Delcastle's stiff body, the young lord's arm crooked and one leg raised to take a next step.

"Does he know what you'll be doing to him, I wonder?"

Settling himself on the ground, Elminster turned his head and looked into Arclath's face.

His answer, when it came, was in Amarune's voice. She sounded half grim and half on the sword's sharp edge of tears.

"Oh, he knows. Believe me, he knows."

Chapter
Twenty-Two

Disputes and Recriminations

Why did I become a hated magister, who argues out policies
Before the throne, disputes and recriminations day-long?
Lad,'tis no mystery I'm skilled at sharp-tongue talk, my
Hard-armored hide thick as a dragon's;
I got both those being husband to thy mother.

> Thorgraunt the Vizier, Act III, Scene I of the play
> *Before the Black Days* by Auhntryn Valavvur of
> Athkatla first performed in the Year of the Voyage

Arclath flung up a hand. "I can *move* again! All gods be
praised! Thank you!"

Amarune's hand remained on his throat, and out of her
beautiful lips—which he'd been about to kiss—came Elminster's deep voice. "Save thy thanks a bit, lad. We're not done yet."

Arclath's eyes narrowed. "Oh? What are you going to do?"

"Storm," El asked, "are ye up for this?"

"Yes," Storm sighed. "It must be done."

"Aye, it must."

Arclath scowled and drew his head back, trying to arch
away. Rune's hand on his shoulder suddenly gripped him
firmly.

"Suppose you explain what 'must' be done *before* you do it
to me, mage."

"We must peer into thy mind to make certain no one's
influencing ye, spying through ye, or using tracing magic on ye."

Arclath stiffened. "I knew it! I *knew* you'd find some
excuse to—"

"So, ye were just as clever as ye thought ye were, and aren't
disappointed now, are ye?" Mirt growled, standing above them.

"He's talking about *enslaving* me, Lord of Waterdeep!" Arclath barked. "Forgive me if I'm ..."

His voice trailed off and his eyes went from furious to frowningly surprised.

Yes, this is what a rude and dishonest old archwizard's mind feels like, El's voice said, in the depths of his own head. The words were a sarcastic growl, but his mind was friendly, as affectionate as any whimsical old uncle. Arclath had a brief glimpse of shining, upswept towers gleaming blue-white in the depths of a great green forest, then a laughing bearded face wearing a state crown of Cormyr, a face that almost had to be the fourth Azoun in his prime ... then an unclad, beautiful lady flying high in the air in the heart of a lightning storm, her hair wild around her and festooned with lightning that seemed to do her no harm, a lady with eyes of triumphant fire and a face like Storm's yet subtly different ... then he was looking down vast dark halls, endless long passages full of too many images to see, let alone count.

"All right, lad, *all* right. Don't try to see all my remembrances at thy first gulp. It's taken me some twelve centuries to assemble them; getting greedy is apt to drive you mad."

Then Elminster's mind seemed to slide *past* him, like a great leviathan of a cruising dragon, a body that went on and on, displaying frightening size and power as it rolled past, and rolled past, and went on rolling ...

Arclath's anger was gone, lost in wonder, and most of his fear with it. He felt sudden discomfort, born of El starting to root around in his mind while he sought to keep gazing at Elminster's ... he saw some dark and terrible things, some gruesome deaths and sadnesses that made him recoil, but he could tell the Sage of Shadowdale was hiding *nothing,* was letting him see and feel whatever he desired.

And Arclath Delcastle discovered he liked the *feel* of this visiting mind. He *liked* this old man. Truly liked Elminster, as he was starting—just starting—to really know him, better than he'd ever known anyone before.

The vast mind turned gently and started to withdraw, the dragon sliding past in the other direction now. He'd seen so little of it, yet beheld enough to know one thing: he could trust Elminster of Shadowdale.

Inside his mind or anywhere.

He was suddenly tearful, lost in a joy he knew was silly yet meant so much. Nobles of Cormyr grow up knowing they can trust no one in the world, and that those who trust others are fools or dupes to be used.

Now, at last, he knew—*knew*—there was one person he could trust.

"Four, lad. There are four, not one," El murmured, holding him in Amarune's embrace. "Storm, thy mother, Rune, and Elminster Aumar. Now stop weeping on me; these are Amarune's best leathers."

Ah, now *there* was a rare sight: war wizards who had some common sense.

Riding the body of his mightiest eye tyrant, Manshoon skulked behind a rooftop cistern, watching the Crown mages turn their watch patrol back from Dardulkyn's mansion.

"Cordon, until full light and reinforcements," he heard one of them shout. "No rushing in. Cormyr needs live heroes, not dead ones."

My, my. A philosopher, too. He'd have to remember to use that mage on special missions, once he was Emperor of Cormyr and Beyond. Or imprison him. Perhaps as a brain in a jar.

Grateful that clouds had drifted in to shroud the stars and make this a dark night indeed, Manshoon floated to the edge of the roof—two removed from Dardulkyn's, with a street separating the wizard's abode from that last roof—and watched Purple Dragons retreat to positions where they could watch around corners for anyone entering or departing Dardulkyn's mansion.

Not that they could see all that well. The lanterns were frequent and well tended in this neighborhood, one of the better parts of the city, but a mist off the harbor was beginning to steal through the streets.

The moment he saw visible haloes of light around the lanterns—meaning the mists were becoming thick enough to glow and impede vision—it would be time.

Ah. There. Patience rewarded.

Manshoon glided forward, eyestalks writhing in anticipation.

So, Elminster, care for a rematch? A second annihilation?

Dardulkyn was on his feet finally, shaking his head and mumbling to himself. From the rubble he took up a long, jagged sliver from a shattered doorframe and leaned on it as if it were a staff.

Leaning as if he were old, weak, exhausted . . . as if he truly needed aid to keep from falling.

Which made Manshoon dare to descend into the half-shell of a riven upper room of the mansion, and from there send forth his mind, slowly and with infinite care.

Are you Elminster, mumbling archwizard? Or another overreaching fool?

The world certainly holds no shortage of those, after all . . .

Manshoon's subtle probe felt something sharp and narrow that was focused on the mind he sought. Then another and another, moving restlessly, but not far. The helmed horrors, who were still surrounding the stricken mage, anxious for orders and purpose. Ten of them in all.

His reaching slid past them, as slow and silent as he could make it. Of old, he'd felt far too many of Elminster's traps close around him . . .

Dardulkyn was aghast, only now crawling out of dazed disbelief that he could be laid so low so quickly and effortlessly by a young lass who moved like a dancer or a purr-posing playpretty.

Elminster. Not this overblown mage, but the spellhurler who'd shattered a few rooms—and this dolt of a Dardulkyn's worldview—at the same time.

His hated foe had done this, either riding the mind of his descendant or, far more likely, cloaking his clone in her shape to escape all blame—for when war wizards used their spells on the real Amarune Whitewave's mind, they'd find she had no talent for the Art at all.

So, this Dardulkyn was no Elminster, and a weak-spirited preener besides. That didn't mean he couldn't be a very useful mind-slave. This mansion, suitably repaired, would make the perfect place to keep all his beholders—the three living ones, the six eye tyrants and pitiful hulk of a seventh, and the five usable beholderkin. After all, if they were ever found, Larak Dardulkyn would be blamed; no one would look further for some other archwizard. Whereas, if they were discovered in Sraunter's cellar, the Crown would quickly ascertain that Sraunter was as feeble at Art as Whitewave, and go looking for a spellhurler in the shadows behind him.

Yes, this would be ideal. Human thralls in the alchemist's cellar, and the tyrants here.

His probe became a brutal surge; Larak Dardulkyn barely had time to register astonishment and cap it with affronted rage before his mind was vanquished and quivering.

"Stand up," Dardulkyn heard his own voice whisper to him, as the helmed horrors all turned to stare at him intently.

"It's time to act like an archwizard for once, and not a sneering bellows of empty arrogance and overestimation. *Be* a mighty mage, Dardulkyn. Be me."

"It's an ironguard ring," Storm explained. "It'll make most swords and other blades pass right through you but do no harm. Don't trust in it overmuch—anything bearing an enchantment will cut you as usual."

She held up her hand to show Arclath she was wearing an identical ring, and pointed at Mirt's and then at Amarune's.

His love reached out to take his hand, letting Elminster flow back into his mind and link it with Storm's—warm yet sad, joyous and, yes, arousing—so he could see and know Storm was telling him the truth about the rings.

Then Elminster withdrew again, leaving Arclath awash with relief.

Storm's mind was dangerous for him. He could *so* easily fall in love with her and lose himself in rising lust ... but crown and throne, it was good to *know* when one was being told the truth. No wonder olden-times war wizards had mind-reamed nobles and everyone else so often.

"What now?" he heard himself asking, as a gentle night breeze rose and ghosted past, rustling a few nearby leaves in his family gardens.

"Now, lad," Elminster replied promptly, that deep voice still sounding ridiculous from his Rune's lips, "we talk. A war council, if ye will. A small, brawl-free one, if we can manage it."

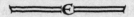

"My name is Rorlyn Handmane, and I am a lionar of the Purple Dragons," the Dragon officer answered the cold demand calmly, as if he'd expected it. "I've been ordered to investigate what befell here and render any reasonable aid you request, Saer Dardulkyn. Explosions and possibilities of magic gone awry are always of interest to the Crown. Mindful of your stature and accomplishments, senior wizards of war have sent me to make inquiries rather than approaching you—an archwizard who may have professional matters you prefer not to let other workers-of-Art examine—themselves."

"Your prudent—for once—discretion, and theirs, are appreciated," the archwizard replied coldly. "Heed these words well, and share them with the other Crown watchers ringing my home before you take them back to the mages who sent you: a rather powerful but peaceful-of-purpose spell went awry, and nothing more. I neither need nor want any assistance in determining details of the resulting damage. What befell is no business whatsoever of the Crown or the wider weal, and for your own safety you should all take yourselves away again. Immediately."

He stepped forward, to the crumbling edge of what was left of the end wall of his mansion, and glared down at the lionar and the three other Dragons who stood with the officer.

The lionar nodded, raised his hand in salute, and replied flatly, "Your words have been heard. As for our offer and vigilance . . . you're very welcome, wizard."

Then Handmane turned his back on Dardulkyn and his mansion, and marched away.

Manshoon had to stop himself from chuckling. Oh, well *said*, brave lionar! He made Dardulkyn's body turn to the helmed horrors floating in a patient arc behind him, and order them—loudly and unnecessarily, for the benefit of the cordon of listening Dragons—to secure the damaged mansion and make very certain no intruder slipped inside.

The beholder body he'd arrived in was hidden in one of the upper rooms that still had a roof, accompanied by a patiently floating beholderkin he could use to return to Sraunter's shop.

Reaching out to the minds of the two nearest horrors, he sent them to begin breaking open a shaft to let his beholder float down into Dardulkyn's cellars.

Leaving the other horrors to defend the walls against every last rat, mouse, or bird that ventured near the riven mansion, he took Dardulkyn's body on a tour of the cellars.

Pleasingly, the uppermost of those lower levels included one large chamber into which had been placed a row of cages fashioned of massive iron bars—cages as large as small huts. A thin, sickly looking griffon was trapped in one, the cage strewn with its shed feathers, but the rest were empty of all but some unpleasant-looking mounds of bones. Good. The beholder—and, once he got them here, its fellow tyrants—could be put into these monster cages.

He'd raise some strong wards around the place—Dardulkyn's were pitiful—but for the benefit of the inevitable farscrying war wizards, some of whom were undoubtedly spying on him right now, he'd make sure his tyrants rested on the floor rather than floating in midair, and kept their eyestalks drooping, so as to look dead rather than alive.

Wards that were nigh worthless, a lot of "impress gullible idiots" décor . . . well, one could but hope Dardulkyn's tomes and enchanted items were a tenth as powerful as the man's mind believed they were. It was high time to see what he'd gained, and if his new dupe had any magic at all that was new to Manshoon the Mighty, Emperor-to-be of Cormyr and Beyond.

Yes, that *did* have a ring to it, it did.

Arclath nodded. "So, talk."

Elminster needed no more prompting. "Lad," he began, "ye've heard from Storm who it was who slew me: Manshoon."

"Another centuries-old wizard. Once ruled Zhentil Keep, rode dragons, wasn't nice. Or so the old tales say."

Mirt chuckled and nodded.

"Those tales lie not," El agreed, "and tell ye almost all ye need to know about the man. Hear now the rest. There have been many Manshoons. When he's slain, another of his selves awakens, and ye must slay him all over again. His Art is very strong, and with it he can easily conquer the minds of others and make them his slaves."

"As you can," Arclath said softly.

"As I can, aye. Yet Manshoon is . . . far less considerate. Where I cozen—"

"Manipulate."

"As good a word for it, aye. Where I manipulate, he coerces."

Storm and Mirt both nodded, so Arclath did, too. "And so?"

"The man loves not just to defeat and dominate—he lives to rule. Zhentil Keep and its farflung tentacles—literally scores of holds, from waystop keeps to cities. To say nothing of Westgate, Ombraldar, and far Shanooth. He isn't just here hunting me. Tired of a Westgate that won't stay ruled but seethes tirelessly with deceits, challenges, and coup attempts—a delight for him for a decade or two but increasingly tiresome thereafter, as he sees the same ploys and clumsy deceptions a fourth and a tenth time, or more—he's set his sights on a brighter prize. He's here in Suzail to conquer the realm."

"Isn't competition for that particular ambition a mite crowded already?" Arclath asked. "How can you be certain of Manshoon's involvement, given all the plots and feuds and Crown-hatreds that have been nursed here for centuries? Centuries!"

"Therein lies the sport. Using various nobles and courtiers as his pawns, and remaining unnoticed until his chosen time to reveal himself. The brawl at Council may in very large part be his doing."

"Perhaps, but could you not be as guilty as we nobles of Cormyr are, of seeing every little chance happening not as what it truly is, but as the latest move in our ongoing feuds with each other and the Crown? You see Manshoon's hand because you expect to, whether or not it's really there."

"I agree," said Amarune, her voice clearly hers and not Elminster's.

"*Rune!*" Arclath cried, reaching for her. "He's let you master yourself again! Why—"

"We're sharing, lad," El rumbled, out of the lips Arclath was leaning to kiss. And grinned. "So go on, kiss thy lady. I'll not look."

Arclath froze for a moment, bewildered—then shrugged, swept Rune into his arms, and kissed her heartily.

After a good long time, she ended it with a smile and looked past his shoulder. "Storm? Mirt? What think you?"

"El's right. Manshoon is here in Suzail, and up to something. Seizing the Dragon Throne will be his goal. Seizing thrones always is."

Mirt nodded agreement. "El has the right of it. As usual."

Rune's smile faded as she regarded Arclath, nose to nose. "Much as I hate to think of an evil archwizard slyly at work in our city, it could very well be true. After all, these three believe it, and they've known this spellhurler and our realm far longer than we have. Whether they're right or not, we *dare* not dismiss their warning as mistaken."

Arclath let out a long, exasperated sigh. "You're right, Rune. Of course. And I should need no one else to remind me of my duty to the realm. Nobles must watch for all perils to fair Cormyr, so we can save our land from itself if the need arises. For the sake of Cormyr and everyone in it, I dare not behave as if this tale of a lurking Manshoon is *less* than true."

Storm spread her hands, but it was Elminster who spoke the words to go with them. "And so?"

Arclath waited for Mirt but heard only silence. With all eyes looking at him.

"We're lost if we try to find Manshoon's mind-slaves among all the lords of Cormyr," he said slowly, thinking aloud. "They're all traitors, in tiny matters or large schemings. Every last one of them will seem as suspicious as they always do. Our rooting among them warns Manshoon that we know of him, and gives him endless opportunities to slay us at will."

He winced, seeing imagined disasters at every hand. "No, we must rally to the Dragon Throne. Return to the palace, try to keep out of Glathra's clutches, and hunt for traces of Manshoon—and his mind-slaves and allies among the wizards of war."

Storm and Rune both nodded vigorously.

"Using my Art and the Princess Alusair's aid to hide from Glathra as much as we can," El put in. "So, ye've brought us into the palace, amid much fun of dodging Purple Dragons and war wizards and hundreds of prying courtiers, lad. Where, with the aid of a score of friendly gods, we find and scour out every last traitor within the walls. Finding no Manshoon, who must be outside the palace laughing at us and thoroughly aware of our every belch, yawn, and need to scratch. What then?"

Arclath frowned. "Above all, the king must be protected. *All* Obarskyrs must, for that matter. Yet, I know not how."

"Heh," Mirt growled, "ye must make all 'hows' up as ye go along. I learned that well, the hard way. It strikes me this realm awash in Crown mages needs a ruling hand that every last wizard of war is afraid of. If the infamous Sage of Shadowdale has to step into Vangerdahast's old boots and become royal magician and court wizard all in one, hated by every noble in the kingdom and feared by every commoner, well . . . so be it."

CHAPTER
TWENTY-THREE

SWORDS COME OUT

The time for threats is past, and so the lords do shout
War is come at last, now all the swords come out.

> from the ballad *The Swords Come Out*
> composer unknown first performed
> circa the Year of Bane's Brood

I f you *do* try to become royal magician, Elminster," Arclath
announced slowly, "even knowing you mean well, I might
be forced to oppose you. You'd be better for Cormyr than
Manshoon, yet you're still an old and mighty archwizard, and
an outlander to boot. Magic has a way of . . . corrupting those
who wield it."

"It does indeed. Yet, if it makes ye sleep more serenely, lad,
know this—I have less than no interest in becoming another
Vangerdahast. Giving certain war wizards a solid kick up
the backside, aye; but, commanding them in the name of the
Dragon Throne, never. I'd as soon herd nobles of Cormyr. If
ye'll forgive me."

Arclath smirked despite himself, and cast a glance at the
towers of court and palace, visible above the rooftops, not all
that far away.

"So, how are we getting into the palace *this* time? It's too
much to hope they'll leave that house behind the stables
unguarded again."

"Ye keep hidden—the lot of ye," Mirt offered. "*I'll* do the
talking. Me, the fat uncouth outlander, who's been out in the
city an' has heard something the Lady Glathra *must* hear.
Herself alone, from my maw straight to her ears, right now."

Arclath rolled his eyes. "And if they don't believe you?"

"Ah. *Then* ye burst out to the attack. Nay, wait a bit! Rune and Storm, scantily clad, dance forth, an' I'll admit I'm really a panderer, bringing 'em in for the crown prince, or Hallowdant . . . aye, Hallowdant's safer. 'Tis a pose I've worked before."

Storm winked at Amarune. "Really? You're sure pandering is just a pose for you?"

"Well, now . . . back in Waterdeep, I'd know what to charge and who to offer—er, ah, *knew*. They'll all be long dead now, hey? Well—"

The awning they were passing under suddenly crashed down atop Storm, with an attacker who landed heels-first, dashing her to the ground.

As their attacker landed, Storm bouncing under those boots, a sword slashed Amarune from behind, flashing up under her left arm and slicing into her side. A pulse of purple light—enchantment—burst from that flashing steel, and Rune shrieked as she fell.

As Arclath shouted something furious and desperate, Mirt charged like a human bludgeon, driving the attacker away from Amarune and stabbing with both his daggers as he bowled the stranger to the cobbles and they rolled together.

Storm's tresses reached out to follow them, but the pair had moved too far—and the attacker, who was taller, faster, and more supple than Mirt, broke free of the wheezing man and up to his—no, her—feet, spinning to stand facing them, a silhouette dark and sleekly curvaceous, with a long, slender, and faintly glowing sword in hand.

That purple radiance brightened into a pale white light and showed them a tall, shapely, and fit woman in tight black leather armor and high boots that were too worn and mold-blotched to creak. Helmless, she had long, wild hair, dead-white skin, and a cruel, smiling face. Her eyes glowed red, and a small patch of mold adorned one of her cheeks.

"I am the defender of Cormyr," she purred, "and Elminster of Shadowdale, for your crimes against this fair realm, your life is more than forfeit!"

She was gazing down at Amarune, who lay moaning on the

cobbles, bright red blood flooding out of her and Storm rising to crouch over her like a grim gate guard, sword drawn and something else—a helm—in her other hand.

"Yes," Targrael added, seeing Arclath's horrified look. "I know. This is the Sage of Shadowdale, not a foolish little minx of a mask dancer. And it's soon to become the *remains* of Elminster of Shadowdale!"

Arclath Delcastle swallowed, then charged at her, drawing his sword with a flourish as he went.

"*I'm* Elminster, disloyal Highknight!" he snarled. "Not this blameless lass! Is *this* how you serve Cormyr?"

Targrael's glowing steel flashed up to turn his blade deftly aside as she hissed, "You *dare* to judge my loyalty, child of a noble? You, spoiled brat of one of the many traitor Houses who seek to sunder our fair realm? *You're* no Elminster! He's a fool, yes, but not *your* sort of a fool!"

Her sword lashed out, but Arclath parried expertly, smiling at the momentary surprise in her eyes—there *are* some benefits to a noble upbringing, and skilled sword-work is one of them—and advanced, pressing her. Out of a spinning clangor of parries, he ducked down into a lunge, then sidestepped her parry to lunge again, driving her back from Rune.

"Keep going," Storm murmured up at him, and he turned his head toward her long enough to see her jam the helm in her hand over Amarune's head.

It was the blackened helm from one of the helmed horrors El had felled. The helm full of roiling fire.

The wild shriek that rang out from inside it, in the instant before Rune jerked wildly in Storm's grasp and then fell limp, distracted Arclath just an instant too long—

The glowing sword slicing at his throat came so close that he felt its chill along his cheek and jaw, a sear so slight it would soon fade, as Targrael sought to slay him—and Mirt rolled right under her, snatching her feet from the cobbles and pitching her helplessly onto her face, her blade falling away *just* before it would have cut into Delcastle flesh.

Arclath whirled back to the fray and saw the death knight at his feet and snarlingly clawing at him, wildly hacking at the cobbles beneath and behind her with her blade and striking many sparks—yet failing to do more than make slices in Mirt's already-ragged boots, as he spun deftly around on one shoulder on the cobbles, away from her.

Arclath drew back his sword to stab her, then turned its edge so its point could seek her neck and throat as he brought it down—just how *does* one slay a death knight, anyhail?

Then he faltered, his blade slowing and drifting aside in the air as something burst into his head.

No, some*one*. Elminster. Ashes were sliding itchingly over his collar . . .

Targrael was up again, an unlovely smile growing on her face as she swung her sword in a vicious slash that couldn't miss.

Damn you, Elminster! Your brain-riding has slain me! You ruthless—

Storm's sword struck aside Targrael's with a shriek of straining steel, and the charging ranger's shoulder slammed into the death knight and sent her staggering helplessly back. Whereupon, Mirt hooked Targrael's planted hind foot out from under her and sent her toppling again.

"*Back!*" he roared, waving both arms wildly. "Keep ye back!"

Storm flung herself away from the bouncing, wallowing death knight, and as Targrael twisted around as swiftly as any angry eel, Mirt drew something from one of the many bulging pouches at his belt—and tossed it right in her face.

Arclath had time to see that it was a palm-sized sphere of rusty iron—and that the lady Highknight looked momentarily bewildered, ere her expression slid into dawning rage. Then the sphere glowed the purple-white of an awakening lesser enchantment of elder palace magics, and expanded with astonishing speed into a widening web of iron hoops, like the bands around an iron barrel. Still holding the shape of a sphere, they fell around the scrambling-to-her-feet Targrael in a cage.

Then they snapped tight again, trapping her, so that Mirt faced a much larger iron sphere from which jutted Targrael's head, her empty hand, the tip of her glowing blade, and one foot, with the rest of her hidden within its widening, now overlapping bands.

"Stlarn it," Mirt growled, weaving to his feet and huffing heavily for breath, "*that's* not going to hold her for long! Not with yon fancy magic blade of hers."

"It doesn't have to," Storm gasped, "if we can reach the palace before she's free! Hurry!"

"But, but—*Rune!*" Arclath protested, even as Storm dragged Amarune to her feet and started to run.

He could see that Amarune was stumbling along blindly, the Harper holding her up and guiding her. Her back and side were drenched with fresh blood, but she moved like someone unhurt, just dazed and unable to see.

Small wonder, that last: her head was still encased in a helm far too large for her, whose flames were fainter and dwindling still more as Arclath stared. Flames that could be clearly seen out the open front of the helm, which had wobbled around to show him the back of Amarune's head.

Was the blackened shell of metal *healing* her? It was certainly losing the fire that had raged in it in the wake of Elminster's horror-rending spell.

Arclath shook his head. He would *never* understand magic . . . and what scared him was the strengthening suspicion that even archmages understood only scraps of it.

"Come *on!*" Storm snapped over her shoulder, running faster. Mirt wheezed, then groaned like a sick walrus, barreling forward in a pell-mell lurching.

Arclath looked at the spitting-with-rage death knight in her iron prison—in time to see her overbalance in her struggles and fall to the cobbles to roll helplessly, snarling curses—then started to sprint after everyone. Catching up to the odd parade all running toward the palace.

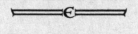

As the last of the wagons rumbled away from Sraunter's alley door, Manshoon helped the alchemist slam and bar it, then ran for the cellar stairs.

He had to move fast; the wizards of war wouldn't refrain from prying forever.

Not with their suspicions aroused, the city full of scheming nobles, and the sort of temper the Lady Glathra had.

A temper he would show her a match for, if it came to that. He was getting a headache already, what with having to dominate and control Sraunter and no fewer than six carters and drovers on three wagons. So soon after promising to limit himself, too. He'd picked the first three teams who'd stopped by the alchemist's shop with supplies in closed wagons that were large enough, not the carters and drovers Manshoon might have chosen at his own leisure.

"Leisure" being something he entirely lacked, just then.

That headache was why Crownrood spellslept in his locked cellar room, and some streets away Dardulkyn was hidden in a closet in his mansion, deep in similar enspelled slumber, while Manshoon trusted—*had* to trust—in the explicit and detailed orders he'd given the helmed horrors to keep all intruders at bay. Including zealous Purple Dragons, war wizards, and for that matter, any Highknights who might be lurking in Suzail and aching to demonstrate their prowess.

Aching mind or not, this darkly handsome human body was strong and supple; he could descend the cellar stairs in three long strides without fear of falling or skidding into an unyielding wall.

Coming to a deft stop by the chair, he turned on his heel and sat, wasting not a moment in his haste to get to where he could stare at his scrying eyes. Three of them could be turned to cover most of the wagons' route without need of going out and casting new scrying spells, and he'd either have to accompany a wagon himself to add the missing dogleg of streets, or risk doing without it. The beholderkin body he'd ridden back here could cast only spells worked by force of will or very simple utterances.

He stared into those three scrying eyes as he bent his will to making them leave the current array and drift to new positions, in a row floating together right in front of him, at the same time as he turned and refocused what they could see in Suzail.

Manshoon's head throbbed with sharper pain. He clenched his teeth, pressed hard fingers against his temples, and glared at the moving scenes of the dark Suzailan night streets as they swam, drifted sideways . . . and then settled into the views he wanted.

He was in time to see the first of the wagons carrying his precious cargo rumble into view from beneath, and on down the street away from his scrying eye's vantage point. It was followed by the second wagon.

It would have been subtler to send the wagons on different routes and approach the still-ringed-by-Dragons mansion singly, in something that was a little less obviously a convoy. It was proving hard enough to keep Sraunter, here at hand, and six other mens' minds at a distance, as those six guided carthorses and steered wagons in a normal-seeming fashion, all firmly in thrall.

Hard, but necessary.

It would be less than wise to have drooling, vacantly-staring, oddly leaning men visible when the wagons approached Dardulkyn's mansion—considering that under the tarps and behind the swing-gates of each wagon lurked the floating body of an undead beholder, bound for his new lair in Dardulkyn's mansion.

Manshoon was trying not to think of what would have to happen when they arrived. He'd just have to put Sraunter to sleep, hope no one came banging at the doors of the closed-up shop—yes, alchemists tended to do business at all hours, but it *was* the darkest, coldest time of deep night—and awaken the distant Dardulkyn to cast concealing magics before he sent his will into the distant death tyrants, one after another, and made each of them move. He dared not trust even the thickest sea fog to hide something so distinctive as a larger-than-man-sized beholder from prying war wizards.

The first wagon was only two streets away from the mansion, just coming into view in his newest scrying eye, the one he'd compelled Dardulkyn to cast before sending the man into slumber.

Coming into view but slowing, as a dung wagon came rumbling out of a side street to block its way.

Manshoon silently cursed all dung wagons and the idiot dungbucketeers who drove them, even as he reminded himself that doing anything to this one was out of the question . . .

The battered old dung wagon stopped right across the street, and men on foot appeared around either side of it. Far too many to be dung collectors or citizens bringing their nightsoil.

Not that citizens wore chainmail and the helms of Dragons, or were accompanied by wizards of war with wands ready in their hands.

Oh, *naed*. Naed naed naed *naed!*

Manshoon slammed clenched fists down on the arms of his chair and stared into the scrying spheres with blazing eyes.

Dardulkyn would still be blamed, yes, but they were going to find his death tyrant.

This first one, at least; he was already coercing the other drovers to turn aside and head toward the docks, the first leg of a long circuit that would bring the other two wagons separately back to Sraunter's rear door.

Dragons shouted sharp orders at the two wagonmen. To halt—which they already had—and to climb down and stand away from their wagon. Soldiers were already holding the bridles of the foremost draft horses.

Manshoon fought down his anger, tried to ignore the sharper and rising pounding in his head, called the spell he needed to the forefront of his mind, worked it but held it firmly in abeyance—"hanging," in the old parlance—and threw his mind from the suddenly stumbling drover to what awaited in the dark depths of the wagon.

A war wizard conjured bright light, harsh and white and flooding everywhere, making all the horses snort and stamp.

Dragons warily clambered up onto the back steps of the wagon, threw the latch on its doors, and hauled them open, jumping down. Then another pair of Dragons leaped up onto the steps and flung the tarps back.

Leaving his staring, rotting, gape-mawed, and ten-eye-stalked secret floodlit, and a secret no longer.

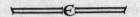

"She's free!" Mirt roared from behind them, obviously struggling to find breath enough to both shout and run. Inevitably he'd fallen behind in their trot to the palace. Not far ahead of him, Storm, Rune, and Arclath had burst out into the Promenade. They were swerving toward an area lit by both lanterns and conjured light around the fallen palace door that smiths and woodcarvers were examining, under the watchful eyes of Dragons.

"Try to get into the palace, or at least past as many Dragons as possible before we're stopped," Storm had just warned them, plucking the now-dark helm off Amarune's head and tossing it to the cobbles behind them. "Targrael wants our blood."

"Y-you surprise me," Rune joked weakly.

Turn back, lad. Now we stand and fight.

The voice in Arclath's head was firm, but no coercion came with it. Arclath nodded as if Elminster had spoken aloud, and whirled around, waving his sword. "Mirt!" he shouted. "I'll stand rearguard! *Run!*"

Targrael was running hard down the street behind the lumbering Waterdhavian, overhauling him with frightening speed.

Run toward him, lad, and be ready to drop thy sword. I need to work a spell while we still can.

"We?" Arclath snapped.

We, as in ye and me. We'll have time for only one, before there're too many palace folk blundering around in the way. Swift, now!

Swallowing down his fear, Lord Delcastle obeyed the voice in his head, muttering, "This had better work, or . . ."

Or we'll haunt each other. Aye.

Shaking his head, Arclath ran. Wheezing heavily, Mirt lurched past him in the other direction. Targrael was a balefully grinning figure some three wagon-lengths away, running closer fast.

Now stop. Right now. Try to go calm. Let me use thy arms.

"Yes, master," Arclath said sarcastically but obeyed. His arms and shoulders moved seemingly of their own volition, a warm darkness that wasn't him rising at the back of his mind, his body dropping into a lunge with sword raised.

Targrael swerved wide and then turned and lashed out with a slash from one side, of course—but Elminster had already cast Arclath's good blade at the cobbles right in front of her racing feet. It clanged as it bounced; she stumbled over it; he sidestepped—and then, with a grace that Amarune might have envied if she hadn't been busy screaming his name as Storm shoved her on into the alarmed Dragons—he cast a spell.

Motes of light appeared in a swift, rushing circle in the wake of his nimble fingers, rushed together into a single pulsing light that flared into a cone of what seemed to be bright sunlight, and caught Targrael full in the face.

When it struck her sword, the blade shattered with an ear-splitting shriek, bursting into deadly shards that flew in all directions. One of them spun right across Targrael's face, and another laid open her shoulder.

She howled in anguish and staggered back.

Snatch up thy sword and run her through. Take care to keep hold of it—she won't fall or seem to be hurt much.

Arclath obeyed and did almost lose his sword as the death knight roared and spun away from him in a frenzy of pain, lashing out blindly with the twisted stump of her sword.

Now run, lad. Don't play hero. Get in among the Dragons.

Arclath obeyed happily this time, and pulling back his weapon, sprinted into a knot of soldiers, most of whom seemed to be glaring at him, their swords drawn.

A handful of reinforcements trudged down the street from the direction of the Eastgate—more Dragons, but not fresh ones. The new arrivals looked exhausted, travel-stained, and far less grandly armored than the palace guardsmen. Some of these new arrivals were behind Arclath, milling around between him and the snarling, shuddering Targrael.

Ahead, Arclath saw his Rune staring anxiously over Storm's shoulder at him. Even as he gave her a reassuring smile and espied Mirt arguing with a Dragon who had grabbed hold of his shoulder, he saw a man whose stern face he remembered from around the palace. At the same time, Storm greeted the man, "Well met again, Sir Starbridge. Will you be needing to see my chest again?"

"You handed us a merry journey back from Shadowdale," he growled. "We've just walked the last leg, from Jester's Green. What's all this? What mischief are you up to now?"

"Trying to keep from being cut down in the street," Storm replied—a moment before Wizard of War Glathra Barcantle thrust her head out of the gap where the door had been, saw Storm and then the others, and snapped, "*You!* Men, arrest these people! Her, and *her*, and the fat man there, and Lord Delcastle yonder!"

Mirt shook off the Dragon he'd been arguing with as if the man were a straw doll, and roared, "*Fat* man? Who're ye calling a fat man, Shrewjaws?"

Whatever reply the blazing-eyed Glathra might have made was lost in her sudden jaw-drop of astonishment, as a Purple Dragon far across the Promenade was flung into the air to crash down among his fellows, and another man screamed in agony.

Heads turned, men gaped—and more Purple Dragons were hurled aside, streaming blood.

Lady Targrael was back on her feet and swinging two swords whose owners wouldn't be needing them anymore. She was *really* angry now, and coming through anyone in her way.

CHAPTER
TWENTY-FOUR

BATTLES INSIDE AND OUT

Tales tell of battles where banners flap, o'er hosts drawn up
In glittering lines on a broad open field, under a clear sky,
To charge together and work decisive butchery. Real war
Is seldom so clean or simple. It runs to mistaken foes, chases,
Falls, foolhead accidents, battles inside and out, and inevitably
Untidy and bloody endings.

Sarnaur the Sage, *Wisdoms of One Old Fool*,
a chapbook first published in the Year of the Bent Blade

Just one? We face *just one?*" a gruff Purple Dragon lionar
demanded disbelievingly. "Well, why haven't you jacks
downed her by now? What by the Rampant Dragon is—"

He broke off to gape as a severed head flew past him
to bounce off the shoulder plates of a swordcaptain nearby,
drenching the man in blood ere it tumbled down to be lost to
sight underfoot. It had been wearing a Dragon helm.

"Sabruin!" he gasped in disbelief. "What manner of—"

Another Dragon fell, and his slayer ran along his toppling body, swinging swords in both hands against the
soldiers now crowding around her and hacking at her
almost desperately.

The lionar gaped again. She looked *dead*, this lone woman
butchering her way through palace guards who should have
been able to withstand a thousand women with ease.

"Sir Eskrel Starbridge," the lionar heard the sharp voice
of the Lady Glathra rising from behind him, "attend me. You
and two of your Highknights. Tell the others to arrest and
imprison the four persons I identified, in our dungeons, and
quell this disturbance. They may call on the services of all the

wizards of war who are here—it seems whoever is attacking, yonder, bears heavy magical protections. I have far more pressing matters to attend to right now than street butchery. Our oh-so-loyal nobles are gathering forces under arms all over the city, and Larak Dardulkyn may be involved."

"Just what *else* befell here, while I was out hunting a false Elminster?" Starbridge demanded.

"Later, Highknight," Glathra replied crisply. "*Later.*"

Lips set in a thin and furious line, Manshoon hissed out the short incantation and sat back to watch what befell in the shifting glows of his scrying eyes.

The blast was sudden and terrible, destroying the wagon and everyone close to it. Knowing what was coming, the future emperor of Cormyr had darkened that particular sphere almost to black, to avoid being blinded; the moment the flash had passed its height, he rekindled it, and was in time to watch the dung wagon spread itself and its contents in a thin, wet layer over the walls of the buildings at the far end of the street.

Of his wagon, the eye tyrant within it, the horses and Purple Dragons and war wizards—with any luck, every last person who might have seen the smallest glimpse of what the wagon was carrying—there was no sign.

Except for a red fog in the air and bedewing the street, not to mention the wide but shallow pit that had replaced the sweep of worn cobbles where the wagon had been standing.

Manshoon watched shards of glass fall in a gentle rain out of the sky, looking for any larger movements that might mean a warrior had survived or a Crown mage had shielded himself somehow.

Nothing. He'd gazed longer, now, than a wounded man could hold his breath. Still nothing.

He'd managed it. Kept his secret, and done it far enough from the mansion that Dardulkyn couldn't be blamed outright.

Not that he considered the reckoning even, between himself and Cormyr. A dozen-some magelings, perhaps twice that many Dragons . . .

The Forest Kingdom still owed him four senior war wizards, or more. Beholders didn't come cheap.

Letting out a breath he hadn't known he was holding, the future Emperor of Cormyr and Beyond looked one last time at the blood-drenched street, reflected that it was high time to check on the other two wagons, and—

Something caught his eye, in another glowing scene. Or rather, a lot of somethings: Purple Dragons, their swords out and gleaming back reflections from some lanterns in a Suzailan street, and a bright and steady conjured glow that showed him the familiar façade of the palace behind it.

They were gathering around a lone, embattled figure, swords rising and falling, rising and fall . . .

Targrael!

In the street outside the palace, taking on a good third of the Crown soldiers in Suzail who were awake at this hour.

Manshoon stared at the battle for a moment more, seeing wizards of war, the hole in the palace wall where a door ought to be, and . . . was that Amarune Whitewave? *Elminster?*

He sprang from the chair, landing at a full sprint, heading for another of his beholders.

A living eye tyrant at the height of its powers should make for a dandy battle. After he made utterly stone-cold certain of his foe, this time.

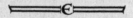

Nay, lad, no more heroics. Not yet.

"So when, Old Mage?" Arclath snapped, seeing hard-faced Highknights shouldering their way through the Dragons toward him. "They'll have Rune in a moment or two!"

Not in this fray, they won't. Head up the street toward Eastgate a bit, then turn in toward the palace. Don't run, or the Dragons will key on ye. Brisk and purposeful—stride like a lionar or an ornrion. That's the way of it, aye.

Arclath held his sword low but ready, staring down soldiers rather than offering them battle, and won his way past more and more of them.

A flash of light reflected off their helms and faces, from behind his left shoulder.

Then another, amid shouts of anger and pain.

Arclath risked a look. Crown mages had tried to fell Targrael with spells, but failed to strike her down as she battled in the midst of so many Purple Dragons. Soldiers had paid the price of those magics, and were less than happy. Their comrades, around them, were angry, too.

Arclath had barely managed to sigh and take another step before he saw something that snatched away his breath and made him freeze where he stood, in one heart-fisting moment.

Out of the nightgloom over the tall buildings facing the palace across the wide Promenade, something as large as a coach was gliding.

Something spherical, with a huge fanged maw surmounted by a lone, malevolent eye the size of a table. Around the sphere curled ten long and flexible eyestalks that were moving into a staring halo of ten gleaming eyes, all of them glaring down at the mailed men in the street.

Rays of magic lanced out from those eyes, rays of ruby and ale-brown, dead white and fell, sickly yellow-green.

And Dragons died. Those who didn't were left to shriek, try to flee, writhe in wild pain, or turn madwits upon their fellows, hacking and crying out in wordless despair.

Save for the small knot of soldiers battling the death knight. The beholder swept over them and left them untouched, in its eagerness to get at the Cormyreans near the doorway.

In its racing, gleefully burbling hunger to get at Rune.

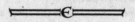

The street rocked under the most foolish of the Crown mage—hurled spells, a blast that flung some Dragons off their feet and forced the rest into ducking and dancing for balance.

At the heart of the frenzy, one sword thrust into the throat of a swordcaptain and the other hacking hard at a desperately parrying telsword, Targrael grinned mirthlessly and went on slaying, never slowing in her endless dance of lunging, slashing, parrying, and spinning around to gut or hurl aside the inevitable clever fools trying to take her from behind.

Something caught her eye, up high behind her right shoulder.

She risked a swift glance at it as she turned that way, taking advantage of the fading aftershocks of that last spell to stab at the faces of men still fighting for balance. A man blinded by a forehead cut is a poor fighter, and she needed as many poor fighters around her as she could acquire, to keep them from overwhelming her with sheer weight and numbers, holding her down, and dismembering her.

As she slew and slew, wondering how long it would take a Dragon officer to summon up wits enough to think of just such a strategy, Lady Targrael took a second look at the movements and revealed light she'd glimpsed a moment ago, high up on the dark front of one of the tall buildings that faced the palace across the Promenade.

Curtains were being pulled aside and tied back up there, revealing the low light and dark fineries of one of the exclusive upper-floor clubs that overlooked this stretch of the Promenade. Faces were eagerly crowding the windows, peering down at the fray.

Well, now. It seemed even drunken, dunderheaded nobles could notice shouts and swordclangs and the street-shaking blasts of reckless spells if such tumult went on long enough. No doubt they were deeming this battle grand and exciting entertainment, and taking bets on who would down whom, and how soon and how bloodily—

Then there were screams from the street around her, and the eager watchers at the windows started to cower back.

Targrael saw by the reactions that the cause had to be overhead, and approaching in silence from behind her, but she dared look no longer, as Dragon swords came at her face and throat from three sides.

When she was done hacking her way out of that particular doom, the eye tyrant had already passed over her and was dealing death to the Dragons beyond.

Could this be Manshoon? There *were* other eye tyrants in the world, and even men who strove to control them, but—

Gazing up, Targrael caught sight of the answer to her question.

On the roof of the club of screaming, fleeing nobles crouched a dark figure, head forward and peering intently down into the mob of Cormyreans.

Talane. Yes, the tyrant almost had to be Manshoon, and this was another of his obedient mind-thralls.

As I once was and never shall be again, she promised herself.

Targrael slashed open the throat of one last Dragon and spun away to sprint toward that club. There would be stairs around the back, and she should get off the open street where Manshoon's pet beholder could easily turn and lash her with its magics, anyhail.

"Talane, I'm coming for you," Targrael whispered as tenderly as any lover, and started running hard.

Behind her, the boots of pursuing Purple Dragons rose in a wild thunder that made Targrael laugh aloud.

Mirt fought for his breath, laying out in all directions with his fists and one of his daggers, as grim-faced Purple Dragons thrust swords or spears or just themselves at him.

Thus far he was winning, if "winning" meant staying alive, on yer feet, an' without too many large holes in yer hide. Tempus and Tymora be with me!

Aye, both of ye. I'll need ye and more, what with all the new war wizards and Dragons streaming out of the doorway in the palace wall. Sent by Glathra or farspoken by their fellows, no doubt, to come rushing to join the fun.

Fighting a stlarning *beholder*, mind ye!

That death knight was still back there, too, hewing her way through a small army of Dragons like a butcher on market day, trying to catch up to *him*. Oh, and El and Storm, too, of course, but it was he an' his little liberated Obarskyr treasure as had imprisoned her just now, an' if he knew enraged women . . .

Speaking of whom . . .

"This is one of them," a deep-voiced Dragon bellowed, pointing at Mirt. "To be taken and chained in the dungeons, by order of the Lady Glathra! So slay him not!"

"Oh, *that's* nice of ye," Mirt wheezed, punching aside a sword and shoving the man who'd swung it into his neighbor, so they both went over in a ringing and skirling of clashing armor plates. "Keep me alive for the mind-reaming, hey? *Nice* little kingdom ye have here, thick-necked barbariaaa*ugh!*"

A swordcaptain had leaped at the back of his neck and brought both forearms crashing down on it as he fell past, at the same time as a snarling telsword swung the butt of his spear ruthlessly through Mirt's fingers, to slam it into Mirt's throat.

Gurgling, Mirt went down.

And promptly got buried under a dozen hard, heavy, and none-too-gentle loyal soldiers of Cormyr. Two of whom then became *very* heavy as the beholder's grayest ray swept along the Promenade, leaving a path of men turned to stone.

Snarling fearful curses, the rest of the Dragons dragged Mirt roughly out from under their transformed fellows and raced for the gaping palace doorway in such frenzied haste that Mirt had time neither to breathe nor to touch even one boot down before he was inside and being hustled along dark passages by hard-breathing, incoherently cursing men of Cormyr.

He let them take him around the first corner before he elbowed one man in the ear, kicked off him to slam the man on his other side into the wall with good, solid, rib-shattering force, and took advantage of his firmly held arms to deliver a crotch-lifting triumph of a kick to the Dragon who turned to confront him—and he broke free.

He wasn't foolish enough to try to get back out of the palace past them. Not when there was a table right handy that could be swept up and used to brain his closest pursuer, then tossed under the knees of those following, to take them down groaning among impaling splinters.

An instant before a deathly white ray stabbed into the palace from the beholder somewhere near, outside—and the doorway became a huge hole in the palace wall that claimed the floor of a stone chamber above and the bodies of at least three Dragons who'd been running after him in one sighing moment.

A fourth soldier, who'd been just about to drop two hairy hands onto Mirt's shoulders to drag the fleeing miscreant down, shrieked as one foot foot vanished in the ray, leaving behind a spurting stump—and fell.

Yelling out unthinking curses of fear, and running as fast as he could wheeze, Mirt of Waterdeep raced deeper into the palace.

"Spread out!" a war wizard was yelling, his voice high with fear and excitement. "Wide apart, so it can't easily get all of us! *Hurry!*"

Now. Elminster's voice was fiercely insistent. *Get to Storm. In by the walls, tell them you're surrendering, act like the beholder has you so scared you'll surrender quietly, sheathe your sword, and get ye to Storm, to touch and hold onto her, just as fast as ye can.*

Arclath slammed his blade back into its scabbard and hastened toward the palace, bowing his head as he stepped around Dragons. "Sorry, can't stop. I'm busy surrendering," he said to the owner of the one hand that grabbed at him, and hurried on.

"Well, I'll be so bold if you really insist," he joked aloud to the heavy presence in his head, "but among politely reared folk, those who rush to touch and hold expect to pay for the privilege, in establishments that exclusively cater to such behavior."

Oh? Since when have nobles of Cormyr been politely reared folk?

Arclath laughed aloud at that and caught a "You're madwits, you are!" stare from a Dragon right in front of him.

By way of reply, as the beholder turned overhead and let fly with more rays, and men shouted and fled, he spread his empty hands and offered hastily, "I'm surrendering, and spell-talking with a friend of mine, a wizard of war who's with the king right now—and who's guiding me where I should go."

The Dragon gave him another strange look then fled. Half a breath before the soldiers beyond him and a good bit of the palace wall beyond them vanished in a flash of eye-tyrant magic, enlarging the open doorway to a gaping hole.

Leaving Storm and Arclath staring at each other across suddenly open street cobbles, with devastation on one side of them and frantically fleeing Purple Dragons and war wizards on the other.

Run!

Elminster's mind-shout was almost deafening, and Arclath put his head down and pumped his arms and really ran, fetching up in Storm's arms—as she caught him to keep him from slamming into the palace wall—a few panting instants later.

The moment Storm was holding him, it was as if a great glowing hearth of light and warmth rolled open in Arclath's mind.

He reeled mentally and was thrust firmly to the task of regaining his balance and breath, just as fast as possible, anchoring himself with one hand on the unyielding stone of the palace wall, as Elminster and Storm communicated in a flashing dance of thoughts too fast for the Fragrant Flower of House Delcastle to follow.

A moment later, he was turning, Elminster firmly in control. Away from the palace, to look up into the night where a great looming eye tyrant was turning, rising, and rolling over to look down on the greatest number of Cormyreans at once, ready to hurl its magics again and permanently deprive the realm of as many Crown soldiers and mages as possible.

To cast a swift, deft, and unfamiliar spell that lanced up to strike the beholder and wrestle it into its true shape, in the grip of a terrible compulsion. A magic that raced around and around the floating horror in a snarling racing of blue-and-silver fire.

The Weave may have fallen, and Elminster and Storm might be Chosen of the mightiest goddess of the realms no longer, but they knew just how to force proud wizards who'd grown up praying to Mystra to obey, even if only for a moment.

The racing fire became a spellburst, a shortlived sun of silver-blue light in the sky over the Promenade, around a writhing beholder.

An eye tyrant that flickered and was a man for a moment, a man falling through the air. Then it was a beholder once more, shuddering and writhing, groaning aloud and then roaring, "I am Xarlandralath, spawn of Xorlughra—and slave of the accursed *Manshoon! Deliver me! Deliver me from this!*"

Then the sun winked out, hurling the beholder high into the air, spinning and writhing.

Arclath heard a gasp, and the strong, longer-fingered hands holding him stiffened—and then fell away.

He turned in time to see Storm fall on her face on the cobbles, crumpling to the street as limp as a wet cloak.

Pain exploded in his head. Elminster's pain.

As he staggered back to the wall to keep from falling, and clawed his way feebly along it, Arclath heard the wizard say weakly, sounding both faint and far off in the echoing depths of his mind, *Storm's done Storm's done get us inside get us away . . .*

He bent to pick her up, or try to, lost his balance, and stumbled a few wild and swift steps back on his heels to keep from falling. They took him around to look out into the street again.

Where the Lord of House Delcastle saw the beholder descending again, wearing a murderous glare and seemingly in control of itself—or under Manshoon's control, that is—once more.

Beyond it, Targrael had turned from trying to get to a particular building, and with a sword waving wildly in both hands, was racing back across the street, wearing a murderous glare of her own. A bared-teeth glare that was bent on the beholder.

Far more glares were being aimed at the menacingly swooping eye tyrant. Every wizard of war on the street had taken a stance and was casting a spell—every last one of them, with the Dragons drawn hastily back to give each one room.

"Now!" a long-bearded war wizard shouted.

And the air itself screamed as half a hundred spells tore through it, to converge in the onrushing beholder.

The flash was blinding and deafening and made Arclath want to fall.

So he did.

CHAPTER
TWENTY-FIVE

RESCUES AND CAPTURES

One man's chained imprisonment is another's deliverance
From oppression; one man's elevation ride another's downfall
Rescues and captures may be two sides of a coin; I've seen
It all far too often to trust overmuch in any god.

> Sagranth the Sour Sage, Act I, Scene I of the play
> *Darantha's Dance With Death* by Lalaya Nabra, Bard of
> Nyth, first staged in the Year of Three Streams Blooded

The royal palace, the Promenade, and the row of buildings
facing the palace across the broadest street in Suzail all
rocked and swayed. A parapet corbel broke off and plum-
meted to the cobbles where it shattered, the shards rolling
ponderously to various halts.

Hardly anyone noticed. Everyone, even as they fell and
bounced amid the shaking cobbles and swirling dust, was
staring up at the beholder above—the eye tyrant at the snarling heart of more than twoscore ravening magics. They tore
and thrust, seared and lashed, and sent a shrieking, fang-
shedding, broken-jawed sphere spinning helplessly away,
shredded eyestalks whirling away from it in a wide-hurled
rain of wet ruin.

Dying, torn open, and spilling guts in a rain of purple gore,
the beholder Talane now knew was Manshoon's slowed as
it reached the zenith of where the magics had hurled it, and
started to fall.

Ravaged and drifting, too wounded to attack anything, but
trying to slow its descent, the beholder tumbled, its central eye
staring at nothing and going dim.

The Cormyreans watched, not daring to cheer yet.

Targrael kept moving, following the path of the beholder, peering hard at it, watching for any sign of Manshoon working a last magic.

It was drifting sideways as it fell, away from the palace . . . toward the rest of the city. To the rooftop where Talane crouched.

Targrael never let her stare leave the ruined tyrant, not for an instant. Would it crash and splatter on that club rooftop, right beside Manshoon's slinking little mind-slave?

It certainly looked as if . . . no . . . no. It was going to drift just far enough to fall past, to be dashed to wet ruin in the street behind, or across the fronts of the shops and balconies of the next building beyond.

Then Targrael's vigilance was rewarded.

She saw the briefest of flashes in the air between the beholder and the dark figure on the edge of the rooftop. Manshoon, plunging into the mind of his Talane.

Talane, who by day was the Lady Deleira Truesilver, resident of a noble mansion that not even the founder of the Zhentarim could hide or move.

Targrael forgot all about the falling beholder. Talane was her new target.

She started to run. Dragons were running, too, and some of them were eyeing her as their swords came up, but she ignored them, sprinting all the faster, heading for the street that ran beside that club, trying to circle around behind the rooftop.

She was in time to see Talane, high above her, make the dangerous leap to the roof of the next building.

"You!" a man commanded from close behind her. "Down steel, or die!"

Targrael rolled her eyes. Did clod-headed Dragons *never* give up?

Still running, she looked back. Stlarn! The man had friends, about a dozen of them, and a war wizard was running with them. Looking neither winded nor afraid in the slightest, to boot. He had a tluining *wand* out!

She'd passed the club and was running along the side of the second building, knowing that Talane was likely several buildings along by now, making much shorter rooftop leaps and acquiring a wide choice of ways down to the street—or deeper.

More Dragons were coming at her down the sidestreets, closing in.

"Stlarn it," she said aloud. "Enough of this! I *will* go to Truesilver House to hunt myself a Talane, but I need that gem from Queen Alendue's cache first, anyhail. If I capture his mind, he can't use his magic on me!"

Rounding a corner she knew, a good six strides ahead of the Dragon who was still commanding her to surrender or taste death, she came upon the wooden hatch she remembered. Plucking it up, she flung it back in his face without even looking and plunged feet-first down the revealed shaft.

She was half a dozen sloshing steps along a noisome sewer quite large enough for tall warriors, heading into the palace by one of the wetter ways, before the Dragon whose face she had crushed with her hurled hatch drew in his last, gurgling breath and died.

Mirt's headlong flight through the palace had slowed to a fast, stumbling lurch, restoring wind enough to him to roar, "Help! Ho! A rescue! Beholder attack! War wizards and Dragons beset! The palace breached! Aid!"

Where *were* all the doorjacks and guards? Usually the stlarned pests were everywhere, like flies on fresh dung, forever stepping forward to politely bar your way, and—

He came to a lamplit meeting of passages that had to be a guardpost, and it was deserted, too. Oh, well, mayhap they were all out there in the street already, and busy dying . . .

An old shield hung on the wall beside the lantern, adorned with peeling paint that had once proclaimed a no-doubt-famous blazon. It was probably a precious relic of some famous old Obarskyr king, a hero of the realm storied in song.

Well, old relic, time to save Cormyr again. Reversing his daggers into a pair of improvised clubs, Mirt started hammering on the shield, belaboring it like a gong until it rebounded repeatedly off the wall, raising a terrible racket.

He could hear the echoes rolling back from six or seven rooms away, setting various distant and unseen metal trophies to ringing in sympathy. Grinning, Mirt dented the shield even harder, paint flying into dust all around him.

A door flew open, and a man staggered through it, face contorted in anger.

A war wizard.

Of course.

Seeing Mirt, he waved his hands imperiously and snarled, "Stop that, sirrah! Madwits! Old fool! Folk are trying to sleep!"

Mirt went right on ringing the shield but used one hand to point back the way he'd come, and then waved the dagger he was holding.

The Crown mage was unimpressed. "Under attack, my left elbow! Bah!"

Snatching out a wand, he marched up to Mirt, planted himself dramatically to blast this noisy nuisance—and collapsed senseless to the floor, struck on the back of his neck by something plummeting from above.

Mirt peered down at the mage with interest, then recoiled. The thing that had felled him looked a little like a wraithlike wisp of something dark, and a bit like a spider. It was unwrapping its long legs—which began to look more like human fingers—from around a ceiling tile it had obviously ridden down on. Spiderlike, it scuttled toward Mirt, who resisted the urge to stamp on the thing with both boots.

Now the wraith looked more like an old man's face, the cloud trailing away in the suggestion of a beard. Beneath that face were definitely human fingers, a hand, rather . . . but the face was walking across the floor on the tips of those fingers.

Aye, the floor; it had come down off the unconscious wizard and was crawling toward Mirt. Who devoted himself to backing away warily.

"Mirt of Waterdeep," the spiderlike thing greeted him dryly. "Well met. Vangerdahast, Royal Magician of Cormyr, at your service. Keep ringing that shield."

Mirt bowed, nodded, and resumed striking the shield, with enthusiasm.

The din was tremendous, almost deafening when the echoes got going, and it wasn't long before someone who looked both groggy and angry lurched around a corner and came striding along the passage toward Mirt.

Watching this second arrival closely for any signs of a wand or a spell being cast, Mirt barely noticed that the spiderlike thing had crept around to stand in the lee of his boots, hidden from the oncoming courtier.

Who shouted, "Cease your noise! Who are you, anyhail, and what do you want? I am Palace Understeward Corleth Fentable!"

The man had said his name as if he expected Mirt to be impressed, so Mirt shrugged and smiled. "I'm Mirt, and I'm ringing this shield to let all the palace know there's a beholder out in the street blasting Dragons and war wizards—oh, and a big hole in the side of the palace, too. Well met."

"Oh?" Fentable seemed less than impressed. "Wait right here. I'll be back with suitable minions."

Whirling around, he marched back the way he'd come.

"He's going to get Dragons to come back and arrest you," Vangerdahast said quietly, from down by Mirt's boots. "Run after him, and smite him cold."

Mirt smiled. This seemed the best advice he'd heard in some time. Drawing in the breath he'd need for a swift lurch down a passage, he hefted his daggers in his hands, pommels up—and did as he'd been told.

When he looked back at Vangerdahast from above the understeward's sprawled body, one spiderlike finger was crooking to beckon him back.

Mirt bent down, grabbed a good handful of palace understeward tunic-front, and gave the royal magician a questioning look.

Vangey nodded, so Mirt dragged the man back to the lamplit shield.

"This man's a traitor to the Crown," the royal magician explained. "Just whom he's working for, and to what ends, I don't know yet—and right now, we haven't time to try to force answers out of him. And the realm needs answers, not all this shouting and chasing about after disasters have befallen. So, I need you to take him down to the royal crypt for me."

Mirt shrugged. "As long as the guards won't try to inter me there, that's fine with me."

"Good. Hold still." The man-headed spiderthing started to climb Mirt's leg. "I'll ride on your shoulder and guide you. It should be unguarded, except by the sealing spells, and I can take care of those. We have some empty coffins there, and anyone put in them is held in spell-stasis. I can think of quite a few persons in this kingdom I'd prefer to entomb there until I'm ready to deal with them, but this wretch is a start."

Mirt chuckled. "Guide me."

"We take this passage, to the bend there. See that square stone, right down by the floor? Kick it with your boot. Another stone should move out a bit, right in front of you. Push in on it, hard, and a hidden door will open."

"Better and better. Is there any treasure hereabouts that no one would miss, hey?"

"No," Vangey said flatly. "Yet the royal magician of the realm *has* been known to reward those who serve Cormyr well."

Mirt followed the instructions, and a door grated open with surprisingly little noise. He dragged Fentable through it and went on, the door swinging closed the moment the under-steward's dragging boots were clear of it.

A bare breath later, just as he was opening his mouth in the pitch darkness to ask the spiderthing on his shoulder for more instructions, he heard a commotion on the other side of the wall.

Many men in boots were hurrying around the corner he'd just vacated, and at least one woman was with them. The Lady Glathra's unmistakable voice was berating them as they went, telling all within earshot that she was simply *spitting* mad, and someone was going to pay for it; and that she wanted to know just who'd dared to rouse this part of the palace, and she'd ring his clanging gong for him, good and hard.

Mirt and Vangerdahast were both wily old veterans, so they waited until the sounds had died away to utter silence before they chuckled. In unison.

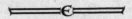

The King's Forest was a cold place at this time of deepest night, shrouded in streaming wisps of mist and awake with eerie calls.

One of those sounds was coming from a shallow dell not far from the Way of the Dragon. It was the deep, loud snoring of an exhausted young lord of Cormyr.

Pillowed on a bodyguard's cloak and lying on the layered cloaks of two more, Marlin Stormserpent was deep in his dreams, wrapped in his own cloak, while his shivering bodyguards stood grim guard over him.

"He's not paying us near enough for this sort o' duty," one of them whispered hoarsely, not for the first time.

"Shut it," came the familiar reply, made more curtly than ever.

"Hear that?" the third bullyblade hissed, sword singing out. "Something's coming—yonder!"

They caught a glimpse of distant blue flame through the trees, and fearfully roused their lord, shaking him and nudging him with their boots in hasty unison.

The master's blueflame ghosts were coming back, and the cursed beyond-dead things obeyed only him.

He came awake as fearful as they were, sweat-drenched and cursing, and had to scramble up to have both Blade and Chalice ready in hand when the two flaming slayers stalked up to him, dragging a hairy mass larger than both of them. It was leaving a wide, wet trail of gore through the leaves and fallen logs, which made the bodyguards look even grimmer and shuffle until they stood together, swords out and watchful.

"What is it?" Stormserpent asked, unenthusiastically.

"You ordered us to get evenfeast. Behold. It's a bear—everything else in the forest fled from us."

The three bullyblades traded silent glances that all said, "That surprises me not," as loudly as if they'd bellowed it.

Stormserpent merely nodded, held up the Chalice and the Blade, and bent his will upon the two ghosts. Who leaned forward as if in belligerent challenge but said nothing.

In eerie silence the noble strained, trembling and going pale ... and slowly, very slowly, the men wreathed in cold blue flames faded away, their last wisps rising up into the two items the lord was clutching.

Stormserpent let out a deep sigh, let his hands fall to his sides, then turned and snapped at the three bullyblades, "Butcher yon bear, light the fire you laid, and start cooking it. You can wake me again when it's done."

Crossing Chalice and Blade across his breast as if he were a priest sleeping vigil on an altar, he laid himself down on the cloaks and closed his eyes.

The bodyguards grudgingly set about following the orders he'd just given. As they bent down around the bear with their daggers out and started sawing, the looks they sent their master's way were almost as baleful as the ones the blueflame ghosts had been offering him, a dozen breaths before.

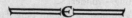

"Cheerful place," Mirt commented, watching Vangerdahast's approach to the double doors cause the expected sigils to glow into eerie visibility. Warning off tomb robbers and fools.

Well, he'd been both, in his day, and probably would be both again ...

He glanced back at Fentable. The understeward looked a little the worse for being dragged down two flights of stairs and along more passages than Mirt had bothered to keep count of, to reach this cold, silent lower cellar.

The doors sighed open, and Vangerdahast said, "Thank you for looking away. Waterdeep is well lorded over, I see."

Mirt managed to quell the snort he usually greeted such sentiments with, and watched a pale glow kindle out of the empty air as the spiderlike royal magician advanced cautiously into a large, dark vault.

"Are there occasional . . . problems?" Mirt asked warily, staying where he was.

"More than a few coffins have been opened since I was here last. I know it doesn't appear that way, but I can tell. Leave the understeward, and come in. I'll need your help with the lids."

"And I'll need your help blasting the undead when they burst out and try to throttle me," Mirt replied meaningfully.

"You'll receive it," came the flat reply.

Mirt rolled his eyes and lurched forward. "Which one first?"

The seventh coffin Mirt opened with a grunt held an immobile, intact-looking man. Who moved not at all in the heart of the faintly singing magical glow that filled his stone resting place.

"*Don't* reach in," Vangerdahast warned.

"No fear," Mirt retorted. "I was just looking for traps."

"He's caught in one. A stasis trap," the royal magician snapped, scuttling to the top of a nearby royal catafalque to get high enough to look down into the open coffin.

"That's the lord warder, Vainrence," he added in a satisfied voice, the moment he'd surveyed the still form in the coffin. "Just step back and leave him be. I'm hoping one of the three remaining disturbed coffins holds Ganrahast. This is the last place in the palace I had left to check for the two of them."

The next coffin contained the royal magician, in the same sort of singing, gently pulsing stasis.

"We dare not disturb them without a senior wizard of war on hand, in case spells are needed, fast. Swift casting is something I can't do, given what I've become."

Mirt regarded the spiderlike mage with interest. Vangerdahast hadn't sounded bitter, only matter-of-fact.

"What do I do with the dolt I dragged down here?"

"Put him in that coffin, and set the lid back into place over him. He'll keep until I have time to cast this same sort of stasis. I can manage it, but slowly."

"Right, and then?"

"Let's go get Glathra. She might as well do something *useful*, for once."

Arclath looked around, wearily. Purple Dragons and war wizards were murmuring triumph to each other. Any moment now, they'd notice one noble lord in their midst—with a mask dancer clinging to him, and an infamous Harper with silver hair everyone recognized at a glance lying senseless at his feet. Storm looked as lost to the world as Elminster was, inside Arclath's own head.

Silent, not answering. Gone.

"Rune," he whispered, into the closest ear of the mask dancer whom he loved more and more with each passing moment, "if I carry Storm, can you take her feet?"

"Take her where?" Rune whispered back. "Into the *palace*?"

Arclath shrugged. Where else could they go? He very much doubted they'd be allowed to depart, if they tried to take Storm across the Promenade right now. Plenty of these men had heard Glathra's orders.

Naed. They always seemed to be wading deeply in fresh, warm naed.

Chapter
TWENTY-SIX

Lies, Chains, and Kisses

Well, lad, ruling a realm usually turns out like
The stormier sort of marriage: it's all lies, chains, and kisses.

> Old King Sandral, Act II, Scene V of the play
> *How Ralindarria Fell* by Ohndravvas Duskingstone,
> Bard High of Darromar, first staged in the Year of the
> Fallen Tower

Ahem, ah, dauntless guardian? Saer Dragon?"

Mirt put what he fondly hoped would be taken for a friendly smile on his face, and lurched up to the palace guard with his hands empty and spread out before him, to show that he was unarmed. The man did not look friendly.

"I'm looking for the Lady Glathra. Wizard of war, usually in a hurry, loud and forceful? Ye know her, aye?"

The Purple Dragon turned his head to give the stout Waterdhavian a long, measuring look, from his untidy hair down to his flapping boots and back up again, before settling in one spot. Mirt saw that.

"Heh-heh. Pay no heed to this that rides on my shoulder. 'Tis a pet, no more. Harmless, I assure ye. Harmless."

Close beside Mirt's ear, Vangerdahast gave a low, warning growl.

Mirt hastened on. "So, saer, can ye take me to the Lady Glathra? Or tell me the way to where she might be found?"

"Why?" the Dragon made reply, shifting his spear from "ceremonial upright rest" to a menacing, ready position. "Who are you, and what's your business with her? What are you doing down here, anyway?"

"Looking," Mirt explained patiently, "for Glathra. I'm Lord Mirt of Waterdeep, visiting my good friend King Foril Obarskyr. As for my business with Glathra . . ."

He leaned forward to give a wink and a friendly leer, but the horrific result made the guard recoil—then flush with irritation at having abandoned his urbane, neutral manner, and snarl, "I don't believe you. Show me your pass!"

Mirt sighed and strode past the man. "I pass," he explained, "like this. See?"

"A jester, eh?" the Dragon snarled, lowering his spear to point at Mirt's ample belly.

"Hey," Mirt said agreeably, steering the spearpoint aside with one hand. "I take it ye're unaware of Glathra's whereabouts? Aye? Well, then, I'll just be—"

"*Halt!* Stand and surrender, you! Lord of Waterdeep, indeed!"

The Dragon made a jabbing movement with his spear, threatening to use it if Mirt tried to flee. Then he stood it against the wall with one hand and drew his sword with the other.

"Consider yourself," he said sternly, "under arrest. As my prisoner, you will accompany me without challenge or violence, seeking neither to deceive me nor to flee from custody. And we won't be going anywhere near the Lady Glathra, believe me—"

Without warning, Vangerdahast launched himself like a striking spider, right into the Dragon's face. The Dragon fell to the floor.

"So, what did ye do to him?" Mirt rumbled, stepping over the fallen guard and hastening at full lurch farther down the passage.

"Enspelled him to sleep, at my touch," Vangey replied. "Dragons didn't *dare* to be that officious in my day. With a visiting head of state, too!"

Mirt chuckled as he rounded a corner and caught sight of another guard, standing to attention against the wall under another lantern.

"So, care to place a little wager on the conduct of this next one?"

"No," Vangerdahast replied flatly. "You provoke them—and I'm just a *pet*, remember?"

Mirt had the grace to wince.

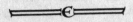

Glathra's reappearance at the greatly enlarged hole in the palace wall caused an immediate clamor, as war wizards hastened from all sides to try to push through the Dragons and speak to her.

"Silence!" she barked—and the Crown mages obeyed, in midword. All around them soldiers blinked, raised eyebrows, or grinned openly.

Despite the way she felt, still lying on the ground in pain and feeling utterly drained, Storm joined in the latter reaction.

Glathra had it, all right. Dominance, with a single word.

Yet the wizard of war wasn't done. "You can report to me later. The engagement here is obviously over, yet I observe my orders have *still* not been carried out, despite an assembly of more loyal soldiers and oathsworn wizards in one place than I've seen for a good long time. So let this disobedience be remedied, forthwith. Use spells to paralyze these three—this mask dancer, Amarune Whitewave; this Harper outlander, Storm Silverhand; and this noble lord of Cormyr, Arclath Delcastle. They are to be taken into custody and chained to the wall in the main Westfront holding cell to await interrogation. Do this *now*."

Storm didn't even try to stir. She was so exhausted that she'd be asleep at that moment if it weren't for the pain. The beholder's searing ray had caught her, though three Dragons had unintentionally shielded her from its full effects with their bodies and had paid the price. The Westfront cell was clean, dry, and well lit, and she could sleep dangling from chains about as well as she could in the street, where she was liable to be walked on or have a cart driven over her.

The war wizards obeyed Glathra with alacrity, probably because she stayed to watch long enough, this time, to make sure her orders were carried out. When the two standing over Storm finished their brief chanting, she felt no more than an immediate numbness. Followed by the inevitable itches she could now not scratch, of course. When she flexed a finger, she found she could move it—though she stilled it instantly to avoid anyone noticing.

The old Harper paralyzing glove. It was still thrust through her belt and must have absorbed the magic that should have frozen her. Which might mean it would again work, paralyzing at a touch, at least once or twice.

"You have no right—" Arclath started to shout, nearby, but broke off as magic silenced him.

"Rights?" a Dragon telsword growled as he struck the sword from the paralyzed noble's hand, to clang on the cobbles. "Don't make me laugh. Rights are what we carve out for ourselves, with the points of our swords!"

"They're all done," a mage reported. It was a voice Storm knew.

"Very good," Glathra replied crisply. "Wizard of War Welwyn Tracegar, you will supervise the conveyance of the prisoners to the cell, and their securing. Dragons, you are to obey Tracegar as you would any battlemaster. Tracegar, see it done!"

"Lady," Tracegar—the owner of the familiar voice—replied with a bow.

Storm tried to act paralyzed as firm hands took hold of her, lifted her, and carried her away.

Tracegar extended his hand. "The keys."

The lionar shook his head. "No, saer. The Lady Glathra said we were to obey you as we would a battlemaster. Save in time of open war's need, no battlemaster would break *that* standing order—the keys are to be retained by a soldier away from the dungeons, to prevent prisoners who overcome a guard from being able to win free of manacles or cells. The prisoners have been secured now—so I go, and the keys go with me."

Tracegar gave the man a glare.

Stone-faced, the Dragon looked back at him.

"The Lady Glathra charged *me* with full responsibility for the prisoners," he snapped, "and I can't carry that out unless I have the keys."

"Then declare yourself regent, saer. Whereupon, you'll have them on the spot. While all of us await the interesting reason you'd soon have to offer the king for your declaration. Saer."

Tracegar gave the lionar a long, cold stare, then snarled and waved at the Dragon to depart and take his fellows with him.

They went, one of them daring to make the low bow extended to regents, on his way out of the cell.

As Tracegar glared at their backs, Storm slipped on her glove.

Like Amarune, she was secured to the wall by ankles and throat and her right wrist, all manacled to wall-rings by chains about a foot long. Their left arms were free.

Men were deemed more dangerous, so Arclath—despite his noble birth—had both wrists chained to the wall. He was between Storm and Rune, sharing ankle and wrist wall-rings, but secured tightly enough that they could never touch.

Storm's hair had been gathered into a rope and then stretched down her back and clamped to a chain that led down to the ring at her right ankle. It seemed Cormyr was taking no chances.

The Dragons had left the cell door open. As per standing orders, Tracegar or his designate would have keys to all doors, so any prisoner seeking to escape would need to cooperate with—or somehow vanquish—the two captors. Courtiers in Cormyr had long ago heard enough bards' ballads not to make the most obvious mistakes.

Except, it seemed, the ones about turning your back on prisoners and gloating.

Tracegar turned to them once again and strolled right up to Storm.

He slowly traced a line down the side of her face, from temple to jaw, with one forefinger as he explained, "I am less than comfortable with any of you suffering this treatment, but there is much peril and uncertainty in the realm right now, and the Lady Glathra needs answers, above all. These manacles are to avoid unpleasantness until the veteran wizards of war the Lady Glathra wants to, ah, meet with you can be roused from their beds. Customarily, chains are unnecessary for persons such as yourselves—but these are extraordinary times."

His face was so close to hers that he was almost brushing her with his lips.

Storm reached out with her glove, kissing him to quell any swift and desperate incantation—and Tracegar stiffened into helpless silence.

"My sentiments exactly," Storm purred in reply, as she wrapped her free arm around the paralyzed mage and swung him around to thump against Arclath. She held him there, against a frozen Delcastle flank, so Elminster could get to work on the war wizard.

"El?"

The Sage of Shadowdale had no way of replying, but she could see by the movements of Arclath's eyes that he'd noticed a healing potion—a shiny steel vial marked with a sun—at Tracegar's belt.

Then ashes were trickling out of Arclath's nose, and Storm knew El was on his way to Tracegar's nose and mouth, to invade and conquer the war wizard's mind.

To work a spell by will alone was beyond Tracegar's skill at Art, but not Elminster's.

Tracegar stiffened, and then his eyes flickered and he was moving, as smoothly and matter-of-factly as if he were an old friend. Taking the vial from his belt, twisting the stopper to break the wax seal but not opening it, then putting a finger under Storm's chin so gently that it was a caress.

Storm opened her mouth obediently, and El made the war wizard pour the healing potion into her slowly and carefully. The familiar warm, then minty-cool flood coursed through her, banishing all pains and aches and weariness, leaving her feeling wonderful.

She sighed out her contentment as Tracegar stepped back and worked another spell, murmuring the words El chose for him aloud as he spell-spoke Vangerdahast from afar, telling him what had befallen.

Then the enthralled war wizard murmured a reply.

"Mirt will bring a coach to the Three Dolphins Door, for the conveyance elsewhere of Wizard of War Welwyn Tracegar with three still-shackled prisoners," Vangey informed Elminster. "Provided you have the good sense, for once, to get out of Suzail fast. All of you."

The alley behind the shop of Sraunter the alchemist was apt to be deserted in the dark, chill hours of very early mornings, but things were different this night. Two closed and loaded wagons stood in the nightgloom, their horses hitched and dozing, and the drover and carter of each wagon sitting like statues with their reins and whips, seemingly lost in personal dazes.

The lithe figure in dark thief's leathers was little more than a shadow until it suddenly mounted one wagon, sat down beside the drover, and kissed him *very* thoroughly.

Whereupon he stirred, turned his head, and told her in a coldly familiar voice, "Go home now, and enjoy what's left of Lady Deleira Truesilver's slumber. Go to ground until I reach out to you again. You are not much suited to my next few battles."

Talane nodded, dared to squeeze the drover's hand in farewell, slipped down from the wagon, and was gone, melting into the night in silence.

She was three streets away before she dared to murmur, "You *might* have thanked me, Lord Manshoon. I merely saved your life. Not much suited . . . *bah*."

She'd expected no thanks, but being left out of the fun rankled.

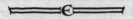

"Got it?"

Mirt winced. "Aye. Not that I enjoy having views of rooms an' passages thrust into my head, mind ye. I can feel a headache coming on."

"If you got yourself lost and ran afoul of the wrong war wizard, you'd soon learn what a *real* headache feels like," Vangerdahast snapped. "Waste no time, mind. The longer you're in the stables, the more loyal Cormyreans you may have to brawl with."

Mirt grunted a wordless reply and set off along the passage.

Vangey smiled thinly at the Waterdhavian's ample back. Well, at least the man had picked the right passage and was heading down it in the proper direction.

At that moment Mirt stopped, turned, and growled, "So, while I'm stealing coaches an' horses an' all, what'll ye be doing?"

"Pretending to be a much younger and more callow wizard of war than I am," Vangerdahast replied, "as I spell-send Glathra a false alarm about intruders getting into the palace to try to slay the king, to draw her—and most of the Dragons and other court mages who are up and awake right now—to the royal wing of the palace. Yet, I'll be far from there."

"Huh," Mirt grumbled, setting off again. "Always take the easy part, wizards do. The *talking*. Always the talking. Some of us actually have to *do* things, ye know."

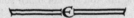

"Where's he going?" Amarune whispered as Tracegar strode out of the cell, leaving them chained to the wall.

He had just ended the paralysis on her and on Arclath, who looked at her now and replied—in his own voice, thank Tymora!—"Elminster's using a spell to ride *his* mind from *my* mind; that's why Storm pressed us together, all that time. He's off to find the guard who has the keys to our shackles, and deal with him."

"Deal permanently?"

"No," Storm put in. "The gods frown on folk who slay unnecessarily—and they send misfortune by way of 'reward.' The Dragon will find a short sleep or paralysis, no more."

Rune was still nodding when Tracegar reappeared and silently freed them all.

"Leave the unlocked shackles on," Storm directed, as her hair, holding its ropelike shape, arched up to feed itself down the back of her neck, inside her clothes, "and move and act as if they're still locked and we're still prisoners. We'll probably run into someone in the passages. We follow Tracegar."

The silent war wizard waved a wand threateningly, his face grim, and strode out of the cell. Looking just as grim and keeping her wrists crossed, Storm followed him, so Arclath and Amarune fell into step behind her.

Behind a door that looked like many others they'd passed was a closet whose door shone with a warning sigil that Tracegar ignored, opening it to display shelves of gleaming vials. Storm gave them one each to drink, banishing all hurts and weariness, then two more each to carry.

Tracegar put the emptied vials in a basket on the closet floor, closed the door again, and waved his wand, pointing along a new passage.

Storm crossed her wrists again and looked glum, so Rune and Arclath did the same as they shuffled along after the silent war wizard, chains clinking.

They were heading for a distant lantern, by a large door that looked like it led out of the palace. Standing under the lantern were four impassive Purple Dragons, watching them make the long, long walk.

As they got closer, two of the guards lowered their spears to the ready, points up and inclined in their direction. The other two set their spears against walls, drew their swords, and stepped forward, looking decidedly unfriendly.

Mirt sighed heavily.

"I know not *which* harness to use, or what horses, either! But I know right well I was ordered to bring a closed coach—like this one, or that one yonder—around to a particular door just as fast as I could. And being as those orders came from the highest-ranking wizard of war ye're likely to find, *I'm* not inclined to disobey them. Why are ye of a mood to, I wonder?"

"Because I've never seen you in my life before," the senior hostler said bluntly, "because you talk like an outlander, and because it's the middle of the stlarning *night* and what you're telling me you want to do would be unusual at highsun! Why don't we just wait for this highnosed wizard to show up himself and demand his coach, eh? After all, it's you he's going to be angry with, not me. I'm just the man responsible for all the coaches and horses and tack here, who's not letting any of them out of my sight without clear orders from *my* superiors."

Mirt sighed. "I was *afraid* ye were going to be like this, an' I want ye to know that I regret what I'm now going to have to do." He rubbed his knuckles, made a fist, and started forward threateningly.

The hostler sneered, stepping back and reaching for a long-tined hayfork—as a massively muscled telsword of the Purple Dragons stepped out of a stall to confront Mirt. "Any trouble, Neld?"

"Yes," the hostler said triumphantly, glaring at Mirt. "This fat outlander is trying to steal a coach—and wants me to harness up the horses for him, first."

"Nay, I'm not trying anything of the sort," Mirt growled, still advancing with his hairy hands balled into fists—and ignoring the looming telsword. "I'm trying to get ye to obey orders that came from the royal magician himself."

"Are you, now?" the telsword asked softly. "Being as the royal magician's been missing for days, I'd like to hear those orders directly from him myself. In the meantime, what's your name, outlander, and what's your trade?"

"Mirt, an' I'm a Lord of Waterdeep. It pays well."

"I'll bet it does, if you acquire coaches this way everywhere you go," the telsword snapped, stepping forward to confront Mirt.

The Waterdhavian was a big man, but the telsword was head and shoulders taller and just as wide, his bulk being muscle and bone where Mirt's was fat and bone. "Well?" he asked silkily. "Still going to try to bully Neld into helping you clout a coach, Lord Mirt?"

"I was asking nicely, but I suppose if local custom demands I bully him, then bully him I must," Mirt growled. "Stand out of the way, Nameless Dragon."

"Heh. My name is Voruld, and I don't take orders from outlander thieves."

"Stand out of the way, Voruld," Mirt growled.

"Or you'll what?"

Mirt shrugged, snatched one of his handy bags of pepper from his belt with the twist that undid its binding, and flung it in Voruld's face. Sidestepping the inevitable blind charge, as the telsword bellowed in pain, he deftly slit the man's codpiece straps with his dagger—and from behind the roaring Dragon, delivered a good hearty kick where it would cause impressive results.

Then he ran up the Dragon's shuddering body, temporarily out of reach of Neld's jabbing fork, stamped on the back of Voruld's neck with both boot heels, and, as the Dragon fell heavily to the floor, snatched some filled and ready feedbags from their pegs and fed them into Neld's face.

Avoiding the fork, he followed the blinding doses of oats with his fists, taking solid satisfaction in hammering Neld to the floor twice. When the hostler seemed disinclined to rise on his own the third time, Mirt took him by one ear and hauled him to his feet.

"I'm in a hurry," he growled with a jovial smile, wiping away spattered oats until Neld could see him out of swelling eyes that were going to be impressively purple-black by highsun, "so I'll refrain from breaking your nose or jaw. If, that is, you get the proper horses harnessed to that coach there, right away without any delays at all. And in case you're thinking of giving me lame horses or the wrong harness and reins or some such trickery, I suppose I should warn you that I've readied coaches in my time. Cut a strap or leave anything important loose or undone or just missing, and I'll break your fingers. Backwards."

Neld swallowed.

Mirt gave him a tender smile. "Yes, I mean it," he added lightly. "And I do believe time is sliding past us, Neld, my new friend. Just like the royal magician's patience. And where I'm a simple man who just knows how to break things, he's a mage who knows how to *really* exact *lasting* revenges."

Neld ran to the nearest tack table. Fast.

Chapter
TWENTY-SEUEN

Bedchambers Invaded

My fiercest battles weren't against orc hordes, or hurling back
Border raiders, nor yet traitor lords' armies; no, they were the times
Ladies wanted my head, over their bedchambers invaded.

> reputedly said by a drunken King Malek of Tethyr to
> three courtiers at a feast in the Year of Burning Steel

G ot you here, didn't it?"

Glathra Barcantle stiffened as if she'd been slapped,
then turned slowly, trembling hands clenched and a wordless,
rising-pitch snarl escaping her lips.

Her towering rage at discovering no danger at all in the
royal wing, that she'd been duped, and that she'd awakened
Obarskyrs for no good reason had not been improved by angry
royal aspersions upon her competence.

She was facing a sleepy King Foril right now, and he continued to be none too amused.

So an unwelcome voice from behind her was a last slapping
insult, by the throne!

"Give me one good reason," she hissed as she addressed a spiderlike intruder that had somehow gotten past several posts of
guards and into the outermost anteroom of the king's own bed-
chambers, "why I should not blast you to your grave, *right now.*"

"You'll be dooming the realm, entirely for your own selfish
ambition and shortsighted stupidity," the black, wraithlike head
atop spiderlike human fingers replied calmly, lifting one finger
to wag it at her disapprovingly. "To put it diplomatically."

The king had caught up a scepter that could do all the
blasting that might be necessary to dispose of all of his guests
and most of the wall beyond them, too, but was staring past

Glathra at the walking head atop the high back of his best guest chair with interest rather than fear.

"Are you who I think you are?" Foril asked quietly. "Vangerdahast?"

"I am," the spiderlike thing replied. "And I needed to lure this noisy wizard up here so I could converse with her before a royal audience. Vastly increasing the chances she'll listen and obey."

Glathra exploded. "*What?* Don't presume to give me orders! Your time is past, old man—by the Dragon, your time as a *man* is past!"

"I serve the realm still. And do so far better than you've ever done, Barcantle. Bluster, highhanded rudeness, and lashing out before you consider consequences is never superior to subtle manipulations—even if you weren't now facing a city full of angered nobles just itching to find provocations. So spare me your shouts, and tender me your ears and whatever small part of your brain you still use for *thinking*."

"How dare—? I've *never* been spoken to—"

"Indeed, and what a problem *that's* created! Now, will you *listen?*"

Glathra folded her arms across her chest and tossed her head. "I don't even know you *are* the infamous royal magician! You look like a construct an ambitious but not accomplished mage might cobble together! The words we're hearing from you right now could be those of any traitor noble, Sembian, or other foe of the Dragon Throne!"

"Or they could be my own. Foril, call to mind the line of verse Queen Filfaeril left to you, written in a locket, but say them not."

The king frowned then nodded. "I remember them."

"'The Crown of the Dragon is a thing so heavy, that I send my love to all who may wear it when I am dust, because only love can hold it high,'" the spiderlike thing declaimed, then asked, "Believe I'm Old Vangey now?"

"No," Glathra snapped, before the king could speak. "Scores of courtiers know those words now, because of various royal scribes and palace gossip and the Highknights' use of parts of it, some time back, as pass phrases."

"Very well," the wraith-spider replied and murmured something too softly for either the king or the wizard of war to hear.

Foril's scepter suddenly vanished from his hand, two suits of armor in the corners of the anteroom stepped down off their plinths and knelt to the king, and a dusty stone statue at the end of the room shifted its pose to hold forth and open the stone book it was carrying, revealing it to be a pipe coffer holding three pipes and four small and rather moldering lines of pipeweed.

"Do you believe me *now?*" the spiderlike intruder asked rather testily. "I come on a matter of some urgency, as it happens, and would rather not deprive the crowned head of Cormyr of any more royal slumber because I'm being challenged to do *tricks*."

"*I* believe you," King Foril Obarskyr said firmly, "and that should be sufficient. What do you want, Royal Magician Vangerdahast?"

"To tell Your Majesty that I've found Ganrahast and Vainrence in magical stasis, down in the royal crypt."

"*What?!*" The king and wizard of war shouted that word together.

"Reduced to what I've become," Vangey continued calmly, "I can't cast the necessary spells if they awaken crazed or hostile or enthralled by a foe of the realm. So, I need Glathra here to gather four or five war wizards of experience and accomplishment, and go down and release them."

"Is this another ploy, old madwits? *Another* deception?" Glathra spat. "What sort of trap awaits us down there, hey? You just want us all gone, so you can rule again!"

"I want nothing of the sort," Vangerdahast snapped. "Other than to know just *why* you didn't search the palace well enough to find them yourself, days ago. I would hate to think you were either that incompetent or that much of a traitor."

Glathra went white. "You *dare* accuse me of treason?"

"Yes. Twice now. I'll do it again, if you're hard of hearing. Foril, will you *please* order this witch to go down to the stlarning crypt and free the royal magician and the lord warder? I don't need to sleep anymore, and even *I'm* getting weary of endless snappish debating."

A sudden commotion erupted outside the doors, the gruff challenges of veteran Dragons overruled by stern orders—and then the doors were flung wide.

Three Crown mages stood there. Seeing the king in his nightrobe, they hastily went to their knees. "Forgive us, Your Majesty, but there's grave peril! Statues and suits of armor—solid stone ones, and empty suits, that is!—are on the move, all over the palace! They're tramping places and rearranging things, and we can't—"

The wraith-spider chuckled, muttered something, then said, "Sorry. That should all stop now. I hope."

The war wizards all stared at the spider-thing, and some of the Dragons behind them raised spears as if to try to stab at it over the heads of the gaping mages.

"Behold," Vangerdahast said gleefully. "Here are the wizards you'll need, Glathra. You might actually reach the crypt before highsun, if you stop arguing and start obeying!"

Glathra glared at him. "I—"

"Can provide us with *no* good reason not to go down to the royal crypt to investigate Lord Vangerdahast's claims," the king said firmly. "Wherefore, I now give you, Lady Glathra, these explicit orders—you are to free the royal magician and lord warder if you find them, and bring them unharmed here to this chamber without delay, that I may converse with them. You are to take these wizards and all of the loyal Dragons outside my doors except Launcel and Tarimmon, there, who will remain as my guardians. Go. Go now. See that this is done."

With alacrity Glathra bowed low and replied, "It shall be, Majesty."

After she'd swept out, she looked back to see if the wraith-spider was offering any menace to the king—but it had vanished.

She hesitated, but the king gave her a cold look. She hurried off toward the nearest stair.

The royal crypt was a long way down from there.

"Th-the Three Dolphins Door," Neld quavered. "Now, will you stop hitting me?"

Mirt gave him a jovial grin and slap on the back that almost pitched the hostler off the coach and onto the rump of one of the hindmost horses.

"Of course," the Waterdhavian agreed. "Down ye get, now, an' run along, an' I'll say nothing at all bad about ye to the royal magician. A pleasure, Master Neld—a distinct pleasure!"

Neld said something in an incredulous voice as he launched himself in a heroic leap out from the drovers' seat to the hard cobbles of the Promenade, quite a distance to one side of the coach.

Mirt gave him a cheery wave and brought the coach to a rattling stop outside the Three Dolphins Door.

Four impassive guards held their positions, spears slanted just so, as if he, his coach, and their dust weren't there at all.

Behind the four Dragons, the double doors that made up the Three Dolphins "Door" started to swing inward.

Smoothly the door guards swung around to face inward, so that whoever was departing the palace would pass between them.

"These prisoners," an officer's voice inside began suspiciously.

"I have my orders," came a flat reply, then the same voice snapped some orders of its own. "Forward. Into the coach. Remember, my wand is ready."

Storm Silverhand strode out of the palace in shackles and dangling chains, her head bowed. The Lord Delcastle followed her, then Amarune, also in shackles. Behind them came the War Wizard Tracegar, his wand in hand.

Storm stopped in front of the coach and waited. After a long span of hesitation, one of the outer-door guards stepped forward, opened the coach door, and folded down its pair of steps. She ascended, and the other two prisoners followed, under the frowningly suspicious stares of all the guards.

As Tracegar got into the coach with them, one of the guards peered up at Mirt, then snapped, "I've not seen you before, and you wear no uniform! Who are you?"

Mirt gave the man a hard stare. "Ask the king. Keep in mind that your low rank will limit the answers you'll get. And may well wind up lower, when you're done asking."

Tracegar rapped on the inside roof of the coach then, so Mirt flicked his whip, clucked to the horses, and set the coach in motion, his stare never leaving the guard's eyes.

Unhindered, Glathra's prisoners were conveyed in stately splendor up the Promenade—and out of her reach.

For a while.

The Lady Deleira Truesilver was not in a good mood. Wherefore, fools and those who merely happened to displease her did well to get themselves out of her sight and stay there. Though it was true she was eye-catchingly beautiful, lithe, and elegant, her exquisitely styled white hair contrasting with her flashing yellow eyes, it was the edge of her tongue and the weight of her formidable wits and character they were apt to remember instead, on nights like this.

To put it plainly, she ruled Truesilver House like a tyrant, and in the so-late-they-were-early hours since her reappearance from her chambers, she had verbally demolished two of her kin and a few servants for various stupidities. Having grown tired of having to find fresh words to find so much fault when it seemed to besiege her on all sides, she retired to her chambers again, dismissing her maids and locking them out.

Certain of her inner chambers had bars as well as bolts, and she used these with the deft vigor of a woman half her age, her movements both graceful and imperious.

When the last door was firmly fastened, leaving her only the windows, balconies, and certain secret passages as ways of departing her self-imposed retreat, the Lady Truesilver turned and began to disrobe as she walked toward her favorite bed-chamber, kicking off her dainty boots and then doing off her gown and petticoats and hurling them aside for all the world as if she were a club dancer.

When she was down to the most scandalously brief of clouts—definitely the fashion of club dancers, and not aging noble matriarchs—she padded barefoot to a particular relief-carved wall panel, did something to the eye of the doe carved on it and then something else to a moon depicted in a panel across the room—and then returned to the first panel, put two fingertips around some gnarled tree roots in the carving, and drew the panel gently open.

The revealed recess beyond was just large enough for her to hide in—she'd done so just twice, and one had been only a short trial—but held, on foldout hooks, things that did not look at all ladylike. She drew them out, one by one, draping them on handy furniture: boots, several weapon-belts, and then some garments.

The tight leathers of a thief.

All that was left in the closet were wigs—long, dark hair that hung on their hooks like cowls—and a coil of dark, slender cord.

She shook out the leathers, reached for the well-oiled, supple breeches—and froze.

The curtains that framed the door to her balcony were swirl-ing, and no one should have been there to make them move.

Someone was. Not of Truesilver House, but someone she'd never seen before. An intruder. Dark, agile, feminine . . . and bearing a drawn sword in one hand and a dagger in the other.

Lady Truesilver glanced over at her swordbelt—*just* out of reach, slung over the back of a chair, with her dagger-baldrics impossibly distant on the lounge beyond—and asked calmly, "Who are you, and what do you want?"

"I am one who has served Cormyr since your grandmother was young," the intruder replied almost mockingly, the voice female, gentle, and at the same time colder than Deleira Truesilver's frostiest tones, "and I want to know your secrets. Talane."

Lady Truesilver stiffened. *No one* should know that she was—

She whirled and fled, seeking her innermost bedchamber and a door she could slam between her and this intruder.

Who shed a dark helm as she sprang across the room like a panther and pounced, slamming Deleira Truesilver bruisingly to the floor and easily overpowering her in a chilling, steel-strong grip.

"Not so fast," the intruder hissed, their faces almost touching. An eerie glow came from between the unfamiliar woman's teeth. "Your death can be easily achieved, but I want what you know first."

"And just how are you going to get *that?*" Lady Truesilver snarled defiantly, arching and struggling, trying to buck her attacker off.

"Like *this*," Targrael replied, opening her mouth to reveal a glowing white gem on her tongue—before she forced Deleira Truesilver's jaws open with iron-hard fingers, and kissed her.

A flash of light erupted as their tongues met that Deleira Truesilver *felt*, like a silent roar of surf crashing through her very bones, and she felt the cold, somehow minty feeling of magic awakening within her.

Her attacker was now more than a stronger, colder body than hers, holding her down. There was another mind in hers, a dark and looming presence growing larger and closer.

Lady Truesilver did not hear the words that Targrael spoke then so much as she felt them.

"The royal magicians of Cormyr left some *very* interesting magics hidden around the palace. This was the one that most interested *me*."

Enthralled and helpless, Deleira Truesilver couldn't move or speak as the dark malice of her foe's cruel, hostile mind flooded into hers, drowning her in shivering darkness . . .

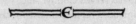

The Horngate, of course, was locked and barred for the night. The stone-faced guards there crisply informed Mirt that they had no intention whatsoever, short of the correct horn-calls from the palace, or the king himself wagging "crown and scepter" in their faces, of opening it before morning.

"All Cormyreans know these rules," one of them added sharply. "Climb down from there, man, and yield up to us your name, your business here, the land you hail from, your passengers—and their destination. *Now.*"

Mirt sighed. "I have my orders, an' they don't sit well with the ones ye're giving me, man. So a little less of the 'now,' if ye *don't* mind."

"But I do mind, saer! Now, there are ten crossbows aimed at you, so I'm going to tell you agai—"

"If ye put a quarrel through any of my passengers," Mirt roared, "'tis yer lives as'll be forfeit, idiot Dragons! Now, down bows, an' pay heed to who's stepping out of my coach!"

His shout rang back at him off the closed gates, and he sat down sweating, hoping very much he'd bought Elminster enough time to think of something.

Under him, the coach made the slight rocking that meant its door had been opened and someone was stepping down.

There was a stir among the guards, and he could see crossbows being lowered. They obviously recognized the passenger who'd alighted.

"Open the gate," came a crisp, simple order.

Mirt hid a smirk. The voice was a very good imitation of the Lady Glathra Barcantle's shrill of excitement, but it was Elminster's very good imitation.

And now the guards were opening the gate, and "Glathra" was climbing back into the coach.

Mirt waited for the rap on the coach roof before he urged the horses forward again, and they rumbled out of Suzail into the last dark hours of the night.

Or were they the darkest hours of the morning?

Even after twenty seasons of leading raids in those dark hours, Mirt had never decided.

He waited until they were out of bowshot from the walls before opening the little hatch that let a drover talk with passengers, and asking, "Where now?"

"We take the coach to the paddocks nigh Eastgate," Elminster's voice came up to him, "and leave it there, hobbling the horses. Then we go for a long walk on Jester's Green, well out from the walls. We'll go well west, around to the Field Gates. Accompanied by this pet war wizard of ours, we'll trudge back into the city through them at daybreak, looking suitably different than we do now. We'll be burying those shackles."

"Oh?" Mirt growled. "What're ye going to make *me* look like?"

"Old Lord Helderstone," Elminster told him. "He has no heirs and has dwelt in seclusion in Sembia for years—no one in Suzail should know that he's dead yet. I know where a handsome fortune in coins can be had, and ye can lord it up in a highnose inn as long as they hold out. Storm will be thy servant. I'll make Rune look like a retired Highknight I recall, who died a few months back, who's now in Suzail and investigating just why rich old Lord Helderstone has returned to Cormyr—in other words, which faction of treason-plotting nobles he's drenching in floods of coins—and the rest of the time she can look like Amarune and be with Arclath, the two of them keeping well away from ye."

"While I do what?"

"Wench, trade, work a few swindles, get rich—in short, be thyself," El replied. "No noble of Cormyr would spend a score of summers in Sembia who did not love coins and the winning of them."

"And what will ye be doing?"

"Trying to hunt down and slay Manshoon, and hold Cormyr together, and find and come to command or destroy all the blueflame ghosts, of course."

Mirt shook his head slowly. "Ye're as crazed as ever."

"Of course."

Mirt could *hear* Elminster's grin.

CHAPTER
TWENTY-EIGHT

A LADY OF GHOSTS

For in my darkest dreams she smiles
Coming for me with skeletal hosts
Her gaze piercing dark, howling miles
My loving Lady of Ghosts.

Mintiper Moonsilver, Bard
from the ballad *My Lady of Ghosts*
first performed in the Year of the Bright Blade

The morning sun was reaching bright fingers in through the windows. None of the dozen senior wizards of war gathered around the long table, which almost filled this locked room on an upper floor of the sprawling royal court, cared a whit about sunlight, however.

Their minds were on darker things, specifically, the foremost current threats to the realm.

The royal magician of Cormyr and the lord warder had been too long absent from such conversations, and there was much to catch up on.

"Of *course* our tirelessly treasonous nobles are brewing civil war in earnest in the wake of this disastrous Council," the Lady Glathra was declaring, "but there are other, smaller players we must now pay attention to."

Ganrahast held up his hand to stop her. "I want you to list them for us in a moment, lady, but first—Erzoured?"

"Our ongoing work to, ah, take care of every crony and ally he develops," a thin and dour mage replied, "continues, and he remains isolated, as he has found himself time and time again. Many of the nobles' factions and Sembian and Suzailan merchant cabals are reaching out to him right now, but he has joined none of them, yet—and all of them fear the possibility he's a spy for the king."

Dark chuckles made note of that irony, ere the royal magician stilled them with his hand again and asked, "Glathra? Those smaller players?"

"Targrael, the death knight who believes herself the true guardian of Cormyr. The rival claimant for that role, the ghost of the Princess Alusair. Whoever sent the eye tyrant to attack us last night. The scuttling wraith-spider—I know of no better name for it—who claims to be the infamous Vangerdahast and certainly commands as much about the palace as that royal magician was reputed to—statues, and the like—not to mention the escaped Elminster, and his companion Storm Silverhand, who for some years have stolen magic from us, in the palace."

"Have any of these joined in common cause with ambitious nobles, while we've been . . . asleep?" Vainrence asked with a frown.

"Not that we know of," Glathra said slowly, after no one else ventured a reply, "yet all of them are capable of such treason."

Ganrahast snorted. "So is any dog or passing falcon. We must avoid raising phantoms and fearing them. The real foes are formidable enough."

"I do have my suspicions about one of us," Glathra added, raising a finger, "though I admit it is early yet for my alarm to have gained any serious substance. Yet, we all follow our hunches or noses or itches . . . and this is my newest."

Ganrahast waved at her to continue. "Raise your suspicions. Please."

"Welwyn Tracegar," she replied bluntly. "Last night I ordered him to take three persons into custody for questioning—Storm Silverhand, Lord Arclath Delcastle, and a mask dancer of the city who seems to be descended from the notorious Elminster, one Amarune Whitewave. He did this but has since vanished, along with the prisoners and a man calling himself Mirt, who claims to be a Lord of Waterdeep. Though that name was better known in Waterdeep about a century ago."

"We can all banish our suspicions about Wizard of War Tracegar," Ganrahast announced firmly, "and leave him be, to operate without hindrance."

Glathra leaned forward to look at him, frowning. "Why?"

"I've taken counsel with Vangerdahast—or what is left of him—and we have agreed on this," the royal magician replied curtly. "Ask me no more."

Eyebrows went up all around the table, but Glathra merely sat back and asked the ceiling, "Will there come a day when someone *else* besides a former royal magician—who richly earned himself a *very* fell reputation—will decide things for the Forest Kingdom?"

"Vangerdahast swore to dedicate his life to guard Cormyr, and he is still guarding Cormyr. Guided by wisdom and experience none of us can match," Ganrahast replied quietly. "In this, I am willing to trust him for a little longer."

"How little?"

"We'll see."

This cellar was beginning to feel like a prison cell. Manshoon paced it, thinking dark thoughts.

He was back in the body of Sraunter, who was given to such gloomy thinking—but the worrying that was consuming him at that moment was all his own.

He could find no trace of Mreldrake or Targrael—or Talane!

Dared he creep back into Understeward Corleth Fentable's mind, using one of his wagon drovers, who supplied the palace with foodstuffs daily, to reach Fentable? And so seek to learn the current thinking of the Crown?

Or was it time to lie low, going nowhere near the palace? He could instead take fresh measure of the war wizards, with an eye to which ones he could isolate and destroy or ruin with scandal, either by entrapment or deceit.

It went against his desires to lurk idle and let others seize power—it had angered him just to return his beholders to hiding in the cellar—but perhaps that was the best path to take over the next few months. He could work through Dardulkyn to keep some sort of watch over the various ambitious nobles ...

He nodded, feeling grim.

He'd succumbed once again to the urge to take a direct hand in things, and the results had been disastrous.

Two beholders gone, for scant gain, and his presence very close to being revealed or at least suspected strongly enough to set the wizards of war to hunting him.

No, lying low and keeping his beholders hidden was best, for a while.

He would work through Dardulkyn—he had, after all, managed to destroy everyone who'd seen his tyrants—and use various lesser thralls, servants and carters, to try to discover just which Cormyrean noble besides Marlin Stormserpent commanded a blueflame ghost.

This stealth should keep him away from Elminster's notice, too. He would wait until the Sage of Shadowdale revealed himself, and then pounce and destroy Elminster again.

"And bury him deep, this time," he told the cellar fiercely, as the shop bell rang and he started up the stairs. "As often as it takes, until he's gone forever."

"Well?" Marlin Stormserpent snapped. It was full morning and foresters would be about, all too soon. His bodyguards should have managed this a *lot* faster.

"Done, lord," came the flat, almost sullen reply. "The huntsman and all six lodge guards are dead."

"Wrap the bodies in the oldest tent of those up in the rafters, and take them to the bear den up by Blackrock, right down in the rocks at its mouth, for the bruins to devour. *Don't* be seen, and don't trail blood from here to there. Leave Ghalhunt here with me."

"As you command," the man replied, almost insolently, and strode away.

Shaking his head in exasperation, Marlin went the other way, to where the doors of the Windstag hunting lodge—his, now, for a few nights at least—stood open and waiting.

Windstag could find another huntsman, and any lout of an armsman could be a lodge guard. It wasn't as if House Windstag lacked coins enough . . .

Ghalhunt at least had sense enough to light and stoke the firewood that had been left ready in the lodge hearth, to drive the chill damp out.

With a sigh of contentment, Stormserpent settled himself in Windstag's big lounge chair, right in front of the hearth, and kicked his boots off, the better to toast his cold and aching feet. He'd always coveted that particular chair . . .

He gave Ghalhunt a nod of thanks as the bullyblade rose from the hearth.

"Just going to fetch more wood in, lord, before any nosy foresters come by and want to know who all the strange faces belong to."

Stormserpent nodded, satisfied. The shed was perhaps ten strides away; Ghalhunt would be back in no time to get a morningfeast going. At the very thought, his stomach rumbled loudly.

He heard the bullyblade chuckle at that as he went out, the door squealing ever so slightly in the man's wake.

The next thing he knew, something had been tossed into the fire, scattering sparks. Something round, that set up an angry hiss. Something that stank of . . . burning hair?

Marlin Stormserpent sat up, rubbing at his eyes. He must have dozed off.

Was that—what *was* that, in the fire?

A log slumped, the object he was staring at rolled over, and he realized he was looking at Baert Ghalhunt's dully staring severed head.

But who—?

He tried to look back behind him, but the high wings of the chair were in his way. Blue flames, cold and tireless, were flickering above and behind them, and he grabbed frantically for the Flying Blade. His fingers closed around the familiar, reassuring weighty curves of its hilt.

Then a man he'd never seen before strode into view around the chair, smiling down at him with sword drawn. A cruel smile on the face of a man wreathed in blue flames.

A blueflame ghost, but not one of his!

Then hard, cold hands took hold of him from the other side of the chair, holding his arms with iron strength. He strained to draw his sword, managed to get it halfway out with a sudden jerk—then felt the coldest, keenest pain that had ever blighted his life.

His hand had been hacked off.

His other arm was grabbed by the man who'd walked around the chair to smile at him, and forced down onto the chair arm. A blade wreathed in blue flames chopped down again, and Stormserpent screamed.

He was lost in pain, he was staring in disbelief at the two streaming stumps of his arms—and above them, standing side by side to smile down at him, three blueflame ghosts. Strangers, all of them.

The Flying Blade and the Wyverntongue Chalice were lost to him. He couldn't call forth his own two blueflame slayers now, to save him.

If it wasn't too late for any saving . . .

He could feel his own life flowing out of him, *pumping* out of him . . .

This couldn't be happening! Couldn't . . .

He was Lord Marlin Stormserpent! Didn't they *know* that? How dare they?

Someone else was strolling unhurriedly around the three ghosts and reaching down long, shapely arms to pluck up the Blade and the Chalice. *His* Blade and Chalice.

Marlin stared up at her in dimming, dying disbelief. Blearily he beheld a tall, slender, beautiful human woman with a cruel face and dark, rage-filled eyes, clad all in black, with a silver weathercloak around her shoulders. He'd never seen her before, either.

As she set the sword and the cup down on a sidetable he hadn't the means to reach, Stormserpent saw the bloody point of a dagger protruding from her black-garbed chest, thrusting out between her breasts.

He was fading fast, his lifeblood flowing out of his useless stumps with every heartbeat. He tried to raise them toward her, and his effort earned him a cold sneer.

"W-who are you?" he managed to gasp.

"The Lady of Ghosts," came the mocking reply. "I gather blueflame ghosts. Yours are a most welcome addition to my collection."

She strode closer. Marlin stared at the blood-drenched point standing out between her breasts in dull, dying fascination.

She smiled. "Like it? I seek the man who put it there. A well-known wizard named Manshoon. You've heard of him, I'm sure, but have you seen him hereabouts? Recently?"

Marlin shook his head.

"Is anyone else in Cormyr collecting blueflame ghosts?"

"One appeared . . . at the Council," he replied weakly, tasting his own blood in his mouth. "No one knows who commands it."

She bent suddenly and took hold of his throat, her grip cruelly tight.

"Do you tell me truth?" she hissed, blue flames suddenly dancing in her eyes.

Marlin shuddered and tried not to choke. "Y-yes."

Eyes burning into his, she shook him.

Then, suddenly, she was telling him a tale, the words whispered low and fast.

"The one called Manshoon literally stabbed me in the back, years and years ago, and as you see, left his dagger in me, pommel-deep. I'm under a curse and cannot die until the spell is broken—so I live in constant agony. *Worse* than what you're feeling now, worm of a noble."

Marlin had just enough strength left to shake his head in disbelief.

"I am driven," she hissed into his face. "Driven by my pain and hatred to seek Manshoon's death. I dare not have his blade plucked out, because doing so will alter the enchantments on my body, and I'll literally rot while staying alive. Undeath may be my fate, but it's one I don't want to choose yet."

Straightening, she hauled the dying noble up out of the chair to stand with her, hanging from her grip on his throat and shoulders.

"I'm on Manshoon's trail," she whispered. "He is *the* collector of blueflame ghosts; he was busy gathering them all those years ago, when we first met. By assembling my own collection, I hope to lure him out of hiding. To me. *Within my reach at last.*"

Lord Marlin Stormserpent stared at her glassily, his eyes dark and empty.

"So," she snarled, "is there anything you can tell me to help me find Manshoon, doomed noble? Anything at all?"

But she was shaking a dead man. While she'd hissed words at him, Stormserpent had died.

With a soft curse, she dashed his limp body to the floor.

The walls of the room, deep on the lowest level of the palace cellars, were furred with dark, sickly-looking green mold, and the air was damp and fetid.

Lord Arclath Delcastle guided the silent and empty-eyed wizard Tracegar to a stop in front of the massive stone table that was the room's sole furnishing, looked around again at all the mold, and rolled his eyes. "Some six hundred rooms down here, and we have to meet in this one?"

His voice was Elminster's.

Vangerdahast might be reduced to a spiderlike thing, but he could still shrug. "No one comes near it. Making it useful. You have no idea how many lovers come creeping down into the cellars for thrill-trysts by candlelight."

"Oh, but I do," El replied gravely. "Believe me, I do."

He looked down at the man lying still and silent on the stone table, with Vangey poised like a protective spider by his head.

Youngish, pleasant-looking, but not overly handsome, Chondathan stock. Clad in the sort of robes favored by war wizards. Breathing very slowly, but senseless. No visible wounds, or for that matter, scars.

"Who's this?"

"Wizard of War Reldyk Applecrown. Young, loyal, a minor wielder of the Art. He's been healed of the wounds he took last night in the beholder fray, but he got caught in a spell backlash and hasn't much of a mind left."

"Brain-burned," El murmured, looking up at Vangerdahast with a silent question in his eyes.

"Your new body, if you want him," the former royal magician of Cormyr said gruffly. "The realm owes you that much. Hells, a lot more. As do I."

Elminster looked at him gravely for a moment. "Thank you."

He inclined Arclath's head toward Tracegar and asked, "You need him up on the table?"

"No," Vangey replied. "Just walk him around it—slowly, mind—as we work on him."

So Elminster did that, as the two of them, riding Vangerdahast's spell, drifted into Welwyn Tracegar's mind together, fogging his memories with spell after overlapping spell so he'd forget all about how he'd helped his prisoners escape. Then they lowered him to the floor and cast simple sleep on him.

"I'll steady you, once you're in," Vangey offered, nodding at the man on the table. "Can't have you getting up and stumbling over Tracegar, and him waking up thinking he's facing two traitor mages and a spider-monster that all need blasting."

El shrugged. "It's what Glathra would do."

Vangerdahast was still chuckling ruefully at that when the young wizard on the table stirred, then started to convulse and thrash.

"Don't try to get off the table yet," he advised. "I have to reassure Lord Delcastle here about what we're up to, first, or he might just decide not to catch you when you start to topple."

Spiderlike fingers rose to point down over the edge.

"Arclath, try not to step on Tracegar, there. He'll look a bit odd with boot-prints all over his face, when they find him sleeping in a bed he shouldn't be in, somewhere in the palace."

"Ah . . . which bed?" Arclath asked carefully.

"One of the ready rooms in the guest wing, I'm thinking, so he'll be found before he starves. My sleep spell won't be broken—assuming the ceiling doesn't fall or the bed collapse—until someone not of us four touches him."

"Four?"

"I'm counting El, dolt of a lordling. *And* his new body. Which isn't really his yet, until he learns to walk and talk with it."

Arclath gave Vangey a disbelieving frown, at about the same time as the man on the table thrust one arm stiffly into the air, tried to wriggle the fingers of that upraised hand, and worked his jaw enough to say, "A bit shaaaky, thusss fahr!"

Rolling his eyes, the noble took a swift step back so he wasn't within reach if the body should lash out suddenly.

"Wise lad," Vangerdahast commented solemnly—a moment before a wild sweep of Applecrown's arm dashed him off the table.

Arclath sniggered, then let his laughter roar out of him.

"That's right, lad," Vangey's voice rose, from somewhere on the floor on the other side of the table. "I like pet frogs that know how to laugh."

Busy and brightly lit palace passages hung with shields and lined with statues weren't Glathra's favorite sites for important policy discussions, but Highknight Starbridge and Sir Talonar Winter had come rushing up to the royal magician while he, Vainrence, and Glathra had been heading to the kitchens for something to eat. She couldn't remember when she'd last chewed food or swigged something more than a goblet of water snatched from a passing maid's tray.

Someone, it seemed, had burst into Staghaven House unnoticed by any neighbors or watch patrols, and had slaughtered Lord Windstag with most of his household servants. And *very* recently—when they'd been found, blood had still been running out of some of the bodies. The Dragons securing the house had recognized a face among the sprawled and slain servants that shouldn't have been there: Palace Steward Rorstil Hallowdant. Worse yet, someone had cast powerful magics on the slain; three priests and a young war wizard who'd cast spells on the corpses to try to learn more about their passing had been plunged instantly into barking, howling insanity.

"There will be no more attempts to cast *anything* on the slain," Ganrahast decreed grimly. "Take the oldest palace supply wagon, convey the bodies all out to the rocks beyond the Westhill, and burn them all there, wagon and all, with guards posted to keep the curious away. I want this done in secret, as much as possible, to keep word from spreading."

Starbridge and Winter nodded, bowed, and hurried off to see to it.

"So who did this, do you think?" Vainrence murmured, watching them hasten down the passage, distant already and dwindling fast.

"Noble slays noble," Ganrahast sighed. "It begins."

"Royal magician," Glathra said darkly, "with respect, it began some time ago. It's only going to get bloodier."

"Blood spilled among nobles I expect," Ganrahast replied, starting off down the passage. "Betrayals and disloyalties among Crown folk are what shake me. And more importantly, shake the Dragon Throne."

"Every one of them," Vainrence murmured, nodding agreement.

"Has every interment in the royal crypt now been examined?" Ganrahast asked him.

"Yes. Nothing is amiss, nothing missing, and there are no more empty coffins. New wards and alarm spells have been cast."

"Have you found Vangerdahast?" Glathra asked sharply.

"No."

"And why not?" Ganrahast pressed him, as if he'd been a disobedient young mageling and not her superior.

The lord warder shrugged. "He doesn't want to be found."

Blueflames left the lodge in an eerily silent procession, with the Lady of Ghosts stalking after them and the Flying Blade and the Wyverntongue Chalice in her hands. She spared not a glance for Marlin Stormserpent, lying dead on the floor.

The room started to fill with the smell of Baert Ghalhunt's scorching head, but it wasn't long before the door opened again.

A lone person came in, hooded and cowled, and made straight for the dead noble.

Murmuring half-sung lines of ballads to himself, this new arrival bent to pick up the two severed hands and put them in a pouch.

"But she had eyes, those nightdark eyes, only for meee . . ."

The singing broke off with a brief grunt as the cowled one bent again—and in one swift, smooth heave, lifted the limp corpse up onto his shoulder.

Then he turned and went out into the forest, ignoring the drips that fell from what had been Marlin Stormserpent as he went.

"For I walk a lonely road, a hidden road, a bright road, yes I walk a . . ."

The soft singing faded, and birds began to whir and call again.

By the time they broke off and the lodge door swung open again, the head in the fire was a blackened thing, more skull than Baert Ghalhunt.

The two bullyblades were hot, sweaty, and very tired. Not to mention hungry. They'd been up all night, and if their mad lord of a master wasn't asleep, they certainly wanted to be.

"Lord Stormserpent?" one of them called, finding the chair—nay, the room, there was nowhere here to hide—empty. He glanced up into the rafters but saw only pelts and trophies, no lurking slayers.

The other bodyguard touched his arm and pointed silently down at the blood on the floor.

There was a lot of it.

"Tluin," the first one swore and hurried to the door that led into the kitchens, to make sure Stormserpent—or anyone else—wasn't there.

He came out shaking his head. "Circle the place."

"Of course," the other bullyblade replied, drawing his sword. "Are you thinking what I am?"

"If you're thinking Lord Mightybritches Stormserpent is dead, and we're out of hire and are likely to be hunted as murderers, then yes."

They gave each other grim nods and hastened back outside.

Never seeing or hearing the cowled one who watched their futile search from behind a distant tree, singing very softly, "Oh, there's nothing so sad . . . as a bodyguard . . . with no body . . . left . . . to guard."

Chapter
TWENTY-NINE

A Different Night

Then out came the moon and what did I see?
His teeth turned to fangs and his eyes burning bright
My darling, my lover a-coming for me
I knew we'd be having a different night.

Zaroanra Deltree, Bard
from the ballad *My Lady of Ghosts*
first performed in the Year of Rogue Dragons

It had been a long night at the Dragonriders' Club, and Amarune was so weary her dances would soon become snoring collapses into patrons' laps if she tried to go on.

The nights all felt long since she'd gone back to dancing.

It wasn't the work; it was the tension.

Everyone was watching each other warily; everyone looked over his shoulder; everyone carried an extra knife or pouch of sand or pepper . . . in the tenday since the Council, a mask of calm had settled over Suzail that no one at all trusted.

There was general brooding, a waiting to see just how and when the fighting would erupt.

No one doubted that it would. Most of the nobles who'd come for Council were still in the city, plotting and scheming behind closed doors, but oh-so-polite to each other on the streets and in the shops.

The good merchants of Suzail—and the shadier ones, too—were making coin hand over fist, feeding and thirst-slaking the fine lords and their maids and jacks and bullyblades, but wondering how soon this windfall would end. And how bloodily.

Right now, Rune was far too yawningly bone-weary to think any more about it. Not that she hadn't thought and thought far too much already.

Her feet hurt the most, as usual.

She rubbed them thoughtfully, curled up on her chair, then rolled out of it to find her clothes. It was astonishing how quickly her own life had settled back into its usual routines. How she'd lived before a certain Lord Delcastle had started taking a *very* personal interest in her.

Not to mention a crazed old man named Elminster and a sinister thief by the name of Talane.

Wincing at that latter name and wondering if she should go home this night, after all, Amarune ran her fingers through her hair to banish the worst of the tangles, yawned farewell to her mirror, blew out the little lantern, and made her way to the door, surefooted in the total darkness.

It seemed a very long time since she'd been the Silent Shadow, peril of the night. Some time in the last few days—had they *really* only been that few?—she'd drifted into being the ornament of a dashing young noble. A spirited lass, but only a lass, coin-poor and bearing a family name that mattered to no one . . .

The guard that Tress had hired to watch over the back door of the club and the street outside, to make sure no one was lurking to endanger her dancers, gave Rune a smile and a nod.

"Safe as it gets," that meant. Stifling another yawn, Rune smiled back, waved farewell, and slipped out through the door.

The street was not empty. A gleaming white coach stood where she would have blundered right into it if she'd come out with her head down, its horses pawing contentedly as they munched at their feedbags. A familiar face grinned at her out of its nearest window.

"Lord Arclath Delcastle," she greeted him with a tired grin. "I hope you're not expecting anything from *me*. Like staying awake, for instance."

Arclath swung the door open and sprang out of the coach to assist her into it with a courtly flourish.

"Nothing of the sort, I assure you. Ravaging your snoring body will bring me all the delight I need at the moment—or to be more serious, Rune, why not spend a night under my roof in Delcastle Manor? Alone, in a guest bedchamber, with the servants knowing you need to sleep just as long as your snoring takes you, and a splendid repast waiting when you *do* rise? Mother won't mind, being as she suggested it. What do you say?"

"I say, 'Yes, please, and thank you *very* much, gallant lord, and wake me when we get there,' " Amarune replied happily, settling herself into the cushioned back seat of the coach.

A breath later, they were rumbling through the streets, and she was nestled against Arclath, talking uncontrollably. "Spilling all your secrets," as Tress would put it.

"I feel utterly mind-mazed, to tell truth," she gabbled. "Settling back into my old ways, as if none of it, the beholder and being in chains in the palace and—and *everything*—was real. Then when I'm alone, it rushes back to me, the bad things, I mean. I'm still afraid Talane will appear when I'm least ready for her, and *really* afraid whenever I return to my rooms that a deadly trap will be waiting for me—or a brutally welcoming thick-neck bullyblade. Then, when I'm out in the sunlit streets again, it's all different, with El and Storm just gone, and all the exciting and important doings they brought with them, too!"

Arclath was nodding, so she rushed on.

"I—I don't feel as if I'd ever dare approach the palace, now, by myself and on my own behalf ... and I *still* don't feel as if I belong to the grand, expensive world of you nobles—or ever will."

Arclath smiled. "Nobles aren't much different from commoners," he told her quietly. "We're just more spoiled and pompous and better fed—and have more coins to waste, and better clothes to waste them in, that's all."

"That's all," she echoed in amusement.

Yet, his words held truth, for she and Arclath's mother were cautiously becoming friends, and few could match Marantine Delcastle for cold, lofty arrogance when she cared to play the noble matriarch to the hilt.

This strange calm that had settled over Suzail had come after a rather large handful of nobles had been wounded in duels and skirmishes, causing some of the highborn to bolt out of the city for the comparative security of their various country seats.

Yet, intrigues were still going on, with nobles hiring sellswords as fast as they could—some of them in more numbers than any impartial observer could possibly deem necessary for bodyguard purposes, or for that matter were allowed under the laws of the land—but it was all happening out of sight, behind closed doors or high mansion or estate walls.

The war wizards were back in control, aggressively leading highly visible Dragon patrols to keep order in the city, clear out undesirables, and maintain an alert garrison against the oft-rumored imminent invasion. All independent mages in Suzail were under close watch, and it seemed as if most commoners—after an initial rush to secure transportation for swift flight, and ready coins for spending in exile—were holding their breaths and just waiting for whatever befell next.

"Which," Arclath gloomily observed, as the coach turned a corner, "is usually some nastiness from Sembia, or something particularly cruel, stupid, and high-handed from one of the senior Houses. My mother would hotly dispute that, but it's true. Everyone who bothers to think on such things can see it." He sighed. "So, who will be the next stone-headed idiot to endanger the kingdom, I wonder?"

"Arclath Delcastle!" someone yelled, as if on cue—and men came rushing up to the slowing coach, out of the night.

Arclath snatched out his sword, and Rune, her heart suddenly pounding, raised one of her knives beside her ear, ready for throwing.

Yet, the man who stepped up onto the coach to rap on the closed window wore a bright smile, and Arclath knew him.

"Well met, lord!" were his first words, as Arclath thrust the sliding window down. "I—we—serve Lord Elbert Oldbridle, who bids us invite you to eveningfeast on the morrow, at the home of Lord Arkanon Nalander."

"Is this an open invitation, Clarn?" Arlcath asked mildly.

"No," was the reply.

"Don't bother to bring your doxy," Clarn added coldly, glancing at Amarune.

Arclath nodded, the Oldbridle bullyblade sprang down off the step, and the coach started to move again.

"What was *that* about?" Amarune asked.

"An invitation to join Lord Nalander's scheme to put someone or other—possibly himself or his son Arkeld, or possibly someone chosen by his Sembian backers—on the Dragon Throne, after young fools like me risk our necks exterminating the House of Obarskyr," Arclath replied grimly. "I'm beginning to think fleeing deep into the forest with Storm and Elminster, and staying there a good long time, is a very good idea."

"What will happen if you don't attend?" Amarune asked softly.

"They'll consider me a foe and treat me accordingly," Arclath replied calmly. "See? Not much different from commoners, after all."

Amarune shook her head and murmured, "You've no idea what common folk are really like, do you?"

Arclath frowned. "Lady," he said sternly, "I have tried hard to stride through life with my eyes open, seeing past the masks most adopt to greet the wider world, and marking the details of many lives and trades and customs, the better to—"

"Oh, I did not say you have not *tried* to look beyond the lives and affairs of nobles, my lord," Amarune told him earnestly. "It is one of the reasons why . . . why I love you. I—I—"

She threw her arms around him, drew him down into an embrace, and hissed, "What're you going to *do?* If not this cabal, which one?"

"None of them," Arclath snapped. "We have our own cabal—you, me, the Lady Storm, Mirt, and your great-grandfather. Plus the ghost of the Princess Alusair, perhaps, when we venture into the palace."

"So, do we turn this coach and head for the inn where Lord Helderstone has taken rooms?"

"In the morning," Arclath told her, his smile surfacing. "Tonight, Lady Rune, you are *mine*."

"There's been no sign of young Lord Stormserpent or his two flaming slayers for days now," Elminster murmured. "I wonder who got to him?"

"You think he's dead?" Storm asked, by way of reply.

That fair evening, he and Storm were strolling along a sweeping, lamplit street lined with noble mansions, neither of them showing Suzail their true selves.

Eccentric old Lady Darlethra Greatgaunt was known as a collector of curios, and an independent-minded walker and huntress. She was also known to always demand the protection of the wizards of war when she was in "godless, perilous, *almost*-as-bad-as-Westgate" Suzail. In the form of a lone mage as her constant escort. A handsome, young male wizard, of course.

Wizard of War Reldyk Applecrown was far from the most handsome mage about the palace, and was far from the most powerful. However, he was happily eager to perform the duty, which was more than most of his fellows had been.

It wasn't that Lady Greatgaunt expected her escorts to set foot in her bedchamber—indeed, she would have been loudly appalled and offended at the slightest hint of such "disgustingly forward" behavior. It was just that she liked to walk. And walk and walk and *walk*. No matter how foul, crowded, dusty, or stormswept the streets of Suzail were when she started down them, she wanted to walk them all. Setting a steady pace that permitted no dawdling or shopping moments, yet never approached what might be termed "brisk."

Wizards seldom tended to be walkers for the sake of walking, and very often discovered that the hard, hard cobbles of Suzail's lanes and byways made their feet hurt. Soon, and a lot.

Wherefore, there was little competition for Greatgaunt escort duty, and Applecrown had spent a long, footsore day—and most of the preceding eight or nine days, too—exhaustively scouring Suzail for a cobble that Lady Greatgaunt hadn't set elegant slipper upon, yet.

For her part, Storm had worn out three pairs of slippers, had frankly grown tired of nodding politely to each watch patrol, most of them so often that she knew every last Dragon and Crown mage by the informal, daily short versions of their names, and was quite bored enough to tear off her expensive gown, snatch the nearest merchant by the hand, and dance with him the length of whatever street they were on.

Lady Greatgaunt, of course, would not have approved of such antics.

Not that she was soon likely to know someone had borrowed much of her wardrobe and been enspelled into her exact likeness, being as she was lying abed in Mirt's lodgings, deathly ill after some unknown noble rival—or one of several much younger Greatgaunt heirs, succumbing to an attack of inheritance impatience—had tried to poison her and almost had succeeded.

Yes, her counterfeit had walked even more energetically than the real Lady Greatgaunt, but she and El had really been spending most of the last tenday exhaustively scouring Suzail for traces of a blueflame item, by walking the streets and covertly casting little pulses of magical fire that should send back an echo if such an item was nearby.

If they'd fashioned the spell correctly, that is. Though after centuries of twisting the Weave to myriad uses, very few folk in all the realms were better suited to probing for unusual magics.

"Dead or fled," El replied now, stumbling in weariness. "I'm about done, lass. Let's get home. Not a trace of anything strong enough to be a blueflame item, down all these streets."

He glanced at her eyes. Lady Greatgaunt looked as leathery and indomitable as ever, but Storm's eyes would tell him what Storm felt like, underneath. She, after all, was the one who'd been anchoring his spells, steadying him constantly; she had to be far more tired than he was. "How are ye, lass?"

"Ready to get home," she sighed, letting her exhaustion show for a moment. "Rub my feet, when we get back to Mirt?

I hope he won't be roaring drunk this time. His snoring drunk is bad enough."

"Heh. Don't ye prefer finding seven or eight warmskirts snoring along with him?"

Storm rolled her eyes. "I do *not*. Seeing their charms—even when they're worn out and snoring, too—makes me feel all the older. I'll grant that Mirt has the stamina of a fresh young stallion. I just wish he didn't feel the need to prove it every second day or so! One of these nights he's going to host the wrong lass, and she'll slit his throat for him and take away everything he's neglected to nail down."

"Which is everything," Elminster agreed. "Well, perhaps tonight will be different."

It was.

Mirt was happily wrapped in the embraces of a willing playpretty when something that felt like his own weight in cold hard stone struck him on the back of his head and sent him down into darkness.

The coinlass beneath him was still drawing breath for a scream when she got a cloak tossed over her head, then received the same stone-to-head treatment.

Men in leather who were bristling with weapons suddenly flooded through Lord Helderstone's rooms, two frowning and alertly peering hired wizards among them.

One of whom suddenly stiffened and snapped, "Someone— no, two people—climbing the stairs!"

"I'll take care of it, Morl," the other mage said. "Keep your scrying going. I want to make sure we get not just the two we can see, but anyone else, too."

The blasting spell he hurled down the stairs then was far more powerful than it needed to be, but he had a fee to earn, and a surviving witness was a curse that could haunt you for the rest of your life in this city.

"You got them, Scarmar," Morligul Downdagger announced with some satisfaction. "Smashed the man right down the stairs and back out of the building. The woman got tangled in the railings, but she's down. Don't see any lurkers yet."

"Keep looking," Scarmar snapped. Pulling out his paralyzing wand, he waved at six or seven armsmen to come with him.

From the head of the stairs he triggered the wand at the sprawled woman, then told the armsmen, "Get out there and find the man I blasted! I want him back in here *fast!*"

They raced past in a wild thunder of boots. Scarmar Heldeth followed more slowly with the rest of the armsmen, knowing Downdagger of Highmoon was guarding their rear; in Athkatla, where he came from, folks who rushed into unknown danger were usually soon known as "corpses."

"Kind of old for a playpretty," one of the armsmen lifting Storm's frozen body commented. "Expensive gown, too."

"Looks noble," said another.

"They said he has a maid," a third one put in, "so unless old noblewomen are suddenly hiring themselves out as coinlasses, this has to be her. She's about the same age as him, right? This is Helderstone's maid, probably dressed up for a night out."

"They're not finding him," Downdagger said suddenly, staring off into the distance.

"Stlarn," Heldeth muttered. "I *hate* loose ends."

Armsmen were coming back to the doors now. He could see by their faces that Downdagger was right.

He looked at his fellow mage, whose face wore the same uneasiness he was feeling.

"Let's be gone from here," he muttered.

Downdagger nodded, then snapped at the armsmen, "Leave the playpretty in the bed, but take Helderstone and his wench to the warehouse—and hurry!"

The armsmen hurried Mirt's limp body down the stairs to where they'd laid the old woman in the gown, snatched her up, and rushed off into the night.

"We should be with them in case they meet with any watch patrols," Downdagger muttered as Heldeth laid a staying hand on his arm. "Besides, the reek of yon dung wagon isn't impressing me."

He would have been surprised to know a scorched and angry Wizard of War Reldyk Applecrown was crouching in the fresh, wet nightsoil on the other side of the weathered boards of the dung wagon's side, listening to their every word—and even more astonished to learn that Applecrown was really Elminster, the legendary dragonslaying and throne-toppling Chosen of Mystra.

As it happened, Elminster wasn't interested in enlightening him. Yet.

"We have to decide what to say about the one who got away," Heldeth snarled.

"Tell him we tarried for a moment because we knew he was hiding, found the fool, and blasted him to ashes," Downdagger snapped. "What else?"

"*You* tell him," Scarmar Heldeth snapped right back. "He only paid me for one night's work—and now that I've tasted this work, I want to be well away from Suzail before he decides to rid the realms of those who could tell others too much of what he's up to. Guard yourself accordingly."

"Huh," Downdagger sneered. "He dare not do that to me. If I die, half the spells that protect him from scrying and prying vanish with me—and his own swift death at the hands of the war wizards is certain."

"Suit yourself," Heldeth replied, rushing off. Two running steps later, he was suddenly surrounded by a winking cloud of sparks. A warding.

Downdagger smiled crookedly. Deep trust, indeed. Yon shielding could only be meant to thwart any spell he might hurl.

He hurled nothing but shook his head and murmured after Heldeth, "Idiot. You could have been rich."

Then Downdagger glanced all around, saw no one watching, and set off in the direction the armsmen had gone. "Well, off to tell the good news."

He looked back one last time before he turned a corner but never saw the befouled, squelching man who'd climbed quietly out of the far side of the dung wagon to skulk slimily after him.

He *did* smell something, but after all, a dung wagon was right there.

CHAPTER
THIRTY
MURDERING LORD HELDERSTONE

We now know some nobles were far from noble,
in principles and purpose; some sought wealth by any means
And some were busy murdering Lord Helderstone.

Alander "Anyman" (a pseudonym)
from the chapbook *Aftermath of the Council of Dragons*
first published in the Year of Deep Water Drifting

I t had been years since he'd had a body that could really
sprint, leap, and go like the wind for a fair while, and
running hard seemed to keep some of the otherwise overpowering chamberpot stench down, so Elminster ran.

If he tried to follow Downdagger—an unscrupulous local
mage-for-hire he'd seen in dockside taverns a time or two, back
when he was busy being Elgorn Rhauligan—he had to admit
that he'd only be able to sneak up on the man if Downdagger
had almost entirely lost his sense of smell. Yet, if he ducked into
a parallel alley and ran ahead of the mage, he would at least not
be seen if the wizard looked back the way he'd come.

El sprinted until he was out of breath, then turned down
a side street to come out ahead of Downdagger. Who *was*
looking back, as he turned into a side street where there was a
covered carriage yard.

The mage gave a low whistle, and five warriors in identical
surcoats promptly melted out of the shadows amid the coaches
and wagons to surround Downdagger. They all moved together,
the mage strutting like a haughty noble, and the armsmen
forming a ring around him and marching like any bodyguard.

They were heading for better streets, where mansions
would be larger and walled, but just then were in a "high

houses" neighborhood of the sort favored by wealthy merchants and nobles who weren't rich enough to, say, buy a village upon a whim.

So, Elminster plunged into the nearest handy flowerbed—it belonged to Lord Relgadrar Loroun, as it happened—to have a good roll, and rid himself of some of the dung and cover himself with the scent of fresh-crushed flowers. At the end of the raised bed was a fountain, and he happily slid into its shallow surrounding pool to rinse himself off, then hurried after Downdagger's procession.

Two streets later, the bodyguard dispersed at the doors of The Three Ravens, a nobles' club Elminster knew. A small, quiet, stone drinking-house much favored for swift and private discussions, and currently the seat of power for the cabal of nobles led by Lord Dauntinghorn.

Morligul Downdagger strode inside as grandly as any highborn patriarch, and Elminster gave him two breaths to order a drink and get clear of the door before he followed.

As the door guards smoothly moved to block the path of this wet and bedraggled stranger, El murmured, "Urgent message for Lord Dauntinghorn," and strode right on, the door guards expressionlessly stepping out of his way again.

Inside, the Ravens was quieter than usual, with many empty tables, but the closed curtains across the entrances to the private booths along the back wall told him every one of them was occupied.

Downdagger was just gliding up to one of those booth entrances—one of the few flanked by two impassive private bodyguards.

"Rorn, Brabras—well met," the mage greeted the guards by name as he slipped between them and through the curtain.

Elminster promptly sat down at a table with his back to the booth and murmured a spell to eavesdrop.

It faded almost immediately, countered by a stronger ward, but not before El heard a man's voice say, "Ah, Downdagger! How did matters unfold?"

An impassive flagonjack appeared above Elminster. "Saer's pleasure?"

"Firewine, one flagon," El murmured. "Mind that it's aged, not last season's vintage or"—he shuddered—"*fresh*."

The server nodded and glided away, evidently taking Elminster for an eccentric lord rather than a commoner who should be ejected.

He returned almost immediately with the flagon, and El made a show of sniffing it critically before nodding and casually dropping a sapphire the size of his thumb into the flagonjack's outstretched hand.

The server's eyes widened, but he bowed low and glided away without a word, correctly interpreting El's "stop" raised hand gesture as a refusal of all coins back.

El was confident that Lady Greatgaunt, the owner of forty-six almost identical sapphire-trimmed gowns, wouldn't miss one gown—and being as three sapphires that Storm had been wearing had ended up out on the street with him after the spellblast, he still had two stones to spend.

A firewine-filled flagon makes an excellent mirror if the light is right, so El had no difficulty at all in seeing Downdagger emerge from the booth again, or of identifying the noble who emerged with him. Kindly old Lord Traevyn Illance. Well, well.

Illance and Downdagger strolled along the line of booths to the line of garderobes at the end of the room, Illance's two bodyguards a careful three paces behind them. Carrying his drink, Elminster strolled languidly toward the same destination.

When the lord stepped into a garderobe, Downdagger hesitated, shrugged, then entered an adjacent one. Elminster worked a silent spell.

The veil of darkness he'd conjured was wide enough to wall off this end of the room from all eyes, thick enough to surround the bodyguards' heads and blind them, and moved in accordance with his will, so he could keep it around them ... if they didn't move too far in opposite directions.

Elminster finished his firewine, set the empty flagon down on a table he was passing, and strode right up to Rorn and

Brabras—whose wildly waving arms and swiftly drawn swords betrayed their consternation at being plunged into utter darkness. They were going to start to shout, so El raced around behind them, touched both of them on the backs of their necks to enspell them into unconsciousness, caught their swords to prevent any loud clangs, laid the blades atop their bodies, and stepped over those bodies—into the garderobe where the wizard had gone.

The staff of the Ravens had noticed something amiss, but all they heard was a brief, wordless exclamation of astonishment from behind an area of obviously conjured darkness.

The senior flagonjack rolled his eyes. These younger nobles! Couldn't wait to rut until they got home, but didn't want anyone seeing their faces as they rode some coinlass—or a noble lass of a rival family. So, a little conjured darkness . . . they'd be using magic to disguise themselves while here in the Ravens, next!

On the other side of the veil, Downdagger emerged from the garderobe, dragged Rorn into it and dumped him *and* his sword in on top of the unconscious Morligul Downdagger, and shut the garderobe door on them both and checked that it would stay shut. It did. The second Downdagger then sat down at an adjacent table and bent his attention in another direction . . . as his veil of darkness moved smoothly into the garderobe he'd just filled up with bodies.

The flagonjacks, staring down the room, saw the darkness vanish, and beheld nothing amiss except a man sprawled on the floor with a sword atop him.

The senior flagonjack started down the room to see what had happened, but he was still a good twelve hurrying strides away when a garderobe door opened and Lord Illance emerged, to find his hired wizard sitting at a table—and one of his two bodyguards sprawled senseless on the floor.

He could see the man's own blade—clean of all gore—was lying atop his body, and there was no blood or visible wounds.

"A *wench* did that," Morligul explained before he could ask, pointing down at the body. "Rorn's chasing her right now."

Illance looked down at the unconscious Brabras, shook his head, sighed in exasperation, and grunted, "Can't even get good bullyblades these days! Come!"

He stalked off, heading for the front door of the Ravens. Elminster hastened to follow.

The third hard, ringing slap brought Mirt awake.

By the burning sensation down that side of his face, previous slaps had been administered with powerful enthusiasm, yet had failed to rouse him.

"I hope ye're a pretty lass," he growled, "because those are the sort of folk I *like* to be slapped by."

He tried to turn his head, which was when he discovered he was bound—by quite a lot of rope, knotted very tightly—to a chair in a cavernous warehouse.

Standing in front of him was Lord Traevyn Illance, wearing an unpleasant smile as he stared at Mirt. The old lord was flanked by five bullyblades in matching surcoats, and another man who looked more like a mage than any sort of warrior. As Mirt looked at all of them, Illance nodded to his five bodyguards, and they disappeared through a door in the wall behind him, seeming rather eager to be gone.

"I think we both know why you're here, Rauligus," Illance said coldly.

"Ye're smitten with me and seek to enjoy my charms in private?" Mirt asked hopefully.

Illance's eyes narrowed. He looked at the mage, then back at Mirt. "Your voice is different, the words you use, too . . . you *are* Lord Rauligus Helderstone, are you not?"

"Have been these too many seasons," Mirt replied cheerfully. "Getting good at being Lord Helderstone, I am."

Illance nodded. "Then you will recall that you owe me a quite considerable sum. Seven hundred thousand golden lions, to be precise. Not to mention ten thousand more on the year-day mark, every year since you borrowed it. *Twenty-nine summers ago.*"

"Aye?"

"You dispute this?"

"Nay."

"Good. Then you should also recall that the entire sum was due if ever you returned to Cormyr. Which you have obviously now done. Probably because you had to depart Sembia in a hurry, thanks to some new foe—and considered me the lesser peril."

"Aye."

"I've heard you've been here in Suzail for almost a tenday, now. Yet, I had to hear it from others, because I heard *nothing* from you. You failed to contact me promptly upon reaching the city to offer me the repayment of my loan, despite such action on your part being a clear part of our agreement. I am hurt, Rauligus. Hurt. Almost as deeply hurt as I've been all these years, living in near penury without my gold. It's been calling to me, Rauligus, as I scrimped and saved and did without . . . but I took what scant consolation I could from the knowledge that my gold was at least in the hands of a fair man, an honest man. A rival, some might even say a foe, but an honest man."

Illance was pacing now, drawling airily, the wizard in the background smiling and enjoying the performance.

"I am that," Mirt agreed happily.

Illance stopped. "Oh? You claim so? How is it then that you shatter our agreement, returning to fair Suzail to live like a decadent king, drinking kegs upon kegs and rolling in perfumed bedlinens with playpretties night after night, without even a word to me? For in that, I do not see the conduct of an honest man. I see the brazen behavior of a *swindler*."

"Nay, nay!" Mirt protested, trying to strain against his bonds without appearing to do so. Gods below, but they were tight. He was trussed like a roast, and every whit as doomed. " 'Twas nothing of the sort!"

"Lies are no more attractive when retold," Illance replied coldly and waved his hand dismissively. "Enough of this. I was hoping for pleading, for desperate bargaining for your life—or at least the retention of some of your limbs—but you seem to have become some sort of happy half-wit. So, hear now your fate—my five bodyguards are going to torture you into yielding up the whereabouts not just of what you owe me, but *all* your properties and wealth. Everything. If you're still alive, we'll put you on a boat to Westgate to be unloaded, naked and broken, onto the docks, to see how long you survive in *that* pleasant den of vipers."

"B-but you sent them away," Mirt pointed out brightly.

Illance smiled. "Oh, they'll be back. Just as soon as they finish enjoying your maid, in yonder room." He leered. "She's really your wife, isn't she? Wearing quite a few sapphires, wasn't she? Oh, yes, I'm expecting them back soon. Yet, we mustn't rush my loyal blades . . . and there *are* five of them."

Mirt let himself look downcast for the first time. He was done. The ironguard ring Storm had given him protected against metal weapons—until, of course, they took it from him—but there were many other ways a man could be hurt. Roasting alive, or breaking most of his bones, one after another, for instance.

"And how d'ye know I won't lie to ye?" he asked. "Send ye headlong into trap after trap?"

Illance smiled thinly. "This handy hirespells mage here will tell me when you're lying. And keep you alive and awake through the pain, so you can enjoy every last moment of it."

The wizard gave Mirt a solemn wink. Then he turned to the door the bodyguards had disappeared through and called, "Done, lass?"

The door opened and Storm stepped through it, dragging the limp body of the largest bodyguard by his throat.

She was barefoot and bloody, the gown torn to shreds that still clung to her largely because the blood was making them stick—but she was grinning.

"Done," she said simply, striding across the room. Behind her, through the doorway, the rest of the bodyguards could be seen strewn senseless all over the room she'd departed.

She was coming for Illance, who after one look at her turned and fled across the room with surprising speed.

El hurried after him, caught him up, and calmly tripped him.

Illance had just time to scramble up to his knees before Storm reached him. Her kick took him under the chin, snapped his head back, and lifted the rest of him right off the ground.

They watched the old lord bounce, out cold. Storm waited until Illance lay quite still before plucking out the noble's belt dagger and heading over to Mirt.

"Hey, now," Mirt said, "ye look dangerous with that fang."

Storm smiled through the blood. "I *feel* dangerous with this fang. Yet, Mirt, why the worry? You always wanted bondage, and bared women to come for you ..."

"Not with knives, and not *me* bound," Mirt protested.

Storm sighed as she set about cutting him free. "Details, details ..."

"Hoy!" Mirt yelped. "Get yer knife away from that! It's *not* a detail!"

Elminster looked up from Lord Illance's body. "Stop playing with Mirt and get over here. Undressing unconscious men is harder than I remember."

"Undressing ... ?" Storm teased. "El, is there something you should be telling me?"

"Just help me get all this clobber off him," El growled. "By Siamorphe, Tiamat, and Waukeen, but nobles wear more costly tripe than they ever did when *I* was playing at being one!"

Mirt shook free of the last few coils and lurched to his feet, wincing and growling at the numbness—and the pain, wherever there was no numbness. "What're ye baring him for, anyhail?"

"I want every last bauble and stitch of magic on him, to take to Alassra," Elminster replied. "Though none of it—even if we amass a cartload of it—will do her as much good as a blueflame item. If I could get one of those before we go to her ..."

Mirt shook his head. "Well, I just want to be free of nobles trying to harm me. D'ye know if anyone *else* in Suzail is likely to treat kindly old Helderstone like this one was planning to? For that matter, what's to stop him trying again, when he wakes?"

El and Storm looked at each other, then shrugged.

"We'll change thy appearance again and give ye another name, so ye can dwell in Suzail free of that particular problem," El told him.

"And we'll spread word that Illance tortured and killed Helderstone, then hid his body, so our kindly old lord here will receive some *very* unwanted attention from the war wizards," Storm added with a sly smile.

Mirt grinned. "The two of ye would have made very good Lords of Waterdeep, ye know?"

El and Storm exchanged glances again.

"As I recall," Storm added sweetly, "we did."

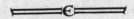

Lady Greatgaunt's rented suite boasted three guest bed-chambers, and although her war wizard escort bedded down in the most distant one, there was no one at all to see that he stayed there.

Particularly in the hours just before dawn, when two tired walkers came home with some wine and a filched wheel of Illance's cheese to share between them.

"So," Storm asked Elminster as they munched and sipped, "how do we find the mysterious noble who has a blueflame ghost up his sleeve? We can't just go from mansion to tower all around Suzail knocking down doors and trying to shake the truth out of every lord and lady we meet!"

El grinned. "No," he agreed, "so we'll lure a ghost to us, instead. I'll use a spell to grace a certain mask dancer with blue flames, and wait for word to spread."

"Tress won't thank you for getting her club wrecked by a blueflame ghost," Storm said quietly. "And young Arclath will probably try to serve your beard up to you on a platter—attached to your head or not—for endangering his love."

"The dancer isn't going to be at the Dragonriders' and isn't going to be Amarune," El told her happily.

"Then who . . ." Storm gave him a sharp look. "*Oh, no, El. Oh, no!*"

"I'd much rather see you barepelt than young Rune, and I'll wager most of Suzail will, too. You're something splendid, lass. Truly. And you don't look a day older than, say, twenty-two summers."

"You *rogue*," she replied with a twinkling smile. "You lying, flattering rogue."

"Aye, that's me," he said serenely. "Shall we go out and purchase a mask?"

"After I've had a good long sleep," Storm replied emphatically. "There's no longer a Weave to replenish us, Old Mage, and I get *tired*, these days. Weren't you 'about done' most of the night ago?"

"I was," El agreed—and fell face-first onto her bed. He was snoring in a trice.

Storm rolled her eyes.

"Now *that's* a useful trick, Sage of Shadowdale," she told him. Then she bent closer and frowned. He really *was* snoring.

She kicked off Illance's boots, wriggled out of his clothes—they fit terribly, and she resolved to burn them before someone recognized them; Suzail these days seemed a city of tireless spies—and cuddled against him.

In his sleep, Elminster stroked her then put an arm around her.

Storm amused herself by trying to undress him, but fell asleep in his arms before she got very far.

CHAPTER
THIRTY-ONE

THE DANGEROUS WORK OF LURING GHOSTS

I cower not at head-shattering spells
And tremble not at invading hosts
For I have walked haunted fells
On the dangerous work of luring ghosts.

> from the ballad *My Long Ghostdance*
> by Eleyera "Lady Minstrel" Dree
> first performed in the Year of the Haunting

Manshoon leaned eagerly forward in his chair, straining to see and hear better.

Or rather, to urge Ironhand, ever so gently, to shift to where *he* could see and hear better.

Manshoon's spell would let him observe what Ironhand was seeing and hearing for just a little longer. He wasn't riding the man's mind, because he didn't want the risk of being where Ironhand was just then.

He had found his best blueflame hunter yet. Imglor "Imhammer" Ironhand was *very* expensive, but worth it. The man was almost as ruthless, careful, and coldly calm as Manshoon himself, and had carved himself out an impressive career as a slayer-for-hire specializing in swift and covert killings disguised as accidents.

No slaying was necessary, this time—only a slayer unmasked. The noble who commanded the lone blueflame ghost that had appeared at the Council.

Thus far, Ironhand had helped make almost certain that three candidates for the blueflame noble were not, in fact, the one Manshoon sought.

At that moment, Manshoon's new hireling had wormed his way onto the roof of a high house adjacent to the one where

Lord Harkuldragon was strutting around an upper room that had open windows. Through which Ironhand could hear a discussion between Harkuldragon and his longtime hired mage, the homely, aging sourface Sarrak of Westgate about the slaying of a certain inconvenient courtier.

The courtier was one whose death half Suzail would greet cheerfully. The pompous Khaladan Mallowfaer, Master of Revels, was no one's favorite or confidant, and as far as Manshoon knew was kinless, had never married, and had never romanced anyone. He'd hired doxies aplenty, of course, but that was an entirely different matter. His inconvenience to Harkuldragon was that he'd inadvertently learned something of the noble's planned treason, and so could expose Harkuldragon, if he so desired. A situation the lord naturally found intolerable.

What had made Manshoon pay far too much to have Ironhand eavesdropping on the noble and his mage was Harkuldragon's grim comment over one too many goblets, at The Three Ravens some nights ago, that if "the usual magics failed" he had "something more to settle scores with."

Harkuldragon could have meant nothing more than blackmail, the fact that he was good with his fists and swift to use them, or that he owned a magic sword of great age and mysterious powers that adventurers of his hiring had once brought him. Or he might have a pet monster, or be able to call in a favor from a mage or two. But then again, it might mean he could send forth his own slayer wreathed in blue flame ...

So far, the converse Ironhand had overheard hadn't suggested blueflame ghosts or anything of the sort, but they were getting to interesting words finally, as Harkuldragon's temper started to slip.

"The man's as greedy and malicious as a *snake*, Sarrak! And as conceited as—*what was that?*"

Ironhand had heard it, too, and leaned out so far in a neck-craning attempt to see and hear that his eavesdropping almost became literal.

Someone had caused the lock on the door of that upper room to burst outward in all directions, showering the room with tiny pattering fragments of metal that would have been deadly if they hadn't been almost dust.

The door yawned open, evidently revealing no one at all outside the room.

"Make whoever it is visible, wizard! Banish invisibility, or whatever the spell is!" Lord Harkuldragon bellowed.

"Done," Sarrak replied a moment later.

"Who—who are you?" the nobleman demanded, hauling out his belt dagger and glaring at someone Ironhand couldn't see. "Wizard, don't just stand there! Smite her! *Smite her down!*"

"I fear he can't, noisy fool. He made the mistake of obeying you—and while he was making me visible, I was casting paralysis on him."

With an easy, almost insolent stride, a tall and slender woman came into the room. She had pale white skin, a sharp-featured, cruel face dominated by large, dark eyes that snapped with simmering anger, and long, long legs. She was clad all in black except for a silver weathercloak that hung from her shoulders, and Ironhand was certain he'd never seen her before.

A woman this beautiful, he would remember.

"Who *are* you?" he demanded, hefting his dagger as he came around the table. "And what do you want?"

"I am the Lady of Ghosts. And fear not, Lord Harkuldragon—my business here is not with you at all. I am here for Sarrak of Westgate."

"Sarrak? *Why?*"

"Your questions grow tiresome. Perhaps you should fear me, after all."

"Oh? You wield no weapon, and I'm protected against spells. Perhaps *you* should fear *me*."

Harkuldragon strode toward the woman, who stood watching him come closer, making no move at all. She looked bored.

Two strides from her the lord suddenly hissed out a curse, shook his dagger hand as he stepped back, then flung the dagger down. "*Burned* me!"

He was flapping fingers that seemed to be dripping melted flesh.

"Protected," the woman said contemptuously. "By Sarrak's spells, no doubt."

Then she moved like a striking panther, charging to take him by the throat so swiftly that Harkuldragon didn't even have time to cry out.

He managed to do so a moment later, when her hard-driven knee into his crotch lifted him off his feet, but thanks to her tightening fingers, his cry wasn't much more than a croak.

As he went down, she got behind him, hands still gripping his throat, and flung herself hard down on his neck, knees together.

Ironhand winced as Lord Harkuldragon's neck broke.

The woman calmly twisted the lord's head around at a gruesome angle as she stood up. Then she walked away, leaving the man dead and forgotten on the floor behind her.

"Now, Sarrak, let us begin. I will see what is in your mind—destroying it in so doing, but that can't be helped. You see, I've heard you know things about Orbakh, who once ruled your city. Things relating to who he really was. A man I seek, named Manshoon."

Manshoon sat frozen in astonishment. What was *this*?

Sarrak emitted a sort of sob as her spell struck him. As she bored into his mind, the magic that was destroying his brain seemed to release him from her paralysis, but too late for him to escape; his limbs were trembling violently and thrashing wildly about from time to time, utterly out of his control.

He staggered back into Ironhand's field of view, tripping backward over Harkuldragon's body and crashing to the floor, where he lay twisting and panting, his eyes bulging and sweat drenching his skin . . . which was going bone-white.

"Please," he blurted.

Ten or twenty of Manshoon's breaths passed before the stricken mage spoke again. "Please . . . please stop."

"I'm sorry, Sarrak, but I must *know* what's in your mind, not just what you choose to tell me. Speak freely if doing so will bring you a little release. It makes my peering easier."

"No!" Sarrak gasped, in feeble defiance. "No."

He fell silent again, except for gasps, until his eyes started to go dark.

Manshoon had seen wizards' eyes do that before, when farscrying Thayan torturers; Sarrak's end would come soon.

"Manshoon," the doomed mage quavered suddenly, through his streaming sweat, his eyes now dark pits. "You live to slay him. You *burn* to slay him. Is this the Manshoon of legend? Why do you hate him so?"

"You seek to buy time and a little relief from pain," came the calm reply, "yet, I'll tell you, Sarrak of Westgate. I hate only one man more than Manshoon—if he *is* a man, at all, or ever was. Elminster, the Sage of Shadowdale."

"How . . . how so?"

"I was Manshoon's lover and apprentice. So was my mother. And my two sisters. Oh, he was a magnificent beast; when he stared into your eyes, there was *nothing* you wouldn't do for him."

The Lady of Ghosts took a step closer. "He ordered them to attack and kill Elminster, and in their battle with the Old Mage—Manshoon watched from afar for his personal entertainment, rendering no aid at all—Elminster slew my kin. I was the youngest and Manshoon's favorite. He held me back. I believe he knew he was sending them to their doom."

She took another step forward, her voice rising a little. "I was enraged, and in my grief turned on Manshoon, incredulous that he'd done nothing. He left me with *this.*"

She tore open her black jerkin.

Between her pale, revealed breasts protruded the bloody point of a dagger.

A wound that should have been fatal. The blood glistened fresh and wet.

"He left me for dead, knowing nothing of the curse I bore that kept me alive. Elminster had cast it on me earlier, to keep me safe from Manshoon's 'murderous cruelties,' he told me— though it was really to give him a spy the lord of the Zhentarim could not slay; so, when Manshoon finally fell he could plunder my mind at will to learn all Manshoon's deeds and treasures and secrets."

Her voice rose into a savage snarl. "He used me. They both used me. They will both die!"

The Lady of Ghosts made a swift, complicated gesture—and Sarrak's head burst like a rotten fruit. She turned away.

"Much more slowly and painfully than I let you perish, wizard of Westgate. But then, your only crime was working for the wrong man. A crime I share twice over."

As Ironhand watched, not daring to move lest he make a sound she might hear, the Lady of Ghosts went to various places in the Lord Harkuldragon's chamber and collected as many hidden magic items from them.

"Thank you, Sarrak," she told the headless corpse. "The entire roster, and how to safely recover them. You saved me much time."

Ironhand heard her walk away, across the floor and out and down the stairs.

He waited a long time before he dared shift his position on the roof and take himself away.

Manshoon never noticed. He was too busy staring into the darkness around his chair, shaken.

"Cymmarra," he whispered. "Is this fallen Mystra's last slap at me? How much do you know of what I am now, Cymmarra? You hunt me here in Suzail, so you know something . . . oh, Bane blast all! *Now* what do I do?"

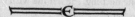

Elminster came awake slowly, feeling the warmth of a loving embrace. Ahh, Alassra, at last . . .

No. These were . . . *Storm's* arms about him, her bare body wrapped around his. They were on her bed, and he wore only Applecrown's breeches and clout.

He rose on one elbow, and she stirred in her sleep then settled contentedly back against him, the side of her face against his breast.

Hmm. Against Applecrown's young, sleekly muscled chest, and flat stomach below. Nothing to compare with her rounded magnificence, of course . . .

Mystra, but she was beautiful! The sun was high—stlarn, it must be almost highsun!—and lancing down through the window to paint her body with bright gold. Her silver tresses were writhing and coiling, slowly and lazily, in their own sensual pleasure.

Such beauty . . .

He was aroused, yes, stirring beneath her and causing her to purr and move against him in her sleep. Aroused, and why shouldn't he be?

Well, because she was his friend, and although she wasn't his daughter, he'd raised her like one some seven hundred years ago. She was his companion, his sword sister, not his lover . . . never his lover . . .

Storm's eyes opened. She gazed up at him along his bare chest, her nose almost touching his belt buckle, and gave him a long, slow smile, regarding him dreamily.

"Even in another's body, El," she whispered, her hair lashing him gently like the tails of a dozen playful cats, "you're . . . a comfort to wake up to."

She had obviously changed what she'd been about to say midsentence. Unsettled, he looked aside before whispering, "Yes."

Then, slowly, he rolled away from her.

Just as reluctantly, she let him go.

As he padded to the garderobe, he growled, "Ye'll make a good mask dancer."

"No," Storm replied, up on one elbow in the rumpled bed. "You will."

Elminster turned around to regard her, a silent question in his lifted brow.

"El," she asked softly, "why don't *you* be the mask dancer? And spell-shift my face and this silver hair that marks me for all eyes, as well as using magic to wreathe yourself in blue flames? Then we'll be two women, not that silver-haired Storm, so the man with her *must* be Elminster of Shadowdale, no matter what he looks like.' We'll still be a lure—just not the lure that tells everyone who's luring."

El blinked. "Oh, now. That *is* better. Well pointed, lass. Aye, we'll do it thy way."

Storm smiled, not bothering to hide her pleased surprise. "Well, now. Progress at last."

Elminster's reply, as he headed into the garderobe, was a rude noise.

Storm chuckled and rolled over on her back, stretching her arms, legs, and hair wide, and flexing them.

She was in the midst of gently groaning as she wiggled her cobble-worn toes, and their aches all throbbed in response, when she heard the unmistakable sounds of the inn's guards admitting someone into Mirt's rooms, across the hall from their own.

Springing out of bed, she snatched a robe around herself and went across to Mirt's forechamber, where Amarune and Arclath were smilingly greeting a still-dozing Mirt.

Who had obviously spent the night snoring in the forechamber's most massive armchair, after wenching and then dismissing the wenches, and *then* enjoying all he could manage of the best decanters on Lord Helderstone's sideboard, which now littered the carpet around his floppy-booted feet.

"Afraid you'd lose them all when you stopped being Lord Helderstone?" Storm asked, waving her hand at the array of emptied glass.

Arclath chuckled, but Mirt's response was a growl that was only a trifle more jovial than surly. Then his eyes focused on her, and he brightened, sitting up a little to properly take in the sight of a barely clad Storm.

"Now *that* fashion I like, lady. Are ye succumbing to my charms at last?"

"No," she replied fondly, "I was finally getting some sleep. And unlike some old rogues around here, I like to occasionally get out of garments I've been living in for days. It gives the lice a little excitement."

Mirt started scratching himself.

"Never saw the point of exciting lice, myself," he growled. "Maggots, now . . ."

"Maggots? I *thought* I heard someone discussing morning-feast!" Elminster put in, from the doorway behind Storm. "Yet I smell nothing sizzling."

"Oh, no?" Mirt leered at them both. "I'll wager something was, in yon bedchamber last night."

Storm rolled her eyes. "How often do you lose your last coin in foolish wagers, I wonder? Where *is* your cook, anyhail?"

She strode into the kitchen—and stopped dead.

The cook's severed head was staring in terror at her from where it sat, beneath a handful of eager flies, in a skillet on a cold and unlit hearth. That end of the room was drenched with blood, but the rest of the cook was nowhere to be seen.

"Someone's sent us a warning," she told the others over her shoulder.

There was a rush to look—and Amarune recoiled, Arclath winced, and El and Mirt looked grim.

"It's more than time for Lord Helderstone to disappear," El muttered. "He had other old foes among the nobles, I'd say." He looked at Mirt. "Sorry, old friend."

Mirt shrugged and grinned.

"Where's the rest of her?" Arclath asked, peering around the blood-spattered kitchen.

"Carried off into undeath," Storm replied crisply, "or left somewhere to make trouble for us in the eyes of the Crown. Let's *move*."

Every now and then, when walking the haunted wing of the royal palace, one came to a high window whose shroudings had fallen to let in the bright sunlight.

Radiance that fell in shafts down into the gloom of the deserted galleries, illuminating thick dust that hung in the air like lazily swirling snow.

Targrael liked the haunted wing. It was more home to her than the cleaner, busier, noisy chambers where the courtiers worked, walked, and talked.

Yet, she wasn't here in this particular corner of the shunned part of the palace this day for a pleasure-stroll.

For years she'd heard rumors of this or that hidden royal cache of enchanted weapons. Most of the tales were overblown, over time transforming a glowing dagger or ring hidden in a hollow bedpost into a small armory boasting many flying suits of armor and figurines that became snarling lions or flying dragon steeds, but she'd found a few palace treasures herself, and learned enough to know that there *were* larger ones. Or had been, once.

Of particular interest was a "marcher in blue flame" mentioned in a long-ago scribe's description of items Salember the Rebel Prince had once publicly gloated over, that had apparently never been seen again since. She'd been hoping the five sages who'd been closeted secretly combing palace records for years now would turn something up . . . and it seemed they finally had.

It wasn't much, just a line at the end of a Jorunhast note: "The three pillars safeguard the most perilous." One more cryptic taunt, most might well term it, but to *this* lady Highknight, it meant something more.

There was just one pillar in this whole reach of the palace sculpted into the semblance of a triangular cluster of three fused pillars.

A pillar that stood like a prow where a little three-room-long side wing branched off the main block of the palace, rooms that on all five floors had once housed senior war wizards, the spell-crafters and researchers too old to ride in hard country and take to battlefields.

The young Palaghard, while still a prince, had once written a note to a young lady who'd caught his eye that "If you need to hide, Druth's pillar swings wide." Now, a wizard of war hight Jereth Ardruth had once dwelt in one of those rooms, and the triple pillar would have formed the endpost at the back of Ardruth's—Druth's—closet.

A stretch, but worth investigating. Blueflame ghosts could be used to bring down House Obarskyr and plunge the realm into years of thronestrife—but blueflame ghosts under *her* command could keep Cormyr strong, the Dragon Throne better guarded than ever before.

The wizards of war had sunk beyond untrustworthiness; the current royals were weak; and the highest-ranking courtiers a more corrupt and venal band of pompous greed-heads than she would have thought tolerable, even to a weak king.

No, it was all up to her.

And with the blueflame ghosts hers, she could at last . . .

This one. This was the door.

Closed and locked, but that meant little to a death knight. Drawing her sword, she positioned herself just so, aiming her blade so it would plunge down the crack where door met frame, and swung it high.

Before bringing it down with all her might, straight and true, to slash through the forged locking mechanism in one great shriek of metal.

Then she gently pulled on the door ring, let the great door swing wide, and went in.

The room beyond was a mess, of course. The windows had broken long ago, and generations of pigeons and whir-wings had nested on the desk, shelves, and bed, winter snows and winds had scattered parchments across the floor and set about rotting them into the moldering ruin of carpet, and the closet was right over—*there.*

Its curtain fallen, its—

The door she'd just forced slammed shut behind her, and a doorbar thudded into place.   Targrael whirled around with a snarl, sword up.

A woman was facing her, leaning indolently on a sword of her own. Someone she knew. The ghost of the Princess Alusair Nacacia Obarskyr. The Steel Princess. The Steel Regent.

"Well met," Alusair said dryly. "I've been waiting for you."

Targrael wasted no time in words. She sprang at her hated foe with a snarl, bright blade singing.

"You traitor and stealer of Obarskyr secrets," Alusair added almost gently, flying up into the air to parry and draw Targrael out into the room.

The death knight charged, trying to pounce and hack the ghost down to the floor in a flurry of slashing swings.

Though the princess might be insubstantial as a wraith, she was solid enough to hold and swing the weight of a sword—even a sword made of her own ghostly self, sharpened momentarily to the strength and keen edge of warsteel. So she could be hurt.

Alusair laughed amid the clang and skirl of steel. "Is that your best, kitchen-cleaver-maid? How many beds did you have to warm to get made a Highknight?"

"I *never!*" Targrael shrieked, stung to speech at last. "You *bitch!* You *evil*, reckless-of-the-realm, rutting *slut* of a—"

Her blade crashed home, right through Alusair's ghostly sword—and right through the ghostly breast beyond, pinning it to the floor.

She crowed in triumph, as Alusair arched and writhed in soundless agony beneath her.

"Ha *ha!* Not so insolent *now*, are you, failed regent! Disgrace to the realm! Overmatched fool of an incompetent warrior!"

Through her open-mouthed, gasping pain, Alusair spat out the words, "Fly, Fang." And then she smiled.

As up through her, up from the moldering heap of rubble she'd been lying on, sprang a glowing blue dagger.

Point first, it sped through Targrael, up through her leathers into her breast and inwards, through ribs, slicing upward like icy fire.

"Meet the Fang of Baerovus," Alusair whispered. "The blueflame treasure you sought . . . the only one we Obarskyrs have. I wish you joy of it, would-be tyrant!" She faded into darkness, a wisp that drifted slowly across the floor, toward the door.

Targrael lashed out sideways with her sword, seeking vainly to slice that whispering shadow as it flew this way and then that, wriggling snakelike out under the door.

But the Fang of Baerovus was caught in her throat and sliding *higher* . . .

Desperately she dropped her sword, reached up with both hands, and broke her own neck, thrusting her head grotesquely to one side to hang limply down her back.

Just in time. The Fang burst up to the ceiling, trailing one of her ears, and struck sparks off the stone there.

Before it arrowed to the door, out through the gap she'd made by chopping through the lock, and away.

She knew by the utter agony, that her wounds would be mortal for one with lifeblood to spill. She felt too weak to do anything more than slump down atop the rubble and whimper.

Chapter
THIRTY-TWO
Old Games and Older Secrets

We Highknights, like many another ruler's dark agents
Go armed in the shadows, and break laws by royal consent
An army of thieves and slayers devoting ourselves
To new threats, old games, and older secrets.

Baerend "Blackblade" Blakshar
Loyal Forever: A Highknight's Tale, a suppressed
chapbook first seen in the Year of the Talking Skull

The oldest, grandest Delcastle coach had thickly cushioned seats, but nothing else to soften rides. Wherefore Amarune was clinging to Arclath to keep upright, with her booted feet wedged against Mirt's knees where he sat facing the noble and the dancer. Loose cobbles on this particular lane were making the coach rattle almost deafeningly as it rushed toward Delcastle Manor, where it had been agreed they'd tarry until Storm or El appeared to fetch Mirt to different lodgings under a new face and name.

"So who *did* kill the cook?" Rune was asking.

"Almost anyone may have," Arclath said bleakly.

"Not so, lad," Mirt rumbled. "The slayers were working for a noble."

"Likely, yes," Arclath granted, "but tell me why you say so. Is it merely one more 'dastardly nobles are behind everything' thought?"

"Nay. They carried off Lady Greatgaunt with no mess or noise. No ransom demands, no snatching all her gowns or the jewels off 'em, no blood or tussle. Following clear an' detailed orders—carefully." Mirt waved a hand. "Therefore, working for nobles, hey?"

"Hey," Arclath agreed with a grin.

"I—" Amarune hesitated, then continued, "I learned much from Elminster's mind, while he was in mine. It's only right you should know as much as we do about all of this. The ghosts, I mean."

Arclath nodded, and Mirt made a beckoning "out with it!" gesture.

"At the Council," Rune began, "a blueflame ghost appeared briefly during the fighting and felled several nobles, specific ones, but then vanished. So, obviously someone in the room was controlling it."

Mirt nodded. "A noble who attended yer Council has a blueflame item."

"A mystery for Elminster, or his old foe Manshoon, not to mention half the ambitious nobles in Suzail, now, to solve, as they all scramble to get that item and control the ghost," Arclath added.

Rune nodded. "Elminster wants it to try to restore The Simbul—you know about her?"

Mirt chuckled. "I do. More'n I want to, but that's another tale."

Rune shook her head. "Not now, I pray you! Manshoon presumably wants the ghost to have another slayer he can send forth, in case he ever runs out of mind-slaves or beholders."

Mirt nodded. "I remember him, too. That one will never be able to resist seeking such power."

"Yes, but he mustn't yet have it, or he'd be using it, not faring forth himself or sending agents. The blueflame ghosts frighten and therefore dominate—and Manshoon *lives* to control and dominate."

Mirt nodded again. "Over the years," he growled, "some things change very little. Names and faces, aye, but the games, nay." He flexed his hands—and a dagger suddenly gleamed in one of them.

He held it up, smiled at it, and told Amarune and Arclath, "Fortunately, I always did enjoy playing these particular games."

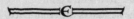

In a place as sprawling, tall, and deep as the royal palace of Suzail, there are forgotten places.

There are also "almost forgotten" spots. One of them was a neglected corner deep in the palace cellars where ancient and mighty interwoven ward spells foil detection magics and hide magical auras, very much as a thick fog conceals small scuttling things.

Targrael thought she just might be the last rememberer of that spot, judging by the condition of a particular ill-mended wall that had been getting worse for centuries. It had two dark recesses, cavities where stones had collapsed out to leave behind holes like missing teeth in an old warrior's jawbone.

One of them was large enough to hold a death knight, one who had managed to unbar the door, escape Druth's room, and make her slow and painful way to the doors of the royal crypt after several long and agonizing hours of crawling. Only her incredible force of will kept her going,

There, as she'd expected, the Fang of Baerovus glowed, as it protruded from the heart of a warding-rune that had kept it from entering the crypt.

She had it with her now.

Oh, this was going to hurt.

Stepping into the little cavern behind the wall, she bent over, choosing where she would fall, making certain she had space enough to lie. The slow, cold drops of water seeping through the stone above her chilled her back as she brushed against them. Yes, this place would do. It would have to.

She undid her leathers above her belt, laying bare her midriff, chose the spot with one careful finger—and slowly thrust the Fang of Baerovus into herself, driving the blade up under her ribs.

Every inch tore a fresh gasp of pain out of her, and she shuddered helplessly.

"I," she hissed at the unhearing stone around, "am a High-knight of Cormyr. *The* Highknight of Cormyr!"

Then the agony overwhelmed her, and she sank down with a moan, trembling . . .

This was her doom, or her last slender hope.

Would her undeath slowly drink the magic of the dagger, healing and strengthening her, despite the agony she now felt?

She dared not move around the palace—where Alusair might find and finish her, or foolish war wizards destroy her. Not as weak as she'd become, even before tasting the Fang.

She would be a long time healing, if this worked at all . . . a very long time.

But then—she smiled coldly—that was the one thing she did have left. Time.

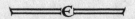

"What was *that?*" a Dragon snapped, his sword hissing out.

"A stone tumbling out of a water-soaked wall," Glathra replied briskly, not slowing in the slightest. "It's why we no longer use this part of the cellars much. Too many springs seeping out of the stones. Walls were built to seal off the worst parts, but that was centuries back, and they fall, stone by tumbling stone, with no one here to care or rebuild. Don't worry, there's quite enough solid rock left to hold the palace in place up above our heads. All four cellar levels and six floors of it, just here."

"I thought I heard someone moan," the soldier muttered, looking behind them. Glathra sighed.

"Lord Warder," she commanded, "you have the right wand handy; are there undead behind us?"

Vainrence smiled, used the wand, and reported, "No."

Glathra turned to the Dragon, the Highknight with her, and the other three Dragons carefully avoiding her eyes. "Happier?" she asked the soldier briskly.

"Yes, lady," he replied, managing to convey not even a hint of a sigh. Or a curse.

"Good." She swept on. "We have much larger worries."

"Loyal blades," Vainrence spoke up, "I presume you've heard the names Garendor, Argrant, Orkrash, Wyshbryn, and Loagranboydar?"

"The sages who've spent years digging through ancient court records, down here somewhere?" the Highknight asked.

Glathra gave him a sharp look, but he added stoutly, "The entire palace knows as much. What we *don't* know, any of us, is what they're looking for. Tidying up and organizing doesn't take years."

"Well," Glathra said tartly, "it *can*, but yes, those five have spent most of their waking hours in certain deep palace cellars doing rather more than putting records in order. They've been tracing royal and noble lineages."

The Highknight snorted, which earned him another sharp look.

"Yes, clever Sir Hawkmantle, they're, as you so subtly hint, *not* merely reading records any commoner can consult in the right royal court offices, any day they choose to. We're hoping these sages can, by referencing recorded incidents from the past, identify nobles who have, or are likely to have, any inherited personal talent for the Art."

"You're hunting the noble who commands a blueflame ghost," one of the Dragons said quietly.

Glathra stopped dead, so swiftly that they almost ran into her, and gave the man a flat, expressionless look. "I see there's nothing at all wrong with your wits, Sir Jephford."

"For years," the lord warder told the ceiling, "our wizards of war have scorned using such methods to learn more about our nobles' mastery of magic, trusting instead to scrying and to subversion of—even placing our own mages among—the House wizards hired by all nobles who can afford to do so. Yet this long-practiced vigilance has thus far failed to identify who controls the ghost who slew nobles at the Council, so . . ."

"You're willing to try other methods," Sir Hawkmantle finished the sentence. He did not add "at last," but his tone of voice made doing so unnecessary.

If the Lady Glathra's glare could have melted manhoods, he would have suffered such a fate on the spot.

The lord warder flung out an arm to bar Glathra's way. "I will go first."

"Lord Vainrence," Glathra began, "there's no need—"

"Oh, but there is," he said firmly. "The little tellsong I cast across the passage here is gone. Meaning powerful magic has been cast, very close by."

"A tellsong? You never—"

"No, I did not. A secret is something one person knows. Once two know it, that 'secret' is better termed 'realm-wide gossip.' Wait here."

Glathra stayed where she was, a little shocked. Vainrence had never been so curt with her before.

A moment later he returned and pointed to two of the Dragons. "With me. You two, guard the Lady Glathra. Swords out."

Everyone exchanged grim looks.

A few breaths later, Glathra was summoned to join the lord warder and learned why.

The passage they'd been following ended in a large room, which in turn opened into a huge storage cellar. The cellar held the records and the room where the sages worked, in a crowded den of chairs, floating glowstones for lamps, and tables.

No longer. Not only were there no men to be seen nor any hovering glowstones, the furniture and every last record had been reduced to ashes.

Including five neat little piles, standing in a line along a great rectangle of ash that marked where a table had been.

The conflagration had raged long enough ago that all smoke and smell had fled, and everything was cold. Yet a lingering, sickly yellow-green glow played and flickered feebly here and there among the ashes, from the magic that had done this.

"Treason," Glathra whispered. "Right here, beneath our feet. Beneath the *king*."

"Stand back," Vainrence ordered, spreading his arms. "I must try to learn what befell here."

Glathra turned and made shooing motions, frowning at the Highknight, who seemed reluctant to move.

He and one of the Dragons obeyed as the lord warder began a long and careful incantation.

Glathra turned back to face him, to intently watch the spell's results. It was hard for any one person to notice all the details when such a revelation took shape, because so much was revealed so quickly ere it all faded. A second casting would be only a poor echo of the first, a third a ghost of the second, and so on.

Vainrence cast the spell unhurriedly, careful and precise, finishing with a careful flourish.

And the world exploded.

Sir Eldur Hawkmantle was quick. As the blast erupted in front of him, he sprang back, trying to twist around in the air—which promptly gave him a hard shove in his ribs and in a whirling instant slammed him hard into a passage wall that had been far behind him.

He lost consciousness for a moment amid the rolling, booming echoes and swirling dust, but when he was aware again and could move, he discovered he and one wincing and groaning Purple Dragon were the only folk coming to their feet.

Vainrence had unwittingly triggered a waiting trap. A blast of some sort that had—he stared at ashen corpses, crumbling as he watched—fried the other three Dragons, because they happened to be closest.

He dimly remembered seeing Glathra and Vainrence scream, brief tongues of flame spurting from their eyes and mouths ere they'd toppled. Wincing at that memory, he went to them.

They were sprawled atop the older ashes, looking lifeless.

Not scorched, outwardly, and nothing about them seemed broken or missing. Unconscious, and quite possibly brain-burned.

"Search," he ordered the dazed surviving Dragon, and set an example by stirring the ashes very gently with his sword.

They found nothing, but the glowstones Glathra and Vainrence were wearing began to flicker and fade, so they grimly hoisted the two stricken mages onto their shoulders and began the long, grim trudge back up to where they could find help.

Someone wanted family secrets kept. Someone who had magic to spare.

Storm came in first, with Elminster right behind her.

Mirt was standing with daggers up beside both ears, held ready to throw.

She crooked an eyebrow at him. "You hate being Heljack Thornadarr *that* much?"

Mirt grinned, resheathed his fangs, and turned to the table behind him, waving them toward a platter piled high with cold roast fowl and a large, lazily steaming bowl of fragrant fieldgreens soup. "Want some?"

"Do Waterdhavians love coins?"

Mirt ladled soup into tankards for them. "So, who'd ye kill tonight? Shall I expect a host of Purple Dragons to soon break down the door, even as the massed wizards of war blast the roof off?"

"No one, and I hope not," Storm replied wearily, sipping soup and discovering she was ravenous. She waved at the food. "Where'd you get all this?"

"Arclath sent a servant with it. Suitably disguised, so no fear. Said he'll send a man around on the morrow to teach me to cook."

El and Storm regarded him with identical frowns of concern, then headed for their bedchamber, snatching up food and taking it with them.

Mirt roared with laughter at their reaction and headed for his own bed, decanter in hand.

After all, only six decanters already lay beside the bed, and his throat was as dry as all Anauroch.

"You should have come to me earlier, you two." The Lady Marantine Delcastle spoke softly, even sadly. "I had *no* idea."

"I'm sorry, Mother," Arclath said gravely. "This is my fault, entirely. Rune didn't even know my name a month back."

He spread his hands. "I suppose every young noble thinks his—or her—concerns about what's ahead for Cormyr, and its noble Houses in particular, are something older nobles don't want to hear, or will challenge or dismiss out of hand. After all, you are inevitably part of whatever we want to see changed, or that we fear won't change, or . . ."

Lady Delcastle nodded, the ghost of a smile rising to her lips. "I recall feeling very much as you do now, when I disagreed with my father. He hurled me into the duck pond. Which is why we no longer *have* a duck pond."

Amarune and Arclath had been sitting with her in the best parlor in Delcastle Manor for hours, explaining what had been going on with the blueflame ghosts—but not their work with El and Storm, or their deepening friendship with Mirt. Lady Delcastle, in a rare friendly, talkative mood, had proven to be a free-flowing geyser of information about noble feuds and alliances and personal friendships and hatreds, from the time of Arclath's grandsire up until last night, or so it seemed.

She was frowning, now, trying to recall something. Suddenly she flung up an imperious hand for silence and brightened. "I remember!"

Arclath thrust his head forward eagerly, squeezing Amarune's hand in an unnecessary signal for silence. His mother noticed and grinned.

"And does that work on her, dear?"

Her son flushed to the roots of his hair, and the Lady Marantine patted his other hand affectionately and said, "Never you mind. Yet listen. The Imprisoners, they were called."

"They?"

"No, I'll not be rushed, dear. Let me tell this my way. I had it in hints and careless sentences here and there, mind you, from your uncles and Baelarra and Thornleia, anyhail, so it's not much."

She paused, tapping her chin, then said slowly, "The Imprisoners were a handful of wizards, here and along the Sword Coast—in Silverymoon in particular, I understand, and no, I know no names—who crafted the spells for blueflame items and started imprisoning particular persons within them, long ago. Before the Blue Fire came and magic went wild."

She spread her hands. "I heard more about all the astonishment—consternation would not be too strong a word—among our local clergy of Mystra."

Arclath nodded. "Because of Aunt Thornleia."

Lady Marantine nodded. "They were surprised, you see, that the goddess did nothing to stop the Imprisoners, either by altar speech or through her Chosen. As if it was meant to be, or necessary for time yet to come, they said."

She leaned forward just as her son had done, to stare hard at Amarune and Arclath. "So, has the time now come?"

The royal magician looked up when she strode into the room, and smiled in genuine pleasure. "Ah, *something* splendid to embrace at last! You're well!"

Glathra blushed. "Thanks to too many healing prayers from more priests than I care to count. I was fortunate—I was merely caught in the backlash of what felled Vainrence."

"The lord warder?" Ganrahast asked quietly.

"Remains in care. Senseless, his mind still roiling inwardly, despite all the spells they've used."

Ganrahast sighed. "And the five sages and all those old records are gone." He waved at the scrying image he'd been intent upon when Glathra had arrived; in its glow, she could see a distant corner of the palace cellars.

"We're scouring out the cellars now. Larandur has found a spell-locked room—supposedly an armory, sealed since Salember's time—that has somehow acquired very recent spells on its door seals."

"So, it's been opened and resealed recently," Glathra murmured, gazing into the scrying image with him. There she saw Wizard of War Naloth Larandur, as tall and expressionless as ever, calmly finishing the casting of a "long-arm" spell to open the sealed armory door from a distance.

The seals obliged and melted away, and the door swung open.

Floating just inside the chamber was a spherical creature with one large eye, a wide and crooked many-fanged maw, and ten eyestalks that glared at the six court mages outside the room as the beholder unleashed its eye-magics.

Rays flashed out, a mage staggered, and then another fell. And Larandur and the other wizards of war hurled magic at the monster, in a great roar of unleashed Art.

The result, in the instant before the scrying sphere burst, was a titanic explosion.

Ganrahast was seated, but Glathra was flung off her feet as the entire palace shook around them, the walls swaying. They could hear minor crashes from all around as various portraits, shelves, and the like fell or toppled.

A great wave of force rolled away out into Suzail, and in its wake they heard the stones groan, in a deep and terrible sound that told them, even before shouting, running mages came with the news.

Part of the palace had slumped down into ruin topped by unstable, yawing passages and chambers, as the cellars underlying them collapsed.

Killing Larandur and the others with him.

The beholder had been another trap.

CHAPTER
THIRTY-THREE

WHEN THE BLUE FLAME DANCES

Come gather round now and take all your chances
Many will rise, from dark debts win free; some'll
Whirl fine prances, some stumble like me; bathe in
Bright unfolding glee as the Blue Flame Dances!

Maerel "Merry Minstrelress" Shael
from the ballad *When The Blue Flame Dances*
first performed circa the Year of the Purloined Statue

Buildings shuddered near the palace. Folk were flung off their feet on the Promenade. A wagon sideswiped an inn amid screaming horses and splintering wood; slates and tiles whirled down from roofs in a deadly rain; stones and windows and whole balconies fell from up high to crash to the cobbles in a ragged, ongoing thunder ... and one wing of the palace sagged with a deep and terrible groan, settling lower into the earth amid blinding plumes of rising dust.

Manshoon sat back in his chair and allowed himself a gloating smile. He couldn't look away from the scrying eye that was showing him the aftermath of the explosion.

"They'll think twice before hurling spells at the *next* beholder they see," he purred. "A hesitation that will doom them as surely as if they blasted it with all they have. Ah, this is good sport."

Chuckling, the Uncrowned Incipient Emperor of Cormyr and Beyond sprang up and strode to another scrying eye to peer at certain nobles who were arguing in a gathering that they believed was private.

"No hint of the blueflame ghost reappearing yet," Manshoon murmured to himself, "but then its minder knows full well that the wizards of war—not to mention far more formidable mages—are hunting him."

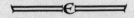

"Storm, it's *us*," Amarune hissed, snatching off the raffish old sailor's hat. "See?"

"Ah, but which 'us'? Surely that fashion disaster in old petticoats with you isn't the lord and heir of a high noble House?"

Arclath chuckled. "Surely it is! Now open that door, or I'll start taking my clothes off to prove it."

"Don't tempt me, Arclath Delcastle," Storm warned him. "You may mean that as a threat, but it sounds more like an enticement to me!" Yet, she threw back the great bolts that held the old warehouse loft door closed, and ushered the two arrivals in. "Welcome to the humble abode of Heljack Thornadarr, Sembian trader."

"Good to be here!" Arclath said cheerfully. "Like the disguises?"

Mirt looked up from a bowl Elminster was peering into, eyed them, and said gruffly, "Well, as a way of telling everyone ye pass in this city that ye're idiot highnoses trying to play at being lowly dockworkers, they're splendid, aye!"

"Hush, old goat," Rune told him fondly, "we didn't have time to find better in the Delcastle gardeners' barn. We have urgent news."

Mirt's jaw dropped.

Then he looked at Arclath and acquired an expression of disapproval. "Ye *didn't*! Already? Barely had her home a night or three, an' ye're thrusting—if that's not too indelicate a word—the next generation of Delcastles out into the world! Ye *might* have *married* the lass, first!"

Rune and Arclath stared back at him, blinking.

"No, no, no, *no*, it's *not* that news!" Arclath burst out hurriedly. "I mean, that news hasn't happened yet! I mean—"

"Oh, this lord is *very* suave," Elminster told Storm, hooking a thumb in Arclath's direction. "Debonair, too. Keep a watch over this one. He's *smooth*."

"If all you jesters will *leave off* for a moment," Rune bellowed, winning their instant silence and attention—which she rewarded with a bright, sheepish grin—"Arclath and I have something important to pass on to you about blueflame ghosts. That we just learned from his moth—from the Lady Marantine Delcastle." She peered at the bowl Mirt had his hands in, and her voice changed. "*What* are you doing?"

"Learning to cook," Mirt replied with dignity, lifting a wet and glistening handful up for display. "Behold—entrails of goat, gutted lampreys, and shucked oysters. All raw but doused in herbal oils an' seven-some spices. As they do it in coastal Rashemen, I'm told."

He waved in the direction of Elminster, who nodded and told Amarune a little absently, "I'm using a spell right now. And watching him learn to cook."

"Arclath," Storm suggested, swinging the massive squared timber that served as a door-bar back into place in its cradles amid a snarling rattle of rusty swivel-chain, "why don't you tell us the news, before these two old rage drakes badger your poor lass into attacking them?"

"Right," Arclath replied firmly, drawing himself up and frowning at Elminster and Mirt. His pose might have been more impressive without the pink, purple, and vomit-green petticoats. "What do you know about the Imprisoners?"

The room went quiet again, and this time the silence seemed to hold a slight tension.

"Lad," Elminster replied quietly, "I know a lot of things. I even remember some of them. Moreover, regarding a rare few, I recall what I dare not tell others, and what will happen if I do. Ye may be young and have years to spend listening, but *I'm* not. So, please don't take it amiss if I ask ye to instead tell me what *ye've* heard about the Imprisoners. Hmm?"

Arclath looked at Amarune. Who repeated, word for word and in a superb imitation of the Lady Marantine's voice that made Arclath's jaw drop and Mirt grin openly, what Arclath's mother had said.

Elminster nodded. "She spoke truth. Every word. I was there."

"*What?*" Arclath snapped. "So why didn't you—"

The Sage of Shadowdale shrugged. "Mystra told me—"

"And me," Storm put in.

"—to leave the Imprisoners be. They were necessary, she said, though she never told us why. They did a lot of 'imprisoning,' though I don't think what we're calling 'blueflame ghosts' were anywhere near all the results of that. I can't tell ye much more, I'm afraid; Our Lady had me working on other matters."

Arclath regained his temper with a visible effort. "So which of her Chosen, if it's not blasphemous to ask, were working on the Imprisoners?"

"Alassra," El sighed.

"The Simbul, legend calls her, or the Witch-Queen of Aglarond," Storm added gently. "One of my sisters. Who is . . ."

"Dead?" Rune ventured.

"Insane. Brain-burned," El said bleakly. "I've thought of how to restore her mind—a dangerous way, by no means certain—but it requires a blueflame item."

"That will be consumed, with its prisoner and all, in that restoration," Storm added.

"Mind ye choose the right prisoner to destroy," Mirt growled, wagging a cook's cleaver in her direction. "That's why I made sure my hand axe vanished, before those two idiot lordlings could find some wizard who knew a way to force me back into it."

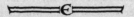

"Here I sit, mad and alone," the high, tuneless voice sang, sounding like a wistful little girl. Then its owner sighed and slumped, to circle her feet in the cold water.

Again. For about the seventy-six-millionth time.

Dabbling in the pool at the heart of the cave that was her prison.

The pool she was chained in, by the chain that was her only constant companion. Her friend.

"My *friend*," she laughed, high and long and wildly, but stopped when the sound of the echoes started to sound like jeering.

Jeering meant Red Wizards, and she slew Red Wizards when she met them.

As she stirred the waters, the massive chain rising and falling with every movement of her shackled ankle, she remembered magic, dreamed of magic . . . and as she did, spell-glows blossomed out of the darkness around her, and rose and fell like questing tongues of flame, lighting up the wet and glistening fissured rock walls of the cave around the pool.

"I am," she announced to no one suddenly and cheerfully, "Alassra Silverhand, once Queen of Aglarond, better known to bards, sages, and just plain folk whispering fright-tales around fires late at night as the mad Witch-Queen who slew armies of Red Wizards. I prefer to call myself The Simbul. It's shorter. Pleased to meet you. And if you happen to be a disguised Red Wizard, prepare to die."

She stood up and struck a pose. Then she tossed her silver hair—as wild and unruly a mane as ever; right now, it looked more like a shrub than a head of human hair—and conjured up a mirror.

A reflective oval of silver as tall as she was, floating upright in midair.

Peering into it, she regarded herself critically. She was naked and besmirched with dirt, yet still shapely. Bony around midriff and hips—the sides of her pelvis stuck up in two sharp humps—but lush and womanly everywhere else, and with those long, long arms and legs that drove men wild.

Hmmph. Had driven men wild. None came to see her now, through all the wards. Once, long ago, one or two had won through, mages with swordsmen, hoping to find great magic.

"Well, so they did," she said aloud, petulantly. "They found me!"

Yet then, of course, they'd made demands, cast spells on her pool, threatened and laid hands on her, assaulted her.

That had been fun. And when she'd grown tired of hurling them around the cave with spells, battered and broken, she'd eaten them.

Foolish, that. They were gone now, and she had no one to talk to. No one but herself, and she was too mad to comfort herself or convince herself of anything.

Elminster.

That was who she needed.

El, her El, back again. Here. Now, with his arms around her.

"Elminster?" she called into the darkness, listening to his name echo into great distances and then come back again.

"El, are you *ever* coming back for me?"

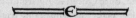

Arclath and Amarune looked at each other and discovered just how pale and wide-eyed they both were. How frightened.

They put their arms around each other, because it was more comfortable that way.

They had heard tales of Elminster since their childhood, and of Fallen Mystra who, before the Coming of the Blue Fire, had been Queen of All Magic, the goddess who somehow was the Weave, though bards disagreed about that. They had heard about the Seven Sisters and the Chosen of Mystra who walked the world doing magic and undoing magic, riding dragons and sundering mountains and . . . and . . .

They knew what they were hearing now was true, yet . . .

Oh, the woman across the room *had* to be older than her young body made her appear. Her eyes and manner marked her as almost thirty summers, perhaps, rather than her shapely twenty, and wiser than many rangers, to boot.

The younger-looking man yonder had worn a far older, bearded body when they'd first encountered him. One touch of his old, dark, and vast mind—that they'd both hosted and seen even more of—would tell anyone that he was far older than he appeared to be.

Yet, it was still rather staggering to hear Storm and Elminster calmly confirming they were, or had been, Chosen of Mystra. A little daunting, too, to hear that they seemed to think they still were.

Fallen from power yet serving a goddess the realms thought was gone, but whom they still talked to and worked for.

It was also more than a little sobering to hear fat, wheezing old Mirt telling the tale of how he was enspelled and forced into a blueflame item in Waterdeep almost a century ago. Against his will but by a foe desperate to avoid being slain by Mirt, one in so much of a hurry to avoid that fate that he laid no spells of compulsion on Mirt—so the Waterdhavian had emerged from a handaxe a few days back, here in Suzail, controlled by no one.

"So who *are* these Imprisoners?" Amarune asked at last, sinking down on the stool beside Mirt to sample the fat man's seafood, er, concoction, and finding it surprisingly good. "Are they still alive?"

El shrugged. "With wizards, one can never tell."

"Heh," Mirt agreed. "Too true."

He turned and hurled the carving knife he was holding the length of the kitchen, to neatly split a melon on the end counter, and added, "Which is why I prefer to rely on more primitive means of coercion and decision making, unwashed lout that I am."

Amarune and Arclath couldn't keep themselves from grinning.

Until Elminster's head snapped up, his eyes flaring with a brief white light. He shook himself like a drenched dog ridding itself of water and announced, "My spell worked. Lord Huntingdown's under attack. Someone's out by day, now, hunting noble lords who can command blueflame ghosts."

"So what do we do?" Rune asked, scrambling to her feet.

"Watch," Elminster replied. "No more. Unless the ghost master everyone's seeking is found. Then we'll watch the great battle that will ensue, awaiting our best chance to rush in. I'll conjure up a scrying eye."

"While noble after noble of Cormyr gets butchered?" Arclath snapped. "In case you haven't noticed, Old Mage, I'm a noble of Cormyr. And even with all our faults, Cormyr needs us. I am *not* going to let the realm discover that the hard way, when most of us are dead and our lands have gone lawless, given over to brigands and warring greedy merchants eyeing lordships."

"So, ye want to run to Huntingdown Hall right now and carve up random folk?" El asked mildly. "And this well help whom, exactly? And how?"

"Pah!" Arclath snarled. "Always the clever words, always the—"

"Being exactly right," Amarune interrupted crisply. "*Listen* to the man, love!"

Arclath stopped midsnarl to stare at her, a bright grin growing across his face.

"What?" she demanded, frowning.

"You called me 'love,'" he murmured.

Mirt rolled his eyes, as El and Storm grinned.

"So, while these two younglings bill and coo for a bit," the Waterdhavian rumbled, "tell me if I have all this straight: The Simbul can tell ye much more about these Imprisoners if she's sane. But to get her that way, ye need to work magic on her, wherever she's hidden, that will drink some gewgaw or other that's the prison of a blueflame ghost. Presumably this gewgaw ye're searching for, that someone in Suzail is hiding."

"Ye have it straight," El confirmed. "More than that, if I'm to recruit the war wizards to serve Mystra—as she has bidden me to do—I *need* The Simbul at my side. No one mage can slay and defeat them."

Mirt spread his hands. "Then what're we waiting for?"

"Some way of finding the hidden blueflame item," Storm explained. "If the various hunts for it go on, the nobles may do that finding for us. Killing many of their fellows in their search. Hence Lord Delcastle's objection."

"That I have *not* withdrawn," Arclath put in, from where he and Amarune stood in each other's arms.

"So, instead of waiting until another dozen nobles are dead—and the wizards of war, Manshoon, and anyone else lurking near who's interested have had another dozen chances to swoop in and seize the blueflame item, we try to lure the ghost master into using his ghost again on ground of our choosing, so as to lay hands on the item," El announced. "The Blue Flame must dance."

"Because using mask dancers as lures works so well," Storm sighed.

"This will be different," El said sharply. "None of us will be on that stage."

"An illusion, sent from afar? They'll see through it in an instant," Storm told him.

"Not an illusion," the Sage of Shadowdale replied and pointed at Amarune. "*She* will be the Blue Flame."

"*What?*" Arclath roared, breaking free of his beloved's embrace to confront Elminster.

"Easy, young lion," the wizard replied, "easy! She'll be dancing on the floor of an empty room somewhere, for me— and before ye get all huffily defensive of her virtue, lordling, know that I intend to have ye standing there as her body-guard, never fear! My magic will make her image, mirroring her movements and wreathed in blue flames, of course, seem to dance on the stage of whatever club we'd most like to see destroyed."

"Destroyed?"

"Aye. When the war wizards, Manshoon, the nobles' various pet wizards, and our ghost master all converge on it to snap at our lure, that club won't last long."

Arclath nodded, then grew a wry smile. "I know a suitable place. Let's do it."

Word spread across Suzail like the howling winds of a shorestorm gale. She who was known as the Blue Flame was going to dance—a performance not to be missed.

No one knew quite where word of this had first come from, but everyone agreed on the where and the when.

It was to happen on the eve of the Festival of Handras, Suzail's annual late-Mirtul reception for the senior caravan traders of the Sword Coast, when it was customary for such far traders and wagonmasters to present "fresh wonders from the Sword Coast" in dockside warehouses, where free food and drink were served to all who came to gaze on the latest goods, curios, and exotic fashions.

And the dance would take place at The Bold Blazon, an exclusive club catering to certain jaded young nobles and socially ambitious folk those nobles liked to drink, trade, and sleep with.

As it happened, the Blazon was not one of Lord Arclath Delcastle's haunts, because the nobles who liked to frequent it included several of his longtime foes and rivals, such as Maerclorn Wintersun—the younger heir Lord Wintersun, not the patriarch—and Kathkote Dawntard.

In vain the proprietor of the Blazon, a greedy, shave-pated, many-earring-adorned snob by the name of Daerendygho Vrabrant, protested that he'd arranged no such performance for Handras Eve or any other night, had never even met the Blue Flame, and did not desire to host such "epicene diversions" at the Blazon.

Besieged with demands from half Suzail to rent stage-side tables, atop the clamorings of all his usual patrons, he hurriedly hired extra security—only to discover that dozens of nobles were outbidding him to buy the "first loyalty" of his security force to obey *them* first, rather than him. In other words, to let those nobles into the Blazon at will, and allow them to bring along extra friends and their own wine, weapons, and anything else they might desire.

Despairing and seeing both ruin and the palace dungeons in his nightmares, Vrabrant went to the wizards of war in secret and entreated their help in providing "unseen security."

Not that Elminster or any of his companions knew about that entreaty until later—though Arclath slowly came to suspect the Sage of Shadowdale had anticipated it.

"Count me out," Vainrence said with a grin, slurring the words.

The eyes of Ganrahast and Glathra met above the lord warder, and it was Glathra who said gently, "We didn't expect you to leap up out of this bed and do anything about it, Rence. We just wanted you to know the particular disaster *we* were wading into, this time."

"After all, once you asked about it," the royal magician added, "we had to admit that, yes, all Suzail *is* talking about it, for you to hear about it in here."

"So who is this Blue Flame?"

"No one knows," Ganrahast replied.

"*But*," Glathra added with wicked glee, "*I* suspect Elminster is behind it, that it's an attempt to flush out the mysterious noble who commands that blueflame ghost—and it's highly likely the Blazon will suffer greatly in the trouble that's bound to erupt."

"Including the trouble we will undoubtedly cause, after your scrying turns up something we absolutely *must* rush in to deal with?" Ganrahast asked dryly.

She widened her eyes into an innocence that fooled no one at all.

"Undoubtedly," she said solemnly.

Chapter
THIRTY-FOUR
Rather Noisy Battles

Why must it always end, these disputes over who has what
Or warms which throne, or gets to bathe or march first
In blood and death and the sowing of fear? Why must there
Always be rather noisy battles?

> Janthress Harroweather, Merchant from her chapbook
> *A Merchant And A Lady: My Thoughts*
> first published in the Year of the Morningstar

The Blazon was packed that warm and breezy Handras
Eve. Half of fashionable Suzail had shown up, crowding the doors to get in. They stood tightly packed along the
walls and between the tables. More, who'd tried in vain to get
inside, were milling around in the streets and down alleyways,
all around.

Inside, all eyes were locked on the stage—that is, on the
small cleared space where a lone dancer was leaping and whirling, her bare body glistening with sweat and ceaseless blue
flames wreathing her body.

There had been no such space a few breaths ago. A despairing Daerendygho Vrabrant had gone to the trouble of having
the Blazon's tiny stage torn down, a new floor installed where
it had been, and new chairs and tables brought in to fill the
space. However, to his open-mouthed horror, several patrons
had suddenly put down their tankards in unison, murmured
magic—and made certain chairs, tables, and the startled diners
seated on or at them vanish. The revealed wizards had similarly
disappeared an instant later, leaving only their tankards behind.

This had not amused Wizard of War Glathra Barcantle,
who was standing on a nearby rooftop trying to oversee a team

of Crown mages, a lot of Purple Dragons, and a covert force of Highknights. She was already uneasy at the dozen-some bands of bullyblades and hedge wizards loitering in the alleyways below, obviously sent by various ambitious nobles. This evening was racing toward *real* trouble.

The sudden appearance of some startled diners, with tankards, platters of fried bustard, the tables those were standing on, chairs, and all their belongings in the middle of one filthy, refuse-choked alleyway did not strike Glathra as particularly helpful, though it made some of the wizards on the roof with her chuckle.

"Just watch for blue flames," Glathra snapped at them, returning her attention to the conjured scrying eye floating in the air before her.

In it, she could see the Blue Flame, whom she'd been entirely unsurprised to learn looked very like a certain Amarune Whitewave.

"Elminster," she snarled, as she kept one eye on the sensuous dance for any sign of something suspicious, and with the other tried to survey what she could see of the crowded audience. "You're behind this, you are . . ."

She could tell Amarune was dancing elsewhere, and magic—Elminster's, for all the gold in the palace vaults—was making the dancer's image appear in the Blazon, and providing the cold, burning-nothing blue flames wreathing it, too.

There! A man among the many along one of the club walls toppled forward, face-first into the lap of a startled drinker at the nearest table, and a blue, flaming glow could be seen behind him. Men started abruptly scrambling to flee from that spot, clawing and shoving, as a figure surrounded in flowing blue flames stepped through the wall, sword first, stabbing ruthlessly at anyone in the way.

Shouts went up in the alleys—other scrying eyes besides Glathra's were in use—and the bullyblades started to surge forward.

Dragons looked to Glathra. "Lady?"

"Stay where you are!" she ordered. "We couldn't get through all the flesh down there, anyhail! Wait and watch, to see *where* we should rush, before we do it!"

Chaos had erupted inside the Blazon. The lone blueflame ghost was stalking through the crowd, apparently seeking specific nobles to slay. Everyone was shouting or screaming, swords and daggers were out everywhere, and men were fighting viciously just to get out of the club, hacking and trampling those in their way.

As the bloodshed grew, tables overturned, and chairs were hurled, the dancer danced on.

A stretch of the Blazon's outer wall abruptly vanished, as some hired mage or other cast a spell no one should use in crowded city streets—and the elder Lord Wintersun, surrounded by a tight knot of bullyblades, charged inside.

He was making for his white-faced and weeping son, who was about seven men distant from the pursuing ghost and vainly trying to get farther away—as behind him, one by one, those seven fled or were hewn down.

Another spell burst right behind the ghost, shooting flames in all directions and flinging the blueflame slayer into the air and halfway across the club. Howls and shrieks arose as the fire spread, and in a trice men who were aflame were staggering helplessly about, tripping over the wounded and senseless.

"Firequench!" Glathra shouted at the four war wizards who'd prepared for that duty. "*Now!*"

Someone else's spell brought another section of the Blazon's outer wall down, and patrons fled wildly, streaming out into the streets in all directions.

"Keep watching the ghost!" Glathra snarled at the senior war wizards standing with her. "Whatever happens, *don't* let it slip away!"

"Uh, Lady Glathra?" one asked, daring to pluck at her sleeve.

"*What?*" she almost spat in his face, fury rising fast. He pointed over the rooftops.

Where a beholder had just risen into view and was floating serenely nearer.

"Lady!" an older, deeper-voiced Crown mage called, before she even had time to gape. "Over here!"

"We *must* get down there!" the ranking Highknight snapped, waving to his men. "Down the stairs! *Move!*"

"*I* give the orders here!" Glathra almost shrieked, but his reply, delivered at the full run without even bothering to look in her direction, was a silent but emphatic gesture of the sort never seen in polite company.

With a wordless snarl of rage, Glathra rushed across the roof to the deep-voiced mage, to see why he'd hailed her.

In the alley below, marching in a line abreast with their swords out and ruthlessly slaying the few bullyblades who hadn't sense enough to flee from them, were *five* blueflame ghosts.

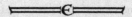

"The Blazon's burning," Mirt rumbled as they hastened together along a sidestreet.

"And not a moment too soon, from all Arclath's told us of the place," Storm replied as they came to a corner where their way joined a larger street. "Now, if I've guessed right, our lone blueflame ghost should be fleeing now and coming right along . . . *here.*"

"Fleeing? I didn't think they ever fled!"

"They do when their commander wants them to, or when they face five of their own kind. See?"

In the distance, down the street, a wall of bright blue flame was moving closer as five ghosts walked abreast, striding swiftly along the street.

"Oh, *naed,*" Storm muttered. "Things can never just be stlarning *simple,* can they?"

She was eyeing the unmistakable shape of a beholder, descending silently in a smooth and unhurried arc, to float just above and behind the line of ghosts.

And in front of Storm and Mirt, about a dozen paces away, a noble was standing facing the ghost who'd been in the

Blazon. The lord was holding something that was glowing blue, something flat and about the size of his hand. The ghost, still walking hurriedly toward him, was fading away.

Its flames pulsed in time with flares of light from whatever the lord was holding.

"Lord *Calantar?*" Storm whispered.

"Ye know him?"

"By sight. I'd never have guessed *he'd* be the . . ."

"'Tis always the quiet ones," Mirt growled, stalking forward and hefting his dagger.

The ghost vanished. A moment later, the cobbles all around Lord Calantar suddenly sprouted war wizards.

"Traitor!" Lady Glathra shouted into the lord's face, trying to grab his hand and the glowing item in it.

"Hey!" Mirt shouted. "Mind out!"

He pointed, and some of the Crown mages turned to look.

They saw the beholder swooping down on them, its many-fanged maw gaping and its eyestalks writhing like angry snakes.

The war wizards let fly with their swiftest, strongest battle spells, chanting and gesturing frantically—as Mirt swept out one arm, caught Storm around her sword arm, and dragged her hastily back.

She was trying to fight free of his dogged, wheezing grasp when the spells started to strike the beholder—and it exploded with terrific force, shattering windows, balconies, and cobbles, dashing their ears into ringing numbness, and hurling scores of folk in all directions, like so many dolls.

Another trap.

Glathra was smashed flat by two of her own war wizards as they were flung into her from behind—and Lord Calantar was sent tumbling down the street to fetch up against a cart, dazed and mumbling.

Storm stumbled after him, the blast having snatched her out of Mirt's grasp, and pounced on the noble. Who stabbed up at her with a dagger as he tried to call out his ghost again. The item in his hand—a belt buckle—started to pulse a bright blue once more.

Storm fended off one thrust, took another in her forearm with a hiss of pain, then lost patience and brought her sword down, chopping Calantar's buckle-holding hand down onto the cobbles. He spat a curse at her and stabbed again, so she swung her sword up and chopped down harder, cutting his hand off.

It was still clutching the belt buckle.

Storm snatched the spurting, severed thing up, buckle and all, and tried to ignore the pulsing blue glow.

She could see the five blueflame ghosts all staring at her and running now, coming for her as fast as they could.

Glathra was on her feet again and running at Storm, too—and was much closer. She was trying to gasp out a spell as she came, but as she trampled on an apparently unconscious Mirt, the Waterdhavian tripped her deftly with one hairy hand. He rose with a grin as Glathra bounced on her face, to shout at Storm, "Go, lass! Get ye gone! I'll try to—"

The five ghosts were almost upon him.

Storm winced, not wanting to see what was going to happen to Mirt—and then, in a sudden flash and a moment of silent, gentle drifting, it was all gone.

The street, ghosts, Glathra, and all.

Elminster's magic had snatched her away.

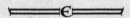

Abruptly, Storm was standing on a hard, smooth, and familiar floor.

She was in the warehouse, holding Lord Calantar's severed hand, and the buckle clutched in those gore-dripping fingers was losing its blue glow.

Elminster was running to her, Arclath and Amarune right behind him. Rune wore her mask but nothing else; the blue flames El's magic had shrouded her in had vanished.

"I—" Storm started to say, but a frowning Arclath snatched up a rickety chair at a dead run and flung it, hard.

Storm ducked aside and the chair smashed right into—Wizard of War Glathra, who had just appeared behind her.

Glathra fell to her knees, spat out a curse, snatched a wand from her belt, and triggered it, blasting—

Elminster, who'd leaped in front of Storm. Flames crashed into him with a roar.

In a trice his familiar face and beard were gone, mere wisps of illusion dashed to nothingness in the flames that tore apart the body that had been Applecrown's.

The staring face of a much younger man was sent flying through the air as Glathra's wand blast flung all that was left of Reldyk Applecrown in a dozen directions.

Severed limbs flew, ashes swirled, and Arclath was flung into a stack of crates, to land groaning.

Storm slid past him across the warehouse floor, silver hair clawing at crates and barrels to try to slow herself.

Nude and weaponless, Amarune Whitewave flung herself on Glathra, backhanding the wizard viciously across the face and snatching the wand away. Glathra made a grab for it and got a hard elbow under her chin instead as Rune twisted away to fling the wand as far and as hard as she could, off into the dim distances of the crate-heaped warehouse.

The two women clawed and rolled for a frantic breath or two before Glathra broke free, sprinted out of Rune's reach, and turned to catch her breath and get out her other wand, the one that paralyzed.

Which was when Storm hit her, launching herself over crates in a wild dive with arms spread wide to make sure the wizard of war couldn't dodge away.

Glathra tried.

They ended up on the floor together, bouncing and struggling. Storm's tresses promptly shackled Glathra's wrists and assaulted her mouth, preventing her from uttering any magic—until the Bard of Shadowdale could get a hand on the war wizard's head.

Ruthlessly Storm slammed the war wizard's head against the floor, then clawed it up by Glathra's hair and slammed it down again. And again.

And again, until her foe went limp under her.

Then once more, just to be sure.

Glathra was far beyond feigning anything. She was out cold.

Panting, Storm rolled away, snatched up the belt buckle—it glowed blue, just for an instant—and cried, "We must get to The Simbul right now! El?"

Elminster's ashes were slithering across the floor like a snake, making for Amarune, but Arclath roared, "No! To me, El! To me!"

The ashes obediently turned toward the young lord.

Who got up, wincing, to call, "Clothes on, Rune! To the palace!"

"Well, the gods smile on us in at least one way," the royal magician muttered as he scooped powerful scepters and rods out of coffers onto the table. "*Something* must have happened to Elminster. They have to walk here, not translocate right past us or up to their chosen palace gate. That will give us time to at least *try* to get ready."

Sir Talonar Winter and Highknight Eskrel Starbridge stood in front of him, already clad in all the magical bracers, helms, breastplates, and codpieces Ganrahast had been able to hurriedly find. He continued on to daggers, swords, and little bucklers, as novice war wizard magelings trotted into the room in a steady stream, bearing weapons, shields, and armor plucked from various walls and stands all over the palace.

"This is a fight to the death," the royal magician added grimly. "Blueflame ghosts are sent to murder our nobles—and now they're coming here, which can only mean they intend regicide. Storm Silverhand, Lord Arclath Delcastle, that mask dancer, and no fewer than *five* blueflame ghosts, who are right behind them—"

He swung around to peer into his nearby scrying eye, to make sure what he was saying was still true. Depressingly, it was.

"—and will try to get into the palace. We must prevent them, at all costs. If they penetrate this far, we must spend our lives stopping them from reaching the king. I will make the final stand, because I must translocate His Majesty elsewhere if all else fails. I'll be sending him alone, because I will not flee this fight."

"*That* is not the royal magician's duty," hissed an unexpected voice, startling them all. They turned to where it had come from—a space too small for any human, behind the table now strewn with enchanted armor and weapons—and beheld a wavering wisp in the air, a faint shadowy presence.

It darkened just a little, becoming a feminine head and shoulders with arms and a sword . . . all of which they could see through.

"I am Alusair Obarskyr," it told them, "and I will fight. Ganrahast, as royal magician, you must see that the realm survives, *not* King Foril. You must *not* lay down your life fighting here!"

"That choice, your Highness," Ganrahast replied politely, "may not be mine."

"It is not," King Foril agreed, striding into the room among the stream of Crown magelings. The bearded head of Vangerdahast rode like a spider on his shoulder.

"You are all to stand aside and let the intruders in," the king of Cormyr added quietly. "They need to reach the Room of the Watchful Sentinel, to use the Dalestride. Let them."

Alusair looked at him. "But—"

"Great Princess, greatest regent Cormyr has ever had," Foril replied gently, "trust me in this, and obey. Please. I *am* king now, after all."

Alusair looked into his eyes for a long while, then nodded and lowered her spectral sword.

King Foril pointed at the novice mages and commanded, "Open the gates, and let Storm and all who follow her in. They are to be allowed to walk the halls unchallenged. Spread the word. *Be swift.*"

Several of the wizards jumped at the ringing severity of those last two words. They landed running, racing out of the room to obey him.

"I hope, Your Majesty, you're not making a terrible mistake," Ganrahast said quietly.

"That's a hope I share," Foril replied without turning. "Nevertheless, it is mine to make."

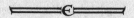

Storm, Amarune, and Arclath walked quickly, in a tight-knit group. Only Arclath kept looking back.

The five ghosts were striding faster, steadily overtaking them. A little behind those blue-flaming figures strode a lone, calm woman unshrouded by blueflame. She was tall and slender, strikingly beautiful despite her cruel face and dark, rage-filled eyes. The bloody point of a dagger protruded from her chest.

King Foril's eyes narrowed. He waved his hand in a signal, and Cymmarra, the Lady of Ghosts, almost vanished under the sudden barrage of spells hurled by wizards of war on all sides, a handful even hastening up behind her.

Wards blazed as bright as the sun—but when that brilliance faded, she was still striding on, unaffected.

As she went past the doorway where the king stood, she raised her hands, a thin and ruthless smile rising onto her face, and started to cast a spell.

Ganrahast, Starbridge, Winter, and the ghost of Alusair all stepped in front of the king to shield him, but that merely changed her smile into a sneer, as she went on spellweaving.

Yet, the air shimmered right behind her and became the archwizard Dardulkyn, his hands reaching out in the last, triumphant gesture of a swift spell.

Before Cymmarra's casting was done, Dardulkyn's spell struck. Its bolt of sizzling force smashed the Lady of Ghosts off her feet and hurled her far down the passage, snarling eerily as it fought with the wardings that armored her against being scorched, melted, and broken. There came crash after hurtling crash as her warded body punched holes in wall after stone wall, until she vanished from view in the echoing distance.

Ganrahast readied a spell to use on Dardulkyn if need be, but everyone else—Dardulkyn included—turned to stare into the scrying eye.

And see the dagger-transfixed woman come to a stop at last, right outside the Room of the Watchful Sentinel.

A bare spear's length behind her, five blueflame ghosts, as they hurried into the room.

Just in time to see Storm Silverhand plunge through the Dalestride Portal, with Amarune and Arclath right behind her.

Cymmarra staggered to her feet, looking a little dazed, and imperiously waved at her ghosts to obey her. Silently and swiftly they surrounded her.

"Elminster," she said with a wry smile. "The heart of all trouble—as always. Get to you, and I'll find Manshoon and all the blueflame I seek. Two deaths within my reach, which I've hungered after for *so* long. Just a little hunting left now. Come, slaves!"

Ringed by her flaming slayers, the Lady of Ghosts vanished through the portal.

"Lord Delcastle and the two women have gone to Shadowdale, to heal a mad queen—and destroy us all," Ganrahast muttered. "The Simbul, who obliterated the loyal Crown mages we sent against her, just as the tales all say she destroyed every Red Wizard she met. If she's restored, she'll surely come here to blast every mage in Cormyr, and all who stand with them."

"I hope you're wrong," Starbridge muttered.

"As do we all," said King Foril Obarskyr. And sighed.

"Nay, *don't* get up," Mirt growled, forcing Glathra back down onto the warehouse floor with one hairy hand. "If ye try again, I may just sit on ye. An' I warn ye, I'm both heavy an' full of wind."

"If you don't let me up," the wizard of war hissed, "I'll see you chained in a deep dungeon for the rest of your miserable *life!*"

"Ah, lass, that's the spirit! Foreplay! I like that sort of spit an' fire! We could use a lass like ye in Waterdeep, ye know? Why don't ye kiss all these gloomy Cormyrean courtiers fare-well and come to where the fresh sea breezes invigorate, coin is king, an' we know how to laugh an' drink an' feast an' wench—well, harrum, that last one may not hold the same attraction for ye as it does for me, but . . ."

"Oh, shut *up*," Glathra told him weakly.

Mirt grinned down at her. "Want some cheese while ye're down there? Wine? We traders know where to get the best . . ."

Chapter
THIRTY-FIVE

Battle and Burial

Then the warhorns cry, the chargers gallop
Lances lowered, and the end comes for all too many.
Battle and burial, that's the way of it.
More lives wasted, and so it goes.

Old Lokhlabur, Act III, Scene III of the play
A Throne O'erthrown by Mandarjack the Minstrel
first performed in the Year of the Hidden Harp

"I don't like this," Storm muttered, peering into the trees all around. "They've *got* to be lurking near, watching us."

"If we tarry, they're sure to arrive. Go in and bring Alassra out," Elminster told her, his grim voice sounding odd coming out of Arclath's mouth. "We dare not try using the blueflame on her in there, with the chain and the wards. I'll guard Rune out here."

Storm nodded, handed him the buckle—it wasn't glowing at all, now—and went into the cave.

"Arclath—I mean El!" Amarune said warningly.

"I see them, lass. Expect me to be hurling spells soon."

Quite suddenly, three warriors had stepped silently out of the nearby trees, blue flames flowing endlessly around their bodies. They held ready swords and daggers and wore wide, tireless smiles.

"Before I get to that," the Sage of Shadowdale murmured, "I'm going to move the cavern's wards over and out past us, at yon ghosts. The ward-magic will roil at a fixed distance before me. I *might* be past controlling it—if I bark or drool or stagger about and say strange things that don't sound like spells, reach out and grab me from behind, then hold me where I stand to keep the magic in one spot."

Rune nodded. He stroked her arm reassuringly—Arclath's gesture, showing her that her lord was sharing his body with El rather than being a silenced slave—and added, "There are at least two more ghosts out there. And she who sent them, a woman with a dagger protruding from her chest. If I don't seem to notice them, keep hold of me and haul me about to move the wards so as to intercept them."

He sank into a crouch, like a knife fighter about to rush the advancing ghosts. "If yon flaming ones come here but emerge not, eventually their commander will be conquered by her curiosity and come looking to see what befell them. Storm can bring me back to my senses; retreat to her if ye must."

He handed Amarune the blueflame buckle. "Take this. If I fall, get it to The Simbul as fast as ye can!"

Rune nodded, unable to keep her mounting fear off her face. The trio of ghosts was advancing in a silent, menacing line, like wary warriors. El retreated before them, putting out an arm to sweep Amarune back with him.

Back they went into the cool gloom of the cave, and the ghosts came on.

The moment the flaming trio was fully in the cavern, El ducked down, hauling Rune with him—and something half-seen that hissed and thundered in the air swept over their heads in a silent, heavy flood.

It swirled around the ghosts, halting them and whirling their blue flames away in a surging chaos of swirling lights and confused sounds, most loudly sharp shrieks like hundreds of harpstrings breaking at once.

The three slayers staggered, hacked vainly at the air, crouched as if caught in a gale—and suddenly were gone, all ragged cries and tatters of blue, fading flame, whirled into . . . nothingness.

Beside Rune, Arclath whimpered suddenly and burst out, "The wolves! And Dalatha, weeping! Oh, her kisses . . . ohhh, broken again. Crowns do that." With every word his voice wavered, sounding like him or like Elminster—or like other folk entirely.

Amarune looked at him, winced, then ducked behind him and took firm hold of his jerkin. Heart pounding, she stood with him in the gloom, waiting.

A long time passed, or seemed to, as Arclath—or Elminster—started to sing. She couldn't make out the words, and the tunes were unfamiliar, but he didn't seem that much different from a lot of drunkards she remembered from the Dragonride—

Suddenly another blueflame ghost loomed up, running hard with his sword raised.

Desperately Rune tugged at Arclath, trying to drag him back—but the ghost was already fading and breaking apart, though it kept on struggling to reach them. Its foremost, reaching hand melted, then the sword arm, with the blade it held, a knee and then . . . all of it.

The singing stopped abruptly, as if Arclath had been shocked by the blueflame ghost's disappearance. Trembling, Amarune held him and waited.

After a time, there came a bright flash from the far side of the roiling magic, and the ward shuddered and seemed to grow thinner.

Another flash. More thinning.

Then another ghost appeared. A tall, cruel-faced woman was walking behind it, working magic as she came. Whenever she finished a spell, it caused one of those bright flashes, melting more of the wards away.

Amarune hastily dragged the lurching man in her arms back to keep the fading, thinning wards around the ghost and the woman.

Suddenly the ghost started to melt, sinking down into the roilings with surprising speed. The woman reeled. She was close enough—five or six strides away, no more—that Rune could see that dagger sticking out of her chest.

Then lightning burst out of nowhere, slamming into the woman from behind and thrusting her into a bulging-eyed dance on tiptoes, wild spasms of agony that ended with her fall, a sprawl on her face that left her lying still.

Fresh bolts of lightning stabbed and ricocheted through the last, thinning wisps of the wards. Behind them, a man— their hurler—was striding slowly into the cavern.

Amarune let go of her Arclath, spun around, and ran deeper into the cave. There was an unpleasant stirring ahead of her in the darkness, as if unfriendly magic was awakening to her arrival.

Caught in its fringes, she stopped and sank down in silence. She was as deep in as she could go and still see Arclath, who was lying in a heap, mumbling and feebly crawling.

She knew the man coming into the cave. She'd seen him once or twice before in the city streets. It was the wizard Suzailans called most powerful mage in Suzail, Larak Dardulkyn.

He strode past the woman he'd felled to stand smiling down at the dazed, incoherently babbling Arclath.

"So, Elminster, it comes down to you and me once more," he said, almost pleasantly. Flexing his hands, he added gently, "Prepare to die, old fool. Again."

Rune swallowed, not knowing what to do, feeling utterly helpless. Should she throw the buckle at him? Well, what good would *that* do?

Almost purring with glee, the man began a spell she couldn't hope to stop—

And then toppled forward, with a sudden shriek.

The woman he'd struck down with his lightning had reached up from the ground with her sword to slash his nearest leg.

"Poisoned," she snarled triumphantly, before falling back exhausted.

On the ground beside Arclath, Dardulkyn rolled, cursing furiously and clutching at his wound.

His rolling became shuddering, and he lost his grip on his leg as he started to convulse. His oaths went incoherent as foam spewed from his mouth.

Rune had seen enough. Heedless of the unseen magic that sang up to claw at her, she turned and raced deeper into the cavern.

Hurrying to get the blueflame buckle to The Simbul.

Cymmarra heaved herself to her knees, the world spinning slowly above her ...

Everything was slow and painful. Everything took so much *strength* ...

She lost count of her weak and staggering tries, but by using her sword like a crutch, she found her feet at last. Only the cavern wall kept her upright after that first, horribly shaky step.

She clung to the wall, whispering prayers she didn't believe in and scarcely remembered, over and over again, seeking strength.

When she felt like she might have found a little, she turned her head and smirked at the two feebly moving men. Dardulkyn's words had made it clear he was Manshoon, and there was no reason she knew of that he might have been wrong about the young lordling being Elminster.

"*Great* archwizards," she sneered. "Not a lot to choose between the two of you, is there?" Shoving off from the wall, she reeled forward, raising her poisoned blade again.

Dardulkyn suddenly sprang up, wild-eyed, and fled, arms flailing. He fell often as he went, but had a frenzied speed she couldn't hope to match.

"The poison will take you," she murmured after him, weak but baleful, "and then I will. After I take care of the Sage of Shadowdale."

That body hadn't moved yet and was right in front of her. One lurching stride, two ... she had to ground the sword and lean on it to keep from falling. Drawing in a deep and shuddering breath, she steadied herself and raised it again.

"One thrust," she gasped. "One thrust, you old—"

Elminster rolled away, then found his feet with the agility and grace of a much younger man.

Arclath Delcastle had snatched back control of his own body. He smiled mirthlessly as he drew his sword, then met Cymmarra's staggering rush with a deft parry.

Slicing two fingers off her sword hand on his backswing, he snapped, "One thrust? I think *not*."

Magic clawed at her like a long-nailed drunkard trying to paw his way to a handy dancer's charms, but it seemed to sigh and fade with her every step. She was fighting her way down a deep, narrow cavern . . .

Amarune pushed on into darkness until she saw a tiny glow of light ahead.

It was coming from a pool of water, where there was much splashing.

Going nearer, Rune saw a chained woman thrashing on the edge of the pool. She had eyes like those of an angry wolf and wore only the great swirling chaos of her long, silver hair, tresses that moved by themselves like Storm Silverhand's hair.

Which it was, in fact, entangled with, Rune saw, the two heads of hair wrestling like hundreds of angry snakes as Storm and The Simbul—this *had* to be The Simbul—struggled with each other.

Storm was trying to drag her sister out of the pool, but The Simbul was stronger in her frenzy, overpowering Storm and dragging them both back down into the waters, time and again.

Now what? Rune discovered she was trembling, not just from the cavern's magic but in deepening fear.

Then Storm saw her—and the blueflame buckle. "Put it in her mouth!" she gasped. "Rune, put it in her mouth, and hold it there until it's all gone—no matter what happens!"

Rune swallowed then started forward. The buckle began to glow again.

With a menacing crackle, The Simbul's hair left off trying to strangle and pinion Storm and reached for the buckle. Her angry wolf eyes flared blue.

Amarune went nearer, trying to keep close to the wall so as not to get easily dragged into the pool.

The Simbul growled at her menacingly, then snapped her teeth at the buckle. Just like a hungry wolf.

Rune dodged her lunges, just as she had dodged so many reaching hands at the Dragonriders'—and, holding the buckle firmly in both hands, thrust it into The Simbul's mouth.

There was a bright flash and a sudden surge of energy that shook Amarune.

The Simbul's eyes spat fire, literally becoming two bright blue flames, and Rune screamed as her fingers and then her arms started to burn, hair sizzling.

"*Hold it in there!*" Storm shouted, sounding desperate.

Rune clenched her teeth, then bent her head and whimpered against the pain. The buckle was melting . . . she thrust its dwindling solidity farther and farther in behind those sharp and angry teeth . . .

Then, abruptly, conflagration and buckle were both gone.

All the struggling stopped, and The Simbul was looking up at Rune with all fury fled and quite a different look in her eyes.

"Lady, I thank you," she said gravely and kissed Amarune's scorched fingers.

That touch sent a soothing, healing coolness through Rune that left her shuddering in amazed relief.

The pain vanished. Her burns were gone.

Then the chain binding The Simbul to the wall melted away in glowing silence.

The freed woman patted Storm in silent thanks and rose, dripping, to stride past Amarune down the passage as regally as any queen.

Near the cave mouth, Arclath Delcastle stood grimly over the Lady of Ghosts, the tip of his sword at her throat. She glared up at him in agony, her hands cut to bloody ruin, unable to fight any more.

The Simbul walked up to the young lord, touched his head, and murmured, "Come forth, El."

Arclath slumped like a limp and empty leather sack as El's ashes, glowing and swirling, emerged from his nose and ears to coil around The Simbul's face and breast.

She laughed in delight, then stepped back and decreed, "Be as sane as I am, and have a body again."

A glow appeared in midair in front of her and faded rapidly into something solid, upright . . . a naked man. It swayed, settled onto its feet, and sharpened into—Elminster, looking old and vigorous but slack-jawed.

The ashes plunged into that open mouth, and the body shuddered all over. Then it opened blue-gray eyes, smiled, and reached out to gather The Simbul into a fierce embrace.

As they kissed, she said to him firmly through their joined mouths, "*Soon.*"

Then she whirled free, bent to the helplessly glaring Cymmarra, and said gently, "Rest, tortured one."

A wave of her hand banished the curse, and the woman transfixed by the dagger crumbled to dust, the dagger sighing into nothingness a moment later.

Then The Simbul headed out of the cavern, waving almost absently at Arclath as she went.

He blinked, stood up, looked around, saw Amarune, and grinned. She rushed into his arms.

Storm and El gently towed them after The Simbul, out into the light—where everyone halted as silence fell again.

A tentacled beholder of monstrous size was hovering in the air waiting for them, glaring eyestalks ready.

Rays spat forth.

The Simbul raised both her hands this time, and those magics twisted in midair into nothing more than a dancing glow.

"*Enough*, Manshoon." She turned to look at Elminster, then regarded the beholder again. "I have remembered much that Mystra told me. The two of you must now work together. Our Lady of Magic commands it."

"Mystra is no more!" Manshoon snarled.

The Simbul frowned. "She is . . . silent, yes, but I am far less certain of her destruction than you seem to be. Yet, her commandment is very clear. You must both gather all the blueflame items you can and use them properly, or the realms will surely fall before the beasts flooding in. The rifts opened in ignorance by those called 'warlocks' are many, and more and more fell powers look to this world to be their new home. More than just the Weave has fallen and been lost."

El listened in thoughtful silence, and Manshoon in growing, eyestalk-quivering fury, as she added, "One archwizard was behind the enchanting of all the blueflame items, using many as his dupes. They were his bid to maintain his own existence, but he built into them the means to watch over all who used the items—for sport and amusement, as well as to effectively compel such wielders."

"'One archwizard'? *Who?*" Manshoon spat.

"The 'Imprisoner' is the one called Larloch. He bound all the magic and essence of three of his servant liches into each ghost-imprisoning item—sacrifices to empower the items."

"*Larloch?*"

The Simbul ignored Manshoon's angry disbelief. "The items are more than extra-dimensional prisons and ghost-controllers. Each possesses a fell power of its own, usable whenever the ghost is imprisoned, and dormant when the ghost is out."

"And if a ghost is destroyed?" Elminster asked quietly.

"The item will crumble," The Simbul replied. "Its magic discharged and forever lost."

"No!" the beholder snarled. "You lie!"

"I do *not* lie, Manshoon. You lie, easily and often, as it suits your desires, and so have fallen into lazily thinking all others must, too. Consider how easy it would be for me to destroy you, rather than spend time telling you this. Consider further my strong temptation to do so. Yet, I refrain. Consider that I do so for this higher purpose, this *necessity* of saving the world we share. Now, will you hear the rest, or will I spell-scourge you until you are humbled and forced to yield?"

The beholder hung silently in the air for what seemed a very long time.

"I ... I will listen," it said at last.

"Wise of you. Mystra and Azuth allowed Larloch's self-serving plan to succeed because they deemed it necessary. Like the lich lord, they saw it as a way of cheating the coming Spell-plague, which they dared not try to prevent as the increasingly unstable Weave raced toward crashing ruin. It needed to be renewed or replaced, and Mystra knew either outcome would destroy her. She also knew she could preserve something of herself and the secrets of the Art she'd inherited—and Azuth could do the same—by insinuating it into the minds of Larloch's liches, and so into the blueflame items."

"Which means ..." Storm said slowly.

Her sister smiled. "Which means the items contain seeds that could perhaps bring back Larloch, or even something ... some*one* more ... if used in the right manner."

"Uh," Arclath mumbled, "I'm not sure Rune or I should be hearing this ..."

Ignoring him, The Simbul went on sternly, "It is imperative blueflame items *must* be wielded to close rifts and restore the balance of Toril, or the ancient Primordials will rise and rage unleashed across the lands ... and inevitably, what will eventually be left will not be the world we know, the realms of humans, elves, dwarves, halflings, orcs, and the rest. Dragons may survive, but probably as enslaved steeds, not conquering wyrms. Their time is past."

She looked from one person to another, staring last up at the beholder, whose rays had faded away.

"El and Manshoon, will you both work to make sure the time of humans is not ended?"

"Aye," Elminster agreed eagerly.

It was another long and silent wait before Manshoon muttered reluctantly, "Yes."

"Good. Starting now would be a good thing," The Simbul told them dryly.

Then she gave Storm a smile. "Thank you for caring for me, sister. I'll return as soon as I can, but long ago I promised Mystra I'd do . . . certain things. I must keep my promises, or I am nothing."

She took a step back. "I go."

Abruptly, without a spell or sound, she vanished.

Leaving Storm, Arclath, Amarune, and Elminster all looking at the beholder hanging in the air above them.

Silence stretched.

"So," El asked mildly, "shall we begin?"

Manshoon glared at him—and vanished, leaving only empty sky behind.

EPILOGUE

Elminster whirled and cast a hasty spell.

Storm started to say something urgent, but Elminster shook his head, waved his hands in a dramatic flourish—and watched Storm, Arclath, and Amarune vanish as his magic took them elsewhere.

Then he ran back to the cave.

He was only a few steps inside when Manshoon's first attack spell stabbed at his back.

It raged against El's ward, shattered it, and the two magics died together.

Elminster kept running, knowing the spot he wanted to reach before—

Manshoon's second attack, a flood of piercing lightning, drove him to his knees, groaning in pain.

El fought to hiss out a small, simple spell, hoping its nature would let him finish it before—

Manshoon smashed him with deadly magic once more.

"Work with you? *Bah!* All my life you've frustrated my schemes, intrigued against me, opposed me!" the vampire shouted. "Work with you? *I think not.* Be entombed, instead!"

Magic clawed at Elminster, and the rock beneath him changed.

"I'll drive you down into solid rock by making it less than solid—in shifting spots, so the weight of the rest of the stone, still hard, will crush your bones to jelly!"

Elminster was sinking, his body tingling, starting to shift at Manshoon's bidding. He had to fight to form a smile.

"I want you to feel pain, Sage of Shadowdale!" Manshoon shouted from above. "*Long, slow pain!* Let your tongue be stilled, your jaw, arms, and fingers all be broken, to rob you of all means to work magic!"

The rock closed over Elminster's head, dark and hissing, Manshoon's magic lancing into his lungs to keep him from suffocating just yet. And to bring him more of its caster's gloating.

"Think you can foil me again? Work another of your sly triumphs? No, a thousand times no! I am Manshoon, and *I will defeat you!*"

"By deafening me? Like any lackspell mageling, ye've certainly mastered being noisy!" Elminster murmured to himself as his body fell entirely back to ashes—and plunged through the fissures he'd been seeking.

The agony was—intense.

Yet, he'd known worse.

It would take him days, perhaps months, to drag himself together again . . . but he'd managed much, much longer patience in the past.

Silently, by many thousands of little ways, he descended.

New magic stabbed after him, thrusting here and there, swift and energetic.

Only to withdraw, finding no trace of Elminster.

"Yes!" Manshoon roared, his voice high and wild. "Bury him deep—and I did! Go godless to the gods at last, Elminster, to fail that judgment and fade, gone forever! Fare you *not* well!"

From some flakes of tumbling ash in a cavern far beneath Manshoon's boots, in an upper cavern of the Underdark, came a faint echo that just might have been an answer to Manshoon's shout.

An echo that sounded rather like the Sage of Shadowdale's chuckle.

ABOUT THE AUTHOR

Ed Greenwood is the creator of the FORGOTTEN REALMS® fantasy setting, an award-winning game designer, and a best-selling author whose fantasy novels have sold millions of copies worldwide in more than thirty languages.

Once hailed as "the Canadian author of the great American novel," Ed is a large, bearded, jolly Canadian librarian who lives in an old farmhouse crammed with over 80,000 books in the Ontario countryside, and is often mistaken for Santa Claus in disguise. Many gamers think he resembles Elminster, but Ed insists he did not model the Old Mage on himself.

Ed was elected to the Academy of Adventure Gaming Art & Design Hall of Fame in 2003, and has been a judge for the World Fantasy Awards. His most popular series include the Knights of Myth Drannor trilogy and the Elminster Saga published by Wizards of the Coast, the Band of Four series from Tor Books, and the Falconfar books from Solaris.

CONTINUE YOUR ADVENTURE

The Dungeons & Dragons® Fantasy Roleplaying Game Starter Set has everything you need for you and your friends to start playing. Explore infinite universes, create bold heroes and prepare to begin— or rediscover— the game that started it all.

DUNGEONS & DRAGONS

Watch Videos
Read Sample Chapters
Get product previews

Learn more about D&D® products
at
DungeonsandDragons.com